SKYBLIND

J.R. FEHR

Jon Fehr

ISBN: 0995162808
ISBN-13: 978-0995162808

SKYBLIND

J.R. FEHR

For all the kids I worked with at Eagles Nest Youth Ranch.

PART I

Chapter One — The Rising Darkness

"For six glorious months the sun blesses the land with light and tranquility; I find it better to pretend the other months don't exist."

—KING TEMCHAR, A.P. 743
SAYINGS OF THE KINGS AND OTHER LORDLY SORTS

"About time! Any longer and I was going to eat your portion," Taylee exclaimed with her mouth full of food as soon as Corwin Medisto entered the shack.

He instantly noticed that his sister was dressed in the nicest blue dress she owned and had her plain brown hair bound into a ponytail with an elegant white band.

I think she even painted her face ...

"Trying to dress older now, I see. You aren't fooling anyone." Corwin grunted as he kicked off his boots by the door.

"One of us should probably look our age, don't you think?" Taylee teased. "What took you so long, anyway?"

"Braed's still sick," Corwin admitted sadly as he hung his jacket on the wall.

Taylee raised her eyebrows in confusion. "Are you still worrying about that sheep? I told you already, she'll recover. We just need more medicine."

"Medicine is not magic," Uncle Jael reminded them from his seat at the table. "It cannot cure all wounds."

"Then maybe we need magic," Corwin said—mostly in jest, though part of him wondered if magic might actually be the answer.

"Be careful how you joke," his uncle replied sternly. "Syyris does not have a sense of humour."

Can god even hear us all the way out here? Corwin wondered.

Life in the Outskirts wasn't easy, a fact Corwin knew better than anyone. But no amount of knowing could have prepared him for the harshness of this sheep virus. There was no official name for it, no known cure or cause, and for the first three months of Day, it had mercilessly swept through their livestock and killed or weakened the vast majority.

Braed will get better, Corwin told himself firmly. *Uncle Jael is just being overly cautious again.*

Though only in his fifty-eighth year, Uncle Jael appeared more and more weary all the time. His hair was the colour of dry ash and his posture showed the burden of many years' hard labour. But he worked hard to educate, train, and provide for them, and, despite the constant pessimism, Corwin knew his uncle meant well.

"Sorry, Uncle Jael." Corwin bowed his head apologetically. "I just wish I could do more to help the sheep recover."

"Some things are beyond our control." His uncle's voice was strained but gentle, and as usual he spoke with a hint of sadness. "Now, come have a seat. Taylee was impatient and started without you, but I made sure to save some birthday hash."

Corwin nodded gratefully and grabbed a plate from the counter.

"Oh, we're having *birthday* hash!" Taylee teased as she tossed a potato wedge into her greedy mouth. "I thought I tasted more festive cheer than usual."

They'd eaten little aside from potatoes, eggs, and beans for the past two months, and it was beginning to take a toll on all of them.

"Hmph!" Uncle Jael scoffed. "If you want fancier meals, perhaps you should find a man who can afford your tastes."

"Someone like … Tray'o?" Taylee's lips took on an oddly mischievous curl.

Uncle Jael narrowed his eyes at her. "No. Someone most *unlike* Tray'o."

At that, Taylee broke out into melodic laughter. "Relax, Uncle. We're only *friends*. But if you must worry about one of us, it should be Cor. He's a 'man' now, but I don't think he's even kissed a girl yet." Taylee laughed.

What do you know of kissing?

Corwin chose to ignore her as he filled his plate with the measly amount of egg and potato that remained. It was a bland and greasy meal – not nearly filling enough – but he ate it with a smile and thanked his uncle when it was gone a minute later.

"Though others may disagree, the journey to manhood takes much more than a kiss or a 16th birthday, I'm afraid." Uncle Jael frowned.

"I imagine the journey to womanhood is equally as challenging. Especially for *certain* silly little girls," Corwin added with a glance at Taylee, who was acting far too smug this morning.

"Oh, dear brother, I haven't been a silly little girl for quite some time." She flashed a grin before grabbing a greasy piece of potato from the table and flicking it at him.

Corwin skillfully caught the potato in his mouth and spat it back at her. Taylee managed to dodge it, but scrunched up her nose in a way that told him she wouldn't dare try throwing anything else at him.

Despite her silly attempts to look like an adult, he would always see Taylee as his innocent little sister—even though he was only a few minutes older.

Uncle Jael remained unusually quiet, largely ignoring their playful banter, and instead kept glancing out the window, which, in reality, was just a medium-sized hole in the wall where the wood had rotted away recently.

"There's work to be done. Neither Mid-Luminous nor a

birthday are excuses to be lazy." Uncle Jael rose from his seat.

"What other excuses do you need?" Taylee laughed, but then, in a quieter voice, added, "And are you sure we should go out? I've heard all sorts of rumours that some Locura were seen stalking around …"

Uncle Jael let out a long and laboured sigh. "Taylee. What do we know about Locura?"

As if insulted by the question, his sister rolled her eyes at their uncle. "Not this again …"

Uncle Jael kept his eyes locked on her and patiently waited for her answer.

"They're evil demons of Night," she repeated the textbook line as if quoting mindless rhetoric. "They hate the sun, they roam the borderlands, and they never come out during Lightspan."

"Why do they hate the sun?" When it came to matters of study, Uncle Jael often had to coax answers out of her.

"Because they're monstrous shadows of humans who don't want their ugliness exposed." Taylee looked miserable. "Uncle, I understand all this, but the *rumours* are spreading that—"

Uncle Jael interrupted her. "I'm interested in fact, not fiction. Why are they monsters, Taylee?"

His sister crossed her arms and looked away.

"It's a result of the curse," Corwin spoke for his sister. "Because they disobeyed Syyris and followed Plyyston."

"I was asking Taylee." Uncle Jael's voice was stern.

Taylee leaned her head back against the chair in annoyance. "Because they disobeyed Syyris," she replied in mimicry of Corwin's voice.

Uncle Jael nodded. "This is why obedience is one of the most important virtues. Those who chose Plyyston's rebellion shared his fate; the Locura are forever bound with him in darkness and despair. If they could live in the light, we would not be able to spend half the year here."

"What about Dark Ones, then?" Taylee asked. "They aren't

cursed."

Why is she so concerned about this? We've never even seen a Dark One before.

"Don't worry, Tay," Corwin attempted to reassure her. "That's why the knights from Pinehouse are on constant patrol."

"Calm down, brother. Who says I'm worried?" Taylee quipped, feigning indifference. "I know Syyris won't let his faithful be harmed. I was only saying there've been strange rumours. That's all."

Corwin shrugged his shoulders. "Uh-huh."

Uncle Jael stood abruptly and glanced again out the window. There was an agitated look in his eye.

He is not himself this morning.

"What is it?" Corwin asked as he watched his uncle grab his tattered leather jacket from the wall.

"Light is not for wasting," his uncle repeated the grim, all-too-familiar saying.

Corwin nodded and pushed his chair back. But before he could get up, Uncle Jael placed a hand firmly on his shoulder.

"I have business in Krydor. Stay, tend the crops and watch your sheep. I won't be gone long." Although Uncle Jael smiled as he spoke, his eyes were uncommonly sad.

"I'll go with you. The crops can wait, and I already checked the sheep."

Between working the farm during Lightspan and schooling in Pinehouse during Darkfall, opportunities to go to town were a rare treat.

"No. I need to do some trading and it's better done alone," his uncle stated firmly.

"Trading, huh?" Taylee raised an eyebrow. "You sure you aren't off to get us a birthday present?"

Uncle Jael shook his head dismissively as he grabbed his satchel and draped it over one shoulder. "Read chapters thirty-three and thirty-four of *The History of Everything and Everyone*. You can skip the rest of your studies. Consider that your birthday present."

As he made his way to the door, Taylee slipped out of her chair and spoke in a strangely cryptic tone. "A break from school is a wonderful present, Uncle. And you know how much I *adore* that book. But, I have to wonder, might there be some *other* present?"

Uncle Jael stopped and turned to look at her. He didn't say anything, but something about the way he squinted his eyes made Corwin think he was uncertain of how best to respond.

"Taylee!" Corwin scolded. "We don't need any presents."

A strange sadness settled over their uncle.

He feels bad.

Corwin couldn't believe Taylee wanted to guilt their uncle into buying them presents from town.

I have the greediest sister in the Kingdom.

Without saying another word, Uncle Jael exited their home.

As soon as the door closed, Corwin spun toward his sister. "What was that about? You know Uncle Jael can't afford to waste Essence on presents!"

"Relax. I never said the present was from him," Taylee said, flashing a grin.

"What's gotten into you this morning? Who else would give us a present?" Corwin was finding her behaviour more annoying than usual today.

The girl turns 16 and suddenly she thinks she can say whatever she wants?

"To you? Probably no one. Me, on the other hand …" Taylee peered out the window to make sure Uncle Jael was gone.

What is she up to?

"So I woke up early, right?" Taylee explained as she crossed the room. "And I overheard Uncle talking to someone. At first, I thought maybe he was just rambling to himself, you know, like he sometimes does. But no, there was definitely someone else here."

"So what?" Corwin tried to sound uninterested, but his voice betrayed him. *We never have visitors.*

Taylee grinned and darted into the bedroom. "They were arguing and didn't notice I was watching. I haven't seen Uncle so upset in a long time. Or Tray'o."

"What?" Corwin followed her. "Tray'o came here?"

Even though they were best friends, Tray'o rarely came out to the farm.

"Sure did!" Taylee beamed. "I didn't catch the whole argument, but Uncle Jael took a wrapped box from Tray'o, who kept saying 'Don't you think your sister would want her to have it?' or something like that. Anyway, Uncle Jael forced Tray'o to leave and then took the box and put it into his satchel."

'Your sister'? What's that supposed to mean?

"Our uncle only had one sister …"

"Yeah, I know. Our *mom*. Try to keep up!" Taylee rolled her eyes as she reached under her bed.

Corwin immediately felt uncomfortable. Their uncle wasn't perfect, but he'd always done his best to take care of them; there was no reason to suspect he was withholding a gift from their long-deceased mother.

And if he was, there had to be a good reason, Corwin decided with confidence.

"Well, whatever that box was, Uncle took his satchel with him, so there's no point in thinking about it. I'm sure he'll show you when he's ready—" Corwin cut himself off.

Taylee had pulled a box wrapped in brown paper out from under her bed, and Corwin's mouth dropped open when he saw it.

"You *stole* it!?"

"Don't be so extreme. Come on, I want to open it with you!" Taylee enthusiastically pushed past him and placed the box on the table.

"Are you crazy? He'll notice if it's not in his satchel!"

"No, he won't. I replaced it with a different box wrapped in similar brown paper. Give me some credit!"

Corwin chose to remain quiet as his thoughts unwillingly

drifted to the mother he never knew. *Kyla. Her name was Kyla.*

She had died shortly after giving birth to them. Corwin didn't know much about either of his parents, and whenever Uncle Jael mentioned their mother, it was always some random memory of a trait or ability, like how she had been fast, and how Corwin must have inherited that from her. Uncle Jael claimed that she had been able to outrun most men, which was a feat that Corwin deemed quite useful, as one of the only other descriptions he'd been given was of her exceptional beauty.

Until now, the only gift Corwin ever received from his mother, besides life, was the ability to run.

"Well?! Aren't you going to come over so we can open it?" Taylee asked impatiently.

Her voice snapped Corwin back into reality. He took his eyes off the box and shook his head. "No. This is wrong. If Uncle wanted you to have it, he would have given it to you before he left. You shouldn't have taken it!"

Taylee rolled her eyes in annoyance. "Come on. Aren't you the least bit curious?"

"No," Corwin lied. He wanted desperately to open the box and see something belonging to his mother. *Uncle Jael took this away for a reason. Obedience is a virtue,* he firmly reminded himself.

"Whatever. I'll open it myself," Taylee said as she reached under her dress, grabbed the hidden dagger strapped to her leg, and in one quick motion, sliced the wrapping off the box.

"Stop!" Corwin tried to grab her, but she squirmed out of his reach and around the table. Then, with a mischievous grin, she flipped open the lid.

Her eyes grew as wide as plates and delight washed over her face. "Incredible!"

"What? What is it?" Corwin asked as he tried to get a better look at what was inside.

Taylee snapped the lid shut and held it close to her chest. "I thought you didn't want to see? I thought it was *wrong*?"

Corwin shook with suppressed anger; it was at times like this that he wondered what it would be like to be an only child.

"Just hand it over!"

His sister smiled victoriously and placed the box into his waiting hands. As Corwin opened the lid, she leaned around him to look again.

"I don't understand why Uncle got so angry when Tray'o brought this," Taylee stated as she slipped her dagger back into its hidden sheath.

Inside the box lay a coiled silver necklace.

At first glance, it appeared to be rather ordinary. But when Corwin pulled it out, he saw that attached to the chain was some sort of metal pendant shaped like an animal.

Corwin held the pendant in his hand to examine it closer, and instantly a cold wave of recognition washed over him.

A Nightwolf!

Corwin gasped.

"What did you do?" Taylee asked as she looked at it in shock.

A high-pitched hissing sound now emitted from the necklace, and the eyes of the Nightwolf glowed white.

Chapter Two — Plyyston's Magic

"We do not worship the past, lest we tempt fate to repeat it."

—ELDER JERAMEE, A.P. 6

<u>HISTORICAL LAWS OF THE FIRST ELDER ORDER</u>

"This is all your fault!" Corwin snapped at her rather unnecessarily as he dropped the necklace. As soon as it left his fingers, the hissing stopped and the eyes of the Nightwolf turned black again.

"My fault? Don't blame me. You made its eyes start glowing. It's probably an enchanted relic! Pick it up and see if you can make it shoot fire!" Taylee exclaimed with glee.

The panic was visible in Corwin's wide-eyed stare.

This is too funny, she thought as she struggled to hide her amusement.

"Are you crazy? No! We have no clue what this does! We need to wrap it up before Uncle Jael gets home," said Corwin as he fumbled with the brown paper.

"We? As far as I can tell, you're the one who opened it. Uncle Jael's going to be so disappointed in you," Taylee teased with her arms crossed.

Corwin shot her a dark look. "You wouldn't dare …"

Taylee couldn't contain herself and so she burst out laughing. "All right, take it easy," she said as she struggled to regain her composure. "It's really not that big of a deal."

"Are you kidding?" Corwin failed to see the humour in any of this. "You stole the present and are trying to blame it on me!"

"It was a joke, Cor. I thought it would be funny to see you freak out, and guess what? I was right."

Corwin struggled to find words. "You're so immature. Help me wrap this up again."

"Why?" she asked as she picked up the necklace and dangled it above the box. "Aren't you curious? Tray'o said this belonged to our *mother*!"

It was almost too good to be true.

Over the years, Taylee had developed a knack for discovering things others would rather keep secret. She attributed this primarily to her clever mind, general sneakiness, and an ability to widen her eyes in such a way that many seemed to find completely adorable; knowing all manner of things was one of her joys in life.

But, much to her dismay, the truth of her own origins was one mystery that remained frustratingly impossible to solve due to Uncle Jael's unwillingness to speak on the subject.

But not anymore. She smiled as she stared deeply into the eyes of the relic. *This will change everything.*

"No. I'm not curious at all," Corwin growled as he grabbed the necklace from her and stuffed it back into the box.

Liar.

Taylee watched with a smirk as Corwin attempted to rewrap the box with the brown paper that she had torn off only moments before. When he was finally finished, it looked like something a child had wrapped. *A blind child.*

"Uncle is going to take one look at that and know you opened it!" Taylee giggled.

"*I* didn't open it. You did!" Corwin exclaimed as he angrily flung the box onto the table.

"Hey! Calm down, angry man." Taylee smiled. Her brother hated when she called him that.

Without another word, Corwin pulled on his boots and stormed out the door.

"Where are you going?" Taylee asked rhetorically as she scooped up the box and followed after him.

Corwin was already several feet away, jogging across the yard and out toward the road that led to Krydor.

Off to tell Uncle, Taylee mused as she chased after him. *He's so predictable.*

As much as she loved to tease him, Taylee really admired her brother. He was trustworthy and honest, and above all he always tried to do the right thing. And, as she suspected, he'd view the *right* thing in this situation as confessing that they opened the present.

Fortunately, that was exactly what Taylee wanted him to do.

"Hey! Hold up!" Taylee hollered as she ran to catch him.

Her brother was no longer jogging, but still managed to walk at an unnecessarily fast pace.

"Don't try to stop me, Taylee. I'm telling Uncle," Corwin warned.

"What are you going to tell him? That we opened a birthday present Tray'o brought for me? That sounds pretty silly," Taylee said.

Corwin stopped and looked her straight in the eye. "There was a reason why Uncle didn't let him give it to you."

"Probably because he doesn't like Tray'o," Taylee reasoned. "What's the big deal anyway? Do you think he's really going to care?"

"Yes, Taylee. Don't you remember what Uncle said? Obedience is a virtue. We can't pray for god's blessings and go around breaking the law." His voice quivered as he spoke.

Taylee recognized the fear behind his words. *This is about Braed again.*

"You know, Syyris isn't going to let your sheep die because you 'disobeyed,'" she spoke confidently. "Our god is not vengeful. He's good."

"Good, yes, but above all he's full of justice," Corwin reminded her as he resumed his pace down the road that ran parallel to their field.

Taylee shrugged her shoulders and followed after him. "Guess there's no talking you out of it."

Getting Corwin involved in opening the present was a stroke of genius. Uncle Jael was sure to be more understanding when Corwin—the "good, obedient child"— confessed to breaking a rule. Forgiveness would come quicker, and with it, answers.

This is almost too easy.

They walked on in relative silence as they passed their sad excuse for a wheat field. The wheat was thin and sickly, and Taylee judged its quality to be slightly worse than the year before. It didn't make sense; no matter how much of their small harvest they offered at the local temple, the crops never saw much improvement.

Uncle Jael often spoke of a time when Syyris would fly over the land and spray the crops with some kind of magic that vastly improved their quality. But many years had passed since their god last blessed the Outskirts, and the wilted quality of the wheat was the evidence of what many, including Corwin, perceived as his indifference.

Not Taylee though. She believed the drought was a time of testing, and felt strongly that Syyris was more interested in growing his children's faith through trials than giving them everything they wanted whenever they demanded it—as nice as that would be.

She was contemplating that idea when she noticed three figures in the distance approaching them on the road. Two, dressed completely in red armour, were clearly knights from the Pinehouse guard. But the one in the middle, wearing fancy clothes instead of armour could only be …

Tray'o, she concluded with a smirk.

Tray'o Sak'ton, a young man of average height, with shaggy black hair, was not what one would expect when imagining the son of a lord, though what he lacked in physical stature he made up for today with a fine white shirt and brown leather vest.

Taylee would have recognized her friend sooner if it wasn't for the unruly facial hair sprouting an inch from his chin.

"You really need to shave," Taylee teased as he came into earshot.

"Now you sound like my father," Tray'o groaned. "Off to Krydor for the festivities? Rumour is there's a sorcerer in town!"

"Sorcery is against the law," Corwin stated in a voice that sounded unusually distant.

"Exactly!" Tray'o beamed.

Receiving no response to his enthusiasm, Tray'o squinted his grey-blue eyes in suspicion before allowing a sly smile to overcome his face.

"I guess I should be wishing you two a happy birthday! Feels good to officially be a man now, doesn't it, Cor?" Tray'o had turned 16 a few months earlier.

"I haven't had time to really think about it yet," Corwin admitted quietly.

Why is he being so awkward? Taylee wondered with irritation. Corwin and Tray'o were practically best friends, though they came from completely different worlds. Where Corwin and Taylee were poor, Tray'o was rich, being the only-born son of Rai'o Sak'ton, a once successful merchant at the Krydor Markets who used his wealth to acquire the title Lord of Pinehouse Castle. How they ever managed to become friends in the first place was still a mystery to Taylee.

"I don't know about Corwin, but *I* am quite excited about finally being 16," Taylee interjected confidently.

"I'll bet," Tray'o replied as he turned his gaze toward her. "You may not yet officially be a woman in the eyes of the Kingdom, but to me, you've always been a lady."

The line was stilted and somewhat awkward. Taylee tried to look amused, but inside she felt more uncomfortable than anything.

"So where are you going, Tray?" Taylee tried to change the subject and glanced at the two guards. They were standing unusually straight and staring blankly into the distance as if unaware of the conversation taking place.

Tray'o avoided eye contact and scratched at the back of his head. "Well, uh, it's a little hard to explain. Basically, I was hoping to have a chat with your uncle."

"Oh?" Taylee couldn't hide her smile. "About what?"

He brought guards with him to try to force Uncle to give me the present? The thought was laughable.

Picking up on her amusement, Tray'o tensed up. "There was a misunderstanding earlier, and I was hoping to clear it up …"

"We know about the present you brought," Corwin blurted.

Ugh! Thanks for ruining the fun.

Tray'o was stunned. "What? You do?"

"Yeah. Taylee found and opened it already."

Tray'o seemed unsure how to respond, and as much as Taylee enjoyed watching him squirm, she was curious to know more about it.

"I saw you talking to Uncle," she explained. "Why did you say it belonged to my mother?"

At this, Tray'o perked up. "Oh, because I overheard my father and Master Lunechair talking, and they mentioned Kyla Medisto. That's your mother, right? Apparently she died giving birth to you two while in Pinehouse Castle."

"We weren't born there." Corwin's voice wavered with uncertainty.

If that's true, why have we never heard this before? Taylee wondered. Master Lunechair was her favourite teacher, mainly because he was so knowledgeable and quirky, but also because she secretly thought he might be grading her better than everyone else. *Could he really have known my mother?*

"Apparently you were," Tray'o continued. "Master Lunechair mentioned he still had her necklace in the vault, so, I snuck in there and took it. Don't look at me like that. If it's your mother's, it belongs with her family, right?"

Corwin narrowed his eyes suspiciously. "What else is kept in the vault?"

"Mostly just random relics from my father's expeditions."

"And you didn't think it was a little strange that they kept a necklace in there with a bunch of relics?"

Tray'o shrugged. "I assume it was kept for sentimental value.

It's just a necklace."

The look on Corwin's face must have given them away, because as soon as Tray'o made eye contact, his grin faded.

"It *is* just a necklace, right?"

Corwin remained silent and looked uncomfortably at the ground.

"We're pretty sure it's some sort of relic," Taylee admitted. "One that doesn't run on Essence."

Tray'o stared at them with disbelief in his eyes. "There's no such thing as a relic that works without Essence," he reminded them.

Silence hung in the air.

"This one does …" Corwin mumbled.

Tray'o exchanged an amused look with one of his guards. "Right. So what makes you so certain it's a relic? How did you activate it if you didn't use Essence?"

"It was an accident. It just turned on when I touched it," Corwin explained.

"You can't accidently activate a relic, Corwin. And why would your mother own one in the first place? They're extremely rare, and valuable." Tray'o frowned. "Let me see it."

Corwin shared a reluctant look with Taylee, who sighed in irritation before handing over the box to Tray'o.

Tray'o stifled a laugh when he saw the poor wrapping job, carelessly tore some of the paper off with one hand and flipped open the lid.

"Careful!" Corwin warned, but it was too late. The torn wrapping paper was already drifting away in the wind.

"It looks exactly the same as when I first took it." Tray'o sounded disappointed as he tossed the box over his shoulder and held the Nightwolf pendant in his hand. The eyes were not glowing anymore.

"I'm not sure of anything," Corwin said as he put what he could salvage of the wrapping paper into his pocket.

"Why did you think it was a relic?" Tray'o asked dismissively.

"The eyes glowed when Corwin touched it, and there was this weird hissing sound," Taylee explained. *Why aren't they glowing anymore?*

"Ooooh, scary! Glowing eyes. What a powerful relic! Maybe you can use it to walk around in the dark," he teased as he dangled the Nightwolf from his fingers.

"Stop!" Taylee shouted as she snatched the necklace from his disrespectful grasp.

But as soon as she touched the pendant, the eyes of the Nightwolf started to glow, and the hissing sound returned.

"There! Ha! Told you," she stated proudly.

Tray'o stared at her with wide eyes. "How ...?"

"That's what we were trying to tell you. It's weird," Corwin said.

"It's more than weird ..." Tray'o looked around nervously. "I think this is ... not of Syyris."

Taylee's heart skipped a beat. "All magic is from Syyris."

"Not dark magic," Tray'o countered. "I think this could be one of Plyyston's relics."

Plyyston. The Devil of Darkness. His name used so casually sent a shiver down Taylee's spine. Suddenly, she didn't feel so amused by the relic.

"You shouldn't say his name." Taylee spoke in a hushed voice.

Tray'o laughed. "I don't think the devil can hear us while the sun's out."

I wish I knew if that were true.

"A relic of Plyyston's ..." Corwin's face went pale. "That's impossible."

"So is a relic that doesn't run on Essence. And yet here we are." Tray'o scratched his head again. "Look, whatever it is, you shouldn't have it. Give it to me, and I'll put it back where I found it," he promised.

Corwin nodded and looked to Taylee.

Is he crazy?

Taylee crossed her arms. "No."

Corwin's eyebrows raised in alarm. "Taylee! Just give him the necklace."

"No! This belonged to our mother! Plus, it's a gift, and you can't just take back gifts!"

Corwin sighed and took a step toward her. "You heard him. We could get in a lot of trouble for this. We don't even know for sure where it came from or what it does. It could contain *dark magic*. Tray can help."

"There's no proof dark magic relics even exist. And besides, I thought you wanted to talk to Uncle Jael? What happened to *confessing*?" Taylee reminded him sternly.

Don't forget where we're going!

Corwin took a deep breath. "We will still confess. But we don't need the necklace to do that. Tray is the one who stole it out of the vault. Uncle Jael will be happy to know it was returned."

"In my defence," Tray'o interjected, "it wasn't really stealing, since I kind of indirectly own the vault ..."

Taylee pressed her lips together and confronted Corwin directly. "Uncle Jael took it away from Tray'o. He won't be happy if we just give it back."

This belonged to our mother! she wanted to scream. *Uncle Jael stopped Tray'o from giving it to me. Why? Did he believe it contained dark magic? And why would our mother have a relic like that anyway?*

There were too many unanswered questions, and this relic was too valuable to just give back.

"You have a better suggestion?" Tray'o asked.

"Fine, Corwin's right," Taylee conceded. "We shouldn't have opened the box. It was foolish, but we can't change that now. We have a responsibility to take it back to Uncle Jael and let him explain what it all means. Maybe he'll explain the connection to our mother."

Corwin was visibly pleased to hear her admission, but still remained guarded. "Uncle has never talked about our mother before," he said. "I don't know why you think this relic will change anything."

"It will," Taylee asserted confidently. *It has to.*

Corwin released the tension in his clenched jaw and shared an uneasy look with Tray'o, who remained captivated by the eyes of the relic, which continued to glow.

"I guess we don't really have any other option," Corwin reluctantly agreed. "Tray, come with us? We'll talk to my uncle first and see what he knows. After, I'm sure he'll happily want you to return it. Deal?"

Tray'o shifted uncomfortably. "Look, just keep it hidden, all right? If anyone busts us with its eyes glowing like that, I'm not sure how much help I can be."

Corwin nodded gratefully.

"Can we please go now? Uncle's probably already made it to town." Taylee was impatient; they'd already wasted too much time debating as it was.

"What about …?" Corwin inclined his head toward the two guards who still hadn't moved.

"Don't worry about them. They're mutes."

"They have no tongues?" Corwin asked in surprise.

Tray'o smiled as they resumed walking down toward the Krydor Markets. "I should clarify. By 'mutes,' I mean they're paid quite well to keep silent."

Taylee faked a laugh. Although she was happy that they were finally moving, she couldn't shake the uncomfortable feeling that her mother's relic might actually contain dark magic.

Chapter Three — The Master's Tent

"Anyone who discovers a relic shall immediately bring it to the Temple for inspection and possible reward. Magic is not for amusement; there are repercussions for its unauthorized use."

—PUBLIC DECREE OF THE SEVENTH ELDER ORDER, A.P. 601

Tray'o was torn between a feeling of ecstasy and terror.

Not only was he indirectly in possession of what seemed to be a relic—a rare and unusual one at that—but, more importantly, he was also in the presence of Taylee Medisto.

Even dressed in that cheaply made holiday dress, she was quite beautiful. He loved the way her soft, brown hair curled gently around her face and accented her high cheekbones, and the way her smile, so pure and sweet, could light up a whole room. And then there were her eyes: large and innocent when she wanted, but mischievous too, and always shifting between greens and browns.

Brown for innocent, green for mischief, Tray'o mused.

She was everything he'd ever wanted in a woman, and more. They'd been through a lot together, yet somehow, she had never seemed to recognize his deep affection. He had silently loved her since the time he almost drowned in the mud-pit as a child and she had rescued him. The memory of her, so cute and muddy, giggling at his foolish mistake, forced Tray'o to tighten every muscle in his face in order to restrain the grin that threatened to possess his mouth.

"You look nice," Tray'o said as he glanced away from her in an attempt to feign indifference.

"Thanks," Taylee replied politely.

Be calm, Tray. Keep it under control. You could all be in a lot of trouble, he ordered himself as he locked his eyes on the road.

The Krydor Markets were in sight now, and Tray'o could almost feel the energy pulsating from behind the famous wooden walls.

While Tray'o almost always found the Markets to be entertaining, there was something uniquely special about going during Mid-Luminous. It was as if the whole area transformed from a ruthless and unforgiving trade town to a thriving world of adventure. Merchants offered special deals, new booths were set up for gambling, and visitors from all across the Outskirts gathered to pay tribute and participate in the festivities. Everyone was united by this one sacred holiday, and in a kingdom that was often set on individualism, this was a very rare and special thing.

On top of all that excitement, they were on a mission to locate Uncle Jael, and learn the story behind the mysterious relic.

"Do you remember exactly what Master Lunechair said about our mother?" Taylee asked as they came up to the giant, wooden gates of Krydor.

"No, not really. Just that she gave birth at Pinehouse Castle almost 16 years ago, and that my father put her necklace in the vault."

"There must have been more," Taylee insisted.

"Probably, but it was hard to hear. They were in another room and were speaking quietly."

"I wish Master Lunechair were here so we could ask him ourselves," Taylee complained.

There's a thought. "Now that you mention it, he is spending the holiday here in Krydor," Tray'o informed them.

"Really? He is?" Taylee stopped and considered that for a moment. "What if...do you think we could talk to him?"

"It's possible," Tray'o reasoned. "I mean, if anyone could tell us more about the origin of the relic, it would be him."

If he doesn't kill me for taking it in the first place, Tray'o mused. It was in times like these that he was grateful for his guards.

"Whoa, hang on," Corwin stepped in front of them. "You can't seriously be considering telling our teacher that you stole a relic from the vault!"

"I told you, it's not stealing because—"

"It's stealing!" Corwin snapped.

Wow. Someone's having a grumpy birthday.

Taylee lovingly placed a hand on her brother's shoulder. "Brother, listen, Master Lunechair has always liked me," she said. "I know he'd understand once we explained how it was a misunderstanding and everything."

"And what if he doesn't understand? What if he tells Lord Rai'o?"

Tray'o laughed. "My father wouldn't care as long as the relic was returned. The *Lord of Pinehouse* is too *busy* attending meetings in Lightspire to waste time on the affairs of the people he supposedly rules." Even though he knew he shouldn't, Tray'o always found it hard to say his father's title without a tone of mockery.

"Master Lunechair … Why didn't I think of that sooner? This could solve everything!" Taylee said.

From the few encounters Tray'o had in the past with Uncle Jael, he understood why Taylee was reluctant to talk with him; her uncle clearly loved them, but was a strict and unreasonable man.

"I'd say it's worth a shot. His tent is right over there. We could stop by before going into the markets if you want." Tray'o pointed to a bright, yellow-striped tent outside the town walls.

"No. We agreed on taking it to Uncle Jael," Corwin insisted.

Taylee groaned in frustration. "C'mon, Cor! Tray'o thinks it might contain dark magic. Master Lunechair knows all about relics, and may know why our mother had it in the first place. Uncle Jael will be happy we went to our teacher for help."

Corwin frowned as he looked from the tent toward the crowded streets of Krydor. "Uncle Jael asked us to stay home—so going behind his back and trying to cover this all up—it's just another way we're disobeying."

"Fine, do what you want. Confess and take the blame—that's fine with me. But Tray'o and I are taking the necklace and going to talk to Master Lunechair." Taylee declared this with all the confidence in the world that Tray'o was going with her.

Which he was, of course.

"Taylee!" Corwin snapped. "You know we aren't supposed to wander Krydor alone!"

"But I won't be alone. I'll have Tray'o and his two silent sentries. I'm sure you can borrow one, if you're worried about being all by yourself."

Corwin narrowed his eyes at her, clearly offended by the implication that he was afraid.

"Don't worry, Cor. I'll make sure Taylee is safe. We'll just ask some questions and clear things up. We'll meet up with you after," Tray'o suggested.

Before Corwin could say no—and much to the relief of Tray'o—Taylee argued his case.

"So it's settled. Everyone gets their way. Happy or not, we're going."

"Fine. But know I don't approve. When I find Uncle Jael in the markets, I'm going to tell him all about this."

"Go ahead! By then, we'll have already sorted everything out and there will be nothing to be punished for, except maybe for you wasting Uncle's time." Taylee giggled as she danced away from him and toward the tent.

"We'll meet up with you soon," Tray'o promised.

Corwin nodded and, without another word, slipped past the gate and into the city.

Snapping his fingers with joy, Tray'o chased after Taylee.

Now if only I didn't have these two oafs following me around, it would be perfect. Time alone with Taylee was rare, and he did not want to waste this opportunity.

Master Lunechair's tent was unique in design: circular, with yellow-striped canvas wrapped tightly around three large beams of wood protruding from a hole in the middle that allowed smoke to lazily escape into the sky. On one side, a triangular hole was cut, and the flap drawn shut.

"Well, Taylee Medisto," Tray'o said with a wink, "shall we see if you're right about your teacher's support?"

"I'm rarely wrong, Tray," Taylee smirked at him as she pulled back the tent's flap.

Inside it was dark, and it took Tray'o's eyes a moment to adjust. The only light came from the hole above them, and a small fire pit burning in the centre. The tent was decorated with furs and brightly coloured pillows, but otherwise it was pretty simple in design.

Looks like something a merchant would live in. Tray'o was disappointed. He had secretly hoped a more intriguing atmosphere might spark some romance for the two of them.

He hadn't even noticed the curled mass of a man lying among the furs.

"Uncle!?" Taylee exclaimed as she ran over and dropped to her knees. Sprawled flat on his back, Jael Medisto tossed about feverishly.

Tray'o could hardly believe it. *Why is Jael here? And what happened to him?*

"Rhem, get Corwin and bring him back here. Quickly!" Tray'o ordered one of his guards, who nodded obediently before slipping out of the tent flap. Of the two guards, Jarv was the better runner, but Rhem often proved more reliable.

"Taylee …" Jael rasped through fits of coughing. "My girl."

"Hang on, Uncle. You're sick. We're going to get you help," Taylee said as she held her uncle's head.

Jael's eyes were wide with panic as white foam started forming at the corners of his mouth and he began to vomit.

He's been poisoned. Tray'o could hardly believe it. He and Jael had their differences, but that didn't mean he wanted the man to die.

All at once, Jael let out a horrid groan as all the colour drained from his face. His eyes abruptly jerked left and rolled into the back of his head as his right hand clenched into a tight fist. His face suddenly turned purple, and his whole body was sent into violent convulsions. Tray'o had seen this once before and knew what had to be done.

"Roll him on his side," Tray'o ordered.

Taylee didn't seem to hear him and instead tried to hold her uncle's thrashing body still.

"His side, Taylee! He's choking!"

As if paralysed by the shock, Taylee would not hear him, forcing Tray'o to reach over and grab her by the shoulders.

"No!" she pleaded as Tray'o pried her away so he could get to Jael.

"Trust me!"

He attempted to keep her away with one hand while struggling to roll Jael onto his side with the other. With great effort, Tray'o finally rolled Jael over so that he wouldn't choke on his own tongue or vomit.

"What's happening to him?" Taylee pushed past Tray'o and retook her position by her uncle's head.

"He's seizing. Watch his neck," Tray'o said as he scanned the tent for something—anything—that could be used to help Jael.

If only there were ocean water … Tray'o recalled that the salt in ocean water could help pass poison through the body.

"Please, god, don't let him die!" Taylee reached into her pocket and pulled out a folded prayer cloth. "Uncle Jael doesn't deserve this!"

Jael continued thrashing, but the coughing and vomiting would not seem to end.

He can't breathe. The feeling of helplessness was unbearable. *Why won't he breathe?*

Suddenly, with several desperate gasps for air, Jael lurched backward and let out a long, painful groan.

And just like that, the convulsions stopped.

The whole tent was still.

Jael's face was still purple and his eyes were void of all life.

He's gone, Tray'o thought and sank to his knees.

It was as if time itself had stopped.

Tray'o struggled to make sense of it. In a matter of minutes, everything had changed, and the world seemed a darker place for it.

How could Syyris allow this? he wondered bitterly. *Who would poison Jael? He has no wealth, no secrets, nothing worth killing for.* Nothing made any sense.

Tray'o tried to clear his mind. Thinking this way usually took him to dark places, and he preferred to avoid a negative mental spiral at all costs. Instead, he focused on Taylee, and felt the loss anew through the sorrow in her eyes.

Her knuckles were white from clenching the prayer cloth, and her face was wet with tears. All the joy and innocence that were once a feature of her face now seemed nothing more than a vague and distant memory.

Will she ever smile again?

"Hey ..." Tray'o wanted to comfort her with his arm, but Taylee shoved him away.

"No! He's not dead. He can't be dead!"

Tray'o wanted so desperately to take away her pain, but knew he was powerless to do anything.

"I'm so sorry," he muttered as Taylee, overcome with emotion, sobbed bitterly into her uncle's shoulder.

"It's not fair!" she screamed. "Wake up! Wake UP!"

But there was still no response. Except for the crackling of the fire and the sobs of Taylee, a painful silence hung in the air.

"Is it because of the relic? I'm the one who used it—me!" Taylee sobbed a prayer as she clung to Jael's stiff body. "Don't punish him because of what I did. I'm so sorry! I took the necklace and accidently turned it on. I didn't know it was Plyyston's magic! I never meant for anything bad to happen. Don't take my uncle, please. Spare his life, please don't let him die!"

Hearing her in so much sorrow broke his heart. Tray'o ran his hands through his hair and tried to think of what to do next, but everything seemed like a blur. How could they go from such happiness to such tragedy in a matter of minutes?

If Taylee was still praying, Tray'o couldn't tell. All he could hear was thumping in his ears from blood coursing through his body and the sound of laboured breathing.

Wait … breathing!

"Taylee!" Tray'o nearly exploded with relief. "Your uncle is still alive!"

"What?" She whipped her head around.

"Look! His chest!" Tray'o couldn't believe he didn't notice it sooner. It was subtle, but Jael's chest was slowly rising and falling.

Taylee's eyes lit up as she noticed it too. "He's alive!"

For now. The breaths were quite shallow. Tray'o knew he was still at risk.

"Jarv, help me pick him up," Tray'o ordered.

"No!" Taylee exclaimed. "Don't move him. He needs to recover!"

"He can't stay here. Whoever poisoned him could come back. His best chance at surviving is if we get him to Pinehouse. My father has medicine there. But we have to hurry," Tray'o insisted.

The look on Taylee's face indicated that she knew he was right but wasn't happy about it.

"Be careful with him," Taylee warned Jarv.

Jarv nodded respectfully to her as he gently scooped up Jael in his arms.

Without wasting another second, Tray'o peeled back the flap of the tent.

But as his eyes adjusted to the light of the sun, he almost wished they'd remained inside.

OOOOOOOOMMMMMMMPAAAAAAAA!

The low alarm blast of a brass instrument boomed through the air and confirmed that his eyes did not deceive him.

The fields that surrounded the Krydor Markets were burning.

Chapter Four — The Day the Night Won

"... there is nothing more dangerous to our survival than pride. Except for perhaps the Locura."

—ELDER JERAMEE, A.P. 6
THE NINE SINS OF NIGHT

Corwin often thought of the Krydor Markets as crowded, but today was taking the term to a whole new level.

"King's gone all out this year!" one merchant shouted.

"... a Mid-Luminous to remember, they say!" another cheered.

Corwin struggled to squeeze past one merchant after another as he pressed his way through the over-crowded street.

"... be a fool to miss out on this!"

"... if I were king, Essence would be cheaper on holidays..."

"... even my cousin is winning today! Been rolling dice for the last year ..."

For the most part, the voices all blurred together into a meaningless cacophony of joy and complaint; any hope of isolating a single voice was rapidly fading, and Corwin wanted nothing more than to shut them all out.

How am I supposed to find Uncle Jael in all this? Corwin wondered right before a rather plump merchant knocked him aside as he rushed by with a crate of apples under one arm.

"Watch it!" Corwin snapped, knowing it was pointless.

No one cares.

Irritated, Corwin crossed his arms, kept his head down, and pushed forward.

I should have tried harder to stop Taylee from opening that box, he thought angrily, cursing his own curiosity and his sister's impulsiveness. If the relic was full of dark magic, the consequences could be dire. *Just when I needed the blessing of Syyris the most...*

By the time he reached the market square, Corwin's tunic was damp with sweat and clung uncomfortably to his body.

Although the market square of Krydor wasn't anything special to look at, it was easily considered the heart and soul of the Outskirts. It was here that all the trading happened; depending on the season, one's entire survival during Night rested in the hands of a greedy merchant dealing in this square.

Most of the time, Corwin felt the square brought out the worst in people. And Mid-Luminous often proved to make things even worse than that.

No wonder Uncle Jael doesn't want us to come here on holidays. This place is chaos.

People of every shape, size, and colour were packed into the square, waving bottles of Essence and screaming curses at one another while attempting to make their trades. At the base of a nearby tree, two shirtless men battled each other with short knives while a group of stout gamblers bet on the winner. In another corner, a man boasted of having captured Locura that you could view for only three bottles of Essence.

This is pointless. Corwin grumbled as he strained to see over the heads of those in the square. He was tall for his age, but his vision was being constantly obscured the crowds.

If I'm going to have any chance of finding my uncle, I have to get higher, Corwin realised, casting his eye to the nearest and tallest structure in Krydor, a watchtower.

All the watchtowers in Krydor were about 50 feet in height, and, like most everything in Krydor, carved mostly out of wood.

"Hello?" Corwin called up the solitary ladder that led to the upper platform of the watchtower.

There was no response, and after a moment of deliberation, he concluded that there was no better option than to climb to the top and try to convince the guard to let him look around.

I'm sure no one will mind, he persuaded himself as he grabbed hold of the first rung of the ladder and pulled his body up.

Rung by rung, Corwin climbed effortlessly. Though only mildly afraid of heights, he found that as long as he kept in steady motion and didn't look down it wasn't so bad.

After climbing higher than he would have personally liked, he finally reached the last rung and eagerly pulled himself onto the platform.

Much to his confusion, the watchtower was completely abandoned.

Even the guards must be off celebrating. He frowned. Not that it really mattered. Everyone knew Mid-Luminous was the safest time of the year. Guards in towers during the Day were fairly redundant.

Feeling quite satisfied with his plan to climb above the crowd, Corwin carefully leaned over the edge of the tower in an attempt to spot his uncle more easily.

From this height, he could see just how vast the crowd really was. There were more people crammed into the streets than he knew even existed in all of the Outskirts. Although he didn't like being so high up, there was a big advantage; from this vantage point, he didn't have to overhear their irritating conversation or find himself jostled by person after person.

As he looked around, Corwin found himself distracted and amused by the gamblers. Whenever they would lose at dice or cards, they would shuffle around angrily and curse their luck before turning around to immediately try again.

Corwin noticed all sorts of people: the proud merchants, almost always overweight and in a hurry; the young men and women, dressed in their finest clothes attempting to attract a mate; and of course, the many musicians, loudly squawking and strumming and banging on their instruments in the vain hope of overpowering the noise of the crowd and their competition.

Corwin was amazed by all the different types of people he could see. *But none of them are the man I'm looking for.*

He let out a defeated sigh and was about to give up his search for his uncle when he noticed a man dressed in red Pinehouse armour, pushing frantically through the crowd.

Corwin's heart leapt into his throat.

It was one of the guards who was escorting Tray'o earlier!

He wouldn't have left Tray unless something was wrong.

Shouting at the top of his lungs, Corwin tried to draw the guard's attention. "Hey! HEY!"

Nothing.

It was useless.

From that height, and with all the festivities taking place below, there was no chance of being heard.

Is he looking for me? Corwin wondered as he watched the guard rapidly scan faces in the crowd and push from one person to another.

Thinking his best bet was to descend from the watchtower and find out for himself, Corwin reached for the ladder and was about to climb down when he detected the faint smell of something burning.

That can't be smoke, Corwin told himself despite his nostrils flaring in agitated protest. *The fire ban in Krydor wouldn't change because of a holiday …*

Once again, Corwin's curiosity got the better of him, and he decided, since he was already up so high, that he may as well check over the other side of the tower and look beyond the eastern wall.

But when he got to the other side and looked over the rail, he almost lost his breath.

Outside the Krydor Markets, pillars of thick, black smoke were starting to rise from all across the horizon.

The fields are burning!

And that wasn't the worst of it.

Just on the other side of the nearest wall, a small cluster of ominous black-cloaked figures were gathering next to a row of what appeared to be cages on wheels.

He didn't have time to analyze the situation.

Scrambling across the platform, Corwin reached for the ladder and started a rapid descent into the celebratory crowd below.

None of them know what's coming, and with no guards to sound the alarm, they could all be burned alive ...

Corwin stopped midway down the ladder as he realised the gravity of the situation.

If he kept going, he could possibly escape before the fire reached the city.

But at what cost?

It wasn't much of a dilemma. Corwin knew what had to be done.

He scrambled back up the ladder faster than he'd descended.

Maybe I imagined it, he desperately hoped as he climbed back onto the platform and ran to the rail.

Much to his sorrow, the fire still raged on, and the black figures were closer now, surrounding the city on all sides. Without wasting another minute, he grabbed the coiled horn that served as the watchtower alarm and pressed one end tightly to his lips.

Inhaling as deeply as he could, he blew into it with all the strength his lungs could muster.

OOOOOOOOMMMMMMMPAAAAAAAA!

He took another breath and blew again.

OOOOOOOOMMMMMMMPAAAAAAAA!

The brass horn, though low in pitch, boomed above the clamour of the crowd beneath him.

Whatever they were doing before, everyone stopped at once and, unmoving, cast their silent gaze up at him.

Why are they just staring? Corwin wanted more than anything to yell into the horn, "*This is an alarm! Run!*"

He was about to sound it a third time when another instrument answered his call. Only this time, it wasn't a horn.

KRAUNCHHHHHETTCH!

The sound was unique—a magnified version of the sound Corwin imagined his sheep might make if they accidently chewed on gravel or on broken glass, and were gasping for air.

He didn't need to imagine what caused the sound, though. He knew the stories.

The call of the Locura.

And just like that, the panic started.

At first it was just one person screaming—a woman, he thought—but her voice was immediately lost among the shrill screams of many more.

KRAUNCHHHHHETTCH!

The timber of the enemy's instrument was paralyzing.

They don't come out during the Day, Corwin's brain insisted. *They aren't supposed to be able to organize like this!*

It didn't make any sense, and yet, there they were, waiting outside the city with cages.

It was rumoured that the Locura fed on fear, and if you showed them that you weren't afraid, they would leave you alone.

Unfortunately, he was afraid, and just below him, people were shouting and beginning to race wildly through the streets, creating enough noise and fear to feed the entire horde of Locura.

Corwin ducked as a black rock soared over the wall and straight into the crowd below, carrying with it an overpowering stench of ash and burning flesh.

That's no rock! Corwin realised as it landed near the base of his tower and exploded into a spray of bright white smoke and fire.

Sorcery!

If it were even possible, the screams increased as more smoking rocks soared over the walls and began to engulf the entire city in smoke and flame.

Corwin wasn't sure what to do; staying in the wooden tower would be useless with the city burning, but climbing down into the fray below wouldn't do him much good either with the white smoke blinding everyone.

Ultimately, he didn't need to decide, because before he could do anything, the base of his tower erupted in flame.

Corwin cursed at the top of his lungs as the ropes that held the beams in place snapped, causing the tower to break free of its foundation and lean dangerously close to the wall.

It's going to fall! Panic shot through his veins as the platform shifted and swayed.

Corwin stumbled backward as he desperately reached for the ladder, the railing, or anything that might keep him from falling.

But it was no use.

The tower rapidly deteriorated under the strain and intensity of the roaring flames, and so, in a frantic act of desperation, Corwin flung himself over the rail just as the tower collapsed against the city wall and set both structures ablaze.

Falling helplessly through the air, he tried to direct his body into the branches of a nearby tree.

Reaching out his hands to take hold of the branches proved worthless. They were old and weak, and snapped as soon as he tumbled into them.

This is it. This is how you die. He shut his eyes as he broke through branch after branch on his way to the ground, which was rapidly rushing up to meet him.

Though falling several feet through the branches of a tree effectively slowed his fall, the velocity with which he slammed into the ground was enough to knock all the air from his lungs and force Corwin into a barely conscious state.

Rolling in agony at the base of the tree, he gasped for air.

Breathe, he desperately ordered his injured body. *Breathe!*

It wasn't easy, but after several desperate attempts and with great physical strain, he was finally able to coax a bit of air into his lungs.

Wheezing and in excruciating pain, Corwin forced his eyes open and struggled to see past the inky black spots that now blotted his vision. Black smoke from the fire, mixed with white smoke from the sorcerers' rocks, swirled together into the sky and eclipsed the

Mid-Luminous sun.

If he wasn't in so much pain, he might have considered it beautiful.

"Get up, you fool!" A familiar voice broke through the fog that was now clouding his brain.

Uncle Jael?

Corwin struggled to focus his eyes on the blurry shape that stood above him.

If he had had the breath or wits to do it, he might have laughed.

Standing above him was some sort of man, but one whose elongated features and gangly frame were more reminiscent of a mythical monkey than anyone Corwin knew.

The man wore a short, pointy black hat that barely covered his greying hair, and a long, wispy moustache sprayed out from under his big, drooping nose.

But with his face shadowed by the hat, and his back to the raging flames and billowing white smoke, he took on an almost sinister look. For a split second, Corwin thought perhaps it was not a man nor a monkey, but one of Plyyston's demon Locura, searching for the Nightwolf relic.

"E don'ave et," Corwin mumbled what should have been words as he struggled to stay conscious.

The man tilted his head and crouched down to get a better look.

The next thing Corwin knew, he was grabbed and tossed over the shoulders of the man, the same way he would carry a sick sheep.

"Lemme 'o!" Corwin tried to speak, but found his tongue quite numb and heavy.

"Keep quiet," the monkey-man demanded.

Silence made no sense to Corwin.

Everyone is screaming, he thought dimly to himself as the sounds of frightened people filled the air.

In this light-headed state, Corwin almost found the chaotic

sounds relaxing – that is, until he heard what sounded like his sister emitting a blood-curdling scream.

"Taee! Wer'eshe?" he blundered the words.

"Stop struggling! I'm saving your life!" the man said.

I'm struggling? Corwin didn't realise he was even moving. *Who is this man?* As interesting as it would be, Corwin realised that there was no way it was a monkey carrying him.

And Locura can't talk …

The man charged through the blinding smoke, around wailing merchants, and over burning booths.

The tent! a voice in his head insisted. *Something about a tent …*

The thought didn't stick, though, for the next thing he knew, they were facing a blazing city gate.

"Ee gonn bern!" Corwin tried to warn over the roar of the fire, but it was no use. Without taking a second for consideration, the mad man rushed through the inferno with Corwin on his shoulders.

Before this, Corwin thought he knew what heat was, but nothing he'd ever experienced could compare to the intensity he felt raging inside the gate.

The smell of burning wood caused his breath to sting, and he had to blink repeatedly to keep from tearing up.

Thankfully, it did not last long.

Almost as soon as they entered, they were free, beyond the gate and outside the city.

"Unol 'ael," Corwin mumbled. *Why won't my tongue work?*

He could still hear the screams from inside the city, and his mind turned to the thought of his uncle, possibly trapped and burning alive in the market square.

"Trust me! We need to get far from here!" The voice of his rescuer was clearer now, but he still couldn't quite recognize it.

The tent. What if Taylee and Tray'o are still in the tent?

It was unlikely still standing, but at this point, he could think of little else.

Corwin tried to lift his head so he could look around. It took a second, but when he located the strange little yellow tent, he wished he hadn't.

Like everything else, it was consumed by flame.

Taylee! Tray'o!

Fueled by anguish, Corwin fought to get free of the man's grasp.

It took quite a bit of thrashing, but he was able to successfully throw the man off balance, causing them both to tumble into the dirt.

Corwin hit the ground hard but didn't feel a thing.

Immediately, shaking himself loose of the man's grasp, he started to crawl on his elbows toward the burning tent as bitter tears formed in his eyes.

KRAUNCHHHHHETTCH!

Corwin looked up.

Clearly unbeknownst to his rescuer at the time of their escape, a single gate of Krydor remained unaffected by the flames, and people streamed out of it, escaping from the city.

We went through the fire for nothing?

It took him a second, but he quickly realised that as soon as anyone escaped through the gate, they were grabbed by the dark-robed figures and tossed into the cages he had noticed earlier.

As the robed figures were so focused on catching the helpless victims fleeing through the open gate, they somehow didn't notice their escape from the flaming one.

Though his vision was still clouded and blurry, he could make out that the robed figures were tall and thin. However the way they stood and moved seemed more human than he imagined Locura should behave.

Dark Ones. There could be little doubt.

And now, in the arms of one of them, Corwin spotted Tray'o and Taylee, struggling to get free as they were shoved with the others toward an open cage.

Corwin was about to shout to them when the hand of his

rescuer covered his mouth. "Quiet, you fool!"

But Corwin simply watch as those he loved were taken captive. Without a second thought, he chomped his mouth down on the hand of his rescuer, who yelped in pain and released his grip.

"Taee! Unn!" Corwin shouted as loud as his injured body would allow.

It was enough.

The Dark One who held Taylee shot a look in his direction, and as it did, Taylee was able to elbow it in the chest and break free of its grasp. Corwin watched with relief as his sister bolted away.

His rescuer did not share his sense of victory though, and forcefully grabbed Corwin from behind in an attempt to toss him over his shoulder again.

But it was too late. A few of the Dark Ones, having spotted them, were advancing.

His rescuer dropped him again and frantically tried to grab something from his belt, but before he could do anything, they were surrounded.

Corwin couldn't see what happened next from his position face-first on the ground, but knew that his rescuer had been defeated when his body fell unconscious next to him.

For the first time, he was able to get a clear look at the man's face.

Master Lunechair?

Corwin rolled himself onto his back and looked up to see three robed figures peering down at him, each holding a staff. Their skin was eerily smooth and pale white, and they regarded him with black eyes and cruel, frozen smiles.

Fear gripped him, but he forced himself to stare back into the glazed, sinister eyes of the nearest one.

Rage is better than fear.

Corwin tried to stand, wanting nothing more than to fight them, but before he could fully right himself, he was struck in the forehead by a staff that sent him sprawling back down to the dirt.

His vision blurred again.

The dizziness he now experienced impeded his ability to resist as his arms were yanked in front of him and his wrists tied together.

Blackness swarmed his vision, and all the rage he'd felt only seconds before seemed to drain out of his ears and into the dirt.

Not rage. Blood, Corwin thought idly as his brain shut off.

Then there was only silence.

Chapter Five — Rise of the Midnight Sun

"I hate 'Dark Ones.' Bloody worshippers of Locura. Somehow, they think offering other humans as sacrifices will earn them protection. A foul way to make a living, if you ask me."

—AALARDIN NEY'RK, A.P. 412
A TRADEMASTER'S GUIDE TO GOODS, GODS, AND GIRLS

Desperate sobbing brought Corwin back to consciousness.

The combined effect of the fall and being struck in the head caused such a horrible throbbing in his brain that he struggled to form coherent thoughts.

The tent, the tent! A voice echoed in his memory.

But he couldn't remember what it meant, or why the voice was so frantic.

His eyelids felt as if they were held down by heavy weights, and only with a great deal of effort was he able to force them open.

The bright gold sun glared down at him through the swaying of iron bars above.

From its position in the sky Corwin suspected that it was still Mid-Luminous, but without familiar landmarks with which to place the sun's location over the horizon, the amount of time that passed was impossible to know.

I've only been out a few hours, he suspected. *But why was I sleeping in the first place?*

Touching his hand to his chest, Corwin realised his shirt was soaking wet. In fact, he was entirely wet, and lying in damp straw inside what appeared to be a giant cage in motion.

As if reading his mind, a somewhat refined and familiar voice spoke up, "I'm guessing that's the Midnight Sun. At least, as far as I can tell. Not that time matters much to you. 'Light is not for wasting,' am I right?"

Slumped opposite from him in what he understood now was a cage, his best friend Tray'o smiled at him weakly. And just like that, all Corwin's memories came flooding back.

Lurching forward, he demanded, "Where's Taylee!?"

But the combination of having just woken up and the movement of the cage caused him to immediately lose his balance and fall helplessly against the bars.

"Easy, Cor. You've been out for a while."

Corwin grunted as he righted himself. His head felt full of jelly, and though his tongue no longer felt as heavy or numb as before, it stung something fierce.

I must have bit it when I fell. Looking around the cage, he realised with some degree of sorrow that he and Tray'o were not alone. About fourteen other dead-eyed strangers stared back at him.

"Taylee? Uncle Jael?" Corwin called out in desperation as feeling returned to his tongue.

No one responded.

"They aren't here," answered Tray'o, stumbling over his words.

What does he mean? Why aren't they here?

Corwin blinked several times as he tried to focus on his surroundings.

Thick, iron bars encased them on all sides. The metal base of the cage was covered by straw and, as best he could tell, it was attached to four outer wheels that were responsible for its motion, creating a kind of carriage. And this carriage wasn't the only one.

A single glance outside the bars revealed several more were trailing behind them, forming what appeared to be a of caravan of carriages filled with captives from Krydor.

But the most alarming part of it all was the dark, hooded figures walking alongside the cages.

"I think this is the Trade …" Tray'o admitted sadly.

Corwin shivered with the realization that what he formerly believed to be a tale used to scare children into obedience might actually be a real thing.

Even though the Locura were commonly believed to be unintelligent creatures cursed beyond any sort of rational thought, there were some humans who chose to worship them. They were known simply as Dark Ones, and were believed to capture people of all ages in order to sacrifice them to the Locura as a blood offering. No one was really sure what the Dark Ones received in exchange; none of the stories Corwin heard ever really agreed on any point other than the fact that there was no return for those taken in the Trade.

A bolt of anxiety shot into Corwin's gut as Tray'o said the name that was already beginning to plague his mind. "So … about your uncle …"

"I couldn't find him," Corwin admitted sadly.

"I know … we did. In the tent. He … he's not well, Cor."

The words were painful, but they didn't seem to take root. Maybe it was the trauma of everything he just experienced, but for some reason, Corwin wasn't surprised. "Oh," was all he managed to say.

"Thanks to your shout, Taylee got away, though …" Tray'o said, confidently at first, but the added, "I think," put her safety into question as well.

My family is lost and it's my fault.

"What happened?" Corwin heard his own voice, but it felt like it was coming from someone else.

"We found your uncle in the tent. He was sick, and then was hit by some type of seizure. I think … I think he was poisoned …" Tray'o cleared his throat before continuing. "I ordered Jarv to carry Jael to Pinehouse and get help when the Locura came … There was so much smoke, I …" Tray'o took a nervous breath. "I tried to get Taylee out safely too, but she was determined to find you …"

"I see." Corwin's voice came out as a whisper.

Poisoned? Who would poison my uncle? Would Syyris punish my uncle for our disobedience?

Tray'o pressed his back against the bars and lowered his head. "I'm sure Jael and Taylee are safely in Pinehouse right now," he suggested weakly.

Corwin nodded, though he wasn't sure his sister could outrun a horde of Dark Ones.

"What happened to Master Lunechair?" Corwin asked after a long pause.

"He's here." Tray'o nodded in the direction of a curled lump in another corner of the cage. "Like you, he's been out for hours."

Corwin stared at the curled shape of his teacher. Something about his presence filled Corwin with a sense of frustration, and he started to shake the man vigorously in an attempt to wake him.

"Don't bother." Tray'o sounded sad. "He took a pretty bad blow to the head trying to protect you."

He rescued me from the city. Why? Corwin sighed and fell helpless back into the damp straw.

The two friends rode in relative silence with only the sound of muffled sobbing and the constant creaking of the carriage to comfort them.

Unwilling to think anymore, Corwin lay back and tried to sleep. However, he found his efforts at getting rest useless due to their exposure to the bright sun and the presence of the Locura worshippers walking alongside the carriages. They had the annoying habit of splashing the prisoners with buckets of ocean water every hour or so. The first two times he shouted at them to stop, but after the third he gave up and resigned himself to reality of their current situation.

The carriages moved at a gruelingly slow pace, and even after half a sun-cycle passed, Corwin could still see the billowing black smoke from what remained of the Krydor Markets.

Everything's gone. He remembered the look of the burning fields, and tried desperately to push the thought of his flock from his mind. *I hope they got away …*

Unable to get any kind of successful rest, he found himself lying on his side and staring mindlessly at a few of his captors.

There were surprisingly few of them—about twelve Dark Ones that he could see—all dressed in the same black robes with the hoods pulled up, casting dark shadows over their white faces. They walked in steady strides next to each carriage without making a single sound.

The thing that was really confusing was that there were what appeared to be several actual Locura walking along with the Dark Ones. He assumed they were Locura because, unlike the Dark Ones in robes, they were dressed mostly in rags, exposing sores and cuts, and all were connected to the carriages by a long chain that was bound around their necks.

Considering the horrific stories he'd heard about them, the Locura actually looked quite human. They had two arms, two legs, and were clearly male or female.

But there were also terrible differences. They moved with an unusual gait, their eyes seemed to be a sickly hue of either red or black, and their pale faces were hard and sharp, almost like burned masks, some with ancient markings and symbols tattooed in various colours of ink.

The most disturbing part for Corwin was the stench; the teeth of the Locura were black and rotted, and their rancid smell was much worse than his uncle's stew the one time that he and Taylee had gone for a walk and forgotten it in the sun.

The memory of Taylee brought a weak smile to his face.

She got away and is probably with Uncle Jael in Pinehouse now, he hoped idly as he rolled over onto his other side and faced his friend. Tray'o was slumped up against the cage with his head hung low.

"I tried to protect her," Tray'o mumbled sadly.

Corwin nodded, but didn't respond.

We are the dead, Tray. There is no protecting the dead.

He had dreaded turning 16, but he never imagined it would be quite like this.

Chapter Six — The Man Who Was Skyblind

"Syyris Sagrado, the bringer of Day.
Who spared our lives for his pleasure alone.
There is no god but Him."

—THE ELDER'S CREED

Run!

Taylee knew there was no other choice; she'd been telling herself nothing else since the attack.

But her legs would no longer listen.

With an exhausted yelp, she collapsed in a small clearing surrounded by pine trees. Her ears ached, her stomach heaved, and the hot tears that streamed down her face only aggravated her further.

There's no time to rest.

She was still being chased.

Two Dark Ones had been following her since she escaped their grasp outside Krydor. Although Taylee proved to be faster, it seemed they had more endurance.

My dagger! she recalled, as she frantically reached under her dress for the blade she kept strapped to her leg.

"Leave me alone!" Taylee screamed as she pulled out the blade, rolled onto her back, and waved it at her aggressors.

The Dark Ones slowed to a stop a few feet away.

"Come any closer and I'll kill you!" she warned in her most threatening voice.

The Dark Ones exchanged a confused look with one another and then burst into throaty laughter.

Go ahead. She ground her teeth. *We'll see whose laughing when this is done.*

Although Taylee had never been in a real fight before, Uncle Jael had taught her a few tricks with a dagger in case she ever found herself in this kind of situation. Whether those tricks would work on Dark Ones was yet to be known.

Completely disregarding her warning, the two Dark Ones pulled out a small net and started to approach her.

"It'll all be over soon," one hissed at her.

Taylee swallowed the lump that was growing in her throat, clenched the dagger and braced herself for a fight.

Syyris give me strength. She was praying silently and trying to anticipate their next move when, suddenly, the crisp sound of a twig snapping caused the two villains to turn and look behind them.

A man stepped out of the forest.

Although he only appeared to be a few years younger than her uncle, his faded black vest exposed muscular arms and gave him the rugged appearance of great strength and vitality. He was at least six feet tall, with broad shoulders and a square jaw that was adored with a rather disgusting beard. His hair was a soft brown colour that contained flecks of grey and hung down to his shoulders in a tangled mess.

Hair much too long for a man, Taylee thought with a frown.

His hands were tanned and leathery. In his right he held a long, sturdy-looking oak staff and in his left he carried a bulky brown bag.

"I think you misunderstood the girl," the man's voice echoed through the forest as he slid the bag over his shoulder. "She asked you to leave her alone."

The Dark Ones hissed and lunged at him.

But the man was fast.

He spun his staff high in the air, crouched low, and cracked it down to sweep the legs out from under the two villains. The Dark Ones tumbled and hit the ground hard.

Though both were winded, one recovered quickly and tried to stand. But before he could fully get up, the man with the staff cracked him across the head and sent him sprawling back down.

"Wait! Please!" the other one cried pathetically, right before the man knocked him unconscious with the bottom end of his staff.

Taylee couldn't believe what had just happened; the two Dark Ones were out cold. "Thank you …!"

"No time. Follow!" the man ordered as he turned his back to her and darted into the forest.

Taylee scrambled to her feet and, without looking back, followed after the strange man as fast as her tired legs would allow.

They made their way deep into the forest for what felt like hours before finally coming across a small creek.

Here, the man paused and knelt down in order to fill a small leather flask with water. After taking a small sip, he passed it to Taylee.

"Again, thanks," she replied as she greedily lifted the spout to her dry lips and swallowed the water in big gulps. It was cool and refreshing, and reminded her just how tired and thirsty she actually was.

"Slower," the man insisted. "You'll make yourself sick drinking so fast."

"Sorry." Taylee handed back the flask and wiped her lips with her arm. "Do we need to keep running?"

"No," the man said as he stared into the trees. "We were not followed. We should be safe to rest here for a while."

"Great," Taylee replied and sat down by the creek. Her legs ached, her breath was short, and her stomach wouldn't stop contracting.

Breathe deeply, my girl. Taylee could almost hear the kind voice of her uncle encouraging her. As a child, whenever Taylee would get winded or run too hard, Uncle Jael was always there to advise her to take deep, deliberate breaths.

But what started off as a comforting memory soon turned sad as she realised she might never hear her uncle's voice again. It was a horrible thought, and because of it—despite great effort—she could not keep tears from forming in her eyes and blurring her vision.

"Everything will be all right. There's no need to be sad anymore." The voice of the man was reassuring, but for some reason it irritated her.

"I'm not sad," she grumbled as she aggressively knuckled the tears out of her eyes, "just … frustrated."

The man smiled. "I understand. You are safe now." He extended his hand toward her. "You may call me Skyblind."

"Skyblind?" Taylee grimaced as she shook his hand. "That's not a real name."

"What is a name but something one is called? Skyblind suits me better than my given name."

"I'm Taylee."

"Hello, Taylee," Skyblind replied. "You have no idea how glad I am to have found you."

Taylee was about to ask him why, when all at once, she noticed three little blue flames burned under his right eye in exquisite detail.

He's been marked!

"Don't move!" Taylee shouted abruptly as she pulled out her dagger once again and leaned away from him. *A criminal! But what kind, and why out here?*

Although she'd never seen a marked man before, everyone knew the warning. Three blue flames under the eye meant danger.

Confused by her sudden apprehension, the man called Skyblind looked at her curiously before letting out a deep sigh.

"Ah, yes. The mark. It's been so long since someone reacted, I'd almost forgotten it was there." He frowned thoughtfully to himself. "You have nothing to fear from me, child. I'm on your side."

Although he did help her and seemed friendly, she chose to remain extra alert.

You should run, she told herself. *But where would I go? And anyway, he'd just catch me.*

Taylee wasn't sure what to do, so she decided to play dumb. "I've … never seen a mark like that before." She did her best to make her voice sound innocent and curious.

Skyblind tilted his head slightly. "You are speaking truthfully. But you know what it means," he stated.

"No, I don't," she lied.

Skyblind stared at her with doubt in his eyes. "You do, otherwise you wouldn't still be waving that dagger at me."

"I don't, I swear! I grew up in the Outskirts and haven't seen anything like that before. It just … scares me."

She could tell by the disappointed look on his face that he knew she was lying. "In Lightspire, when a man is exiled from the Kingdom, the Elders mark him to warn anyone he comes in contact with that he is dangerous and untrustworthy," he explained as he methodically touched each individual flame with his finger.

Taylee couldn't believe he was being honest about it. *He knows I know, that's all. He has to be honest.* "So you're telling me you're dangerous …?"

"By nature, all men and women are dangerous, Taylee. But most people are able to hide their marks."

She lowered the dagger slightly but kept a firm grip. "Why were you exiled?"

"That is a long and painful story that we do not have time for now. But I can promise you, it was not because I did anything evil or harmful."

Taylee wanted to believe him, but the mark kept glaring at her. *He is dangerous—he even told you. You need to run!*

Despite the frantic voice in her head, something about the way he spoke so honestly and gently captivated her attention. *A dangerous man doesn't speak like this. He speaks like my uncle.*

Even still, she couldn't seem to quell the fear in her heart.

Search his eyes. It's the only way you'll know for sure, Taylee concluded. With great reluctance, she forced herself to look past the mark and meet his gaze.

The eyes of the man called Skyblind were unlike any she'd ever seen before. They were deep brown and gentle, yet stern, glowing with an intense inner light that could in no way be described as safe, yet was not malicious either. She couldn't put her finger on what it was about this man, but something about his presence brought comfort.

Even though he was marked, she felt her trust in him return.

If he wanted to harm me, he could have easily done so by now, Taylee realised and lowered her dagger. "I'm sorry for being rude. I just… I've been through a lot."

"Indeed," he said as he slid the brown bag from his shoulders and pulled out a metal pot and a few logs of wood. "Does it have to do with why those men were chasing you?"

"Yeah," she mumbled. "I got lost trying to get away from them and the fire."

"What fire?"

"The Locura. They attacked Krydor … and my uncle … he …" Her voice quivered.

At the mention of the Locura, Skyblind furrowed his eyebrows and silently worked his mouth. "Interesting," he replied at last. "Well … do not fear them. You are safe here with me. Help build the fire and I will prepare a meal for us."

Although she had no real reason to believe him, something about his words caused the tension she had been carrying in her shoulders to release.

A minute ago she was desperately trying to figure out an escape, and now, she sat comfortably across from him fixing a fire while he prepared to make some stew in the pot.

"Do you … live out here?" she asked as her voice and curiosity strengthened.

"In a sense, yes," Skyblind answered as he stirred the stew with wooden spoon. "I've been living all around the wilderness for many years … too many years." His voice was sad.

"Because of the mark?" Taylee asked carelessly. She knew it was rude, but she couldn't help herself; her curiosity was growing more and more with each passing second.

Skyblind poured some of the stew into a wooden bowl but gave no answer. "Eat this," he instructed, passing her the bowl.

It wasn't until the tasty aroma of freshly cut potatoes and carrots wafted to her nose that her stomach rumbled.

Taylee licked her lips and eagerly devoured the stew. It wasn't particularly delicious, but after eating nothing but hash for weeks, it felt as though she was eating from the King's own table.

The two ate in silence, and when the stew was gone, and her offers to help clean up continually refused, Taylee resolved to recline by the fire while Skyblind scrubbed the bowls clean with dirt and water from the creek.

Everything felt about as normal as possible—not counting his unnerving mark and their current location—until he finished cleaning the final bowl.

Without a word of explanation, Skyblind crouched on his knees, lowered his head to the ground, and gradually rocked back and forth while making guttural sounds in his throat. It reminded her of what she'd seen some people do when they worshipped at the temple of Syyris. But there were no icons here, nothing visible to worship or hold, and yet Skyblind continued in what could only be prayer.

After several minutes of earnest rocking, he returned to his spot by the fire and pulled a small, worn, and dirty red book out of his bag.

"What were you doing?" she asked when it felt appropriate to speak.

"Giving thanks," Skyblind responded as he opened his book.

"Giving thanks? To what?"

"To *whom*," Skyblind corrected her. "To God."

Something about his answer made Taylee uneasy. "Obviously to god. But with what idol? Syyris can't hear you without one," Taylee reminded him.

I wonder if I should lend him my prayer cloth?

Skyblind cast a sad glance at her and shook his head. "Let heathens to their idols haste, and worship wood or stone. But my delightful lot is cast where the True God is known." The words flowed off his lips as if he'd spoken them a hundred times.

He speaks blasphemy like poetry. Taylee was shocked. "I don't understand, don't you worship Syyris?"

"No."

"But … you have to! There's only one god—Syyris—and he sent you to help me. You're an answer to my prayer!"

"You're right in saying there is only one God, but his name is not Syyris."

Taylee tensed up. *Is he a Dark One after all? Has he come for the necklace?*

As if reading her mind, Skyblind reassured her with a smile. "Relax, child. His name is not Plyyston, either. I worship the True God—the God of both Day and Night."

Taylee hesitated. "What you're saying … I've never heard anyone say such a thing. Day and Night are separate forces. There isn't a god of good *and* evil."

Skyblind locked eyes on her and closed his book. "You are young, Taylee. There are still a great many things you do not yet know."

Though the man spoke in a gentle way, she didn't like the implication that she was young and ignorant.

"I see." Taylee turned away from him and stared deeply into the fire.

But as she watched the leaping flames, her mind wandered to all the things she really *didn't* know, like what had happened to her uncle, the nature of the mysterious relic, and the truth about why her parents had left them.

Maybe he's right. Maybe I really don't know anything.

After a moment of heavy silence, she worked up the courage to ask the question that was now plaguing her. "What makes you think that Syyris is not god?"

Skyblind sighed. “Syyris is an idol, and cannot speak; my God is living and I have heard his voice.”

Taylee bit her lower lip. *Is this why he was marked? For denying Syyris?* It was strange to think that anyone would even consider denying the existence of their god. *He's not a Dark One … but has time alone in the wilderness driven him mad?* She wasn't sure that madness was the better option.

“God spoke to you?” Taylee asked uneasily.

“Yes. In a dream. After many long years He has finally shown me how to make His name known.”

Taylee shook her head in disbelief. “Dreams don't mean anything. They're just dreams.”

“This was not a normal dream. It was how I knew where to find you, and how I know your brother will not be killed.”

“Nice try.” Taylee couldn't help but be skeptical. “There's no way a dream could tell you all that.”

“As I said, it was no normal dream,” Skyblind looked up and stared deeply into her eyes. “In it, God showed me many things—including the relic you found.”

Taylee froze. *He must have seen me with it. He's trying to trick me.*

“I don't know what you're talking about,” she said in as casual a tone as she could muster.

“Yes,” Skyblind replied confidently. “You do.”

Taylee watched with confusion as Skyblind stared up into the sky and hummed softly. It was a soothing tune, and in any other circumstance she would have been quite captivated by the melody, but right now the abruptness of it was more of an annoyance, and Taylee longed for it to end.

When he finally finished, he grasped his book and kissed the cover. Taylee was torn between her desire to trust him and her doubts of his sanity. *Whether sane or not, somehow he knew about the Nightwolf.*

“What does the relic mean, then? I have to know,” she demanded abruptly.

After another excruciatingly long pause, Skyblind made eye

contact. "It means you and your brother are miracles. It means the age of Syyris is finally drawing to an end. It means God has heard my prayers."

"That's not what I'm asking." She frowned. "I was told the relic belonged to my mother. But why? Why would she have it? Does it contain dark magic?"

Were my parents Dark Ones? She wanted to ask it out loud, but suddenly felt afraid that saying it might make it real.

"You asked me what it meant, not what it is or where it came from. Now you must rest and regain your strength. We have a long journey ahead of us."

Taylee froze. "We?"

"Yes. God brought us together for a purpose; we must follow His lead."

Taylee couldn't believe what she was hearing. "I appreciate you giving me something to eat, but I can't go with you. I have to find Corwin and my uncle."

"They will be fine." Skyblind spoke as if there wasn't a single doubt in his mind. "If you come with me, I will tell you everything you want to know."

"Everything, huh?" Taylee crossed her arms. "Even about my parents? And the origin of the relic?"

"Yes, Taylee. Everything."

He's serious, she realised as she looked into his eyes again. They were not the shifty eyes of a liar, nor were they wide with madness; they were the open, intense eyes of a man who truly believed every word he was speaking.

Taylee hesitated. *He was right about me having a relic. What else does he know? Could he actually be hearing from some other god?* The offer to go with him and find out was tempting.

But her uncle needed her help, and Master Lunechair. Her teacher had been captured with Corwin and Tray'o. While Skyblind possibly had answers, Master Lunechair certainly did.

"I'm sorry," Taylee said as she stood up from her place by the fire, "but I can't abandon my family and friends."

For the first time since their meeting, Skyblind seemed confused. He let out a long sigh and cast a questioning glance to the sky.

"But," Taylee said with a sly smile, "you could come with me. I could use help if I'm going to free them."

Skyblind shook his head. "The help you need does not come from man."

She continued talking as if she hadn't heard him. "Once I know for certain my family is safe we can discuss this journey of yours again. And you can tell me all about your god."

"You tempt me. But I am called in a different direction."

Taylee shrugged and tried to make herself sound as indifferent as possible. "That's fine. We'll just go our separate ways then."

Skyblind stared at her intently as he rubbed his beard with his thumb and forefinger.

He doesn't want me to leave him.

"You'll go after the Locura alone?"

"Guess so," she replied.

"Are you certain that's wise?"

Taylee shrugged her shoulders. "Probably not. But unless you help me, I don't see any other option."

Skyblind worked his mouth back and forth as if he were chewing his next words before speaking them. "You walk a dangerous path, Taylee Medisto," he reluctantly stated as he stood and snuffed out what was left of the fire with his foot. "If you're serious about this, we must go now before the shadows are reinforced."

Ha! I win. She beamed. "I'm ready whenever you are."

Skyblind did not share her enthusiasm. "This will not be easy. Pray that God has mercy on this diversion from His will."

"Of course. Syyris is full of love and has mercy on all his children," Taylee replied confidently as she helped him gather his things.

Although they didn't worship the same god, and it was clear this man was marked and perhaps delusional, Taylee was overcome with confidence that he was the answer to her prayer.

Chapter Seven — The Cost of Curiosity

"Ours is not a selfish god, like Plyyston, the Devil of Darkness, who sinks the sun to blind creation; Syyris dwells among us on the sacred Island, where the elect are called to share in his glory."

—HECTOR THE HOLY, A.P. 730
A TOME OF TRUTH

By the time the sun had made its full rotation around the sky, Corwin was feeling beyond annoyed; his teacher, Master Lunechair, still hadn't moved, and the pangs of hunger were starting to take their toll.

Without having had anything to eat since Mid-Luminous breakfast, he was beginning to feel the all-too-familiar gnawing in his stomach and rawness in his throat. Having grown up as a poor shepherd on the Outskirts, the ache of starvation was nothing new. However, it was a lack of water that aggravated his body to new and infuriating levels. As his uncle always warned, "You can go weeks without food, but only a few sun-cycles without water."

Other than Tray'o and Master Lunechair, Corwin didn't know anyone else in the barred carriage. Nor could he recognize the people trapped in the one that led the caravan, nor any in the several that trailed behind.

The Krydor Markets weren't located far from his home, but because Corwin spent most of his time working with the sheep or being schooled in Pinehouse during Darkfall, he didn't have much interaction with those who lived in Krydor.

Everyone more or less kept to themselves as the hours dragged on. In fact, aside from Tray'o, no one had said a word to Corwin, or to anyone else for that matter, for the entirety of their captivity. That was probably why it was so startling when he suddenly heard soft and ominous singing coming from one of the men in his cage.

"How slow a death does the sun die?
It sinks forever in the sky.
Around us, circle, then descend,
A little closer to Light's end."

Corwin looked around the carriage but couldn't immediately figure out where it was coming from. It wasn't until the next verse started that Corwin noticed the lips of a short, hairy man moving.

"Now Darkfall rise, and oh how sweet,
The nectar of a god's defeat.
For in the dark, all men are blind;
Death needs not eyes for man to find."

"Wonderful. A minstrel," Tray'o mocked. "Do you take requests?"

The hairy man furrowed his brow and tilted his head in their direction. "I could sing 'The Dragon and the Troll.' Your father always loved that song," he sneered.

Tray'o frowned at the reference to the banned song, but managed to refrain from saying anything else. The hairy man took the silence for approval and, with a quiet chuckle, resumed his creepy song.

"Somebody shut that fool up. He'll rain damnation on us all. As if things could get any worse …" a familiar voice groaned.

"Master Lunechair!" Corwin smiled and touched his teacher's

arm. "You're awake." *Finally. Now we can get some answers.*

"Leave me alone." His teacher tried to shield the sun's glare with his hands. "I have no words for the dead."

"It's me, Corwin, one of your Night students. Remember? You were trying to rescue me from Krydor."

Master Lunechair looked up at Corwin for the first time and squinted as if he were struggling to focus. Then, a slow smile crept across his face until suddenly, without any logical reason, he burst into high-pitched laughter. The volume of the laughter rang through the cage and caused the hairy man to end his eerie song immediately.

Has he lost his mind? Master Lunechair was always a bit eccentric, but this was something else entirely. Whatever head trauma his teacher had received in their escape was clearly confusing him.

"Hey! Teacher! Focus!" Tray'o snapped his fingers repeatedly in the man's face. This startled the teacher, who blinked several times in surprise before abruptly rolling onto his side to vomit into the straw.

Thanks, Tray. Another wonderful thing to smell. Corwin wrinkled his nose in disgust.

After the teacher finished heaving his last meal, he wiped his mouth with his sleeve and lethargically propped himself up on his elbow. "Why are we in motion?" he asked as he closed his eyes and pressed a finger to his forehead.

"Dark Ones raided Krydor. We're their prisoners," Corwin said.

For some reason, the reference nearly caused his teacher to break into erratic laughter again. "Be calm, children, Master Lunechair will protect you. There's nothing to fear from shadows."

Corwin glanced out of the cage at the Dark Ones and chained Locura who kept steady pace beside the rolling carriages. They appeared to be in some sort of trance—dead eyes locked straight ahead—and as far as he could tell, they did not speak to one another. The thought that one or several of them had likely slaughtered his sheep caused a sick ache in his stomach, bringing with it pangs of anxiety for what they also might have done to Uncle Jael and Taylee.

These are not shadows; shadows cannot harm.

"You took a pretty bad blow to the head. Maybe you should rest some more …" Tray'o suggested.

"No!" Master Lunechair responded with abrupt seriousness. "We've wasted too much time as it is." He locked eyes on Corwin. "You have it, yes? The relic?"

He knows? Corwin held his breath. "I … uhh …"

"Speak truthfully! I'm not angry. I already know Tray'o stole it from the vault."

At this, Tray'o sat up straighter. "That was all a misunderstanding. I didn't know it was a relic when I took it," he argued in yet another attempt to defend his actions.

"I don't care about that." Master Lunechair waved his hand at Tray'o. "You activated it somehow. Didn't you? Be honest, Corwin, I need to know how you did it."

Corwin hesitated. "Yes … just by touching it."

Master Lunechair seemed to like this answer. He smiled and leaned back against the bars. "Incredible."

"But," Corwin scratched the back of his head, "I don't have it now … Taylee … she and Tray'o were trying to find you to ask about it when the attack happened."

"Yeah," Tray'o added, "we went to your tent but instead found Corwin's uncle … he was poisoned, so Jarv took him to Pinehouse for help."

Master Lunechair let those words hang in the air for a minute before casually responding, "He was not poisoned."

Corwin leaned forward. "How can you be sure?"

"I'm a keeper of knowledge; I know a great many things."

"So he's still alive."

"Alive, yes. Living, no," Master Lunechair replied. "By now, I'm sure the illness has placed him in a deep and unshakeable slumber."

"Unshakeable slumber? What type of illness causes that, and how did he get it?" Corwin was almost afraid to hear the answer.

Master Lunechair let out a contemplative sigh before speaking. "Jael came to me with what he thought was the relic in order to return it. But when he opened the bag and found it was missing, he wisely concluded that Taylee must have taken it out. Shortly after that conclusion, he was struck down with the illness. That's how I knew the relic had been activated."

The explanation hit Corwin like a ton of bricks. "Are you saying Uncle Jael is sick because the relic was activated?"

Master Lunechair nodded. "What did you think would happen when playing with a relic of Plyyston?"

That's not fair!

"Hang on. They didn't know that was what it was!" Tray'o protested.

"It doesn't matter," Master Lunechair stated with frustrating indifference. "Once activated, there was no stopping the consequences. Why do you think the Elders insist on controlling relics? Not only does the past contain great and powerful mysteries, but also dangers beyond anything we can fully comprehend."

"Why Uncle Jael?" Corwin asked. "Why wouldn't Taylee or I be affected?"

Master Lunechair shrugged. "Perhaps it was cursed to harm a loved one. No one really knows the way dark magic works."

An unshakeable slumber caused by illness. Will he ever wake again? It was almost too horrible to believe.

"How can we make things right? There must be a way to wake him."

At this question, Master Lunechair smiled. "There is only one with the power to absolve sin and heal the broken."

Silence hung in the air. Corwin didn't need to say the name out loud; the answer was obvious. *If Syyris didn't heal my sheep from sickness after all our prayers and offerings, what hope is there for my uncle whose been made sick as a result of our sin?*

Tray'o crossed his arms. "I don't want to be the downner here, but don't you think god has bigger things to worry about?"

"'Who else holds the keys to life and death? Syyris Sagrado, the bringer of Day, who spared our lives for his pleasure alone'—that's what we chant, is it not?" Master Lunechair said.

"I didn't take you for the religious type." Tray'o frowned.

"We're all religious, boy. We just don't all worship the same things. All magic—light and dark—comes from Essence, and Essence from the sun. The sun was made by Syyris, therefore Syyris is the only one with the power to undo the effects of dark magic."

Corwin glanced outside the cage again and stared at the sickly field. "Syyris is a god of justice. We didn't mean to, but we sinned against him by using that relic. Why would he decide to help us?"

At this, the teacher slid over to Corwin and firmly grasped his arm. "Don't lose hope! You are right when you say that Syyris is a just god, but his judgement can be appeased."

Corwin wasn't so sure.

"How exactly do you think we can change the mind of a god?"

"As I've just told you," Master Lunechair replied, with the same annoyed voice he used in class when he'd have to repeat some concept that the students did not understand. "Dark magic can only be undone by the god of Light. We have to destroy the relic in the Temple of the Holy Flame. Then, and only then, will your uncle be healed."

Though the teacher's words filled Corwin with dim hope, he wasn't sure it was even possible. *I've never heard of anyone but an Elder entering that temple before. Plus, how would we even get there? But if it's true …* He wanted to believe that there was still hope for his uncle, but he couldn't shake the feeling that it was an impossible quest.

"Oh, that's all?" Tray'o voiced Corwin's doubt. "So you're saying we *only* have to escape our Locura prison, find our way back to Taylee, somehow get all the way to the restricted Island, and then destroy the relic in the ancient fires of the Temple of the Holy Flame. Sounds easy."

Master Lunechair did not appreciate the sarcasm. "I never

said it would be easy. But it will be significantly *easier* if you follow my instructions and keep that smart talk to yourself."

There has to be a better way.

"Why don't we just give the relic to one of the Elders to destroy?" Corwin asked.

Though the question was meant to be sincere, Master Lunechair laughed. "An Elder would never destroy a relic—even one of Plyyston's. No. If you want your uncle alive again, destroying it yourself is the only way."

Corwin looked up. "Do you honestly think it's possible?"

"Yes, Corwin." Master Lunechair smiled. "I have been there before. I know it's possible."

The optimism of his teacher was encouraging, but it didn't make much sense.

"No one but the Elders can get inside that temple," Tray'o reminded him. "When would a teacher ever be allowed inside?"

"You think yourself wise, but there is much you do not know. Stop doubting and trust me!" Master Lunechair snapped. Then, turning to Corwin, he spoke again with a softer voice. "I am only trying to help you."

"I know, and I'm sorry," Corwin apologized. "I just … It's all a little hard to believe. Why would you even want to help us?"

Master Lunechair placed his hand on Corwin's shoulder. "Jael is your uncle, but he is also my friend. I want him alive as much as you do. Besides, I feel partly responsible for the relic falling into your hands in the first place. You see … I convinced Rai'o to hang on to it. Because of me, Jael and all of you got caught up in this mess."

Corwin's heart skipped a beat as he suddenly remembered the whole reason they had taken the relic in the first place. "Is it true it belonged to my mother?" he asked.

Master Lunechair looked away as a strange sadness filled his eyes. "Yes."

So it's true! The confirmation filled Corwin with excitement and dread. *But why would she have a relic of Plyyston …*

"Where did she, uh, get it from?"

Master Lunechair stared intently at him and silently worked his mouth before speaking. "No one knows where she found it. When she died giving birth to you, we discovered it on her body and recognized its design. We couldn't figure out how to activate it, so we stored it away with the other relics."

"You knew my mother, then? What was she like?" Aside from Uncle Jael, Corwin had never encountered anyone who'd actually met his mother.

"She was a special woman. Impatient, and inquisitive." The teacher massaged his forehead. "No more questions, I want to rest now. My head is killing me, and if we have any hope of escaping, I must be at my best."

"Please, just a bit more. I don't know much about her," Corwin pleaded.

Master Lunechair lay down again and turned his back to them. "Not now."

"But ..."

"Later!" he snapped rather abruptly.

Corwin sat back in irritation, but knew from experience that demanding more answers from his teacher never did any good. Uncle Jael always said that teachers only became teachers because they craved power, and having answers that others needed was just another way of keeping it.

He's right. We need him rested, Corwin reminded himself. *If we can escape, and find Taylee ... maybe there is hope for Uncle Jael after all.*

He wanted to believe it was possible, but it was hard to see past the grim reality of their current imprisonment.

"What do you think?" Corwin quietly asked Tray'o.

"Not worth thinking about right now," Tray'o replied dismissively. "We need to focus on surviving, and if we're lucky, escaping."

Corwin nodded in agreement and looked down at his teacher, whose eyes were closed. He already seemed to be drifting off into a restless sleep. *True. This isn't worth thinking about until we're free, if that's even possible.*

Pressing his back against the bars, Corwin tried to get comfortable as he let his eyelids fall shut.

But before he could fall asleep, Tray'o poked him in the side.

"Ow!"

"Something's happening." Tray'o kept his eyes locked on the Dark Ones outside the cage.

"How do you know?"

"I just do. They're worried." Tray'o spoke of the Dark Ones as if he'd studied them all his life.

Worried? They're hardly human.

"They can't be worried if they're not ..." Corwin started to say, but as soon he started speaking, one by one, the carriages came to a grinding halt.

Chapter Eight — The Kaag'ari

"Never forget the sky: it haunts the land as it spreads out across endless horizons, a reminder that, like it, our potential is limitless."

—LORD GEORDAN KAAG'ARI, A.P. 743
SAYINGS OF THE KINGS AND OTHER LORDLY SORTS

"What's going on? Why are we stopping?" a frantic woman asked from her huddled position in a corner.

VAROOOOOOOOOOOOOOOMMMMMMM!

A trumpet blast pierced the sky.

VA VA VA ROOOOOOOOOOOOOOOO!

A second one answered.

Rescue? It seemed too good to be true.

Corwin leaned as far forward as possible, pressing his face up against the bars.

The sun reflected off something metal and green in the distant bushes, and he could hear what sounded like shouting.

No, not shouting ...

Screaming.

It was coming from the Dark Ones at the very back of caravan. The screams were immediately followed by the clanging of metal as a sudden barrage of arrows shot out from the trees.

The Dark Ones exchanged confused looks before abandoning the caravan and scattering in all directions.

"An unexpected surprise," Master Lunechair murmured with

a sadistic gleam in his eyes.

Corwin turned to face Tray'o. "I think we're being rescued!"

A sigh of relief burst from the desperate prisoners, who now looked at Corwin with smiles of gratitude, as if he were the hero who had somehow orchestrated their deliverance.

"See, Cor! I told you we didn't need to worry. My father's men would never abandon us," Tray'o mused, leaning back with unjustified confidence.

The sounds of battle continued, but from his location inside the cage Corwin was unable to see exactly what was happening. The commotion was too far at the end of the caravan.

But then everything changed.

The screams were overpowered by cheers.

At first it came from the very rear, but soon, the next caged group cheered.

The cheer moved down the line, from carriage to carriage, until it came from the one directly behind them.

Corwin watched with shock and awe as his sister came running over and unlocked their cage door with a giant ring of keys.

"Taylee?" Tray'o exclaimed with delight.

She didn't respond, likely because she couldn't hear him over the shouts of jubilation as she flung open the door.

Corwin desperately tried to get out but was pushed back by the frantic crowd, who were forcing their way out of the cage by any means necessary.

"Run for your life! If you want to be saved, run!" the hairy minstrel screeched as he shoved people aside and frantically ran toward the Dark Forest in the distance.

By the time Corwin and Tray'o were free from the cage and on solid ground, every one of the former captives of their group—minus Master Lunechair—had scattered.

Not wanting to waste a second, Corwin rushed through the crowds and straight toward Taylee, who was now opening the door of the final cage.

The people poured out and murmured a hurried "thank you"

as they too vanished into the forest.

But even after saving all those lives, Corwin could tell from her sagging shoulders that his sister was disappointed.

She doesn't know where we are.

"Taylee!" Tray'o hollered as he jogged ahead of Corwin.

"Tray'o …? Is that …? CORWIN!" Taylee dropped the ring of keys she held and ran straight at him. Tray'o spread out his arms as if to receive a hug, but was disappointed to have Taylee completely bypass him and leap straight into her brother's welcoming arms.

"You're alive!"

"Yeah, we're all right. What are you doing here? How did you get those keys?" Corwin asked, searching the immediate area for any remaining Locura or Dark Ones who might try to take them again.

"My friend, Skyblind! We arrived just as the fighting started!" Taylee announced as she pointed behind them. Corwin turned and noticed for the first time the battle taking place at the rear of the caravan.

It was a clash of black on green—Dark Ones fighting what appeared to be knights in emerald armour.

That's why the caravan stopped. They must have come rushing out from the Dark Forest. Corwin had never before seen knights like these, fully armed and armoured, clad in what could only be the blazing green plated mail of a knight of Lightspire.

It took him a second, but then, all at once, he became aware of another, smaller battle taking place.

Standing in the midst of a dark cluster of Dark Ones was a man in a tattered brown cloak. He stood taller than the enemy, and was wielding a flaming wooden staff. His brownish-grey hair flew about wildly on his head as he spun and beat them back with the flames of his staff.

Dodging left and right, he captivated their bloodlust as they desperately tried to rip him open with their clawed hands and weapons. Though he defended himself well, he was outnumbered, and for some reason, the knights were not helping him.

“For an old guy, he sure can move,” Tray’o admitted with a hint of admiration.

“We have to do something!” Taylee exclaimed, running in the direction of the battle.

“No!” Master Lunechair appeared abruptly and grabbed Taylee by the arm. “We must leave.”

“Hey!”

“There’s no time to argue, they’ll see us soon!” The teacher sounded strangely frantic.

“Let go of my sister!” Corwin demanded.

“Corwin, Taylee, you must trust me. I don’t have time to explain what is happening here.”

“We can’t just leave him!” Taylee shouted as she pulled free of Master Lunechair’s grip and started running toward the fray.

Master Lunechair gritted his teeth and cursed under his breath. In one swift motion, he reached into his cloak and pulled out a silver, palm-sized, cylindrical object.

“Such a waste,” he murmured as he threw the object over Taylee’s head into the crowd of Dark Ones, adding a hasty, “Cover your eyes, old man!”

Corwin didn’t think the warning applied to him, and watched foolishly as the object hit the ground and unexpectedly exploded into bright, blinding white light.

Sudden, shrill ringing in his ears, combined with the blinding light, caused Corwin to lose his balance and stumble backward.

All at once he was deaf and blind.

Magic!?

He tried to focus his eyes but could see nothing but white. He was completely disoriented by the flash.

Focus! He shouted in his mind as he vigorously knuckled his eyes and dropped helplessly to his knees.

It took at least a minute before Corwin was able to hear anything other than the high-pitched ringing, which was gradually replaced by muffled shouts, the clanging of metal, and a loud, steady thumping.

"… hear me?" Taylee's voice called from the whiteness.

"Taylee! I'm blind!"

C'mon Corwin. Open your eyes!

Slowly, ever so slowly, dim shadows started to form in the whiteness.

Good. Don't stop. See!

The blinding whiteness began to fade, and before long his vision cleared enough for him to see the outlines of scattered bodies in the dirt.

One flash and all this? Corwin marveled as he struggled to regain his vision and balance. *Master Lunechair isn't just a teacher … he's a sorcerer!*

The revelation was horrifying; according to what he knew, the Elders were the only ones sanctioned for the use of magic relics.

Although the enemy was clearly defeated, Corwin was dimly aware that he was being surrounded by green shapes that formed in the cloudiness of his vision.

It took a full five minutes for Corwin's vision and hearing to completely return, but in that time, it seemed as though the green knights had slain what remained of the Locura blinded by Master Lunechair.

There was no sign of the teacher anywhere.

When Corwin was finally able to make eye contact with Taylee and confirm that his eyesight had returned, she left his side to run to the man she called Skyblind.

Their rescuer had knelt to the ground, desperately gripping his burnt, black staff for support. He was clearly exhausted, and his exposed arms dripped with blood from cuts inflicted by the Locura.

"Are you okay?" she asked, dropping to her knees to meet his eyes. The man nodded and forcefully lifted his shaggy head.

"Just catching my breath, dear one," he assured her, and a small smile spread across his face. "I assume one of these is the brother you were so determined to save?"

"Yes! Corwin, meet Skyblind!" Taylee exclaimed, eager to introduce the two.

Corwin managed to stand and, with great effort, approached the man with his hand stretched out in gratitude. But before he could get too close, a loud and accented voice commanded his attention.

"Do *not* touch that man!" the voice ordered with a ferocity that was quite unfamiliar.

Confusion washed over him. *Who are these knights?* Their armour clearly identified them as knights of Lightspire, yet they had surrounded Corwin and his friends, and every spear was pointed in their direction.

Stepping out from among the knights was a one with jet black hair, flaming green eyes, and smooth, silky white skin. "A marked man is not to be trusted, even if he is old, wrinkly, and stinking of urine," the emerald-eyed knight sang, his voice light and melodic. It was followed by the cruel, throaty laughter of the knights.

"I know my terms. My intention was not to cause any—" Skyblind was mid-sentence when the knight punched him in the mouth.

Taylee let out a scream that was quickly stifled by Corwin squeezing her shoulder. *Don't do anything stupid, Taylee. These are the King's men,* Corwin tried to communicate with his eyes.

"You've not only broken the terms of your exile, but you've caused me a great deal of trouble. Those were my prisoners to free." The knight spat. "Now they're lost and running through the Dark Forest all because of you."

Taylee, unable to resist anymore, broke free of her brother's grip and looked up in defiance at the one who was threatening her friend.

"He's marked, but he hasn't harmed me!" Taylee insisted. "He risked his life to help me. An evil man wouldn't do that."

The knight in charge turned his attention toward her and smiled cruelly, smacking his lips together in a way that made Corwin even more uncomfortable than he already was.

"Whatever lies he put into your pretty little head, forget them! This man is a criminal. His tongue drips with honey but underneath he is dangerous. We are Kaag'ari, and speak no lies. You're safe with us now." He pointed to Skyblind. "Seize him!"

The so-titled Exile did nothing to resist the knights as they held him down and beat him unconscious with their gauntleted fists.

Corwin wanted to help the old man but knew they were completely powerless. His only option now was to try and protect his unconstrained sister, who was likely to get all of them killed if she didn't control herself.

"There's nothing we can do," Corwin whispered as he grabbed Taylee and turned her away from the violence.

The knights carried Skyblind away as the leader turned his attention back to Taylee. He eyed her up and down before calling to the knight nearest him, "Don't forget our guests. They've been through a horrible ordeal."

Firm hands were suddenly placed on their shoulders, and the three youth were shoved forward.

"As much as I love our new escort—you all look great in your armour by the way—I think I'll pass on the 'hang out time' and just head home before it gets too late," Tray'o lightly announced.

One knight answered, "We *are* taking you home."

Though the words sounded positive, Corwin sensed the truth; they were going to a *new* home: Lightspire, the Royal City of Anaciencia and the Centre of the Universe.

Tray'o shot a knowing glance at Corwin. "At least we're safe now."

There was no response.

Between his sister's constant seething and the old man being mercilessly dragged behind them, Corwin wasn't convinced they were safe at all.

Chapter Nine — The March to Lightspire

"The Dragon of Pinehouse
Was brought down low.
Not by might, not by magic,
By a fat little troll."

—AUTHOR UNKNOWN
FROM THE BANNED SONG, "THE DRAGON AND THE TROLL"

There were few things Tray'o despised more than being forced to go somewhere against his will; having a group of grumpy knights do it along a dusty trail was one of those things.

He was, however, quite happy to be traveling to Lightspire instead of wherever the Locura caravan had been taking them, and the reunion with Taylee made the trip tolerable. However with Corwin walking between the two of them, Tray'o found he needed to casually lean his head backward in order see her out of the corner of his eye.

Her eyes were downcast, and her face grim.

Cheer up, Taylee. Things could be worse.

The sight of her looking so sad and hopeless caused Tray'o to lose focus and stumble over a rock.

"Steady, boy! Eyes forward!" One of the knights behind him ordered as he poked Tray'o with the end of his spear.

Tray'o grunted and, rather despairingly, complied with the command to turn his attention back to the wearisome trail.

They walked on.

And on.

And on some more.

This was the furthest Tray'o had ever been from home before and he found that, much to his disappointment, it wasn't all that different. Despite its name, Pinehouse Castle didn't have that many actual pine trees around it. Even out here, on their way to the Centre, they were still surrounded by bumpy little hills, fields of dull yellow-green grass, and sickly patches of bush.

But as sparse as this was, Anaciencia remained the only place on the planet that held any form of life—or so his teachers claimed. "Everything else is in ruins!" they would constantly insist, likely in order to discourage exploring the Borderlands, "It's all just land ruined by the curse of Plyyston."

One thing Tray'o was never really sure about was what made everyone consider the Kingdom of Anaciencia such a great, habitable location for human civilization. As far as he could tell, there wasn't much to be proud of. Just Lightspire at the Centre, the outlying communities, some farming sectors, a few castle garrisons in the Outskirts, and then the Island in the Great Bay. Surrounding the kingdom in all other directions beyond the Outskirts were the Borderlands, which contained the haunted Dark Forest and the unending sands of the raging Red Desert. Though he'd never actually been there, his father had traveled through them once, and would often share all about the adventures and treasure that lay unclaimed within. Exploring the Borderlands was how his father had made his fortune.

Years before Tray'o was born, Rai'o Sak'ton returned from his adventures in the Borderlands with many relics. For each relic he turned in, the Elders rewarded him with vials of Essence. In less than a year, he was one of the wealthiest men in all of Anaciencia.

But his father was not satisfied with wealth alone, so he bought himself a sizeable army and seized Pinehouse Castle for his own. Lord Draken, the former Lord of Pinehouse, demanded the King restore his rightful castle, but Rai'o was smart and used much of his wealth to buy the King's affection. Draken was executed for "failing to control his subjects," and Rai'o gained the title of Lord and Warden of the Outskirts.

Because of all this, Tray'o grew up the wealthiest boy in the region but he was far from the happiest. Even though he was Rai'o's only son, and the heir to Pinehouse Castle, Tray'o and his father did not get along.

Rai'o took any and every opportunity to remind his son that he had "worked" for everything they owned, and all Tray'o had done was be born. It was almost as if his father despised the fact that following his eventual death, Tray'o would inherit it all.

Ironically, Tray'o wasn't all that interested in his father's wealth; he was interested in Taylee.

"Ah, stalking your prey," Rai'o mused the time he caught Tray'o secretly watching Taylee study in the Pinehouse Library. *"Perhaps there is more of me in you than I thought."*

"Hardly." Tray'o tried to play indifferent, but his father had a way of getting under his skin. "And don't call her prey."

"But she is, and you're the hunter. We see what we want and take it for our own. There's no shame in a little lust, boy. I wouldn't be a lord without it, nor would you have ever been born."

His father's voice, even in his memory, drove Tray'o to subconsciously clench his fists.

"This is not the same. Taylee is not just some conquest to me."

"She is, boy. You just don't know it. You want her now, but soon, you'll grow bored and find a new one, just like I did with your mother."

Tray'o hated it when Rai'o spoke so poorly of the woman who gave him life.

"No, I won't. You're incapable of loving anyone but yourself. But not me. I can love. And I choose Taylee," Tray'o proudly announced.

This made his father burst into obnoxious, guttural laughter.

"Foolish boy. She's a poor girl who is lucky to even be allowed into my castle. The commoners exist for the serving and pleasing of their lord, not for loving and marrying. So take her into your bed if you insist, or I'll buy her as a slave if she resists you. But don't confuse your lust with love."

He knew he should have let it go, but degrading Taylee in such a way practically drove Tray'o mad.

"If you're free to take women from the breeding camps, why can't I marry a commoner? No law forbids it!" He foolishly exclaimed in his defense.

Tray'o would never forget his father's cruel smile as he quietly exited the room.

The very same sun-cycle, Rai'o took an unscheduled trip to Lightspire and proposed a new law to the Court that no lord or lady of Anaciencia should ever be permitted to marry below their rank.

The King casually passed the law, and with it shattered any hope of a life of love for Tray'o.

Why did I fight him? A man like that can't understand what it means to love.

Sometime after the law had passed, Tray'o learned the true reason for his father's negative reaction to his interest in Taylee. Although the King had officially granted Rai'o rule and title following Draken's execution, most of the other lords of the Kingdom refused to recognize him as a true lord and mocked him on a regular basis. If Tray'o married Taylee, it would only serve to reinforce their arguments that Rai'o was still a commoner himself. Marrying Tray'o to the daughter of another lord was the only chance Rai'o believed he had at being truly respected.

Because of all this, Tray'o spent very little time at Pinehouse during Day, and took every opportunity he could to visit the Krydor Markets with Taylee and Corwin. There he was free to be himself.

And be with the ones I choose.

Life at Pinehouse had its charms, but Krydor felt more like home. He enjoyed the various smells, the passion of the vendors, and the people who traded there. They were quite unlike the men and women of his father's castle: spoiled, indulgent, and drunkards of Essence.

No, in Krydor, Essence was more than just currency or pleasure; it was the difference between life and death.

And now Krydor is gone. Tray'o felt a pang of sadness as he remembered the way fire had consumed the town.

Father will use this as leverage to demand more military support. He will rebuild Krydor in his own name, and profit from the loss.

Knowing he would never again see the one place he'd been free to be himself left a foul taste in his mouth, and so he ground his teeth together and evicted his father from his thoughts.

At least I'm with Taylee now.

The group of knights continued uneventfully marching them across the struggling plain.

Occasionally they would come across another man or woman who, like them, had escaped the Locura Trade, and by the end of the first full sun-cycle there were a substantial number of refugees mixed with the knights.

Still no sign of Master Lunechair. So much for all that talk of helping Jael. The disappearance of the teacher was as much a mystery as the magic flash he had thrown at the Locura.

As they marched, their rescuer, Skyblind, remained unconscious, dragged along by his arms behind two bored knights. Tray'o wanted to say something about the cruelty of his treatment but was too afraid of the man in charge.

It took longer than it should have, but Tray'o finally recognized the leader as Lord Daraak Kaag'ari—a lord of power, influence, and considerable oddity.

Instead of marching like the other knights, Lord Daraak seemed to strut down the road, with one leg very clearly coming before the other. His tall and disturbingly shapely appearance, mingled with his fair complexion, green eyes, and bouncy black hair, caused Tray'o to think of him as some sort of a comical goblin from a childhood fairy tale. He debated with himself as to whether or not he should mention the resemblance but, much to his personal dismay, concluded it would be in everyone's best interest if he remained silent.

"Why are you smirking?" Corwin asked abruptly.

"Oh, no reason."

"There's always a reason with you," Corwin insisted.

"Ha. I guess I'm just thinking about how much *fun* we're going to have once we get to the Centre," Tray'o lied, hoping his words came across sarcastically.

Though, now that I think of it, there probably will be a lot of fun there. That is, assuming we don't die of exhaustion first.

"How you doing, Taylee?" Tray'o asked in an attempt to initiate some communication with his childhood crush.

"Fine," she replied glumly.

The old man is upsetting her. Tray'o knew it.

"I'm sure Skyblind will be all right. And hey, at least we're all together now, right?" He grinned in an attempt to brighten her mood.

Taylee did not reply.

Maybe a joke will help.

"So, I didn't want to say this before, but the *real* reason I was smirking was because of the way—" Tray'o began, but was interrupted by a knight's louder than necessary shout.

"No talking!"

Grumpiest knights in the Kingdom, Tray'o grumbled to himself as he swallowed his comment.

They walked on and on for what felt several hours, resting only once to eat some thick, red goo out of a small bag. The taste was foul, it was very sticky, and it left a deep longing for more. But Tray'o was in no place to complain, and he really didn't like the snide looks he kept getting from Lord Daraak.

A man more fit to be Lord of Dancing with legs like that.

The sun seemed to crawl around the horizon as time dragged on, and it wasn't until it was all the way behind their backs, casting dark, looming shadows, that Tray'o thought he noticed a glimmer of light in the distance. Thinking it to be a hallucination he tried to ignore it.

"What's that?" Taylee asked, pointing in the direction of the glimmer.

Oh good. I'm not losing my mind.

"Please let it be the city," Tray'o murmured. His legs ached and he was dying of thirst. It had been nearly two sun-cycles since he'd eaten anything solid, and yet it felt like years.

The mere thought of real food caused some sort of hope to spur him on and Tray'o marched a bit more confidently.

Surely there is bound to be a feast waiting for us, the starving refugees of the Krydor Massacre. He could picture the news spreading throughout the Kingdom. *Maybe we'll even be regarded as heroes?* He knew it was too much to hope for.

As they approached the light, it grew brighter and brighter, until all of a sudden, it seemed to separate into three lights emitting from three enormous white towers.

The Three Towers of Lightspire, Tray'o realised. Their journey was almost at an end.

"We're stopping," Corwin observed suspiciously.

"So? We've stopped before." Tray'o didn't mind another rest.

Corwin pursed his lips. "Yeah, but we're almost there. Why stop now?"

Tray'o shrugged.

"One of the knights probably needs to relieve himself and needs help getting out of his armour."

Corwin didn't seem to see the humour in that.

Everyone's so serious. C'mon, man. Lighten up.

"M'Lord!" a knight called from the distance, and just like that, Lord Daraak began strolling over.

"What is it now? Another refugee?"

"No, m'Lord. We found a man in the armour of Pinehouse Castle. He carries a dead man on his shoulders and demands to speak with you."

Tray'o felt his heart skip a beat.

Jarv!

"Why should I care what a knight of Pinehouse wants?"

The knight shifted uncomfortably and said, "He seems quite … suspicious."

Lord Daraak lightly drummed his fingers across his chest plate.

"Make it fast. I'd like to be out of this dreary land and back in my bed before too late."

"Of course, m'Lord. Bring the prisoner!"

Prisoner? I thought we were refugees.

Tray'o felt somewhat relieved when he saw the flash of red armour that signified a knight of his hometown. But his relief was replaced with shock when the man was dragged nearer.

It's not Jarv!

"Release me! We are not enemies!" Master Lunechair spat as he struggled to get loose of the knight's grip.

Clearly dressed in Jarv's ill-fitting red armour, the teacher's age and scrawny body betrayed him. *My father would not employ such weakness in his guard.*

"Somehow, I do not believe this one is a warrior," Lord Daraak teased, yet, even though he was right, Tray'o didn't think Lord Daraak looked like much of a warrior either.

Not surprisingly, the knights failed to see the irony and chuckled at the sight of Master Lunechair.

"A Dark One in disguise, then?" one knight asked.

"What else could he be?" Lord Daraak hummed.

"Here's the dead man he was carrying," another knight stated as he dropped a man on the ground at their feet.

"Uncle Jael!" Corwin and Taylee exclaimed in unison as they rushed to their uncle's side.

Jael lay stiff, but there was still colour in his face, and he appeared to be lost in deep sleep rather than dead.

He's still alive. But what happened to Jarv?

Tray'o could only speculate that his loyal guard had been killed trying to get to Pinehouse. It was the only thing that made sense. *Master Lunechair wouldn't have killed him, nor would he have had any reason to do so.* But the more he thought on it, the more uncertain he felt.

"What shall we do with the Dark One?" a knight asked.

Master Lunechair, aghast at the accusation, let his mouth fall open. "I'm *far* from a Dark One!" He sneered, "And if you'll only listen, you'll understand that this man is not dead. He is sick, and I'm trying to help him."

Lord Daraak regarded Jael's unmoving body with cold indifference.

"Looks dead to me," he stated.

"He's alive!" Taylee exclaimed with tears in her eyes. "Listen! He's breathing!"

Lord Daraak listened for half a second and shrugged indifferently.

"Fine. Bring him with us. I'm sure we can find some use for him when he recovers."

"No!" Master Lunechair growled. "He's mine to protect. Now if you'll kindly allow me to take my Lord's son and his friends, we'll be on our way back to Pinehouse to get this man the help he needs. You would do wise not to interfere." Master Lunechair spoke with the stern authority of one telling the truth, but Lord Daraak had not yet discerned the identity of Tray'o, and so he broke out into uproarious laughter.

"And who," he managed between gasps for air, "is your *Lord's son*? Is there a fat boy among us who I somehow missed?"

Tray'o hesitated and weighed his options.

Up to this point, he hadn't revealed his identity to the knights. Part of him liked remaining anonymous; it allowed him to stay with Taylee, spend some time away from his father, and see more of the Kingdom.

On the other hand, he was getting tired of Lord Daraak's attitude, and loved the though of letting him know that all this time they'd been mistreating another Lord's son.

Imagine the look on his face when he realises his mistake. The thought was too funny to resist.

But before Tray'o was able to declare his title, Lord Daraak regained enough composure to speak again.

"Listen here. I am Lord Daraak Kaag'ari, Second Blood to the Throne. 'Lord' Rai'o has failed in his duties to protect the Outskirts, and as such, no longer has any authority. If you are truly his man, your time in the shadow of the troll is over. If you are a Dark One, we'll know soon enough. Either way, you belong to me now."

The knights chuckled as they shoved Master Lunechair toward the other refugees.

No longer any authority? Tray'o frowned and exchanged an uncertain look with Corwin. *This is not good.*

"Wait! Stop! You don't understand!" As Master Lunechair struggled to get free, something fell loose from within his armour.

It was a silver cylindrical object.

Uh-oh.

One of the knights bent down and picked it up in his hand.

"No!" Corwin stood but shouted his warning too late.

The object exploded in the knight's hand and everyone was knocked backward by the blinding blast.

The only things Tray'o remembered clearly after that were the commotion of the knights staggering around, a man screaming at the bloody stump which only seconds ago had been his hand, and Lord Daraak ordering the prisoners restrained.

You can't treat me this way. I'm the son of a lord, Tray'o thought dimly as a knight rushed over and kicked away his consciousness with the tip of his boot.

Chapter Ten — Being Infinitesimal

"Before asking good questions like 'Who am I?' or 'What's my place in the world?', you must first remember who your family is and where you came from; that's the only way you'll ever know where you're going."

—THE FIRST HOLLAND, A.P. 12
THE HOLLAND FAMILY HEIR BOOK

Silence.

There was no sound, no colour, nor any light.

Nothing remained to fill the deep void in his mind.

There was no room for thought, nor any sense of awareness of self. He—if he was a he—was drowning without lungs in an endless black sea, or perhaps floating without a body in some vast and empty abyss.

Wherever he was, and in whatever state of being, he had never felt so alone.

"Who are you?"

A sharp, impatient voice pierced the darkness.

Attempting to move, breathe, or do anything at all, proved to be nothing more than an exercise in futility.

"Know your name," a soft but firm voice whispered in his mind.

Was it his own voice? He couldn't be sure.

I know my name, he called back to the abyss, though there was no sound. *I know my name!*

So what was it then?

Co …

Cor …

"My name … is Corwin … Medisto." The words were heavy, and dropped awkwardly off his tongue.

"Where are you from?" the impatient voice asked.

"I am … from the Outskirts … near the Krydor Markets. I lived there … with my uncle and my sister … until we were attacked," his voice wavered uncontrollably.

Am I talking? Corwin struggled to think clearly. His mind felt small and compressed, as if it were occupied by some other entity that had complete control over his speech.

"Why have you come here?" The voice was annoying, and Corwin didn't want to answer but was powerless to stop himself.

"I came here … because my home … was attacked … by Locura."

This time, there was a longer pause between questions.

"Who reigns supreme in the sky and holds dominion over the earth?"

"Syyris Sagrado … the Bringer of Day," Corwin's tongue answered immediately.

"Do you love him?" the voice shot back.

Corwin was startled. He'd never been asked that before. "I … I don't know," he answered honestly.

Silence.

"Have you ever been to the Ancient City?"

Corwin didn't know how to answer. *What's the Ancient City?*

"Have you ever been to the Ancient City?" the voice asked again. It was aggressive, and Corwin knew he should be saying something.

"I don't know what that is," his voice answered at last.

Then there was nothing.

No more questions.

No more intrusive voice.

No more sound.

Corwin felt his consciousness slip away, and he resumed

floating in the darkness that relentlessly consumed his mind and body.

The darkness was cold, lonely, and empty.

Corwin was beginning to wonder if he'd died and this was the afterlife.

"*It isn't,*" the soft voice answered with confidence.

Then something changed. A white speck drifted past.

Then another.

A third speck drifted past.

Suddenly, instead of a few specks of light, it was as if someone threw back the blinds. Bright white light flooded Corwin's sight, blinding him temporarily.

His non-corporeal self was surrounded by a swarm of swirling, spinning white flakes that seemed to dance in the air. The flakes floated in every direction: above, below, to the right and the left. Each flake had a mind of its own, and drifted wherever it pleased before fading away into light.

It was peaceful and unique, and he didn't even care that he was alone.

"*You are not alone,*" the soft voice whispered.

No, I'm not, he agreed. *This is a holy place; god is here.*

After resting in that place for what could have been hours, the light eventually faded, and Corwin gradually returned to his body.

A dream ...? He sluggishly opened his eyes to more darkness.

His whole body felt stiff and sore, yet a strange sense of calm lingered in his soul.

But as Corwin lay in the darkness and tried to recall the details of the strange dream, he found little he could retain. It was like trying to grasp water; the more he struggled to remember, the more the dream slipped through his fingers, until all that was left was the vague impression of floating white specks.

It was just a dream. I need to get up. Light is not for wasting, he told himself as he tried to stretch his sore muscles.

It took a minute before Corwin realised that he was not at home in his own bed.

Where am I? What happened? And just like that, the feeling of calm faded and was replaced by dread as all the memories of the last sun-cycle flooded over him.

He sat up abruptly and looked around. He'd been lying on a floor mat in a dark room for an indeterminate amount of time, though his aching body indicated he'd been there for a while. The only visible light in the room emitted from a hole in the floor in the far corner where the top of a ladder was visible.

On his left were three mats. Two were empty, and on one was the barely noticeable outline of a sleeping man. Corwin's eyes took some time to adjust enough to recognize the shape.

Uncle Jael!

Corwin crawled over to his uncle, who lay unmoving on the mat. He wore a soft brown sleeping robe that covered him from head to toe, and although he was placed in a pose that gave the impression of a peaceful slumber, Uncle Jael was clearly not well; his face was pale and drained of all colour, and the quiet sounds of his breathing were laboured and heavy.

"I don't know if you can hear me …" Corwin's throat constricted as he tried to speak. "I'm so sorry for what happened to you."

It broke his heart to see his uncle sick like this, and he desperately longed to make it end.

Corwin pressed the tips of his fingers against his uncle's forehead to brush some stray hairs away from his face and frowned when he felt the hard, dry coolness of his skin.

"Your hair is getting long." Corwin sighed. He'd give anything for a pair of scissors just to trim it. Uncle Jael hated when his hair grew over his eyebrows, but they'd been so busy lately that there hadn't been time to cut it sooner. *He wouldn't want to be seen lying here— helpless—with hair growing all over his face.*

It wasn't fair. None of it was. Corwin didn't care what Master Lunechair said about the mystery of relics and the evils of Dark Magic; Uncle Jael shouldn't have been punished for something they did.

"Don't leave me Uncle Jael … please … if you can hear me,

wake up," he pleaded. "You're all we have … I'm not … I'm not ready to lose you. I can't … I …" His voice gave out. It was too much.

Maybe we're the ones being punished after all. Maybe losing him to this slumber is how the curse is meant to torture us. The thought nearly brought him to tears.

Bleary-eyed and full of sorrow, Corwin lay his head on his uncle's lightly rising chest and once again felt the slow, rhythmic beating of his weary heart.

Thump thump.

Even though it was faint, the feeling was comforting.

Thump thump.

It reminded him that Uncle Jael was still alive.

Thump thump.

A prisoner in his own body.

Corwin lay like that for a long time, not moving or speaking or even really thinking, but feeling the slow beat of his uncle's heart against his head.

You can end this, you know. You can save him, Corwin reminded himself.

But how? I can't just leave him when he's like this. I don't even know where we are, he argued back.

Staying won't help him either, he insisted. *Take comfort knowing that if he sleeps, he probably dreams.*

It was something Corwin hadn't considered until just now.

Not present in the body … but where is his mind?

If Uncle Jael was truly trapped in a deep slumber, it made sense that he could be dreaming. "Can you see them? The floating white flakes?" he asked as he thought back to his dream. Though he couldn't remember much more than an overwhelming feeling of calm it was without question the best dream of his life.

Unless … Maybe it wasn't a dream at all, he thought abruptly. *Maybe it was a vision … a reminder from Syyris that even trapped in a world of sleep, Uncle Jael is peaceful?*

It was a comforting idea. After all, if he was going to figure out how to save Uncle Jael, it would take time, and knowing that he was resting peacefully eased some of the stress and urgency.

Corwin, stirring for the first time in what felt like an hour, leaned forward and gently kissed his uncle on the forehead. "It's our fault this sickness fell to you … but we can make things right again."

How far will I go to save him? Am I willing to give up my own life? He cringed.

Master Lunechair's plan to destroy the relic in the Temple of the Holy Flame made sense, but would be incredibly difficult. The Island itself was a sacred place, and not accessible to anyone of his status.

And even if I manage to get there, I'll still have to find the temple, and then come face-to-face with Syyris himself. This filled Corwin with fear. While seeing god would be incredible, it was something only an Elder was permitted to do.

If he truly wanted to save his uncle, it might mean breaking some serious laws.

There's no way around it. Corwin was resolute. *If I don't try, his life will be over. No one can sleep forever.*

"Be strong and wait for me. I … I'll do whatever it takes," Corwin vowed. Uncle Jael was the closest thing to a father he'd ever known and if it meant he needed to risk a life in prison to storm the gates of Syyris' island temple to save him then so be it. The relic needed to be destroyed. "You will be well again, I promise."

As he sat there in the dark next to his stiff, unmoving uncle, Corwin suddenly became aware of the sounds of a door slamming shut, followed by muffled voices beneath him.

The unexpected sounds jolted him to his feet, though he immediately regretted his action.

Blood rushed straight to his head.

His vision clouded, and Corwin dropped back down.

Easy. Not so fast.

Corwin struggled to steady himself and regain his composure. His legs were stiff and uncooperative, almost as though he'd never walked in all his life.

After expelling far more mental energy than should have been necessary, he recovered enough strength to stand and stagger to the ladder.

He tried to move as quietly as he could manage in order to more easily hear the voices below. One he recognized immediately.

"… saying I didn't really make the choice?" Tray'o asked.

"Ya did! But ya be sayin' only what be truth," a harsh yet melodic older voice cackled.

"So it's not possible to lie?"

"Ha! No good be callin' him the Elder of Truth if ya could!"

Tray'o laughed. "Remind me not to invite him to my card games."

He's... happy, Corwin realised at once.

Deciding it might be best to wait at the top of the ladder and listen until he could accurately judge the situation, Corwin knelt down and pressed an ear to the floor.

"Why ya not be wantin' to be Lord, though, hmm? That be makin' no sense to me."

"My father is many things, but innocent is not one of them," Tray'o replied. "Whatever his fate, I got the better end of the deal."

"Let's see ya be sayin' that aft' ya taste me wife cookin'!" the old man exclaimed, punctuating the statement with a hearty "Ha!"

The silence that followed was interrupted by Tray'o clearing his throat. "So … exactly how long do we have to stay here?"

The old man laughed much too loudly, and for far too long, before finally replying, "Bored already, are ya? Ha! I not be offering much, but it be better than the street! Ha!" Then, abruptly, the old man shouted louder, "Don't ya agree, other boy? C'mon down. No need be shy."

Corwin held his breath.

"He's awake? Corwin?" Tray'o called.

No point in hiding now.

"I'm here," Corwin reluctantly admitted from the safety of the loft.

"About time!" Tray'o snapped. "Get down here! We have things to discuss."

Chapter Eleven — The House of Holland

"If you wish to never be a slave, remain single and chaste; there is no higher cost to your freedom than the love of a woman."

—HECTOR THE HOLY, A.P. 730
A TOME OF TRUTH

Even after wandering around with the quirky old man for the last hour, Tray'o still couldn't shake the voice that haunted his memory.

"Do you—in all fullness of truth and sound mind—choose to renounce your claim and deny your rightful title?" the Elder of Truth had demanded from the shadows.

He could hardly believe the question. Stay a lord and share his father's fate or renounce it all and live as a common man. *Common, but free to marry whom I choose.*

It didn't matter that he was under the influence of a truth spell; his heart and his head had screamed the same thing.

"Yes."

A single word was all it took to strip him of the thing his father spent a lifetime acheiving.

When Tray'o awoke from the interrogation it was with a smile plastered on his face. At first a big part of him feared he'd dreamt the whole thing, and he kept checking his finger to confirm the Pinehouse ring was really gone.

No ring, no claim. It was all real and yet felt too good to be true. Tray'o Sak'ton was no longer the future Lord of Pinehouse Castle.

Of course he would miss some things—like the wealth and the power—but a lifetime with Taylee was worth every castle and all the lordship in the Kingdom. *After all, what good is any of it without love?* He couldn't keep from grinning. *Now all I have to do is find her.*

Since waking in the loft next to Corwin and Jael, Tray'o had done nothing but engage in the most tedious conversation with the elderly owner of the house, a short, shriveled man named Holland. But even now— after returning from a long walk around Lightspire—he was no closer to knowing the location of Taylee.

With his floppy white hair, big red eyes, and pale skin as wrinkly as a raisin, Holland made for the most unusual old man. Typically, Tray'o was suspicious of men who talked too much, but there was something in Holland's eyes that spoke of a deep, uncommon sincerity.

Unfortunately, Holland seemed more interested in sharing jokes and random anecdotes than anything valuable, and it wasn't until Corwin finally woke and joined them at the table that the old man started to get slightly more serious.

"Other boy! Now we can be beginning. I be called White Holland. White, like the colour of me hair, and Holland, like me papa! Ha!" Holland cackled as he extended his thin, veiny hand.

Corwin exchanged a look with Tray'o, who shrugged back. "He's harmless. So far."

Corwin nodded and cautiously shook the old man's hand. "I'm Corwin."

"Pleasure be mine. Now sit, we have much to be talkin' about!" Holland indicated an empty stool.

"My uncle …" Corwin trailed off as he took his place at the table.

"He be restin' here, with us. No one be knowin' what be happenin' to him, but I be makin' sure he stays safe." The man beamed.

Corwin nodded, but by the look on his face, Tray'o knew he was unsatisfied with the answer.

"I be living here in Lightspire me entire life. This here be the House of Holland, named for me great-great-great-great-great-great-great-grandfather, the First Holland, but we be callin' him Holland the Proud, ha! We all be named for him."

Corwin raised his eyebrows. "You're all named Holland?"

Here we go again. Tray'o sighed.

"E'ry one of us! Holland the Proud wanted we be knowing who we come from." The strange man beamed.

"I thought it was stupid when he first told me too," Tray'o admitted to Corwin.

"I don't understand," Corwin replied. "How can you know whose who when you're all together?"

"That be easy! We be having second names. Holland the Wise, Old Holland, Red Holland, Holland the Tall, Holland the Mighty, Holland the Not-So-Mighty," he laughed.

"What about Holland the Who-Cares?" Tray'o teased.

Corwin punched him in the shoulder much harder than necessary. "Tray'o was just joking," he apologized. "We are grateful to be able to rest in a home full of such rich history."

Go on, Cor. Butter the old man up.

Holland grinned. "Of course. But ya be doing more than restin'. Ya two be placed here to be living durin' yer training."

What? He never said anything about that before. "Training" sounded like work to Tray'o. He frowned at the thought. The life of a commoner was supposed to mean being free of duty and able to do whatever he wanted.

"What are you trying to say?"

"Not sure how to be putting this ..." Holland scratched his head. "Ya men now, eh? Ya belong to Lightspire, so ya must serve."

Tray'o groaned. *Why didn't I seen this coming sooner? The knights weren't there to rescue us from the Locura Trade. They were only interested in enlisting slaves.*

Tray'o crossed his arms. "Don't tell me we're slaves now?"

"Oh no! There be no slaving here, ha! Just willin' workers. The sun don't be giving no Essence for free, after all. Ya be seeing soon. Ya two be carefully assessed and yer placement will be real nice, I'm sure. Ha!" Holland cackled.

A heavy silence filled the air. *I didn't give up my title just to have some other man tell me how to live my life.*

"Where's Taylee?" Corwin asked abruptly.

Holland stared back at him, as if trying to register what was asked. "Who?"

"My twin sister," Corwin said impatiently.

"Ah, sister, er, yes, well, my home be only open to young men, ha. Yer uncle be being a special case, seein' as he be, uh, recoverin', an' all. Taylee be placed elsewhere."

"Like where? I'd like to see her," Corwin insisted.

You and me both, Cor.

"Ha! Who be knowing? Like I tell your friend, there not be many options for a young orphan girl in Lightspire. Oft' they end up at the breedin' camps. If she be lucky, maybe she be hitched to one of them knights. Ha!"

"We've been over this. She's only 16," Tray'o reminded the old man with a tone of annoyance. The thought of Taylee at the breeding camps or married to one of those brutish knights was more than he could handle.

"And she's not an orphan," Corwin added. "My uncle is still alive."

Holland nodded slowly. "Orphan, wrong word, but ya be knowin' what I be meaning." He scrunched up his nose. "16? Right. She be too young for the camps or a knight, ha! I be not sure. She maybe be put to work in a kitchen somewhere until she be turning 17," Holland suggested with a shrug. "Truth of it is, I just don't know. Ya be asking the Elder of Wisdom, I s'pose."

"Elder of *Wisdom*?" Corwin asked.

Corwin, you're embarrassing yourself.

Tray'o hadn't paid much attention when his teachers taught the history of Anaciencia, but even he knew the titles of the Elders.

Although he himself had no opinion of the great wizards, his father always said they were nothing but control freaks.

"Eh? The Elder of Wisdom? One of the Elders. Ya know them. Wizards. The six who be speaking with Syyris. They be running the Academy, on the Island. Ya know them?" Holland asked with concern.

"Of course," Corwin replied with a distant look in his eye.

He's thinking about Jael. Tray'o wondered if that man would ever wake again.

"Neither of us knew much about the goings-on in the Centre when we lived in the Outskirts," Tray'o explained in an attempt to make his friend seem less ignorant.

Holland rubbed the side of his face and exhaled deeply.

He's confused. Tray'o smirked. *Welcome to the club.*

If the old man was truly confused, he did not stay so for long, and turned his attention toward some bowls of stew of which Tray'o had been keenly aware since he first woke.

"Ha. Ya be in trouble, then. Here, time for eatin'. The Elder of Wisdom not be going easy on ya, and he be takin' no excuses." Holland offered them each a bowl and Tray'o ate his greedily.

The stew was delicious. It was made of some kind of thick, plum-tasting cream jelly, with chunks of dried raisins, apples, and star-berries. The stew melted as soon as it touched his tongue, and the liquid gently coated the deep, raw recesses of his throat. Holland said it was an ancient family recipe and called "pluma."

While Tray'o finished his bowl and dug into a second helping, Holland explained to Corwin what he and Tray'o had already gone over earlier in more detail.

Apparently, the Locura were becoming more and more aggressive, and in the last two sun-cycles, the entire Outskirts had been raided and burned, forcing all surviving residents to take refuge at Lightspire. Rai'o was somehow blamed for it, and as Lord and Warden of the Outskirts, he would be facing trial for his failure.

Certainly grateful they let me opt out of that experience.

Holland then went on to explain how the King had decreed

that all males between the ages of 14 and 18 be trained for placement, most likely in the military to fight the Locura and take back the Outskirts.

It was a lot to take in, but Tray'o couldn't help but smile. As strange as it would seem to everyone else, losing his title as future Lord of Pinehouse was quite possibly the best thing that had ever happened to him.

Once I find Taylee, we can run off together and be free to live our lives however we please. There was no way he would let anyone force him into military service.

Holland said that there were other options for service—like builders, smiths, or stewards—and if they worked really hard, they might rank among the best and brightest of the trainees and be taken from Lightspire to the Academy, which was on the Island.

The mention of the Island piqued Corwin's interest, and he sat up straighter. "I'm sorry for my ignorance, but my uncle never told me much about what happens when you go to the Island."

"Ha! Probably 'cause it be a one way trip. No one who goes there be comin' back to talk, ha!" Holland explained. "My boy be called there. I not be seein' or hearin' from him since. Been told he be doin' important work there for the Elders."

"Sounds like a glorified form of slavery," Tray'o quipped rather hastily.

Corwin's glare seemed to indicate that it was an insensitive comment, but Tray'o chose to stay oblivious to his friend's judgemental, nonverbal cues.

"Ha! That be something!" Holland chuckled. "Nah, boy. The ones who be goin' to the Island be being giv'n the high honour. The Island be where Syyris be livin', after all, and they be with him forever. The lucky ones be goin' there." Holland stood and moved over to the window, where he stared and became oddly silent.

Corwin shook his head at Tray'o, who responded by mouthing the word "what?" before getting up to grab a third helping of pluma.

"What is your boy's name?" Corwin asked, then, as if suddenly remembering the family history, adding a hasty, "I mean, his second name."

The old man did not move. "He be born Holland the Healthy. But now, he be called the Last Holland."

The title hung in the air with the uncomfortable feeling of finality, and, as if sensing their discomfort, Holland turned and explained the meaning.

"There be no marriage on the Island, and me wife be too old for more sons. The line of Holland be endin' with him."

Tray'o was stunned. "Why no marriage?"

"Marriage," Holland sighed, "be leadin' to children. And children be changin' man. One with child be unable to be servin' Syyris undistracted. Singleness be the sign of holiness, the Elders be teachin'."

The Island sounds more like hell than heaven. Tray'o grunted. He already wasn't planning to try hard in training, but now, more than ever, he was determined to fail.

His thoughts drifted to Taylee, and he deafened himself to the rest of the conversation between Holland and Corwin.

Could she really be married off to some knight? Or sent off to the breeding camps to birth children for scum like my father while I serve in singleness?

The thought—though horrible—was not worth entertaining; there was no way he would let such a thing happen.

Later, up in the loft, as Corwin attempted to carefully spoon-feed some pluma to the sleeping Jael, Tray'o placed a comforting hand on his shoulder.

"You don't need to worry. I'm going to find Taylee," Tray'o promised. "Things are about to get so much better for us. You'll see."

Corwin nodded, but from the look in his eyes, it was obvious he was doubtful.

I will find her, he swore to himself. *I'm better than a lord now; I'm the man who will marry Taylee Medisto.*

Chapter Twelve — Return of the Exile

"It's only a matter of time before Syyris will fail you, and when that happens, my words will be remembered; no idol can withstand the weight of worship."

—PRINCE ELLIAN E'MONTON, A.P. 712
PUBLIC COURT RECORDS

"I thought you wanted to see the trial." The woman who introduced herself as Daeni would not stop nagging as she pushed Taylee past massive stone pillars and down one corridor after another.

"I do!" Taylee squeaked.

"Then move!"

It's not my fault. Not only had she never been in the Royal Palace before, but every step was made difficult due to the flowing blue and black dress that she was currently tripping over.

I'd be moving faster if you hadn't forced me into this ridiculous outfit.

Granted, it was the most beautiful dress Taylee had ever worn, but far too poofy, long, and uncomfortable for her taste.

She couldn't complain out loud, though, because Daeni wore an identical dress—and she had hiked hers up in bunches around her hips so that she could move faster. It worked fairly well, but looked absolutely ridiculous, so Taylee couldn't bring herself to do it.

I wonder if Corwin wound up with someone to boss him around.

Taylee still wasn't quite sure what had happened after the

stranger in the darkness asked her a bunch of annoying questions. All she knew for certain was that she had been placed under the care of Daeni, some palace attendant who had volunteered to watch over her until she was old enough to be married. Taylee wasn't fond of this arrangement, but despite only knowing Daeni for a short time, she had a feeling that any argument with her would not yield pleasant results.

Daeni was a bulky woman, taller than most men, with a firm build and arms like tree trunks. Her short, curly hair clung to her head in tight, controlled ringlets, and her eyebrows were trimmed and sculpted arches.

But regardless of her manly and rigid appearance, something about her caring nature and firm-but-loving attitude caused Taylee to feel a measure of respect for the woman, and so she did her best to obey.

They were currently on their way to the throne room, where Taylee had been told that Skyblind was about to be judged by the King.

"So, Skyblind … he's not a popular guy around here, is he?" she asked timidly as they turned down another corridor.

Ever since the burning of Krydor, Taylee couldn't seem to shake the uneasiness in her chest which quieted her otherwise optimistic spirit.

Daeni did not respond, but continued to prod her forward until they came at last to a set of big red doors.

She reached for the door, but before opening it, Daeni hesitated.

"A marked man does not have friends. It is not likely to go well for him in there. Are you absolutely certain you wish to be in attendance?"

"Of course!" Taylee said. *What kind of question is that?*

She couldn't understand why anyone would want to hurt the man who helped rescue her brother and a bunch of other innocent people from the Locura, even if he was marked for some past crime.

Daeni nodded and pushed open the doors.

What Taylee saw next took her breath away.

Even in her wildest imagination, Taylee had never dreamed a room could be so large. The ceiling, which was round and coloured blue like the sky, extended so high into the air that she might have thought they had stepped outside if not for the four walls enclosing the room. Each one was painted from end to end with the most colourful and intricate images Taylee had ever seen. It took her a minute to realise it was one long mural that started with a depiction of a bright sun, developed into an image of men and women building a city and then going to war, and then was followed by what could only be Syyris battling the dark shadow of his brother Plyyston.

Our history.

The Bringer of Day was painted across the wall as a sparkling, fire-breathing, dragon with translucent, silver wings and a semi-transparent black halo circling his green, scaled body. Taylee had never before seen a depiction of their god, and something about it struck her with holy fear.

Suddenly overwhelmed by the feeling that everything she'd ever said or done was being observed and judged by that image, she quickly turned from it and to the commotion in the middle of the room where a cluster of people were gathered.

They must be the King's Court! Taylee tried to recall what Uncle Jael had taught her about this place, but very little was coming to mind.

She did recall that the Court was made up of lords and ladies from the various regions of Anaciencia, and they met before the King regularly to present gifts, to ask for things, or, as was the case today, to observe justice.

Slightly elevated above the crowd on a round platform were the backs of a semi-circle of seats—seven in total, but only three were being used. The men sitting in those seats were dressed in identical black robes, but they each wore a different coloured sash over their right shoulder – one purple, one green, and one orange.

The three men in black must be Elders.

And in the centre of the platform, elevated a foot higher and facing the semi-circle of seats, sat a rather overweight man on a massive golden throne. The King's chair—encrusted with rubies, carved out of what appeared to be solid gold, and with a back that rose ten feet in the air—was easily the most impressive thing about King Temchar E'monton, aside from his flashy, red-gold crown that was shaped like flames.

He's ... fat. She frowned.

Her disappointment arose mostly because she'd never met a king before and had always pictured one to be strong and muscular. *Or at least handsome.*

This king, however, had nothing with which to impress except for the size of the sagging, bloated belly that bulged out of his shirt.

As she tried to avert her eyes, she noticed Lord Daraak standing tall and alert next to the throne. He wore a dark green velvet robe and seemed to be guarding a prisoner who lay sprawled at the foot of the King.

Not Skyblind though.

Taylee recognized the man almost immediately. "Lord Rai'o?"

"Quiet, child, or we'll leave immediately. It's a privilege to be here, not a right," Daeni snapped as they made their way over to join those in attendance.

Lord Rai'o was different from his son in almost every way. While Tray'o was kind and adventurous, and generally fun to be around, Lord Rai'o had grown contemptuous and lazy. He was a greedy and selfish man whose fatness rivalled that of the King. But here, at the foot of the throne, he appeared quite weak and pathetic.

For Taylee, the most disturbing part was not Rai'o's presence, but seeing how he was dressed. Normally, Lord Rai'o preferred to wear the finest silks and furs, but here he was, on his knees before the King, stripped nearly bare, with only a thin white sheet and his rolls of fat to cover his nakedness.

"If you'll only listen to reason, you'll see that I had noth—" Lord Rai'o said before he was struck across the face by Lord Daraak.

"Will 'reason' restore our lands? No? I thought not," Lord Daraak sneered as he looked up at the King. "Are you ready to pronounce judgement?"

The King's droopy eyes struggled to remain open as he mumbled, "Judgement? Yes. Fine."

There was a short pause before the Elder with the purple sash stood and cleared his throat.

Taylee disliked him as soon as he stood. She could tell by the grey slashes in his hair that he was old, but somehow he maintained the appearance of youth in his wrinkle-free skin and straight posture. He had a long, bird-like nose below which sprouted a wispy grey moustache. His narrow, beady eyes blinked rapidly as he regarded the Court with a less-than-subtle air of superiority.

"Before the sight of men, and in the name of the great Syyris Sagrado, you, Rai'o Sak'ton, former Lord of Pinehouse Castle and Warden of the Outskirts, are declared unfit to rule. You allowed the Locura to sneak past your defences and burn much of the King's land, thereby putting all of Anaciencia in danger. You will be taken to the Island where you will be sacrificed to Syyris on an altar of fire. May he have mercy on you in the afterlife, for this Court has none left to give." The Elder pronounced this judgement with the ease of many years' experience.

"No! It wasn't my fault!" Rai'o screamed, but his voice was drowned out by curses from the crowd.

And just like that, his trial was over. Rai'o was hauled out of the throne room by several guards who ignored his futile pleas for mercy.

The Elder wearing the orange sash—a skinny, gentle looking man with a flowing white and yellow beard—said to the Court in a voice of mild boredom, "I am of the opinion that the Outskirts are no longer habitable. They have been given over to the dominion of the Locura, due to the wickedness of Rai'o. Lightspire is our only refuge now. Let us continue to find solace in the presence of Syyris, and trust him to lead our armies in revenge."

The crowd erupted with cheering and applause.

"They cheer for murder?" Taylee was shocked.

"No, child. They cheer for justice," Daeni responded.

Taylee furrowed her brow. *Rai'o was a Lord. What chance does Skyblind stand against such justice?*

"Are we done yet, Kaine? I'm tired," the King whined.

The purple Elder, referred to as Kaine, could hardly hide his look of contempt.

"We still need to deal with the captive Exile," he sternly reminded the King.

"Oh, right. Of course. I'm eager to see what time in the wilderness has done to a criminal my father banished." The King slumped casually in his seat as if he were sunning himself on a rock.

King Temchar doesn't care in the least about what happens here, Taylee thought as disappointment filled her heart.

The Elder with the green sash nodded to some nearby knights. He was beardless, bald, short and stocky, but Taylee saw very little else that made him distinct or interesting. In fact, he was quite possibly the plainest looking man she'd ever laid eyes on.

"Bring in the Exile." His voice was shrill and sharp.

Taylee stood on the tips of her toes in order to gain a better view over the heads of the people in the Court.

"What are you doing?" Daeni demanded.

"Can we go closer?"

"No. Stand still. We're close enough," Daeni insisted. "No matter what happens, stay by my side."

Taylee rolled her eyes. "You act like you don't trust me."

Daeni frowned, but did not say another word.

On the other side of the room, a set of solid oak doors opened and Skyblind was ushered in.

He was wearing the same brown cloak from when he fought the Locura, but it was now torn and bloodied. Exhaustion pained his face, but still he managed to stand proud, almost as if he were a lord himself.

Better fit to rule than half of these, I'll bet.

As he entered and was marched toward the throne, some of

the Court openly cursed him while others just murmured to themselves.

"Behold, an Exile returned home," one of the knights mocked, giving Skyblind a hard shove that landed him on the platform directly between the throne and the three Elders.

Not a good start …

"Years in the wilderness have not been kind to you, Exile. Your hair is streaked with age, though you foolishly work your body in an attempt to deny it," the King said, followed by snickers from the crowd.

"Yes. Much time has passed. Last I remember, you were but a small child. Strange, in all that time, it seems the only part of you that's really grown is your belly," Skyblind calmly observed.

Taylee stifled a laugh.

The Elder with the green sash cleared his throat and locked eyes on Daraak, who responded by swatting Skyblind across the face with the back of his hand. This resulted in the purple Elder flashing his teeth in what could only be a grin.

"Who is that man? With the green sash and the yellow beard," Taylee whispered to Daeni. She couldn't understand why they were treating Skyblind so poorly.

"Agar, the Elder of Peace," Daeni explained stiffly.

Peace? Somehow I doubt it.

"What about the one with the bird nose? The purple one."

Daeni grunted in annoyance. "Kaine, the Elder of Justice."

Taylee thought about that for a minute. "I don't like him. Or any of them, really," she admitted.

"That's fine. They probably wouldn't like you much either. Now hush!"

Despite having just been slapped, Skyblind maintained his composure quite well and held his head high.

This is stupid, I can hardly see from back here. Taylee glanced at Daeni out of the corner of her eye.

The woman was completely focused on Skyblind.

She's distracted, Taylee realised. *Now's my chance.*

Without making a sound, Taylee slipped into the crowd and eased her way closer to the front.

"Don't speak as if you know me," the King growled.

"But I do know you," Skyblind replied calmly. "And you know me."

Taylee was much closer now, and could see them clearly.

"I do not remember you," the King droned, as he mindlessly fiddled with a silver chalice by his side. "What is your name, Exile? For what crime did my father mercifully mark instead of kill you?"

Skyblind stared the King straight in the eye. "I believe you when you say you don't remember. You were young when I was exiled. But you do know me … brother."

The word "brother" rang through the halls like a bell, and with it came gasps and murmurs from the Court.

What did he just say? Taylee felt as confused as the rest of them.

"It can't be …" King Temchar spoke softly. Where before he appeared casual and indifferent, he now leaned forward and examined Skyblind with an intense curiosity. "Is that … really you?"

"Yes, Temchar. I have returned."

What started off as whispers and murmurs from the Court now erupted into full shouts of derision.

"Liar!"

"Kill him!"

"Impossible!"

Though Elder Kaine looked just as confused as everyone else, he faced the Court and violently stomped his foot on the ground in order to regain control.

"Quiet down!"

Skyblind is the King's brother? It was hard to believe. Taylee had never heard of the King having any siblings. *Though if he was exiled I doubt they'd make it known publically.*

Once the crowd finally settled down enough, Elder Kaine turned his attention back on Skyblind.

"You were told to never return," Elder Kaine warned.

"That is true, Kaine," Skyblind agreed. "I hope you understand that this was not my intention."

"Liar!" Elder Kaine spat. "I know exactly why you returned. Are you so foolish as to think you could take the throne for yourself?"

"No," Skyblind replied firmly. "You know I was never interested in the chair. It is suited for my brother."

King Temchar seemed to like the answer, and leaned as far forward as his bulging gut would allow.

"Then are you willing to submit yourself to my authority? You admit that—even though you are older—I am the true king?"

Skyblind did not respond.

Elder Agar nodded to Lord Daraak, who struck Skyblind a second time.

"King Temchar has asked you a question," Lord Daraak shouted.

Skyblind wiped the blood from his lip.

"I am not here to challenge your claim, brother. But neither will I bow to you. There is only one King, and his name is not Temchar."

There was a bit of murmuring in the Court, but it was quieted by the bird-nosed Elder Kaine, as he gestured for the audience to be still once again.

"You are quite right. *Syyris* is our true king. We all worship him, even King Temchar. I am glad to hear that you have finally come to your senses ..."

But before he could finish, Skyblind raised his voice and said, "I do not worship Syyris. He has no more claim to the title of God than do you, Kaine. Nothing has changed. Syyris is a relic—something made to be used and controlled. I worship the One who is unmade, the Father of Heaven, God of both Day *and* Night!" he declared.

The Court gasped, and several people tried to grab at him, enraged with his blasphemy.

Stop, stop! You're making things worse! Taylee could hardly believe her ears. She knew he believed in another god, but she never imagined he would outright deny Syyris right in front of the King.

"Ellian E'monton," Elder Kaine addressed Skyblind, "you have been charged for breaking the terms of your exile and attacking Lord Daraak and his knights, and now you add blasphemy to the list?"

Skyblind took a step forward and glared at the Elder of Justice. "I am no longer Ellian. You stripped that name from me when you stripped away my rights as Prince. I am now, as you once declared: Skyblind."

The Elder with the orange sash and big beard raised his eyebrows in bewilderment. "You were called 'sky blind' because as a child you constantly denied the god you saw for one you could not. But that is not your name. Choose your words carefully."

"Call me what you want. I will not waste another moment in prayer to your empty idol again." Skyblind turned to face the Court. "Listen to me now. I have been to the Island and have seen what the Elders are doing there. Syyris is an illusion—a tool they use to control you. If I could bring you his lifeless body as proof, I would. But now, I stand here, prepared to die so you may know the truth. My life is in the True God's hands."

Taylee watched the three Elders intently. There was only silence and a look of contemplation on their faces. Then, a small, cruel sneer parted Elder Kaine's lips.

"Let us test him. If your god is real, let him speak in your defense." He raised his eyes to the ceiling. "Oh god of 'Day and Night', if you truly exist, come and save the life of your only prophet. Because if he dies, you die with him."

Taylee's mouth dropped open as Elder Kaine stepped off the platform and grabbed a staff from a nearby guard. Then, in one swift motion, he swept Skyblind's legs out from under him and knocked him flat on his back.

Elder Kaine tossed the staff to Daraak, who, after reading the look in his eye, used the staff to repeatedly strike Skyblind in the face.

The Court erupted into cheers and laughter as the Elder of supposed "Justice" allowed Daraak to beat Skyblind viciously, while the King sat idly by, visibly more intrigued by the silver chalice in his hand than the brutality happening at his feet.

This can't be happening! Taylee could feel the anger rising in her gut. Not only had Skyblind rescued her in the forest, but he had fought to save her brother from the Locura.

And then there was the relic.

He said he knew what it was. He said he would give me answers about my parents. I can't just let him die … But what can I do?

Unfortunately, she didn't have any power here.

But he does. Taylee looked up at the King. *If he understood that Skyblind hadn't come back by choice, and that he helped me, I bet he would stop this!*

But approaching King Temchar was dangerous.

There must be another way.

Before Taylee could figure anything out, she was unexpectedly grabbed from behind; Daeni had found her.

"Let me go!" Taylee squealed as she tried to break free.

"Foolish girl, I warned you to stay close," Daeni snapped. "We're leaving."

"No! I have to help!"

"There's nothing to be done. This place is not safe."

Taylee struggled to get away from the woman's tight grip as she was dragged kicking and screaming through the cheering crowd.

They love violence. Taylee recognized the joy in their eyes as they watched the assault on Skyblind. *Maybe I can use that.*

It was a long shot, but Taylee was out of options.

Without giving it a second thought, she spotted the angriest looking man nearby and kicked him in the shin as hard as she could.

The man let out a howl, grabbed his leg, and spun around. Daeni looked up at him apologetically, but it was no good; the man shoved her hard, knocked her into some others, and set Taylee free in the process.

She didn't want to waste this opportunity and stayed low, kicking more people in the shins as she moved.

Far faster than she expected, the entire room erupted into violence; the members of the Court were now shoving each other, shouting, and breaking into fist fights.

It was the perfect distraction.

Taylee darted in and out of the crowd, hoping to lose Daeni in the process and create enough chaos that she could get close to the King.

Unfortunately, she was not invisible, and before she knew what was happening, angry hands were laid on her and she was knocked to the floor.

"Hey! Stop!" Taylee cried for help, but the lords and ladies around her were overcome with bloodlust and could not hear. She covered her head with her arms in an attempt to protect herself as the members of the Court mercilessly kicked and stomped at each other and hit her in the process.

Thankfully, it didn't last long.

Almost as soon as the fighting began, a loud shout was heard, and the chaos that started as a trial came to an immediate halt.

Chapter Thirteen — Enter the Princess

"A boy becomes a man at age 16, but a girl isn't a woman until 17. What kind of sense is that? Show me a boy at 16 more mature than a girl at 16, and I'll show you a Locura that loves the sun."

—LADY SILVER E'MONTON, A.P. 705
A WORLD WITHOUT WOMEN

"Is this how my father chooses to rule his court? With a defenceless man beat to death at his feet while others fight like drunken fools? This is not the Blood Room, and we are not Locura!" a woman shouted as she confidently entered the room.

At her appearance, the crowd that had been fighting only moments before quickly dispersed and made room for her to pass while the King sat taller on his throne.

"My sweet daughter, what are you doing here? This is an important trial, no place for—" The King was interrupted by his daughter's contemptuous laughter.

"Are you quite mad? Lord Daraak brings the Exile and you call this an important trial?" she asked with a certain fury that caused Taylee—after she had wiped away the blood from her nose—to look up and have hope.

She is nothing like her father.

The Princess couldn't be more than 17. But with her high cheekbones, striking blue eyes, and soft, fair skin, she had an almost ageless quality about her.

Her hair was long and vibrant, and Taylee watched in awe as it seemed to shimmer and reflect the different shades of light from the room. The result was something between a whitish blonde and a stone black, melding together in such a way that it was impossible to identify her natural hair colour.

She approached the throne with confidence, but was blocked by the Elder of Justice, Kaine. "Tame your tongue, Princess Salana. If you must know, this man is not just any common criminal, but your father's brother—your uncle—returned from exile."

Princess Salana hesitated as the weight of those words settled on her. "If that's true," she said after a moment, "then it's even more reason to treat him with respect."

The crowd murmured their disapproval.

"You aren't listening," Elder Kaine growled. "This man returned of his own volition. Not only did he break the conditions of his exile by doing so, but he also attacked Lord Daraak and his knights in the Outskirts. He was captured and brought here to be judged."

Taylee, enraged by the blatant lie, wrestled her way through the crowded floor and rushed to the platform, trusting that she might have an ally in this Princess Salana.

"That's a lie!" Taylee exclaimed, boldly approaching the princess. "I found him living alone in the Dark Forest. He was in exile, like you all wanted, but agreed to help me rescue my brother from the Locura after I begged him. He's the one who saved all the people who were trapped in the cages, not the knights! They came afterward and arrested him for no reason!"

"Is this true?" Princess Salana asked, staring directly at Lord Daraak, who was leaning casually on a staff and examining his painted-green fingernails. He looked up briefly—though never meeting her eyes—shook his head, and returned to the apparently more engrossing study of his nails.

Elder Kaine scowled. "Who is a girl from the Outskirts to challenge the word of a lord? What reason has Lord Daraak to lie?"

"Many reasons, I'm sure," Princess Salana snapped. "Until this discrepancy is resolved, the law forbids you from passing judgement. Every person is entitled to a fair trial."

Elder Kaine let out a long, irritated sigh. "Even if what this girl says is true, it doesn't matter. No matter how noble the intentions of Ellian, or 'Skyblind,' as he chooses to be called, he broke the conditions of his exile by returning."

"To save your people from monsters!" Taylee argued, but before she could say more, Princess Salana held up her hand, indicating that Taylee should remain silent.

The Princess stood silently for a moment, contemplating all that was said. "Father, really. Is any of this necessary? Send my uncle back into exile and let's forget this whole matter. Not only is he a harmless old man, but he's your *brother.* Aside from me, he's the only family you have left," she insisted.

Even when angry, Princess Salana held her chin high, her clear blue eyes maintaining a level of complete calmness and remaining steadily fixed on the King.

Taylee found herself shocked at the captivating beauty of the Princess, and she felt a twinge of jealousy. *I wonder if I could ever look like her.*

Taylee had never really cared much about whether others thought she was beautiful, but in the presence of the Princess, she suddenly cared a lot.

"I don't know …" The King shifted his weight and leaned against the arm of his throne. "I suppose this is getting a little out of hand. Perhaps you are right."

"Might I remind my King that Syyris does not abide injustice?" Elder Kaine interrupted. "Exile will not suffice anymore."

"What justice is there in condemning a man to death when his only wrongs are belief in an imaginary god and protecting a young girl from Locura?" Princess Salana shot back.

As if no longer interested in his nails, Lord Daraak pushed off from the staff he was leaning on and strutted over to Taylee.

Quite to her surprise, Lord Daraak started to run his fingers across the small of her back. Taylee was terrified, and her body went stiff as she found herself paralysed by his invasive touch.

“My dear King, if I may address the court?” he asked with a deep grin, turning to fix his cloudy eyes directly on Taylee’s face. He did not look away from her as he spoke. “The Exile is a dangerous man, and we would be foolish to allow him to leave this place and continue to corrupt the minds of sweet young girls like this one. It isn’t her fault, after all. I have seen the way he works his foul lies to sound like truth. Deception is one of the Nine Sins of Night. Whatever she thinks has happened, I assure you, she has been tricked.”

The lust in his eyes was fierce, and even though she didn’t like his attention, Taylee could feel her face burn red.

Take your eyes off me. She ground her teeth together to keep from speaking.

“Of course,” Lord Daraak continued, turning his gaze toward the King, “given some time alone, I believe I could help guide her memories to more accurately line up with reality.”

“Hmmm … That does sound wise …” the King mindlessly agreed.

Princess Salana flung Lord Daraak’s hand from Taylee’s back, causing her to let out a startled gasp as she realised she hadn’t been breathing. Taylee immediately stepped away from Lord Daraak and closer to the protection of the Princess.

“It is the wisdom of fools that corrupts a kingdom.” Princess Salana spat at Lord Daraak before turning to look directly at Taylee for the first time. “How old are you?”

“I just recently turned 16.”

“Then you are thankfully not yet of marrying age. How have you come to be here?”

Before Taylee could respond, there came a small yelp from the crowd, and Daeni hustled over. “I’m so sorry, my Princess. I was given charge of this girl after she was brought to the Palace. I didn’t expect her to interrupt the trial or I would never have taken her here. I’m so very sorry for our intrusion.”

The Princess regarded them both for a moment. “This girl is to stay with me under my protection until the truth of this event can be properly determined. I intend to keep her far from the clutches of this moral filth my father so loves to entertain."

The King shrugged his shoulders and nodded casually in approval.

Lord Daraak bowed low to the Princess in what Taylee decided could only be mock submission. "As always, your wish is the law."

"If you're both done competing for attention," Elder Kaine interjected, "we can move on to the fact that this girl's contradictory testimony is irrelevant. The guilt of the Exile in other matters has already been determined. He openly admits to worshipping another god—a god of *Night*!—and he stands in defiance of King Temchar. I have been given authority to pronounce judgement in the name of Syyris, and that is exactly what I intend to do."

Skyblind hadn't moved since he'd been struck. Only now, as the attention of the Court was fixed back on him, did they notice that he was quietly rocking back and forth and mumbling under his breath.

The King leaned forward and asked with a certain mischief in his voice, "What is my crazy brother doing now?"

Skyblind mumbled something inaudible in response.

"What was that?" Princess Salana asked.

He mumbled once again.

"For the sake of Peace, speak up!" Lord Daraak cursed.

"… in your hands …" Skyblind whispered in a slightly more audible voice. Then he stood and lifted his face to the King. "I request a private audience with Temchar," he spoke with such authority and volume that this time everyone could hear.

A hush fell over the Court; no one dared to speak. *Is he allowed to do that?*

The shock in the air was palpable.

The King, who was once again overcome by his short attention span, seemed to be unaware of the question.

Agar, the Elder of Peace, finally spoke when it became clear the King wasn't going to respond.

"You mean, without any of *us* present?"

Skyblind nodded, and repeated his request.

This time, King Temchar took notice. “Me? Alone? What for?” he asked.

“I have a message from the True God for you. And I must deliver it in private. Will you hear it?” Skyblind asked.

The room erupted with gasps and murmurs of distress at the reference to a message from another god. Some shouted and demanded that the Exile be executed on the spot.

What is he thinking? We had it under control.

Taylee could see that Elder Kaine was upset by the way his fists tightened at his sides, though his face registered a look of calm.

The King, however, who probably hadn’t been amused by anything like this in years, seemed quite fascinated by the whole thing. He thought for a few seconds, then grinned. “Sure. Why not?”

“My King! You cannot be serious?” Elder Kaine shouted over the exclamations of shock from the crowd.

Princess Salana turned and addressed everyone herself. “You’ve heard him. My father wants to be alone. Clear the room!”

Taylee had a hard time hearing anything after that due to the groans and complaints that came from the Court. Reluctantly, everyone filed out into the grand halls. She was about to follow them when she felt a firm hand grasp her forearm.

“No. Come with me.” The Princess directed her to another door in the back.

Thank you. She wanted to say, but held back, for fear of seeming like a silly little girl in need of rescue.

She watched timidly as Princess Salana spoke a few private words to Daeni before leading the two of them out of the room and into another long hallway.

With one last glance over her shoulder, Taylee caught a glimpse of Skyblind.

He was alone with the King, except for Elder Kaine and Lord Daraak, who appeared to be stalling. But within a matter of seconds, they too were forced to leave.

The door shut behind her.

But instead of following Princess Salana and Daeni, Taylee gave into her curiosity, pulled free of the Princess, and peeked through the crack in the door.

The room was completely silent.

All that could be heard in the empty and enormous chambers was the laboured breathing of the King and his brother.

Before Daeni was able to pry Taylee away from the door, she heard King Temchar eagerly ask about the message, and Skyblind respond ominously, "Brother, you have displeased my God."

PART II

Chapter Fourteen — Becoming Elite

"It is forbidden for an Elder or any who serve on the Island to take a wife or have a child. There can be no distractions if one is to serve Syyris faithfully."

—HECTOR THE HOLY, A.P. 730

A TOME OF TRUTH

A cold wind rose up from across the Great Bay and blasted its way over the 100-foot walls and down the cobblestone streets of Lightspire.

The wind was nothing new; but it was the cold, with its bitter chill, that caused the roaming citizens of the city to pull their hoods tightly over their faces.

All except for Corwin Medisto, who seemed to be the only one in the entirety of the city that kept his hood down. He was impervious to the cold kiss of the wind mainly due to the steady trudge he made up a worn, well-used path.

The path wound its way through the city and up to an innumerable amount of houses and shelters that adorned the base of the wall. Most of them were made of stone, with a few exceptions carved out of dark wood. But regardless of the material, every house had one thing in common: the roofs were all covered with shiny white plates that reflected sunlight back at the Three Towers.

As Corwin made his way up the path toward one of the wood houses, he cast a sad glance back at the three enormous, smooth, white pillars that shot straight up into the sky. The two on the ends were smaller, while the centre tower, Lightspire, the city's namesake, loomed highest in the sky.

His eyes left the Three Towers and moved to the sun, which seemed to hang lower in the sky than last time he checked.

Night is on the way.

Sixty-two sun-cycles had passed since the attack on the Krydor Markets, and although he'd lived in Lightspire for nearly as long, Corwin still felt like a stranger in this land.

In accordance with their orders, Corwin and Tray'o were faithfully attending the same daily testing and training seminars as all the other young men and women their age. It was a fairly boring process, and Corwin initially found little about the Lightspire Masters and their rigid teaching style intrigued him. However he obediently arrived on time for the lessons, hoping that if he made a good enough impression, they might eventually answer his questions about what had happened to Taylee.

In all the time he was in the city, she and the relic remained lost to him, and Uncle Jael showed no signs of improvement—although his host, White Holland, seemed optimistic that if they kept training and serving things would turn around.

When Corwin had first arrived in Lightspire, he thought "White Holland" was an unusual name, but after being introduced to the other youth in his training group, it turned out that naming people after colours was a theme here. The most common colour names were Bleu, White, and Rede.

There were other names as well. Old names, like Summer, Autumn, Wynter, Hael, Snow—words that had no real meaning anymore, nor Corwin the knowledge to comprehend them. In the old legends and fables there were things called "seasons," one in particular where the land was blanketed in a cold white fluff that fell from the sky and burned like fire on exposed skin. *Snow.* According to the stories it hadn't fallen on Anaciencia in a thousand years. But those were just stories. Everyone knew there were only two seasons, the ones the singers called the Long Day and the Black Night.

Another common naming theme among the other Centre-born youth that stuck out to Corwin was mythical birds, such as Phoenix, Raven, Hawkeye, Griffin, Dragon, and Sparrow.

Of all the 42 recruits that Corwin met in training, the girl named Sparrow was by far the most interesting.

Standing next to the other recruits in line, Sparrow towered at least a head higher than the majority. She wore baggy clothes that hid her thin frame, and tied her black hair into a long, thick braid that hung neatly down her back. Even without taking height into account, her tan skin, deep brown eyes, thin, curved eyebrows and sharp nose were enough to make her stand out among the crowd.

She was born to be an Elite.

During the first training sun-cycle, the Master of Peace had wanted to see an example of everyone's fighting ability. Corwin had virtually no experience in combat, so he did fairly poorly in this exercise, but that was no surprise to him. What was a surprise, however, was how Sparrow's skills with a bow and arrow. Within the first minute of target practice, she'd put all the boys to shame.

The next sun-cycle they had worked with the Master of Mind and focused on mental ability. This was an area where Corwin was able to shine.

The youth were presented with a series of complicated puzzles and tested to see how quickly they could solve them. Corwin wasn't the fastest, but he was in the top five, and after that, the instructors seemed to regard him with moderate attention.

The Master of Mind, in particular, was insistent that Corwin sign up to be tested for the Elites. But up until the last few sun-cycles, becoming an Elite had been the furthest thing from his mind.

"G'd day, boy!" Holland shouted from another room as Corwin entered the house.

"Hello, Holland. How is my uncle?"

"Restin', he be restin'." Holland's voice sounded sad.

No change. He frowned.

Every time he returned from training, Corwin secretly hoped

his uncle might have woken or shown some sign of improvement. But it was always the same report.

The medicine isn't helping, he thought bitterly as he placed the freshly purchased bag of medical herbs and spices on a nearby table.

"Get me anything special?" Tray'o flashed a grin as Corwin entered the kitchen.

Tray'o and Holland were in the middle of washing some pots in a basin of water, a sight that still shocked him whenever he saw it.

The former Lord of Pinehouse up to his arms in soap.

The fact that Tray'o was now a commoner still did not feel right.

"Just more medicine. The healer suggested we try Tac'ak berries again."

Holland bobbed his head and smiled his toothy, hopeful grin.

"Gross. Forget it. I'll grab snacks later on my own." Tray'o pulled his arms out of the soap, wiped them on a rag, and cracked his knuckles. "Ready to head out? I thought we could try searching the taverns around the Palace before our second class."

Corwin hesitated. "We've gone over all that area already."

"So? We could have missed something. Maybe someone noticed something new."

"Maybe," he said as Tray'o walked by and pulled on his boots.

Over the course of the last week, Tray'o had become obsessed with the thought that Taylee must be inside the Palace. It was one of the only places they'd been denied access, and even though Holland insisted it wasn't likely, Tray'o remained determined to find out.

"Be making sure ya be goin' to class, yeah?" Holland's voice cracked through the house. "It be important if ya be wantin' good placement!"

"Don't worry about us. We'll get there," Tray'o replied as they stepped out of the house. "Eventually."

His friend's enthusiasm was lost on Corwin, however, and the best he could manage was a weak smile as they shut the door and made their way through the mostly empty streets.

Although they'd lived in the city for quite some time now, Corwin still couldn't believe the size and enormity of Lightspire. There were at least 8,000 people that lived behind the walls, according to what the Master of Ages taught in his history lessons, and yet lately it did not feel crowded.

Corwin suspected this was due to the season. Where Mid-Luminous was a time of celebration, they were now nearing the end of Lightspan, with less than thirty sun-cycles before the sun dipped all the way beneath the horizon and the beginning of Darkfall. From here on out, Essence would be in high demand, and so everyone in Lightspire was probably working extra hours to earn as much as they could to survive the Night.

And somewhere in this city my sister is hidden.

At the beginning, finding her had been an exciting challenge and an excuse to explore, but now, with the season drawing to a close, it seemed more and more like a hopeless dream.

"Holland has a point," Corwin admitted. "We really should make it to class on time for once."

"Relax. It's not that big of a deal. We'll just swing by the Palace and ask around. What's gotten into you, anyway?"

"I just … I'm starting to doubt we'll ever find her, Tray." The words were painful, but they needed to be said.

"How can you even think that? Of course we'll find her. We know she's here in the city somewhere."

"We've been looking for weeks."

"And? It's a big city," Tray'o insisted. "We just have to keep at it. It's only a matter of time before—"

"Before what?" Corwin snapped. "Before we fail all our courses because we were running around instead of studying and are given some awful placement?"

"I'm glad you aren't a fortune teller. Why the sudden pessimism? You know we need to find her. She's still, you know … got the necklace." Tray'o said the last bit under his breath so anyone walking nearby wouldn't hear.

If only I'd kept it and not Taylee …

"I've been thinking that if we don't find her soon we'll need to figure out another way to help Uncle Jael."

"There is no other way."

"There might be …" Corwin rubbed his neck nervously. "I've heard good things about the benefits of being an Elite."

As expected, Tray'o did not look pleased. "Obviously you're joking."

"No … I've been considering signing up for a little while now."

"That's insane. You can't go."

"Why not? Holland's son joined the Elites."

"And no one has seen him since!" Tray'o snapped.

The silence that hung in the air was painful. *Why is he trying to make me feel bad about this?*

"Look, Tray …" Corwin stopped himself when he realised he didn't know what he wanted to say.

"Look at what? If you do this, you're not only abandoning Taylee but also your uncle!"

"Wherever she is, I'm sure Taylee is better off than she would be with us. And I'm not abandoning my uncle," Corwin stated firmly. "If I joined, it would be to save him. The healer told me that the family of those serving in the Elites are taken care of for life. They're given the best medical attention, and provided for in a way that no berries or herbs could ever do."

Tray'o shook his head. "You know what Master Lunechair said. Destroying the relic is the only way to break the curse."

"Well, maybe he was wrong. We haven't seen him in a long time. We have no idea where Taylee is …" Corwin sighed. "This seems like the best option for Uncle Jael to be well again. Syyris is a just god, and he—"

"Syyris is a *just* god, is he?" Tray'o interrupted. "Tell me, what justice was there in your uncle getting sick in the first place?"

"That's different." Corwin didn't like where this was going. "He got sick because I activated a cursed relic. One that you brought to my house, by the way."

Tray'o narrowed his eyes. "Fine, so what justice was there in my father being executed for a Locura attack he had nothing to do with?"

"Tray'o, we have to have faith that everything happens for a reason." Corwin tried to sound convincing, but even as he said the words, he felt uncertain of the truth in them.

"Sure, Cor. Things happen for a reason. That *reason* is that people are selfish, people are proud, people are stupid! You're a fool if you think god wastes his time on us. Face it, Cor. Syyris Sagrado abandoned us to our own devices years ago. We're on our own. All we have is each other, and if you join the Elites, you're throwing that all away." With that, Tray'o spun on his heels and started walking in the direction of the Palace.

He can't be serious.

"What are you doing?" Corwin called after his friend.

"Don't worry about me. Go to class, find a Master, and beg him to let you be an Elite," Tray'o cursed under his breath as he walked away.

Corwin was stunned; he hadn't expected that reaction. "Maybe I will!"

If he gets arrested for poking around the Palace, it'll serve him right, Corwin thought angrily as he watched his friend disappear down the path that veered toward the flat-topped castle made of beautifully carved white stone.

The back of the Palace was connected to the main city walls, but the front was surrounded by smaller, 10-foot white gold walls that not only protected the Palace from unwanted visitors, but also contained some sort of unique garden. Corwin could not see the garden for himself, but the tops of colourful trees were visible over the walls, and the way they swayed in the wind made Corwin think of hands beckoning him to follow.

He considered it briefly, but shook the thought away.

Tray'o doesn't understand, that's all, Corwin asserted to himself. *We've been searching for so long. This is the best option. After all, what's a better sign of repentance than sacrificing everything to serve Syyris on the Island?*

It seemed like a good plan to him, but it broke his heart to think that becoming an Elite would mean he'd never see his uncle or Taylee again.

If that's the price I must pay to make things right, then I will pay it, he resolved sadly as he turned his back on his friend. *Tray'o will see. Becoming an Elite will change everything.*

Chapter Fifteen — A Fresh Discovery

***"If you want something—if you truly want it—
then nothing can stop you from getting it."***

—ELDER RHAMSEY, A.P. 230
THE NINE SINS OF NIGHT

"Hello, Pinehouse. Late again. Are you trying to make me look good?" Sparrow teased with a cocky smile as Tray'o approached the training hall. He frowned when he saw her leaning against a pillar at the top of the stairs.

I don't have time for this. "Is Corwin still in there?"

"He's just finishing up with one of the instructors. You missed another test, by the way."

"Who cares," Tray'o said as he darted up the steps. "I've got more important things to do."

Unlike Corwin, with his moderate success in class, Tray'o was failing miserably—a fact that their classmate Sparrow loved to bring up at every chance she got.

But Tray'o didn't care what she or anyone else thought. All he cared about was seeing Taylee again. Too many sun-cycles had passed since he saw her last, but after what he had just learned, things were looking a whole lot brighter.

Now to tell Corwin the good news. Hopefully he hasn't signed up for the Elites already.

"You know," Sparrow mused as Tray'o got to the top of the

steps, “if you spent half the time that you waste at taverns and walking around the Palace studying, you might be a half decent student by now.”

Her words stopped Tray’o dead in his tracks.

She was right—he’d just come from the Strangled Goat, a shady but popular tavern in the city. Tray’o had learned early in his time at Lightspire that if you wanted information, the Goat was the place to go. Unfortunately, no useful information on Taylee had ever turned up, but his earlier fight with Corwin had put him into such a negative mood that he went straight there to spend a few hours drinking and asking around.

Normally he wouldn’t care if anyone knew where he went, but something about the way she spoke made Tray’o uneasy.

“You’ve been following me?” he accused.

“You aren’t interesting enough for me to follow. I just happened to see you before I left for class.”

Tray’o raised his eyebrows and crossed his arms. “Right. ‘Cause you’re the type of girl who frequents taverns before her special training in the Elites.”

Sparrow took a step forward and locked eyes with him. Her smile vanished and in an instant she became deadly serious. “You have no idea *what* kind of girl I am.”

Tray’o swallowed hard and fumbled for words to say. “How I spend my time is my business. I’d like you to stay out of it,” he managed at last.

Just then, Corwin walked casually out of the training hall and toward them, staring intently at some multi-coloured cube in his hand. Sparrow, upon seeing his approach, smirked and brushed past Tray’o.

“Sure thing, Pinehouse.” She flipped her braid over her shoulder. “The last thing I’d want to do is intrude on your sad little life. Just watch your back. Dark One spies are everywhere. Only our actions prove whether we are trustworthy or not …” Sparrow let the sentence hang as she strolled away.

What does she mean by that? “Right, sure, whatever you say,”

Tray'o grumbled as he watched her leave. "And, hey!" he added with a shout, "Stop calling me Pinehouse!"

Sparrow laughed as she disappeared around a corner.

He hated when she called him that; it reminded him of home.

"What do you make of her?" Tray'o asked as Corwin approached.

"Sparrow? Seems all right. Why? Was she giving you a hard time for skipping class?"

"Don't joke. You'll be happy I did when you hear what I learned," Tray'o snapped. Even though the news was good, he still felt irritated with Corwin for abandoning him.

"Tray, I know it's hard to understand, but one of the Masters just told me I have a good chance at becoming an Elite. We have no idea where Taylee is, and honestly, I think this might be—"

"But that's just it!" Tray'o interrupted. "I found Taylee!"

Corwin dropped the cube. "What? Are you serious?"

Good, you do still care about her. "Well …" Tray'o searched for the best way to spin his news. "I haven't *technically* found her."

Corwin blinked a few times, picked up the cube, and started walking down the steps.

"No, wait, listen! I haven't found her, but I know where she is," Tray'o called as he chased after his friend. "She's in the Palace!"

Corwin narrowed his eyes suspiciously and said, "How do you know that?"

"A knight told me!" Tray'o exclaimed. "I mentioned her description at the Goat, and he said he saw her in the Court with that Skyblind guy. She's in the Palace, Corwin, just like I keep saying."

Corwin looked confused and slid the cube into his jacket pocket. "He was certain it was her? Was he drunk?"

"Of course he was drunk, but that doesn't mean he didn't see her." Tray'o tried to sound calm. "We can go, right now. I found a way for us to sneak over the wall and into the Palace garden."

"What? You want to jump the wall? Are you crazy?" Corwin frowned. "What if we get caught and are imprisoned for trespassing? You know what happens to people who get caught sneaking into the Palace? They get locked away for life. No trial."

Tray'o flared his nostrils in frustration at his friend's lack of courage. "We won't get caught."

"It's too risky."

"Too risky? So you're fine to just leave her in the Palace?"

"She's probably safer there than anywhere else," Corwin replied.

Tray'o couldn't believe his ears. "Right. About as safe as a prisoner can be. Do you know what they'll do when she turns 17? She's a girl from the Outskirts and she'll go to the breeding camps—the knight confirmed it. But I guess I misjudged you. I thought you still cared about your sister."

Corwin spun around. "What are you talking about? Of course I care about her!"

"Well I care about her too! That's why we have to try. I can't lose her! Not like this." Tray'o spat the last word off his tongue as if it were venomous.

There was a minute of silence where the two stared intently at one another.

Tray'o could feel a bead of sweat dripping down his forehead, but he refused to break eye contact to wipe it away.

Corwin, visibly conflicted, groaned and scratched his head vigorously. "I can't risk being caught, Tray. My becoming an Elite might mean Uncle Jael could get well."

"Elite medicine *might* help, but if you find Taylee and destroy the relic, you know for a fact that your uncle Jael *will* get well."

Corwin looked away.

Come on, man. Don't make me do this on my own.

"It's such a long shot …"

"I promise, Cor, we won't be gone long," Tray'o insisted. "No one will even know or care. When we find her, I'll keep her hidden and safe at Holland's, and you can take the relic and do your Elite thing. Just destroy it when they take you to the Island."

"And if we don't find her?"

"We will, and we will bring her back," Tray'o persisted, firmly grasping his friend's shoulder. "If nothing else, she deserves to see

Jael and to know that he's still alive."

After all we've been through. Come on! He wanted to shout. But he could feel Corwin's resistance weakening.

"I don't know ..."

All right Corwin. Tray'o grit his teeth. *This is for your own good.*

"Don't worry. I have a perfect plan, and it can't fail," Tray'o lied. "I need you to trust me."

Corwin looked up and made reluctant eye contact. "You're absolutely sure you can get us in and out undetected?"

Tray'o grinned and placed his arm around Corwin's shoulder to help guide his friend down a different path.

"Oh yeah. We'll be completely fine."

Corwin nodded, and, with one last glance, looked over his shoulder at the training hall. "You better be right about this."

"You worry too much, Cor."

Chapter Sixteen — An Unexpected Meeting

"I pity any woman who declines my company; I am constantly with myself, and I must say, it is quite delightful."

—LORD DARAAK KAAG'ARI, A.P. 743
SAYINGS OF THE KINGS AND OTHER LORDLY SORTS

This is the dumbest thing I've ever done. Corwin took a deep breath.

"Are you ready?" Tray'o called from the tree on the other side of the Palace wall.

"Give me a minute. And don't shout!" Corwin said as he stood up on a branch that seemed liable to break at any second.

Against Corwin's better judgement, he'd climbed with his friend up a large, black tree which grew outside the wall that surrounded the Palace garden. Across from the black tree, inside the garden, grew another tree with somewhat sturdier-looking branches that almost extended over the wall.

Giving many reassurances of their safety, Tray'o had insisted that they could use the branches of the two trees to leap over the wall and climb down into the garden. The plan was actually pretty decent, except for one small problem: although Corwin had climbed trees before, he no longer felt as confidant with heights as he once did, largely due to his incident in the watchtower at the Krydor Markets.

"Just hurry it up, yeah?"

"Yeah, yeah."

Corwin took a deep breath and tried to clear his mind of any fear.

On the count of three.

One.

He closed his eyes.

Two.

He clenched his fists.

Three!

With one rather desperate sounding grunt, Corwin leapt out of the tree and over the Palace wall …

… and missed the branch entirely.

Flailing his arms like a starving Locura, Corwin tried frantically to grasp at something to stop his fall. But every branch he touched snapped immediately, and so he continued to fall, bringing with him a flurry of broken branches and leaves.

Corwin tumbled down helplessly, directly into some prickly bushes at the base of the inner Palace wall.

"Are you all right?" Tray'o called in a hushed voice from the tree.

Corwin sat up and shook his head in disbelief.

Aside from a few scratches and a bump on his head that would likely turn into a nasty bruise, he seemed to be unharmed.

"Oh sure. 'The branches are strong, Cor, trust me,'" Corwin whined in his best Tray'o impersonation.

"Hey! Not my fault. You did it wrong," Tray'o hissed defensively as he dropped down from one branch to another with significant ease until he landed next to Corwin with a soft thud.

"See? Simple. Do you honestly think they'd let you into the Elites with a pathetic jump like that?" Tray'o teased with a confident smile before brushing his shirt clean and extending his hand to help pull Corwin out of the bushes.

"Thanks for the friendly support," he growled. "Let's get moving in case someone heard us." Corwin was already feeling the weight of their trespassing, and the last thing he wanted was for them to be caught.

"In case someone heard 'you', not 'us,'" Tray'o corrected. "But don't worry. I don't think people in the Palace really visit this garden. It always sounds empty when we walk by."

"That doesn't mean anything."

Tray'o shrugged and, without another word, wandered away from the wall. Corwin wanted to stay irritated, but, as he followed after his friend, he found himself too enraptured by the beauty of the garden to stay mad.

This place is incredible.

Yellow, blue, and red flowers, bigger and brighter than Corwin thought physically possible sprouted up out of the earth and bloomed proudly next to equally bright and colourful fruits that dangled from trees. It seemed almost as if here, in the garden, colour took on a whole new energy of its own. Even the grass was vibrant, green and soft to the touch, much different from the brownish, dry brush they were accustomed to in the Outskirts.

Taylee must love this, if she is actually in the Palace, Corwin thought to himself as he looked around.

"Can you believe this place?" Tray'o asked. "Even my father's castle didn't have flowers like these."

"I've never seen anything like it either. But, we should hurry. I don't want to waste time."

"You're right," Tray'o agreed as he plucked a shiny red apple off a tree and took a big bite. "Any ideas where she'd be?"

"What? Me?"

"Well, yeah. She's your sister. Don't you have some kind of twin power that lets you sense when she's near?" Tray'o asked with a mouthful of fruit.

Not that again. Corwin groaned. "For the last time, no! This was your idea. You said you had a perfect plan."

Tray'o blinked a few times, then tossed the half-eaten fruit over his shoulder. "My plan was to come here and hang out in the bushes until she showed up," he answered as he wiped the fruit juice off his lips with the sleeve of his shirt.

"That's ... not a plan."

"Why? If she's in the Palace, then of course she'd come here at some point." Tray'o extended a palm toward one of the yellow flowers. "Taylee loves nature and stuff."

"That's idiotic. What if she doesn't have free reign around the Palace? What if she's in some work program? What if the garden is off-limits to her?"

"I prefer not to think about 'ifs.' But, *if* she doesn't come around, I guess we'll have to sneak inside and look for her." Tray'o smirked. "Have some faith. She's here somewhere, it's just a matter of time before we find her."

I should have known better. "I'm starting to think I made a mistake trusting you."

Tray'o looked like he was about to respond, but, all of a sudden, his eyes grew wide, and before Corwin knew what was happening, Tray'o took off running in the opposite direction.

The next thing he knew, his hair was grabbed from behind and his head yanked back.

"Ow!" Corwin exclaimed as his legs were kicked out from under him and he was thrown onto his back.

Stunned, Corwin blinked and tried to focus on the sun above him, but it wouldn't stop spinning, and almost as quickly as he was knocked down, a silhouetted figure stepped over him and blocked all the light.

The figure promptly knelt on his chest and held a ruby-encrusted dagger to his throat, promptly causing all Corwin's thoughts of resisting to vanish.

"I've got this one. Go after the other!" The voice of his attacker was female, and it commanded some other unseen person.

"I can explain …!" Corwin gasped as a small, white-gloved hand pinched the skin under his chin.

"You don't belong here." The woman's voice was stern, but her face soft. As she knelt over Corwin, the ends of her long, shiny hair lightly dangled against his face. The sensation of it completely captivated his attention, and as he stared up at her, he realised he couldn't discern if her hair was blonde or black.

Magic hair? A sorceress? "I … um …" Corwin stuttered, unable to find words.

She was staring intently at him now. Her eyes were swirling, sparkling blue-green spheres that seemed to drink him in.

Time seemed to stop all together.

Corwin could feel his cheeks grow red, and so he tried to grin in an attempt to appear casual. He instantly regretted the decision, however, as it resulted in him being slapped hard across the face.

"Did I say you could smile, Dark One?"

Don't be an idiot! Corwin raised his open palms in submission. "I'm no Dark One. My name's Corwin, and I'm a student," he blurted, now very much aware of the dangerous situation.

"Why should I believe you?"

"Uh … I don't know … I guess … if I was a Dark One, would I have been so easy to catch?"

"Easy for me to catch—yes. Dumb enough to let yourself be caught—probably not." She smiled ever so slightly.

Good. There's a person under that tough attitude. Use that and you might get out of this in one piece, Corwin's inner voice encouraged.

"If I let you up," she asked after a brief pause, "do you promise not to try and run?"

"I promise," Corwin squeaked in a voice as harmless-sounding as he could manage.

The woman stared deeply into his eyes as if trying to read his mind, then, slowly withdrew her dagger and stood.

"I'm really sorry about the intrusion. I can explain everything!" he stated as he scrambled to his feet.

She arched an eyebrow at him and crossed her arms impatiently.

"Oh, you're waiting for me to explain? All right, um, well, my sister, she was taken here. At least, we think she was."

"We?" the woman narrowed her eyes.

"Uh, my friend Tray'o and I. He's the one who ran away …" Corwin scratched the back of his head. "Right, so, uh, anyway, we all lived in the Outskirts and were captured by the Locura and then rescued and brought here and separated. My friend Tray'o thought that maybe she might be here. My sister, that is. I didn't mean any harm, really. I just want to find her." The words came out rushed and in a bit of a jumble, but he thought she must be able to recognize that he was telling the truth.

The woman regarded him silently for a minute before tossing her hair over her shoulder. Even though he had seen Taylee do the same thing before, the simple act now appeared almost violent due to the woman's intense nature. "Your friend should not have run. Only the guilty run from authority."

"No, he shouldn't have. You're absolutely right. He was probably scared when you …" Corwin hesitated to find the right words, "… brought me down."

"Hmm."

I'm doomed. Straight to jail, if she doesn't put some curse on me first, Corwin thought fearfully as he wiped a smear of sweat from his forehead.

"Will you come willingly? Or do I need to restrain you again?" she asked at last.

"Oh," Corwin looked around nervously. "Where do you want to go? I mean … I could just leave the way I came …"

"No, no. You jumped over the wall. You must have wanted to stay and be a guest of the King. He has a few rooms set up for situations like this."

Corwin tilted his head skeptically. "He does?"

"Oh yes. There's always room in the cells. Come along." She pointed toward a path with the tip of her dagger.

Prison. You're done. It's over. No relic, no Elites, no Island, no saving Uncle Jael.

The thoughts overwhelmed him.

I could run, he thought briefly. But, judging by the ease of her takedown, it seemed likely she could easily catch him again.

Just be honest and cooperative. She might be willing to reason with me, Corwin decided. "I'll go peacefully."

The woman nodded, and soon the two of them were walking side by side down a cobblestone path through the garden.

"I'm not just any student, you know," Corwin announced in

an attempt to sound important. "I'm on the list to be tested for the Elites."

The woman stifled a laugh. "You don't know who I am, do you?" She sounded almost pleased.

"Um … no? I'm sorry. Should I?"

"No, I suppose *you* shouldn't. My name is Salana."

Good, a name. Maybe she's warming up to me.

"Hi, Salana. It's nice to meet you. I'm really sorry about this whole thing. I honestly meant no harm," Corwin blurted his feelings, hoping that perhaps his honesty would awaken some sympathy in her.

"You meant no harm, that I believe. But you broke the law. I don't know about the Outskirts, but here, there are consequences for such things."

Corwin sighed. *It's hopeless. She's not the type to budge.*

Talking any further seemed pointless, and so he resigned himself to following quietly after her.

The woman named Salana lead Corwin down the path, over a bridge, and through the main doors of the Palace.

The interior of the Palace halls was quite impressive. Giant, golden columns rose to the sky, and ancient paintings adorned nearly every inch of the walls. But this was not the time to view artwork. Corwin couldn't get a good look at anything, anyway, due to Salana's pace.

She marched him down one corridor after another and up a winding set of stairs until at last they came to a door.

Salana stopped there and looked at Corwin.

He hesitated, then realised she was waiting for him, and slowly pushed it open.

Inside was not at all what he had expected. Instead of a cell, he seemed to be standing in a bedroom. Though lightly furnished, it still contained a dusty wooden bookshelf filled with old volumes and manuscripts, a dirty brass mirror, a silver washbasin, and a lopsided wooden desk.

And directly in the middle—taking up most of the floor

space—was the biggest and fluffiest bed Corwin had ever seen.

If this is how they do prison in the Palace, then maybe being caught isn't such a bad thing, he thought with a measure of confusion. "I don't understand … I thought …"

The door slammed shut behind him.

"Answer me one question, Corwin, and answer it truthfully." Salana's voice took on a whole new edge, almost as if she were desperate instead of angry. "What is your sister's name?"

Corwin's breath caught in his chest. "Taylee. Her name is Taylee Medisto."

And just like that, the tension in Salana's shoulders relaxed, and an actual smile crossed her face. "Then we have much to discuss."

Chapter Seventeen — What Happened to Taylee

"Without laughter, there are only tears; without tears, we can never know joy."

BLEU'S FABLES AND FOLKLORE: THE CRYING GIANT

"This is Taylee's room?" Corwin exclaimed in shock.

"She stayed here, yes," Salana replied.

It was hard to believe—somehow, after they were separated, Taylee had been given placement in the Palace and allowed to live what looked like quite a comfortable life with Salana, who Corwin assumed was some spoiled daughter of a Court official with major control issues.

Taylee wasn't at all the prisoner Tray'o assumed her to be. I hope palace living didn't ruin her. He frowned at the thought of his sister lounging around in fancy dresses and eating grapes in the garden. *Did she even try to contact us?*

"Where is she now? I have a lot of questions for her."

Salana pressed her lips together and walked over to the desk. "So do I. Unfortunately, we don't know where she went."

"I don't understand. You said this was her room."

"It was, up until recently."

Corwin tensed. "What happened?"

"We don't know much," Salana replied as she traced the top of the desk with her finger. "Taylee was a faithful attendant to me. She was given a lot of freedom within the Palace, and with it, she chose to visit two individuals on a regular basis. One goes by the title 'Skyblind.' Are you familiar with him as well?"

Skyblind. Her bearded Exile friend. Corwin had completely forgotten about him after their separation.

"Somewhat. He was instrumental in helping us escape from the Locura."

Salana nodded. "Good. That's what Taylee said too. Your testimony will be helpful now that she's gone."

Testimony? Gone? "What happened to my sister?"

Salana narrowed her eyes in what could only be irritation. "The other person she visited was one of your former Masters, in the cells. I didn't like her going there, but your sister has a strong will and insisted he was harmless."

Former Master? Corwin furrowed his brow. *She must mean Master Lunechair. I suppose he was here too.* A memory of his teacher attacking Daraak and the Kaag'ari knights flashed before his eyes. *It makes sense that they'd imprison him for that.*

"From what we can determine," Salana continued, "two suncycles ago, Taylee aided him in escaping from his cell. Both have been missing ever since."

"She … freed him?"

"So it seems," Salana sounded as bothered by it as Corwin. "Do you have any idea where they might have gone?"

"No, not really," Corwin wondered suddenly if they might be going to destroy the relic without him. "Unless …"

"If you know anything, I need you to tell me."

Corwin lowered his eyes. "I'm pretty sure they're going to the Island."

Salana stared at him blankly. "And *why* do you think they would try going there?"

If I mention the relic, she might try and take it to the Elders. Corwin nervously scratched the back of his head. "I can't say."

Salana studied his face for a minute before speaking. "It doesn't matter. You're wrong. The only way to the Island is by boat, and there's no chance an escaped prisoner and a girl with an arrest warrant could manage to get on board."

"They'll find a way," Corwin insisted. "Master Lunechair is some kind of sorcerer."

At this, Salana raised an eyebrow and said, "I highly doubt that."

Her better-than-you attitude was starting to get to Corwin, but he knew he didn't have a lot of leverage in this situation. "I know it's hard to understand, but I need to get to Taylee. I'm fairly certain that she'll try going to the Island. Please, if you could just take me there …"

Salana shook her head vehemently. "Absolutely out of the question; the Island is restricted."

"Then take me to the dock … if she's hiding around there, she'll see me and …"

Salana pushed herself away from the window and turned to face him with a ferocity that indicated she was not used to being argued with. "If your sister is trying to go to the Island, like you insist, then she will be caught at the docks and brought back to me."

Corwin cringed. *Uncle Jael's life is on the line. If they get caught and the relic is discovered, it could be the end.* "If you just let me go, I promise you, I can smooth things out."

"No. I have other plans for you."

"Plans? What do you mean?"

"You will stay here and testify to the Court in Taylee's absence of the things you saw Skyblind do."

"What? Stay here?" Corwin suddenly felt very uncomfortable. "I'm sorry, but, I can't. You don't understand …"

"No, Corwin, you don't understand. You have no choice in the matter," Salana growled as she brushed by him and pulled open the door. "There is no further use in discussing this. I will return later. Be grateful I'm allowing you to stay here. I just as easily could have taken you to a cell." Without another word, Salana slammed the door shut and locked it behind her.

Wonderful. Corwin sighed and looked around at what was essentially a prison anyway. But, all things considered, it was actually a pretty nice room. *She's right. It could be worse.*

The first thing he thought to do was search for the relic. After all, if this was Taylee's room, it seemed plausible that she may have hid it somewhere.

But after a lengthy search of every drawer, cupboard, and corner of the room, he resigned himself to the fact that she had in fact taken the relic with her, and was most likely in the process of securing a spot on a boat with Master Lunechair.

He'll keep her safe. Maybe he'll conjure up some magic and find a way to the Island ... It doesn't really make a difference if it's Taylee who goes and not me. All that matters is that the relic is destroyed, he told himself as he flopped face first on the bed.

It was softer than he expected, and he found himself pleasantly surprised by the way his body slowly sank into the cozy mattress.

But the comfort only cultivated his growing irritation with Taylee at how—after having what must have been an incredibly easy time here the last two months—she was now off doing *his* job.

I'm the idiot who activated the relic. It was my responsibility to destroy it.

As much as Corwin wanted to linger in these thoughts, he knew they weren't productive, so he rolled over onto his side and tried to distract himself by speculating on whether or not Tray'o had eluded capture.

Time dragged on, and Corwin, feeling no better about his current situation, decided he may as well try and get some rest.

All of Corwin's feelings of anger toward Taylee and Tray'o faded away as he let his heavy eyelids fall shut, and before he knew it, he drifted off into a peaceful and much-needed sleep.

His awakening, however, was far from peaceful.

Chapter Eighteen — A Sky Ablaze

"... And so the world was bathed with fire,
for the Ancients committed the unforgivable sin:
They worshipped magic over god."

—ELDER JERAMEE, A.P. 6
HISTORICAL LAWS OF THE FIRST ELDER ORDER

He felt the hair on the back of his neck rise.

Don't move. Don't breathe, Tray'o warned himself as the hulking knight walked right by the bushes where he lay hidden.

Tray'o had managed to elude capture so far by hiding in various trees and bushes and constantly staying on the move. But he was starting to get annoyed, and his pursuer—a tall, dark-skinned knight with a thick build and an unforgiving face—was not giving up the hunt. With each new hiding place, Tray'o sensed his luck was running out.

Just give up already, Tray'o cursed the knight's persistence.

His first impulse was to blame Corwin for all this.

He probably let himself get caught by that woman just because she was beautiful, Tray'o thought grimly. *He didn't even try to run.*

Corwin was probably the fastest runner he knew. But when it counted? *"No, no. I'll just surrender." Unbelievable.*

After a few minutes of searching the surrounding area, the knight jogged away to search another corner of the garden.

Now's your chance. Move again! But as Tray'o rose to a crouching position, he realised he wasn't sure where to go next.

You could always leave. Tray'o frowned as he considered the unpleasant option. Leaving the garden wasn't the end of the world; it would just mean he'd have to try to come back again later. But at this point, he was far closer to the Palace than the wall, and even if he could manage to sneak all the way back to the wall undetected, the thought of leaving felt like giving up on Taylee.

And then he saw it; across from him, near a crystal blue pond, was one of the tallest trees in the garden, with thick, orange leaves. The branches looked firm enough to hold him, and the coverage was better than any of the hiding spots he'd used so far.

If I get up into that tree without being spotted I could maybe hide there and safely wait him out, he resolved.

Feeling confident with his new plan, Tray'o listened carefully for any sound of the knight's return.

After a long minute, and when he was certain the knight was not nearby, Tray'o took a deep breath and darted out of his bush.

He moved swiftly toward the tree.

With each step, he was careful to make no sound.

I'm practically invisible, he mused as he avoided leaves and twigs and stepped only on soft grass.

But his confidence did not last. Almost as soon as he started moving, he caught sight of something in his peripheral vision.

No!

Someone was charging straight at him!

Tray'o felt his heart leap into his throat as he tried to get his speed up, but it was too late; the other person had a head start. He lifted his hands in vain defence as he was tackled hard from the side.

Tray'o slammed into the ground.

He tried his best to get free, but the other person was prepared, and before he could say a word or catch his breath, his arms were yanked behind him and a thin rope was rapidly tied around his wrists.

"Wait, please, you don't understand!" Tray'o pleaded. But it was no use.

Once his captor confirmed that the knot was tight and he couldn't fight back, she let out an annoyed chuckle. "This is not what I expected, Pinehouse." The voice of Sparrow rang out. "In fact, I'm a little disappointed."

Sparrow? The voice of his classmate confused him. "You?" Tray'o coughed as she pressed his cheek into the grass. "You have to let me go!"

"Why? Scared of the big, mean knight?" she replied in a mocking voice. "You've got to be the *dumbest* Dark One I've ever met."

Wait... what?! "Is that what you're doing? You think I'm a Locura spy?" Tray'o exclaimed as she forced him up and to his feet.

Sparrow, still smirking, raised her eyebrows in amusement as she spun him to face her. "Of course I do."

"Why? What did I do to make you think that?"

"For starters, you're rebellious, disrespectful, and sneaky. You constantly skip class to spy around the city. And, more obviously, you snuck over the wall in what can only be an attempt to spy on the Palace. I warned you, Pinehouse. Our actions speak to whether or not we are trustworthy." Sparrow smiled as she looked around. "Hey! Akoro? I've got him!"

Tray'o swallowed nervously. If the knight had seen the takedown, there was no sign of him yet. *There's time. You can still get out of this. Convince her!*

"My name is Tray'o Sak'ton and I grew up in Pinehouse Castle, as you so love to remind me. I'm not a Dark One, I swear. I came here to find my friend. Her name is Taylee. She's been missing for months, but I'm positive she's here."

Sparrow looked at him silently as she considered his words, then shrugged in a most irritating, apathetic way. "Dark One or not, you broke the law by coming here. The Court will decide what to do with you. And in the meantime, I'm rewarded. So it all works out in the end."

Rewarded? Tray'o growled as the realization hit him. *She's sold me out for extra credit. I can't believe it.*

Tray'o wanted to argue with her, but all hope of escape faded as the large knight stepped out of the bushes and approached them. "Good work, Elite Sparrow," the knight's voice boomed.

Tray'o tried to put on his most persuasive smile. "Hey, big guy, I know this looks bad, but I promise you, I'm not a spy or anything."

The knight regarded him with as much indifference as Sparrow and said, "You are not allowed here."

"I realise that, but if you'll allow me to explain, I think—ow!" Tray'o grunted as Sparrow shoved him to his knees.

"Stop talking!" she snapped with an unexpected urgency.

I knew she was going to be a problem. He frowned. *If she thinks she can shut me up with threats and shoving, she can think again.* "No! You have to listen to me!" he exclaimed angrily as he struggled to get back to his feet.

But before he could stand, the big knight shoved him back down.

"Quiet." The knight's voice was so loud and so deep that somehow the very trees themselves shook when he spoke.

No. Not his voice … that's something else, Tray'o suddenly realised as he felt the very earth beneath him tremble.

"Syyris." Sparrow fell to her knees in reverence.

SHHHEEEEEEEEEEEEEEEEEEEEEE!

A loud whistling sound rang out, and a white trail of light shot straight up from somewhere beyond the Palace.

Tray'o watched the light as it soared higher and higher into the sky until, without warning, it exploded into a blinding spray of red and blue lights that were followed by a *BANG!* seconds later.

Sky Fire! Tray'o could hardly breathe.

He'd long heard rumours of the holy Sky Fire, but had never witnessed it with his own eyes.

As he stared up, more and more lights shot into the sky, creating a cacophony of whistling, screaming, and exploding sounds mixed with the most incredible light display Tray'o had ever seen.

He seemed to be the only one watching, however, as Sparrow

and the knight both fell flat on their faces and rocked back and forth, whispering words of praise.

Sparrow must have noticed him not bowing out of the corner of her eye, though, because she suddenly addressed him harshly. "Pinehouse. Do they worship god in the Outskirts?"

"What? Of course."

"Then bow your head and worship. He approaches!"

Another explosion flashed.

This is your chance. They're distracted. Run! Without a second for hesitation, he jumped to his feet and took off as fast as his legs would allow.

Running was difficult with his hands tied behind his back, but he managed to maintain a good pace and create some distance between him and his captors, who did not seem to be following.

I just need to hide somewhere long enough to cut the rope, then I can ... Tray'o didn't have time to finish the thought.

Like the sound of a thousand charging knights stampeding across a bridge, or a lightning bolt violently striking a metal pan over and over, an impressive yet deafening roar exploded all around him.

The sound was as painful as it was shocking, and with it came an oppressive, swirling blast of wind. It pressed violently against his back and forced him to quit running and fall helpless to his knees.

Though it hurt his skin to do so, Tray'o turned his face to the wind and squinted his eyes up at what could only be Syyris Sagrado, the one he'd been told to worship all his life, descending from above the Palace.

At only one other time in his life had Tray'o ever seen any evidence of the presence of Syyris.

He was a young boy at the time, tied to a post in the courtyard of Pinehouse Castle, the place where his father occasionally struck his back with a stick in the name of discipline. He couldn't remember the specific excuse for that particular beating, but he clearly remembered the anger he felt when he looked up through teary eyes to see a billowing streak of smoke far off in the sky. It was a rare glimpse of their god in flight, one which many would probably consider a sign that god was watching. But for Tray'o, it served as nothing more than evidence that Syyris Sagrado was a god who remained indifferent to injustice.

But this time was different; Syyris wasn't a faraway streak of smoke. He was directly overhead, hovering about 20 feet up with colourful explosions erupting around him on all sides.

Syyris was narrow, sleek, and wingless, with dark green, shiny skin that brightly reflected the light of the sinking sun and the colours of the Sky Fire. His single eye was massive, black, and cold, and he was staring down at the city.

And as if to remove all doubt of his holy and divine nature, a few inches above his body shimmered what could only be described as a black, translucent halo.

I thought the halo only existed in paintings.

Tray'o thought about running, but found himself paralysed by both feelings of terror and awe. He wanted to keep looking up, to defy the sight before him, but the roar was so loud and relentless that he feared Syyris was angry, so he shut his eyes, bowed his head, and waited for the rage to subside.

This isn't real. It can't be. He wanted so badly for it all to be a dream—some wild delusion brought on by an exotic flower in the Palace garden or something. It was the only thing that would make sense.

But no matter how badly he wanted to deny what he was seeing, he knew it was impossible; this was happening. Syyris Sagrado was present and active. For the first time in his life, he could physically look up and see the face of god.

He never cared to show his face before. Why now?

There were so many things he wanted to say. Yet his mouth was dry, and words would not come.

He's angry. Does he expect me to confess? But why should I? I haven't done anything wrong. Syyris was the one who abandoned him. He was the one who allowed his father to abuse him, Krydor to burn, Taylee to be taken. *He should ask me for forgiveness.*

Without realizing it was happening, words came pouring out of his mouth. “Leave. Me. Alone!” he shouted as he faced the wind and forced his eyes open. It felt good to shout, even though he could hardly hear his own voice.

The roar grew so loud that Tray’o feared his ears might burst.

“Go!” His eyes burned as he stared at the face of god but he refused to look away. “You say you’re good, but you’re not! If you were, you’d allow me to be with Taylee! So do it, then! Do it! For once in your life, do something!”

Tray’o felt empowered by the act of shouting and so continued shouting at the top of his lungs, “Do something! Lead me to Taylee! If you are truly god then—”

Before Tray’o could say anything else, he was knocked painfully to the ground as Syyris unexpectedly dropped a few feet and shot a hot blast of air straight into his face.

Then, without a single word of response, Syyris tilted forward and shot straight up into the sky and off to some other part of the city.

The roar and the wind subsided, and, as quickly and unexpectedly as it all started, it was over.

Syyris was gone.

When Tray’o finally was able to open his eyes and stir from the ground, he realised that Sparrow was standing next to him, staring off in the direction where their god must have flown.

Her hair was a tangled mess, but otherwise she appeared to be unchanged. “Get up, Pinehouse.” Her voice was distant but cold.

Tray’o did not have the strength left to argue, and so, for the first time in a long time, he did what he was told.

Chapter Nineteen — In the Company of Ellian E'monton

"Although Syyris grants kings their kingdoms, he does not abide ingratitude. Even a king must know his place."

—ELDER JAXIX, A.P. 303
THE FALL OF THE KINGS OF KAAG'ARI

Corwin gasped loudly as his eyes shot open and he launched himself out of bed. The next thing he knew he was shivering uncontrollably in a corner with icy cold water dripping down his face.

"What do you know about the Exile?" Salana demanded. She stood scowling directly in front of his bed. Her fingers curled around a now-empty water basin that she clutched like a weapon.

"What's going on?" Corwin's teeth chattered as he spoke. *Did she even try to wake me any other way?*

"What do you know about the Exile?" she repeated the question.

Corwin's mind raced to catch up. "I don't … who?"

"The man who calls himself 'Skyblind.'"

"Oh. Umm …" Corwin stammered as he tried to slow his uncontrollable shivering. "Barely anything. He rescued us from some Locura, but I didn't really talk to him."

She put down the water basin. "Is he trustworthy?"

Why is she asking me all this? Corwin couldn't figure out what was going on, but her tone and his rude awakening caused him to feel very uneasy.

"I have no idea. Probably. Taylee seemed to like him," Corwin grabbed a nearby cloth and dried off his face. "What's with all the questions? And, did you have to throw water on …" When he pulled the cloth away, Salana was gone.

Great. Now what? he wondered as he stared at the now-open door.

Corwin, feeling quite confused, dried what he could of the water from his clothes and exited the room.

Glancing to his left, he spotted Salana moving briskly down the corridor. He briefly considered going the opposite way, where he could find his way back to the garden, climb over the wall, and try to forget that this whole mess happened.

But then what? Tray'o had probably been captured too, and without help there was no way he'd ever get to the dock in order to find Taylee. For better or worse, cooperating with Salana was the best and only real option he had.

"I didn't tell you to follow," she barked as he caught up to her.

"I, uh, thought it was kind of implied. You know … when you threw water on me."

Salana narrowed her eyes at him but didn't slow down to argue.

"Stay close and don't ask questions."

I wouldn't know what to ask in the first place.

He followed her through massive corridors, down lengthy stairwells, inside a secret chamber, and around the various statues and visual art that filled the castle, the whole time staying out of sight of any knights or palace attendants.

Corwin didn't bother trying to figure out what was going on, and resigned himself to simply follow the incredibly beautiful yet annoyingly willful woman on her quest wherever it led.

At long last they arrived at a set of ominous black stone doors, which, when opened, led to a dimly lit stone spiral stairwell leading downward. Torches adorned the walls and provided the only source of light as they descended deep into the darkness below.

Wafting up from the depths was the rancid smell of urine, rotting flesh, and something else Corwin couldn't quite identify. It was a struggle to keep from gagging.

Salana, who was clearly aware of his discomfort, smirked at him as they proceeded down the stairs. “You boys from the Outskirts should be used to foul smells.”

“No one could ever get used to smells like this,” he said as he followed down the infernal stairwell. He only hoped that whatever was at the bottom was not as disgusting as the odours led him to believe.

The stairs seemed ancient; every stone he stepped on was worn smooth from years of steady use. The dim light provided by the torches on the walls illuminated very little of the path, which had the unpleasant effect of causing Corwin’s other senses to go wild.

It was the sounds that bothered him the most.

He could hear echoes of dripping water splashing from somewhere below, mixed with metallic clanging and what he feared could only be the groans of men and women. He tried to remain calm, but the farther down in they went in their winding decent, the worse everything became.

Thankfully, the stairwell did not descend forever, and at last they came to the lowest level and were standing in front of a rotting oak door.

It was locked, but Salana had come prepared, and pulled out a set of silver keys on a small ring.

After turning the correct key and popping open the lock, she pushed the door open and led Corwin into the next room.

It was a long hallway just as poorly lit as the stairwell, but with one stark difference: they were no longer alone.

All along the walls stood sturdy iron cages filled with dirt, hay, and malnourished people of all ages. Some were men, but there were also women and even children locked away, all sharing the same starved and desperate look in their eyes.

She’s taken me to the prison after all! Corwin took a nervous step backward.

“Help, please.”

"Water!"

"Kill me."

The cries of the prisoners were horrible, and Corwin wasn't sure what to do.

"Ignore them." Salana spoke as if she read his mind. "They all belong here."

Though Corwin was quite unsettled by the condition of these prisoners, Salana didn't even seem to notice, and she continued to walk past each cage until finally arriving at one near the end.

For a split second, Corwin feared she was going to lock him up, but he felt a mix of relief and guilt when he realised that the cage she stopped at was already occupied.

Inside, a man sat cross-legged in the shadows. His hair was long and covered most of his face, but Corwin could see the mark of a criminal. "Hey, that's Skyblind!"

The man raised his eyes and regarded them silently before letting his head drop down once again. "I am in prayer. Come back later." His bold honesty was startling.

Salana wrapped her fingers firmly around the iron bars and said in a voice as cold as ice, "My father is dead."

Skyblind's voice was troubled as he replied with the simple and confusing words, "I know."

"Well! What have you to say about it?"

Skyblind was slow to speak. He let out a long and deep sigh, stood up, and stretched his arms. "The king had been ill for several weeks."

"Yes. That is true. I'm told he was made ill by the hand of our god for listening to you and your blasphemy."

Skyblind said nothing to her, but instead turned his attention to Corwin. "You look familiar."

"Oh," Corwin said. "You helped my sister rescue me from Locura. My name's Corwin."

"Of course. It is good to see you here. Taylee must be happy."

"I, uh, haven't seen her yet …" Corwin stopped talking when he felt the intensity of Salana's glaring eyes.

"This is not a friendly reunion. You will listen and you will listen carefully. Any minute now, a group of knights will arrive to part your hairy head from your body. There is little doubt that you will be found guilty for treason on the highest level. You are being blamed for the death of the king." Salana's jaw tensed as she spoke. "Because you are my father's brother, if you tell me truthfully what really happened, I may be able to help."

Wait … what? Corwin wasn't sure he had heard right.

Skyblind shut his eyes and said, "If death is what is required of me, then die I shall, though I have done no evil, and justice will not be served."

Salana kicked the cage in frustration.

"So … your father … is the king?" Corwin asked nervously.

"I told you not to ask questions," she said.

It's true. He could hardly believe it. *How did I not figure that out sooner?!*

Corwin dropped to his knees and bowed his head. Where once he'd seen her as a controlling and selfish force, he now recognized her as royalty, and felt quite unworthy to be in her presence.

"Princess. Forgive my ignorance. I didn't realise." He spoke her title in a tone of reverence, but was surprised to see that Salana looked annoyed at his revelation and impatiently waved him to his feet.

Did I bow wrong? He wasn't sure what the procedure was as he'd never met royalty before.

"And you two are related?" he asked as he looked from Salana to Skyblind.

"Yes," Skyblind answered. "Salana is my niece, though we've met only recently."

"So then … if the king is dead … doesn't that make—"

"Corwin!" Salana snapped. "Would you like this prison as your home? Be silent!"

"Sorry," he mouthed quietly.

"My dear Salana. If you seek the truth, I will give it, though I make no promise that it will ease your pain or bring you peace,"

Skyblind spoke grimly. When she nodded, he continued speaking. "It was not my intention to return here. As you know, I was caught and taken before your father as a criminal on trial for my life. In that moment, I took the opportunity to speak truth into the heart of my brother and thereby try to free the Kingdom.

"I shared with your father the different revelations I've been given in the wilderness, and my knowledge of the True God. I shared with him how Syyris is no more than a false idol—a tool the Elders have been using to control him and the E'monton clan for years."

At those words, Salana scoffed, but Skyblind didn't seem bothered and he kept speaking. "At first, he too was skeptical, but in time he understood that what I said was truth. The Elders, of course, were not pleased, and as soon as your father started refusing to bow to the image of Syyris, everything changed. I did not kill him, but his death is my fault. My God entrusted me with a task, but I chose selfishly. It was not my place to speak to Temchar. If I had remained silent in the beginning, he would not be dead now." His voice with thick with grief.

"What happened?" Corwin couldn't stay quiet. "How did the King die?"

"I have no proof," Skyblind replied after a brief pause, "but I believe the Elders have been poisoning him in an attempt to return him to their control. Today, when Temchar refused to sound the call to worship, Elder Kaine instructed Lord Daraak to suffocate him, with a promise that Daraak would be given the Kingdom through Salana's hand in marriage. Daraak eagerly complied, and I was blamed for the murder of my own brother."

Corwin's thoughts ran wild in the silence that followed. *How can Syyris be a false god? There are countless years of history that prove his existence, not to mention the various sightings. To doubt or question him is the greatest of all sins. How could Skyblind say these things, and how could the King believe them?* It was something beyond comprehension.

"What do you think?" he asked Salana cautiously.

She frowned, but did not scold him for asking a question this time. "I've listened to the Elders all my life," she spoke tentatively. "They have advised my father on the will of Syyris for the Kingdom a thousand times, and I've never questioned any of it. Only recently have things begun to get confusing—" Salana suddenly stopped talking, and her attention shifted to the entrance of the prison.

There was some sort of thumping in that direction, followed by what could only be whimpering. Although the sound was muffled through the door, it seemed likely that someone was descending the stairs.

Without hesitation, Salana pulled out a thin dagger from inside her sleeve and gripped the handle tightly.

"What are you doing?" Corwin asked. "You're the Princess. You don't need to be afraid of—"

"Quiet!"

Corwin looked to Skyblind, whose mouth moved silently in what was probably some prayer to his mysterious god.

"What's wrong, Princess?" a prisoner mocked. "Frightened?"

Unlike the prisoner, Corwin didn't see fear when he looked at her. He saw something much more dangerous—desperation.

The lock turned abruptly and the far entrance door creaked open, revealing a large human shape in the shadows.

Chapter Twenty — Escape from Lightspire

"Fear is counted among the Nine because it alone has the power to cripple one's will."

—ELDER RHAMSEY, A.P. 230
<u>THE NINE SINS OF NIGHT</u>

Without so much as blinking, Salana hurled her dagger across the room and at the hulking shape forming in the shadows of the doorway.

A knight! Corwin realised as the man swiftly blocked the dagger with his armoured forearm and knocked it to the ground aggressively.

"What I have done to deserve such cruelty?" The man's deep and uniquely accented voice boomed through the prison.

The relief was visible on Salana's face as she recognized it. "Akoro! I'm so sorry, I thought you were someone else ..."

"No, I am not someone else. I am only me, and my prisoner."

Corwin's mouth dropped open as the largest and darkest man he'd ever laid eyes on stepped out from the shadows and pushed a much skinnier and younger man to the ground.

"Tray'o!" Corwin immediately left Salana and ran to his friend.

"I'm glad to see you aren't in chains yet," Tray'o grumbled. "Did you explain why we're here? This oaf won't listen to me."

"Yeah. It's ... complicated."

The knight who Salana had called Akoro approached Salana. "I would have come sooner, but, there were … startling rumours …"

"I already know," Salana said.

This visibly shocked the man. "It is true, then?"

"Yes. My fa … the King is dead."

Akoro immediately dropped to one knee and bowed his head in submission, followed by Tray'o, who was probably just trying to score some bonus points by looking respectful.

"Then you are now my Queen, and I am in your service," Akoro affirmed.

Queen Salana … Corwin tried to picture her sitting on the throne, but he was still struggling to imagine her as a princess.

A queen should be old. Not young and beautiful.

"I appreciate the gesture," Salana's smile was small and sad, "but the Elders will never let a woman rule the Kingdom alone."

"What choice do they have?" Tray'o said. "You're next in line."

Salana scowled him.

Guess it's not just me she doesn't like asking questions.

"It seems things are far worse than we could have expected," she said to Akoro. "Ellian has told me that the Elders have promised to marry me to Lord Daraak in exchange for his part in the murder of my father."

Akoro touched the hilt of the enormous sword strapped to his back. "Murder?! Are you certain?"

Salana exchanged a look with Skyblind before answering. "Fairly certain, yes."

"Wait a second," Tray'o interjected. "The Kaag'ari lost their claim to the throne. They can't just take it back by marrying you."

"They can if Syyris allows," Corwin said. Although he didn't really know Salana, he thought she would probably be a better ruler than Lord Daraak. *He can barely rule his own hair. How could he manage a kingdom?*

"Pray that this is not god's will," Salana stated firmly. "I do not wish to marry my father's murderer and usher in a dark new age."

"But how can you possibly know his will?" Tray'o asked again.

"He won't speak to us, so the Elders claim to be his voice, right? If they've decided you have to marry Lord Daraak, how can you argue?"

Salana grunted her annoyance, but it was Akoro who boomed a reply, "By divine word, the E'monton clan are entrusted with the rule of Anaciencia. I do not believe this would change now."

"But how can you *know*?" Tray'o asked earnestly. "He doesn't speak to us!"

I've never seen Tray'o so invested in a discussion about Syyris before. Something was agitating his friend.

"You're right," Salana said after a brief pause. "If Syyris wishes me to unite with a Kaag'ari, then I will have to hear him say it for myself. If he doesn't, then the deception of the Elders will be exposed and Syyris will have to judge them for the murder of my father.

"And if Syyris is not real, as Ellian suggests," Salana added with a glance at the Exile, "then we will be the ones who hold the Elders accountable."

Akoro nodded with determination and touched his fist to his heart. "You will not be alone. I am yours to command."

"Thank you, Akoro." Salana smiled gratefully and turned her attention to Corwin. "It looks like you may get your wish after all."

Corwin couldn't help but grin. *Hopefully Taylee is still at the docks.*

"Salana," Skyblind spoke kindly, yet firmly. "The conclusion you have come to is good. But how do you plan to get to Syyris?"

Salana sighed in annoyance. "There is only one way to the Island, as you know: my father's ship, *Deliverance*."

"Hmm." Skyblind stroked his beard. "That will be risky. You are the first real chance the Kaag'ari have to reclaim the throne. Tell me, when you heard of your father's death, did anyone try to stop you from leaving?"

Salana arched an eyebrow. "Two knights insisted I wait in my room until things were sorted out. But they couldn't stop me."

"As I suspected," Skyblind leaned forward. "The Elders know

you will not easily marry. If you're caught, there's no doubt you will be locked away until they can force the wedding on you. If you want to get to the Island, I humbly suggest you go another way."

Akoro growled. "There is no 'other way,' marked man."

"As a matter of fact, there is," Skyblind replied calmly. "You could get there by going through the Ancient City."

Akoro did not appear to appreciate this suggestion. "This prisoner speaks madness. My Queen, if we leave immediately, we may be able to get to *Deliverance* before Lord Daraak knows it is missing."

Skyblind shook his head in disapproval. "Even if you could avoid capture by Daraak's knights—who are most certainly looking for you as we speak—and then somehow convince the captain to sail you across, I don't believe the Elders will allow you access to the Island."

"What choice do they have? She is the Queen. It is her right!"

"Unfortunately, that is not yet true," Skyblind reminded him. "Salana is not queen until the Elders affirm her publically."

"That is just a formality."

The knight looks ready to explode, Corwin thought.

Thankfully, Salana beckoned Akoro to be silent and addressed Skyblind herself. "It may not be official yet, but no one will question that I am the rightful heir to the throne."

"Indeed, you are," Skyblind agreed, "but that does not mean you are safe. Look what happened to me when I rebelled against the Elders as a child."

"That's different. They said you succumbed to madness. And besides, you had a brother who could take your place. My father has no living children but me."

All at once, Skyblind became deadly serious. "If they were willing to mark and exile an innocent child, and murder an uncooperative king, what do you think they will do to you when you try to leave or refuse to marry Lord Daraak?"

Salana worked her mouth back and forth as she considered his words. "But your suggestion … it makes no sense. The Ancient

City is the dwelling place of the Locura."

"Yes. Which means it's the last place Daraak would expect you to go," Skyblind stated. "Trust me, as your father trusted me. I can lead you safely through the city and to the Island using the Batale'ord Bridge."

Corwin had no idea what they were talking about, but he hated the thought of going a different way. *Taylee will go to the docks. That's where we need to go.*

"That is a rumour, *not* a real bridge," Akoro corrected.

"It is real. I met the man who built it."

Silence hung in the air.

Even the prisoners are quiet. This is probably the most entertainment they've had in a long time.

"Do you really think you can lead us safely through?" Salana asked at last.

"Yes. I know it." Skyblind smiled, but not the smile of a man who had just won an argument. It was forced, more like that of a man who had just accepted a necessary but heavy responsibility.

"My Queen, you cannot be serious." Akoro stood between her and Skyblind's cage. "The danger is too great."

"It seems we're in danger no matter what," Salana spoke to Akoro, but held her gaze directly on Skyblind. "I fear Ellian is right; even as an E'monton, I have no power without the support of the Elders. My only hope is to appeal to Syyris, and to do that, we will have to evade their notice."

Akoro clenched his jaw. "As you command, I will obey."

Corwin suspected that Akoro had more to say, but the big man held his tongue and instead walked over to the cage where Skyblind stood watching.

"If you are deceiving her, I will kill you myself," Akoro threatened.

"If I were deceiving her, I would want you to kill me," Skyblind replied sadly.

Akoro grunted a laugh and pulled out a set of keys, which he used to unlock the cage.

"Hold on," Tray'o approached Salana. "If there really is some secret bridge, then why haven't the Locura used it to attack the Island before?"

Before she could say anything, Skyblind answered, "Because the door to the bridge is locked." He turned his eyes toward Corwin. "But we have the key."

"What?" Corwin exchanged a confused look with Tray'o. "Me?"

"Not exactly," Skyblind stepped out of the cage and into the corridor. "Taylee holds the relic that opens the door."

His words sent a cold shiver down Corwin's spine. *He knows about the necklace? How much did Taylee tell him?!*

Salana sighed. "Then your plan is no good after all; Taylee's been missing for two sun-cycles."

At the mention of Taylee, Tray'o grabbed Salana by the arm. "What do you mean she's missing?!"

Akoro immediately rushed over to pull Tray'o off of her, but Salana easily broke free of his grasp. "Do not touch me again," she warned.

Corwin moved over to them and spoke quickly in an attempt to ease the growing tension. "Salana says that Taylee freed Master Lunechair from prison. They vanished sometime after that …"

"Are you kidding me?" Tray'o snapped. "That doesn't make any sense! Why didn't anyone say anything about this sooner?"

In an instant, Skyblind's entire demeanour changed; deep concern washed over his face. "This is very bad news." He started to pace around. "The one you know as Lunechair is not a safe man. I suspected his true nature when he threw that Flash, but this confirms it."

"Confirms what?" asked Corwin. For the first time, he detected true urgency in the voice of Skyblind.

"I'll tell you everything I know about him on the way. If we hurry, we may be able to catch them before it is too late."

"What? No." Salana crossed her arms. "I need to speak with Syyris as soon as possible. Even if we knew where they were, I can't afford to waste time chasing after my runaway attendant and her teacher."

"You don't understand." Skyblind's voice was stressed. "He is taking her to open the door to the bridge, and if we don't stop him, there won't be a kingdom left for you to rule."

Chapter Twenty-One — Taylee's Mistake

"Be careful when choosing friends; friendship is influence, and influence is power."

BLEU'S FABLES AND FOLKLORE: THE FRIEND WITH NO FRIENDS

The fact that the sun was hanging low in the sky did very little to affect the relentless heat of the Red Desert, and the streams of sticky sweat that poured down Taylee's body caused her shirt to cling to her back in a way that made sleep quite impossible.

She hated the sweat more than almost anything else that crossed her mind. *Except maybe the Locura.* She rolled over and draped her arm over her eyes to try and block out the light. It had only been two sun-cycles since she'd left the city of Lightspire with Master Lunechair, but she was already regretting the decision.

Sleep. You just need rest, that's all. Unfortunately, she was not used to sleeping on the ground in the middle of the desert, and her efforts were mostly in vain.

"Are you ready to continue?" Master Lunechair's dry and raspy voice shocked her out of her half-awake half-asleep state.

Already? She knuckled her eyes. *Maybe I slept after all?*

They'd stopped to rest next to a large boulder that provided the only shade for miles; Taylee, who could not remember the last restful sleep she'd had, did not want to leave it.

"A few more minutes?" Her words came out harsh, and so she

forced herself to cough. *Great. My voice is drying up, too.*

Master Lunechair scanned the horizon and gazed up at the sun, likely trying to gauge how much time had passed since they'd stopped by the boulder. "Hmm. No. Slept much too long. Maybe seven hours. We need to keep moving. Anyway, we're nearly to our destination. It won't be so hot there."

Taylee hid her face against the boulder. "I'm so tired."

"Taylee," he spoke firmly. "Every minute the sun sinks lower in the sky, the likelihood of getting the answers you seek is drastically reduced. Is that what you want?"

Not this again.

Master Lunechair didn't say anything else, but she could practically feel his eyes burning a hole in the back of her head.

"Ugh. Fine. We'll go," she mumbled as she groggily pushed herself up from the ground.

"Good girl." His cracked lips spread into a rather creepy-looking smile.

Gross. She turned away from him. *How did I let myself wind up here?*

The transition from the Outskirts to forbidden territory had happened so gradually that Taylee wasn't sure at what point the rough, rolling hills of her childhood turned jagged, or when the patches of brown grass disappeared altogether. But not long after that, they were wandering in the vast and empty wasteland known as the Red Desert with nothing but oppressive heat on their backs and dry dirt at their feet.

At least here was some mild relief. But, as much as she wanted to stay longer in the shade of the boulder, she knew her former teacher was right. She was keenly aware of the fact that the sun was currently hanging only a few inches above the horizon—an extremely uncomfortable position for it to be in as they wandered so far from civilization.

I think Darkfall happens sooner here. This is truly Locura land.

"How much farther is it?" she asked as she left the comfort of the rock and followed after him. "You're sure he'll be there, right?"

Master Lunechair coughed violently as he tried to clear his throat, then pointed to something in the distance and said, "See those rocks?"

Taylee followed his finger with her eyes. "I don't know ..." She squinted. "Maybe. I think so ..."

"That's the border."

"Border? Of what?" All she could see was a thin line of what was apparently rocks far off on the horizon.

"The border between this land and the Great Bay. Come along. If we keep a steady pace, we'll be there in a few hours."

Finally. The thought of being cool again brought some measure of relief to her weary body. *I hope it's not true what they say about sea water being undrinkable.*

"And to answer your other question," he spoke after a minute, "Yes. I know he will be there, as long as we hurry. We meet whenever the season changes. Now, no more questions, please. We need to save our voices," he instructed.

It's not like there's much to say, anyway.

Ever since they left Lightspire, the conversation between her and Master Lunechair was reduced to him calling out annoying things like, "Almost there!" and "Don't slow down now," or, worst of all, "You'll have your answers soon!"

He seems to be enjoying this, she observed early on. *I wish Corwin was here.*

They walked and walked and walked some more, and Taylee found the only way for her to pass the time was to allow her mind to wander.

She wondered how Skyblind was doing. Ever since his private audience with the king, she had seen very little of him. The two were always off alone together, talking in the throne room. Princess Salana was extremely resistant at first, but Taylee did her best to convince her that Skyblind was a safe and honourable man, despite his devotion to a strange god.

Although she lamented the loss of time with Skyblind, she was happy he could be reconciled with his brother. Instead, whenever she wasn't working for the Princess, Taylee would sneak away to visit with the only other person she knew might have answers about her mother and the relic: Master Lunechair. Unfortunately, he'd been locked up ever since they arrived at Lightspire, and remained in a rather foul mood in the depths of the prison.

Remembering this caused her to think back to the last real, meaningful conversation the two of them had, the one where he convinced her to break him out of jail.

"What was my mother like?"

"Hmm?"

"My mother," Taylee repeated. "You said you knew her. That's how you had her necklace."

"Oh," Master Lunechair let out a long sigh. "We've talked about this before."

"Tell me again," she persisted, adding a quick, "please."

"It was a long time ago." Master Lunechair twirled his mustache between his fingers as he looked at her from behind the bars of his cage. "Your uncle brought her to us at Pinehouse during Night. He wouldn't stop banging on the door, crying for mercy. At first, Lord Rai'o wanted to send them away, but then he saw your mother was pregnant and realised they might be in true danger.

"It turned out she was in labour, and shortly after we let her in she gave birth to twins—you and your brother, Corwin. She gave us the necklace as payment, as it was all she had of any value, but none of us knew it was a relic at the time." He stopped playing with his mustache and broke eye contact. "She died of an unknown illness sometime later."

Taylee chewed her bottom lip. "But what was she like?"

Master Lunechair blew air out off his nostrils and rubbed one hand against the side of his face. "Oh, I don't know. Nice, I guess. Very sweet. Innocent—like her daughter." He shot her a sideways glance. "I don't remember."

Taylee smiled half-heartedly. It wasn't much, but it was more than her uncle had ever said, and served as the most concrete evidence she had so far that at least one of her parents was not a Dark

One. "So, why do you think she had a relic?"

"Ah!" Master Lunechair's eyes lit up. "Now that's the real question. Why, indeed, would a woman from the Outskirts have a relic—and one shaped like a Locura icon, no less?"

His words pierced her heart. "That's what I've been trying to figure out."

"A worthy quest. I always suspected there was something uniquely special about it." He looked away again. "Sadly, now that I'm locked up here, I guess we'll never know."

Taylee tilted her head. "What do you mean by that?"

Master Lunechair started to pace around his cage as he spoke. "When Corwin first told me about the relic, I planned to take him to someone who could help ... but then Lord Daraak found us, and here I sit, trapped in this infernal prison."

"Who would be able to help?" she asked in surprise.

"A friend," he leaned in close. "I haven't seen him for some time, but he's trustworthy. He's the one who helped Lord Rai'o gather all his relics. If anyone would know what the necklace does or why your mother had it, it would be him. He might even know how to help your uncle."

Taylee could hardly contain her grin. "What's his name? I'll tell the Princess. She could summon him to us here."

"No." Master Lunechair stopped pacing and spun to face Taylee. "She cannot know. No one can. He's been in hiding for many years. If anyone knew where he was, he would be certainly be killed."

"No, not Princess Salana. She wouldn't do that if I explained—

"She would," Master Lunechair snapped. "Do you think they listened to me when I explained my case? Look where I am. If you hadn't brought me water and food, I might even be dead by now."

"I told you, I'm trying to get you out," Taylee insisted. "The Princess says you have to stay here until your trial before the Court. I will stand as a witness for you and explain everything, and then you'll be free."

"We don't have time to wait for that. My friend does not know what happened to the Outskirts," Master Lunechair explained. "Every

year, before Night, we meet and I bring him to Pinehouse for safety in exchange for the relics he's found in the Red Desert. But there is no safety anymore. Darkfall will descend soon. If we wait much longer, and I don't meet him as scheduled, my friend will certainly be found by Locura and killed."

"But … we have to wait; there's no other way."

"There is," Master Lunechair clutched the bars of his cage. "Release me and I will take you to him myself."

His words sent a shiver down her spine. "I can't do that!"

"You must! If you truly want to know the origin of the necklace and why your mother had it, then you need to release me."

Taylee chewed her lower lip. "If I do this, and we get caught, I'll be imprisoned myself."

"We won't be caught. I know a secret tunnel that will get us out of here undetected," he insisted. Then, in a more serious voice, he added, "Taylee, if we wait much longer, you'll miss out on the opportunity to get the answers you deserve."

"How can you be sure this guy will even know what the relic is if you don't?"

This made Master Lunechair smile. "I'm just a teacher. But the man I speak of is none other than Logan Rome, the former Elder of Knowledge. He knows everything there is to know about relics."

Taylee, even now, struggled to believe it was possible.

According to what she knew of political history, the last Elder of Knowledge had desired relics more than he desired Syyris and was sentenced to death. But, right before his execution, he had somehow escaped and gone missing from the Island. Unable to find him, the remaining six Elders decided that instead of electing a new Elder of Knowledge, they'd remove the position forever, as the study of knowledge was deemed too dangerous.

That was over 16 years ago; no one had heard from him since. *And somehow, Master Lunechair is his friend?*

After that revelation, Taylee had left the prison to ponder his words. It took a bit of time, and more pestering on his part, but eventually she came to the conclusion that Master Lunechair was the only chance she'd ever have at finally getting answers, and so she freed him from his cage.

But now that they were out here, wandering in the middle of nowhere, she was beginning to doubt she'd made the right decision.

It took many more hours of steady walking before Taylee finally got a good view of the rocks that made up the "border" Master Lunechair spoke of, and another several hours before they were finally standing at the base of them.

It appeared to be less of a border and more of a cliff, with a slightly elevated outcropping of rocks overlooking a valley; Master Lunechair wasted no time in scrambling up the rocks.

Finally. Taylee rubbed the soles of her feet. The climb didn't look too strenuous, but even still, she waited at the bottom.

"Do you see him?" Taylee called out as Master Lunechair stood on top of the rocks and looked over to the other side.

As was his habit of late, he didn't reply, but instead waved his hands, beckoning her to join him.

Taylee mumbled her reluctance as she took hold of the rocks and hoisted herself up. Surprisingly, the climb was considerably easy, and after walking for so long, it proved to be a nice change. But, when she finally got to the top, what she saw nearly caused her to lose her breath.

Down in the valley, in all its thundering glory, the ocean spread out endlessly into the horizon. It was deep blue in colour and reflected the narrow red rays of dying sunlight across its surface like a mirror.

"I can't believe it," Taylee said in awe.

Crashing white-tipped waves were speckled all across the surface, and the sound of the water as it thumped against distant rocks churned up an impressive roar unlike anything Taylee had ever heard before.

She wanted nothing more than to run straight down into the valley and lose herself in the cool, refreshing beauty of the sea. That is, until she noticed an ominous land mass in the middle of the Great Bay, which was shrouded in a cloud of thick white fog.

The Island. Taylee swallowed hard. Hidden behind that fog was the sacred home of Syyris Sagrado. "The Great Bay is so … beautiful."

Lunechair laughed and a mocking smile spread across his face. "I think the ocean has eclipsed your vision, dear one. Look!" The teacher pointed down into the valley with a flourish of his hands.

Taylee turned her gaze downward, but failed to understand. Far below them, in the shadow of the cliff, was an oddly grown, unruly forest, which spread out to the edge of the Great Bay. The forest was patchy and seemed uneven, almost hilly, as parts of it were significantly higher than others.

Wait … those aren't hills. She realised all at once that the forest was growing over something man-made. *Ruins!*

Completely overgrown by wild trees and bushes were the ruins of what must have been a very old city. The forest reached through, over, and around the foreign structures, which were black, square, and narrow.

It was one big ruined waste, one half overgrown with bush and the other half submerged in water, but even still it held a haunting sense of intrigue. Taylee suddenly longed to know what secret mysteries were lost within that city.

"The Ancient City, home of the first people and the birthplace of Essence. Drink it all in. At your feet, true magic awaits." The words rolled off Master Lunechair's tongue as if he'd spoken them a hundred times.

"Essence wasn't born here," Taylee corrected him. "Essence comes from the sun. It is the gift of Syyris to us."

Master Lunechair's top lip curled upward. "Yes, that is what you were told to believe. But it is not entirely true. The ability to harness Essence was developed here, by the first sorcerers in the earliest days of the Kingdom. Essence is fueled by the sun, but channeled by the Elders. This is the entire reason why Lightspire was even created.

"Tell me, Taylee, did you honestly think that the Three Towers of Lightspire—or the *mandatory* reflective roof tiles on every home—were merely tradition? Or perhaps decoration? It is ancient magic by which those towers absorb the strength of the sun."

"I don't understand. If that were true …"

"Then the entire people of Anaciencia are deceived. It's quite tragic, really. They spend their entire lives working, trading, and praying for Essence—the magical currency that fuels their lamps and heats their homes—when in reality, the very roof above their head does all the work."

Taylee could hardly believe her ears. "I refuse to believe that."

"Believe what you will; my words abound with truth. The nature of Essence is the very reason why the great Elder of Knowledge loves this place so much. He sought to discover the ancient magic with which the Three Towers were built, and then to recreate it as a source of energy greater than the sun. He was close to doing it too, but the other Elders were too narrow-minded to see the beauty of his vision."

I hope we don't have to go there. Taylee looked to him, then back down to the city. "Your friend … he lives in the ruins?"

As soon as she asked her question, Master Lunechair broke out into uproarious laughter. "No, Taylee. The Ancient City is now the home of the Locura."

His words shot adrenalin straight into her heart. "What? Are you kidding me? We can't stay here! What if they find us?"

"Sweet girl, that's nothing you need to worry about."

He's lost his mind. I think the heat has literally fried his brain. Taylee took a step backward. "Why's that?"

"Because … they've already found us," he said, grinning at something directly behind her.

Taylee spun around and saw the shadowy figure of a man dressed completely in black, watching them from a few feet away.

And he was not alone.

Chapter Twenty-Two — The Outskirts and Beyond

"The lands beyond the Outskirts contain both ruin and reward; though any man who dares to go is no subject of mine."

—KING ATTILAN, A.P. 390
SAYINGS OF THE KINGS AND OTHER LORDLY SORTS

Considering they were traveling with an escaped prisoner and probably the most wanted woman in the Kingdom, Tray'o was shocked at how easy it was for them to flee Lightspire.

After agreeing to Skyblind's plan, Salana took them all through a secret staircase that lead to an underground labyrinth of passageways far beneath the prison. If it were only him and Skyblind, Tray'o was certain they'd have been lost in there for months. But Salana seemed to know the way, and after walking for quite some time, they eventually came out in the middle of a dry field where all they could see of Lightspire was the dim glow of light from the Towers.

"Whoa. We made good time." Tray'o was surprised, especially when he remembered how long it felt getting there in the first place. *Perhaps the tunnel made it easier?*

"No matter, we've got a long way to go," Salana insisted as she turned away from the city and, with Skyblind, started walking toward the Outskirts.

Or what's left of them.

It felt strange to go back to his homeland, especially now that the Outskirts were officially considered Locura territory. It took almost a full sun-cycle, but when they finally arrived at what used to be the Krydor Markets, Tray'o felt his heart break inside his chest. There wasn't much left, just a pile of rubble and ash.

Tray'o hated seeing it this way; Krydor had felt more like home to him than Pinehouse ever did.

And now there's nothing left.

Thankfully, he did not have to look at it for long; this was not their destination, and Skyblind insisted that they keep moving in order to catch up to Master Lunechair and Taylee.

And so they continued to travel, beyond Krydor, past the charred fields and ruined cropland, straight toward the heart of the Red Desert, the true territory of the Locura.

Where we will find Taylee, Tray'o told himself as he took another gruelling step over the dry terrain.

The land beyond the Outskirts could only be described as a cruel and unforgiving wasteland devoid of life. There were no rivers here, no settlements, no farms, and no people. Only stumpy hills, sizable rock outcroppings, and dry, patchy areas of grass.

The low-hanging sun had only circled them once since the group left the prison, but Tray'o was already beginning to feel exhausted. Although his feet were certainly blistered, and each step was more painful than the last, he felt somewhat uplifted at the thought of rescuing Taylee. But the fact that she needed rescuing at all still confused him.

I've known him my entire life, Tray'o thought with a frown. *How many people did Master Lunechair deceive? Was my father in on it too?* Skyblind's revelations were hard to swallow, but, despite the absurdity, they made sense.

"Do you really think it's true?" Corwin asked early in their journey. "You knew him better than me."

"The Princess seems to believe it," Tray'o shrugged. "I mean … it explains his strange behaviour. And the Flashes."

"But … if it's true, your father must have known. How could he have not? Do you think he was hiding him?"

"Maybe." Tray'o hated thinking about any of this; the whole thing put a sour taste in his mouth. "What I don't understand is … why now? He had the Nightwolf necklace this whole time. Why didn't he take it sooner?"

"Maybe he didn't know how it worked." Corwin wiped a bead of sweat from his brow. "Remember how it only seemed to turn on for me and Taylee? Maybe it only works for us, and that's why he took her."

He'll regret that decision. "I don't care who he really is. If any harm comes to her, I'll kill him myself."

"Good luck," Akoko boomed from his position at the front of the pack. "You couldn't even stop a girl from catching you."

The memory of Sparrow knocking him down caused his cheeks to burn. "I let her catch me. Hiding from you was getting boring."

This made Akoro laugh, but he didn't say another word.

Skyblind continued to direct the group at a steady pace over many hills and barren rocks, insisting that he knew a shortcut and that they should be able to catch up to Master Lunechair if they hurried.

His name's not really Lunechair, though, and if Skyblind is right, he's more than Master. Tray'o found it incredibly difficult to grasp the full weight of what it all meant.

They pressed on into the desert for many miles without stopping for more than five minutes at a time. It seemed that Akoro resisted breaks almost as much as Skyblind—though it was clear his desire for speed was for fear of Lord Daraak's pursuit.

"We must keep moving. They will be searching," Akoro repeated often.

The knight was always on guard and constantly watched the horizon for any signs of movement.

Even though Akoro was the one who had arrested him not that long ago, Tray'o felt some degree of security having the incredibly terrifying and brutishly large man in the group. He was like a giant from one of the old tales, with arms as thick as tree trunks;

Akoro stood a great deal taller than anyone Tray'o had ever seen in his life.

The most comforting thing about him though, was his great-sword; strapped across his back and occasionally reflecting the light of the sun, it was as long as Tray'o was tall. He suspected that with it Akoro could easily strike down an enemy before they could get close enough to fight back.

If they were going to encounter any trouble, Tray'o was convinced that Akoro was the only one who would be able to save them.

The Princess could probably hold her own in a fight, too, he thought as he remembered how quickly she had taken down Corwin in the garden.

Tray'o hadn't been able to get a very good look at her in the shadows of the prison, but out here in the wild, her beauty took on a fierce look.

The woman's hair was so fine and smooth that it seemed to shimmer and shift between the deep black that Tray'o was sure it was, into a fine white-gold colour that practically danced and reflected all the brightness of the sun. When he asked her about it, she simply replied that her hair was actually dark blonde, but the black-white shimmers were a result of some magical hair liquid she'd been forced to use her entire life.

Although she was a great beauty, the thing that impressed him the most was the way she managed to continue at such a rapid pace while maintaining the look of dignity and grace that emanated from her. She was a woman worthy of the title Princess.

Or Queen. Or whatever she is now.

Tray'o found he had to constantly avert his eyes from her elegant form in order to stay faithful to the image of Taylee which urged him onward.

But Corwin was single, and it was obvious from the beginning of their journey that he'd developed quite a liking for the beautiful Salana.

Tray'o couldn't help but smile as his best friend drew closer and closer to her, until at last as they walked side by side.

"It's quite draining. All this walking, I mean," Corwin announced a little louder than necessary.

"Are you tired? Tell me you don't need to rest again."

"Me? Oh no … I just figured maybe you were."

She raised her eyebrows. "Why would I be tired?"

"Oh …" Corwin fumbled for words. "I just thought you might want a break or something."

"Because I'm a woman? Or do you think my high birth has made me soft?"

"No, no. I just mean … I'm just impressed with the progress we've made already."

"Really?" Salana looked away. "You're easily impressed."

Corwin scratched his head as he searched for something to say in the silence that followed. He seemed oblivious to the small smile that Salana tried to hide, but Tray'o was not: he knew the difference between a woman who was annoyed and one who was amused.

"I'm … sorry about your father."

"Why? Were you involved with his murder?"

"W-what?" Corwin stammered. "No! Of course not!"

"Then you have no reason to be sorry," she replied distantly.

"I just meant … I know how hard it is to lose someone you love."

"I appreciate the sentiment, Corwin. But this is not the time to grieve."

The conversation died immediately after that.

Corwin tried again an hour later, and their interaction followed the same rise and inevitable fall for another mile before he finally gave up on his attempts at flirting and resigned himself to walking silently beside her.

They walked and walked and walked some more, but, eventually, even Akoro agreed that it was time they make camp to sleep.

"Only a few hours," he insisted as they came to a stop in the middle of nowhere. Ironically, he was the first one to fall asleep.

"I'll stand watch," Skyblind announced once it became clear how tired everyone was.

"It should be fine if we all sleep …" Salana ventured.

"I don't mind. I need time to pray," Skyblind explained as he crouched down to his knees and bowed his head.

Before lying down himself, Tray'o spent a few minutes watching as the Exile gently rocked back and forth, mumbling words into the dirt. When he finished, he took out a small red book and flipped through it. At first Tray'o thought he was skimming for a particular page, but then he realised Skyblind was letting the pages brush his nose as he breathed them in.

It was a strange and unnatural act, but not interesting enough to warrant losing sleep over, so Tray'o turned his back to the man and picked a spot on the ground to try and get some sleep.

The guy's nuts, Tray'o decided as he struggled to get comfortable. *I just hope he's not just leading us out here to kill us or something.*

It seemed that Corwin, however, was more fascinated by the man than sleep; almost as soon as Tray'o closed his eyes, Corwin opened his mouth. "What do you prefer we call you?"

Oh great. They're going to talk.

"My true name is Ellian E'monton. You may call me whatever you wish."

"Why did you introduce yourself as 'Skyblind' before?" Corwin asked curiously.

"'Skyblind' was a name used to mock me as a child when I refused to accept the flying idol I was told about. But what was meant as mockery, I received as praise," he said.

Even though he really wanted sleep, Tray'o found he couldn't resist joining in the conversation. He sat up and said, "Why'd you get exiled in the first place? Weren't you first in line to be king?"

Skyblind turned his head slightly, but kept his eyes focused on the horizon. "Because I do not worship Syyris."

"Yeah, I know that much. But why? What made you stop believing in god?"

Skyblind immediately turned his full, wide eyes on Tray'o. The blazing red sun reflected off the sweat that soaked his face, and with the lack of sleep and his hair as disheveled as it was, he looked quite crazed. "I never stopped believing in God; Syyris is not God."

An awkward silence hung in the air.

"What other god is there?" Tray'o asked. "I was taught that Syyris defeated Plyyston during the Purge, like, a thousand years ago."

"I do not believe in Syyris or Plyyston. I believe in the true, living, forgotten God." Skyblind's voice grew louder, and his hand trembled slightly.

"Forgotten god, you say. Maybe he wouldn't be forgotten if he showed himself," Tray'o teased.

"He reveals himself every moment, but we cannot see him. He is invisible to the human eye," Skyblind spoke in reverence.

"Invisible?" Tray'o scoffed. "You'd rather believe in an *invisible* God than in Syyris, who you've seen?"

Skyblind did not look impressed. "Hence, the name *Skyblind*."

Tray'o laughed. "That's crazy."

"Tray! Be respectful," Corwin scolded.

"I cannot see God. But I can feel Him. Like the heat of the sun when you close your eyes. Although you cannot see it, you feel the warmth," Skyblind continued. "And He speaks to me. It is my desire to make Him known, if anyone will hear me. That is why I have been exiled; that is what I shared with the King."

"Well … it got him killed, so it couldn't have been all that helpful," Tray'o said.

Skyblind stared at him blankly, then, without a word, rose from his position and walked away.

"Hey—it was just a joke!" Tray'o called after him, but Skyblind did not turn back.

"Speak to me again when you're ready to have a serious conversation," Skyblind stated. "I'm going to find us some food."

And with that, he was gone.

"Wow." Tray'o folded his hands behind his head and stretched.

"What's his problem?"

"You offended him," Corwin said.

"Over that? Then he's too sensitive."

"Corwin is right," Salana announced from her curled spot on the ground a few feet away.

Great. Her too. Everyone has to take everything so seriously.

"Come on. You have to agree that he's speaking madness."

"Maybe. But even still, you should go easy on him," she stated. "His story is unpleasant."

"You know his story?" Corwin asked.

"Of course I do," Salana rolled onto her side to face them. "He's my uncle. I must have heard it a hundred times."

"Can you tell us?"

Salana took a deep breath. "No. We need to sleep."

"Please? I really think it'll help to understand him more," Corwin practically begged.

Help who? I don't care about the Exile's sad story.

Salana didn't say anything, and just when Tray'o thought maybe she'd fallen asleep, she sat up and broke the silence. "When he was 10, and my father 6, they went on a hunting trip with my grandfather. Somehow, Ellian became lost and separated from the group. He was found several sun-cycles later, a captive of two Locura. He was never the same after that and kept raving about the Locura god.

"The Elders tried to set him straight, and even took him to the Island to meet Syyris face to face. But it didn't help. In fact, it made things worse. He then started insisting that Syyris was a fake. That's when the people of the Court nicknamed him the 'Sky Blind' Prince.

"For a year my grandfather remained unwilling to see what was clear to everyone else; Ellian had been infected by the Locura disease. It wasn't until he was caught freeing Dark One prisoners from their cells that grandfather finally agreed that his son was beyond hope. Ellian was marked and cast away to live with the creatures he so loved."

"If that's true," Tray'o interjected, "then why do you trust him? Aren't you afraid he's a Dark One or something?"

Salana shook her head. "When my uncle first returned, I sought to defend him purely because I saw injustice. But, things changed once my father took him into his counsel. Beyond all reason, my father started to trust him. He told me that he regretted Grandfather's decision, and, much to my disbelief, he thought there might be truth in Ellian's story of another god.

"My father wasn't a great King, nor was he particularly wise. But he was still my father, and in the end, he trusted Ellian with all his heart. If Ellian, or 'Skyblind,' as he likes to be called, were a Dark One, or evil in any sense, he could have killed my father numerous times. Do I think he's sane? Of course not. But whatever religion he's adopted seems to require honour and duty, and right now, he is helping us.

"And if he tries to lead us to harm …" she added with a glance at the sleeping knight, "be grateful we have Akoro."

"Interesting …" Corwin replied.

"Yeah. Fascinating. Thanks for the bedtime story." Tray'o stretched his arms, rolled onto his back, and shut his eyes.

"Ahem." Salana cleared her throat.

"Huh? What?" Tray'o asked when he looked over his shoulder and saw her staring straight at him.

"You caused our first watch to leave. That means it's your turn."

"Aw, yeah right," Tray'o whined. "You said before that we didn't even need a watch."

"That was before you irritated my uncle," Salana growled.

She can't seriously hold that against me.

"That wasn't my fault."

"Actually …" Corwin chimed in. "It kind of was."

Great. So much for friendship.

"Whatever," Tray'o grumbled as he sat up and turned his back to the group. "But as soon as he returns, I'm going to sleep."

"You'd better hope he returns soon, then." Salana smirked.

Yeah, yeah. We'll see. Tray'o yawned. He was tired. More tired than he'd been in quite some time.

Forcing him to stay awake while everyone else got to sleep just because Skyblind was sensitive was ridiculous. In fact, if Tray'o wasn't so exhausted, he'd probably try to do something about it.

There's no one around here anyway. What's the point of having a watch when we're way out in the middle of nowhere?

Tray'o yawned again.

Why couldn't Corwin just go straight to sleep? If it wasn't for him starting up that conversation, then Skyblind would be the one sitting here now and I'd be sleeping.

Tray'o felt his eyelids grow heavy.

Maybe I can just rest my eyes and listen for any sounds.

He gently shut his eyes; the relief was immediate.

Yeah. This isn't so bad. My eyes don't need to be open to hear if anyone approaches, he thought as he let his head drop.

But almost as soon as he lowered his head, he drifted off into a deep and much needed slumber.

When Tray'o eventually woke, it wasn't to the sound of Skyblind returning, but to the feeling of cold steel pressed against his neck.

Chapter Twenty-Three — Sparrow

"Essence is a gift from the sun, but it is not free. Love works in a similar way; everything good has a cost."

—AALARDIN NEY'RK, A.P. 412
A TRADEMASTER'S GUIDE TO GOODS, GODS, AND GIRLS

Since witnessing the burning of Krydor and being displaced from his life of comfort almost two months prior, Tray'o had experienced some frightening things, but none of it—not the shock of being in the Locura Trade, nor the cruelty of the knights, nor the loss of Taylee—could compare with the fear he felt in this moment.

"There's no need for violence, yeah?" Tray'o tried to say, but his negotiation attempt only caused the knife to press deeper into his neck.

"Release him, or there will be trouble," Akoro growled. But it was an empty threat, because even though he was armed with a greatsword, a crossbow was aimed directly at his head.

"No sudden moves," Sparrow warned.

She stood behind Tray'o and used his body as a shield, with a sharp dagger in her left hand pressed against his neck and a crossbow in her right that she aimed at Akoro. The rest of the group—including Skyblind, who, judging by his armful of vegetables, must have just returned—were fully awake and stood in a tight, defensive circle.

It happened so fast. With Tray'o sleeping and Skyblind off

gathering food, no one was awake to see Sparrow's approach, and before anyone was aware of it, she'd taken them hostage.

This is all Corwin's fault. He desperately wanted to blame his friend, but he could hardly remember why at the moment.

"Princess Salana and the Exile will return with me. If you comply, the rest of you can leave here unharmed," Sparrow explained, rotating slightly to keep everyone in sight.

Salana locked her eyes on Sparrow and scowled. "I am not accustomed to being threatened by a child."

"Yet you have no problem acting like one."

"Excuse me?" Salana took a step forward, but stopped when Sparrow aimed the crossbow at her.

"Why are you doing this?" Skyblind put down the vegetables and raised his hands in a non-threatening way. "We are not your enemies."

Sparrow scoffed. "I've been ordered to return you and Princess Salana to the Court."

"I didn't take you for a Kaag'ari lover," Akoro's voice boomed out.

Great, thanks Akoro. Next time, do you think we could try not angering the girl with the knife to my throat?

"I wasn't given this order by Lord Daraak, but by Kaine Lanley, the Elder of Justice."

Salana exchanged a look with Skyblind and said, "I see."

"So," Sparrow continued, "since the others were not mentioned, if you two cooperate, I'll allow them to return to their nest—or whatever you Dark Ones call your ruins."

"I already told you … I am not … a Dark One!" Tray'o said through gritted teeth and laboured breaths.

"Don't try arguing, Pinehouse. I don't care what you have to say."

"He's right!" Corwin insisted. "We aren't Dark Ones!"

"Look, I don't care about you two, all right?" Sparrow exclaimed. "I just want the Princess and the prisoner. That's it!"

"Am I allowed no say in this? You *are* still loyal to me, no?"

Salana crossed her arms.

"I am loyal to the Kingdom. Right now, my duty is to return you."

"And I will return. But first, there is something I must do."

"Sorry Princess, but I need to do this," Sparrow warned. "I'll do whatever it takes to bring you back."

"Put the weapons down. You don't understand." Corwin stepped in between Sparrow and Salana.

Good thinking, Corwin, Tray'o thought sarcastically. *Stand in front of the girl who already thinks you're a Dark One.*

"Don't try to be a hero, Corwin. You're lucky I'm offering to let you live instead of killing you for treason, though, as far as I'm concerned, you've all betrayed the Kingdom."

"What treason have we committed? We merely accompanied the Princess, who has come of her own free will," Corwin reminded her.

Sparrow regarded them all sternly. "I don't care what reasons you have; I've made my intentions clear."

Akoro's upper lip curled as he spoke to Sparrow with disgust. "You are the one who betrays the Kingdom, not us. And you do it all in exchange for *rewards*?"

This seemed to catch Sparrow off guard. "What? Are you kidding me?" she exclaimed. "From where I'm standing, I'd say you're the betrayer! Freeing prisoners and kidnapping the only heir to the throne? I should have just delivered Tray'o myself."

"Enough!" Salana stomped her foot. "This is a waste of time. You have two options. You can accompany me on my quest with the promise that I will *eventually* return with you, or you can remain a puppet of the Elders and die the fool they want you to be."

Sparrow looked around from person to person, likely calculating the odds of her ability to defeat them all.

We could definitely overpower her. But not before she cuts my throat and takes at least one other person out with that crossbow.

"Why should I believe you?"

"Because if you don't, you will die," Salana seethed.

Come on girl, use your brain. Tray'o tried to will his thoughts into Sparrow's head. *Surrender this foolish plan.*

"Give me your word," Sparrow demanded after a short pause.

Salana raised her eyebrows. "My what?"

"Your word! Promise that you'll *both* return with me after you get whatever it is you're looking for."

Salana let out an irritated sigh. "Yes."

"Say it!" Sparrow insisted. "Say you promise!"

By the way Salana clenched her jaw, Tray'o could tell she was struggling to stay composed. "I *promise* to return with you—once I'm ready."

"And I get the credit," Sparrow added hastily.

"Yes, of course. The credit will be all yours."

Sparrow seemed to like this, and loosened her grip on Tray'o ever so slightly. "What about you, Exile?"

Skyblind hadn't said much the entire time, but by the look in his eyes, he was lost in his thoughts.

Come on, don't say anything crazy.

"If by the end of all this you still wish to take me back, I will go."

Although it was kind of a strange answer, it seemed to appease Sparrow, and she finally lowered the crossbow and released Tray'o.

Thank Syyris. He immediately made space between him the girl who had now caught him twice.

"Don't try anything stupid. I still don't trust you two," she warned, her eyes darting between Tray'o and Corwin.

Tray'o cleared his throat and rubbed his neck. There was a small cut from her blade, but otherwise he didn't seem to have any injuries.

"You okay?" Corwin asked.

"Meh," Tray'o shrugged. "I've had worse, shaving."

Now that Akoro did not have a crossbow to his head, he swiftly moved to Salana's side and said, "I do not think this is wise."

"No one cares what you think," Sparrow scrunched up her face and pushed past Akoro. "Stay close to me, Princess. I won't have you die and cost me my placement."

Salana, though clearly irritated, did not argue. "Whatever you say."

Even though Sparrow had put away her weapons, and technically everything was better now, the tension in the air remained quite thick, so Tray'o felt it was his duty to try and lighten the mood.

"Well, now that we're done with all this silliness, I think I've earned myself some much needed rest," he playfully announced as he lowered himself to the ground and casually folded his hands behind his head.

No one seemed to appreciate his attempt at humour, though, and instead of smiles, he received scornful looks.

"No. We move," Akoro announced. "If one found us, others will be coming."

"None could get here as quick as me," Sparrow stated proudly. "But I agree; let's get this done and over with so I can collect my reward."

Her cocky attitude was annoying, but Tray'o found something attractive in the way she was so confident and fearless.

If Taylee wasn't my soul mate ... Tray'o stopped the thought before it went any further. *Sparrow is attractive, sure, but unpredictable. Unpredictable girls, while always a good time, are nothing but trouble.*

Chapter Twenty-Four — The Fallen Elder

"As of this Day forward there will no longer be an Elder of Knowledge. The seventh chair will remain in the Court as a reminder of what happens when one places more value on relics than Syyris."

—ELDER KAINE LANLEY,
PUBLIC DECREE OF THE ELDER COUNCIL, A.P. 731

Something about the methodical rhythm that emanated from the ceiling kept Taylee in a perpetual state of drowsiness.

She lay unmoving for what seemed a lifetime, drifting back and forth between levels of awareness and dreaming, while never fully touching either realm. The droning was low, deep, and powerful; the Sound was all she knew here. There was no pain, no sorrow, no suffering. Nothing seemed to have any real importance beyond the confines of her unmoving body or the relentless hum that was gradually invading her soul.

The Sound was not just something she heard; it was part of her very existence, which is why it hurt so badly when the pulsing came to an unexpected and sudden halt.

Taylee's eyes flew open. "No!"

She felt cold, naked, and vulnerable.

Taylee sat up and frantically scanned the room in an attempt to locate the source of the invisible drone.

Come back!

But it was no use; the room was completely empty.

Taylee's eyes darted up to the ceiling.

Maybe it came from up there?

But the ceiling was smooth, with rounded edges, and was at least five times her height; if the Sound came from up there, she had no hope of reaching it.

She'd been lying flat on the floor in the middle of a poorly lit and eerily vacant room for an unknown length of time with no memory of how she had gotten there or where she was; darkness shadowed every corner, and the only light came from an Essence-powered white torch that burned next to her on the ground, which, even though it did spill a bit of light on the floor, illuminated little else.

Where am I? How long have I been here? She wanted to cry.

Without the Sound to keep her company, Taylee felt very afraid, and so she pulled her legs close to her chest in an effort to warm herself while praying desperately that it would return and lull her back into peaceful sleep.

She rocked back and forth in that position for several minutes before finally hearing something. It was a loud, bright clicking that rang out from the other end of the room, up and across the rounded ceiling, and down to the wall behind her.

Suddenly, the clicking turned to a high-pitched shriek as two doors slid open. She was stunned; she hadn't even known those doors existed.

A blazing, unnatural white light pierced through the open doorway, causing her to shield her eyes in order to keep herself from being blinded. But as her eyes adjusted to the light, she became aware of two shadowy figures approaching.

At first, she thought it was Corwin and Tray'o, coming to rescue her, and so she sat up straight.

I have to look brave, Taylee commanded herself, despite feeling very much the opposite.

But, as the figures drew nearer, she noticed that the bright light coming from the doorway did nothing to illuminate them; these figures were solid black and had no discernible faces.

All at once, she was filled with terror. *Locura!*

"Stay away from me!" Taylee screamed as she desperately

pushed away from them.

She slid farther and farther, but soon her back came in contact with an icy cold wall and she realised there was nowhere left to go.

And still the figures drew closer.

"Hey! You don't need to be afraid of us!"

Taylee froze.

"Who said that?" She attempted to sound brave, but the words came out strangled and thin.

As the shapes moved closer to her, the light from the torch splashed across the face of what was clearly a teenaged boy.

It's not a Locura! Taylee let out a sigh of relief.

The boy looked young—about Taylee's age—and was slightly chubby, with dark, curly hair and a soft, innocent face.

"Who are you?" she asked tentatively.

The teenager grinned. "My name's Marlo! And this is my sister Royael—but I just call her Roy for short." The one who identified himself as Marlo spoke in a friendly voice and immediately put Taylee at ease.

Careful. Just because he's not a Locura doesn't mean he's safe.
"Are you," Taylee hesitated, "a Dark One?"

"A what?" He exchanged a confused look with the other figure—a slightly older girl with pitch black hair that hung over her face and covered most of one eye. Taylee judged that she was not chubby like her brother even though she wore a bulky, black jacket and baggy pants.

"Don't know, don't care," Roy responded plainly. "Get her up. They're waiting."

And just like that, all the fear came flooding back. "Who's waiting? Tell me where I am!"

"Hey, hey," Marlo dropped to his knees. "Don't be scared. We'd never harm you."

Everything inside her wanted to believe him, but something still felt wrong about all this.

"Why is that?" she asked nervously as she watched Roy out the corner of her eye.

"Because you're the answer to our prayers!" Marlo flashed a grin. "Can I help you up? The Fallen Elder is waiting to meet you."

Fallen Elder? That must be Master Lunechair's friend! Taylee realised with some measure of relief. "Oh … I see. Good. Will Master Lunechair be there too?"

"Who?" Marlo tilted his head.

"Master Lunechair," Taylee emphasised the name. "The man who I arrived with."

"Oh, cool! Is that your brother's name? Is he here too?" Marlo's eyes danced with energy.

"What? No." Taylee worked her mouth back and forth. *How do they know I have a brother?*

Marlo and Roy exchanged another confused look. "Oh. What did you say his name was? Master Lune-chi-ar? Never heard of that guy …" Marlo struggled to pronounce the name.

"We were told you were alone," Roy answered grimly.

Maybe Master Lunechair made himself invisible, or used one of those Flash things again to escape. The thought wasn't terribly comforting because it only meant that he had abandoned her to be captured by Locura. *He's smart; he wouldn't just let himself get caught by Dark Ones. He must have some plan. I just have to play dumb until he comes back to get me.*

"Right …" Taylee rubbed the side of her head. "I was alone. Sorry. I'm just feeling a little confused …"

"No problem! Things will make sense soon. Are you able to walk?" The compassion in Marlo's voice was genuine, and even though Taylee did not want to trust these two, the attention he gave her caused the tension in her shoulders to relax a little.

"I'll be fine," she replied as she lifted herself off the ground with the help of the wall. Her legs were stiff, and it took several seconds for her to steady herself enough to regain her balance.

"Follow me," Roy said, "and don't try anything tricky. We will use force if you try to run."

Taylee lightly bit her tongue to keep from saying anything. *Play dumb. Play dumb. Play dumb,* she reminded herself over and over. If these Dark Ones were trying to make her think they were on her side, Roy was doing a poor job of it.

But, Taylee felt strangely weak—likely from being under the control of the mysterious Sound—and knew that her best bet was to pretend she trusted them and go wherever they took her until Master Lunechair arrived to rescue her.

Everything was a blur as she was led down several long white hallways and up a few sets of stairs, until they came at last to a door that opened to the outside world.

At least she thought they were outside. A cool breeze gusted past her and brushed against her skin, and the air felt fresh and clean.

But it's too dark. We can't possibly be outside. Unless …

… the sun had set.

The realisation hit her hard.

"It's Night?" she exclaimed at once. *How long have I been here?*

"What? Oh, no, not yet," Marlo matched her pace and walked next to her. "We're in a valley. Things always look darker here."

This place just keeps getting better and better.

As Taylee's eyes adjusted to the darkness, she realised they weren't in just any valley, but deep within the ruins of the Ancient City, surrounded by unnaturally tall and wide buildings that loomed above and around them. Taylee had never before seen anything belonging to the Ancients, and so found herself completely at a loss when she recognised that what she initially assumed were hills and trees were actually old monuments, structures, and towers.

Everything here was strange. The road she walked on was hard and in very poor condition, with large holes and broken chunks of stone scattered all over the place, the structures around her were enveloped in an overgrowth of bushes and plants, and the air itself carried an odd aroma of ash, iron, and salt.

"This is the home of the Locura …" she shuddered.

"Ha! I forgot about that name," Marlo chuckled. "Yeah, we

don't really call ourselves that."

Taylee's breath caught in her chest. *What's wrong with these two? Now they think they're Locura?* Up until now, she'd been convinced they were Dark Ones pretending to be normal humans. *But, he just claimed to be the same as a soulless demon? Be careful, Taylee. Who knows how long they've been out here,* she warned herself.

"Oh. I'm sorry," she tried to sound apologetic. "Locura is the only name I've ever been told …"

"Nah, don't feel bad. Doesn't bother me." Marlo shrugged.

"What—uh—*do* you call yourselves?" Taylee asked after a brief minute of silence.

"Good question!" Marlo laughed. "I don't really know. Humans I guess. We don't really use labels as much as they do where you come from."

"I see …" Taylee tried to casually glance around and check to make sure there weren't any real Locura nearby, but it was too dark to see anything clearly.

"Locura is just a name The Seven made up to make us sound inhuman," Roy abruptly stated.

"Oh," Taylee swallowed the lump that was growing in her throat. "What do you mean by 'The Seven'?"

"Elders. Back when there were seven. But yeah, I guess we should probably call them The Six now, since the seventh Elder fell."

Taylee tried to sound casual as she said, "Oh, of course. That makes sense."

I hope Master Lunechair finds me soon. These people are crazy. She started getting nervous again when she noticed they were coming up to a wide flight of steps, which led to a building made of white marble hidden under several layers of bush growth.

"It's really cool to meet you," Marlo said with a smile.

"Yeah. I'm happy to have met you too." Taylee wasn't sure how long she could keep up this agreeable attitude.

"Does it feel weird? Talking to a 'Locura' after years of thinking we were monsters?"

"I—uh—don't …" Taylee wasn't sure how to respond.

Thankfully, Marlo kept talking. "See, we aren't anything like what you've been taught," he continued as they reached the base of the stairs and began to walk up. "Long ago, there was a war, right? My people lost and were, you know, separated from yours. Many of my ancestors were wounded, mutilated, burned; they were outcasts, branded as demons for not worshipping Syyris, and left to die in the wilderness.

"They were forced to survive underground in these ancient ruins, but somehow, they survived! Soon, they were a thriving nation, and we've lived peacefully in secret for hundreds of years ever since, which, if you ask me, is pretty cool." Marlo seemed way too happy to share his version of history.

Taylee wanted to feign interest and keep playing dumb, but all the talk of the Locura being peaceful humans caused her to boil with anger, and she couldn't restrain herself any longer.

"Have you lost your mind?" she snapped. "The Locura aren't peaceful. They're monsters who burned my homeland!"

Roy looked over her shoulder and narrowed her eyes. "Impossible."

"It's true! I saw it myself."

They were now at the top of the stairs and directly in front of the bush-covered marble building, but Taylee refused to take another step.

If they think I'm going in there, they can think again.

"Taylee, no, my people would never do anything like that." The pain was thick in Marlo's voice. "I promise you. We are peaceful."

He truly believes that, she realised when she stared into his eyes and saw the truth of his words. *What goes on here? Are all Dark Ones brainwashed like him? Is that what the Sound does to people?* The thought actually made her pity them.

But as soon as he placed a hand on her back and tried to guide her toward the open door of the building, the feeling of pity was replaced with anger.

"Don't touch me!" She slapped his hand away. "I'm not going with you any farther."

"Oh, really?" Roy positioned herself in front of Taylee.

Taylee scrunched up her nose in an attempt to look tough and mean. "Really."

Roy wasn't scared though; she crossed her arms and leaned to the side. "You don't have a choice."

Ha! We'll see about that. "What are you going to do if I refuse? Kill me?"

Roy sneered. "Ooh. Tempting."

Even though Taylee had never been in a real fight, the thought of getting into one with this Roy girl was really starting to appeal to her.

"Hey—wait!" Marlo stepped in between the two of them. "We aren't going to hurt you!"

"Uh-huh. Tell that to your brother—oops, I mean, sister," Taylee mocked. *This might actually be fun.*

But before anything could happen, a familiar voice rang out and cut through her anger like a knife. "Children, children! This is a time for celebration, not fighting."

Taylee's eyes grew wide with surprise and then relief when she saw Master Lunechair step out of the marble building and into the limited light.

"Finally!" she exclaimed. *Now we can get rid of these two and get some real answers!*

But the confusing thing was that Marlo and Roy didn't seem to be frightened by his presence; in fact, they almost looked as relieved as she felt.

"There, see?" Marlo smiled at her. "The Fallen Elder is here now. He'll explain everything to you."

Wait—what?

"Hello, Taylee," Master Lunechair took a step toward her and gave her a grin so large that it practically split his face in two. "It's nice to *officially* meet you. You may call me Logan Rome, formerly, the Elder of Knowledge."

Chapter Twenty-Five — The Cliff That Overlooked the Valley

"The secret to happiness is a combination of contentment, and ... ah, forget it. Happiness is overrated."

—HOLLAND THE HOMELY, A.P. 678
THE HOLLAND FAMILY HEIR BOOK

"The Great Bay ..." Corwin could hardly believe his eyes; after hours and hours and hours of walking, they'd finally arrived.

"It's beautiful, yes," Salana admitted as she climbed the final bit of the rock outcropping and joined him on the edge. "But I don't see any bridge leading to the Island."

"Maybe it's invisible." Tray'o tried to brush the dirt from his clothes. "Like Skyblind's god?"

Not that again. Corwin had hoped Salana's lecture would put an end to the mockery.

"It would not be much of a secret bridge if it were easy to see." Skyblind gestured toward the ruins of what could only be the Ancient City, deep within the valley below. "The entrance to the bridge is down there; the bridge itself runs underwater."

"Under ... the water?" Corwin asked.

"Is that a problem for you?" Akoro growled.

"No, it's fine," Corwin answered nervously. "It's only—Tray'o and I ... don't know how to swim."

For the first time since joining them, Sparrow burst out laughing. "Some Elite you would have made."

"We grew up far from any body of water …" Corwin continued, feeling somewhat ashamed of his confession.

"Do not fear," Skyblind responded graciously. "The bridge will keep the sea away."

"Sounds like quite the bridge." Tray'o shielded his eyes from the sun and looked down into the valley. "But there's still one problem: we don't know where Taylee is."

This was a fact that seemed to trouble Skyblind as much as Tray'o, and the man let out a contemplative grunt. "No. I had hoped we would have caught up to them by now."

"So what's the plan, then?" Salana asked. "We can't just walk into the Locura nest and start shouting her name."

"Locura nest?" Sparrow's eyes darted between Salana and Skyblind. "No one said anything about going down there."

"It's always been the plan," Salana said. "You're free to leave if you're too scared."

"Ha!" Sparrow laughed. "Elites don't get scared. But going down there is suicide."

"There is no danger," Skyblind said. "We will have safe passage."

Sparrow arched an eyebrow. "How can you guarantee that, Exile? Going to try to convince your little Locura friends not to eat us?"

"In a sense, yes," Skyblind replied calmly. "Now if you can keep yourself together, we have some descending to do."

He turned away from her and started walking toward a path that Corwin had not noticed until now. It was uncomfortably narrow, and ran down the other side of the cliff.

"Hmph." Sparrow crossed her arms as Salana and Akoro followed him. Though she looked angry, her face was almost pale.

"Don't tell me the world's mightiest *Elite* is scared of a little height?" Tray'o quipped as he brushed past her.

"Watch your mouth, Pinehouse. I could still kill you if I wanted to."

"Sure you could," he laughed as he disappeared down the trail. "Girls will find any excuse to be close to me."

Sparrow growled and reached for the dagger that hung by her side.

"Hey, come on, he's just playing around." Corwin stepped in front of her.

She snarled at him, but released her grip on the dagger. "Whatever. He's just lucky I let him keep his tongue," she grumbled as she made her way somewhat tentatively over to the trail that led down into the valley.

Although Sparrow was now technically a part of their group, it was clear to Corwin that her presence was merely tolerated by the others. In the entire time since she had joined them, she hadn't spoken a single friendly word.

If she wants to isolate herself from everyone, that's her choice. Corwin wanted to leave it at that, but he couldn't shake the feeling that he should at least try and reach out to her.

"Why do you act like that?" Corwin asked as he followed directly behind her.

The path Skyblind had chosen was narrow and steep—much steeper than the one they had climbed to get out of the desert—which forced everyone to descend one after the other in a straight line. Sparrow was in front of him, but she moved at a much slower rate than the others in front of her.

"Why do I act like *what*?"

"You know, the grumpy, tough girl. You're pushing everyone away with your negative attitude."

This made Sparrow laugh. "Oh, am I? What a tragedy, no one loves me! How will I ever sleep?"

"You don't need to be sarcastic. I'm trying to help."

Sparrow stopped on the trail and turned to face him. "If I ever need help from a farm boy, Locura-loving, Elite-pretender—who can't even swim—I'll let you know. But until then, I'd rather not have your irritating little voice buzzing in my ear while I'm trying to focus!"

With that, Sparrow spun on her heels and attempted to resume descending the trail, but, without warning, her foot caught on a loose stone.

"Ack!" she cried out, as part of the stone path broke away under her feet and she slipped uncontrollably toward a cliff off the side of the trail.

Her arms flailed about as she attempted to grab something to stop her fall. Corwin instinctively reached out to grab her, but the combination of his momentum and her panic caused her to take hold of his arm and accidently pull him off the trail with her.

"Corwin!" Tray'o shouted as he turned—but it was too late.

The two of them tumbled down the side of the cliff in an uncontrollable slide and at an alarming speed, bringing with them a cascade of rocks and dirt.

No, no, no, no!

Corwin dug in his heels.

No good.

He frantically grabbed for something.

Nothing but loose stones and dirt.

This is it!

He tried to push the fear away.

Sparrow was completely white.

We're going to die!

Corwin shut his eyes.

He tried to curl himself into a ball to soften the fall.

It didn't help.

His body slammed against the side of the cliff.

Over and over.

With no end in sight.

Until—

The cliff suddenly got soft.

It started to even out.

He gradually slowed.

And slowed.

Until Corwin could roll no farther.

Everything went black.

The next thing he knew, he was waking up to the sound of

voices. "Corwin! Sparrow!" The distant voice of Tray'o called out from somewhere above.

He lay still.

Unmoving.

I'm ... alive?

Corwin forced open his eyes.

They'd tumbled down the entirety of a rocky cliff before hitting what seemed to be a grassier bit of land that gently sloped down into the valley.

His head was pounding, but he didn't seem to have suffered any serious injuries. However, judging by the pain in his arms and back, he could almost certainly look forward to some nasty bruises.

"Sparrow?" he called out as he searched the area.

It didn't take long. He spotted her a few feet away, sprawled face first in a pile of dirt and rubble.

"Are you okay?" he asked as he stumbled over to her.

She did not move, but her fists were clenched together so tight that her knuckles were completely white.

"Sparrow?" Corwin asked as shook her shoulder.

"Get. Your. Filthy. Hands. Off. Me," she groaned.

Corwin let out a sigh of relief and waved his hands up in the air, shouting to the others, "We're okay!"

"Stay there!" Salana shouted back.

Where else would we go?

"You're an idiot," Sparrow said as she tried to push herself up out of the dirt. Although she appeared to be relatively unharmed, Corwin noticed that she grimaced when she moved and her left arm lay stiff at her side.

"You shouldn't move, you could be injured."

"Ha!" she scoffed as she forced herself up and onto her back. "I'm not injured. A stupid boy just fell on me, that's all."

"What? You're blaming me for this?"

Sparrow lay her head back and shut her eyes. "I had it under control."

"Oh, really?" He pulled back the sleeve of his shirt and

showed her the marks where her fingernails had dug into his arm when she pulled him off the cliff.

Sparrow let out a weak "Ha!" but didn't say anything else.

Maybe I should have let her fall, Corwin thought in annoyance as he glanced back up the cliff. The others were carefully descending at a more rapid, but cautious pace. They were fairly high up, but not nearly as high as the fall felt.

Unless I was knocked out for longer than I realised …

"They'll be here soon," he thought out loud.

"Thanks for the update."

Corwin wanted to be compassionate, but he was getting sick of her attitude. "What's your deal? I just about died trying to save your life!"

"My life will never need saving from a farmer."

"Shepherd," Corwin corrected her through gritted teeth. "I'm a shepherd."

"Oh. So a smelly farmer then."

Everything about her exasperated him to no end.

It's just her defence mechanism, he reminded himself.

"You really don't like me, do you?" he asked after taking a minute of silence to calm himself down.

"You're nothing special; I don't like anyone."

"Why?" He'd never met anyone so antagonistic toward others in his entire life.

"People are distractions. I've got bigger things to deal with." Although her eyes were open, she refused to make eye contact.

"Bigger things like what? Trying to win over the Elders?"

For the first time in a long time, Sparrow actually smiled. "There are worse ways to make a living."

Corwin scratched the back of his head as he tried to think how best to form his next words. *She needs to know. It's the only way she'll cooperate.*

"You know, the Elders are kind of the bad guys."

"Oh yeah?"

"Yes. They instructed Lord Daraak to kill the King, and now

they want to force Princess Salana to marry him."

Sparrow shrugged. "I doubt that's true. And anyway, what difference does it make? The Kingdom needs a king."

"Yeah, but …"

"But nothing." Sparrow pursed her lips together. "Despite what you might think, Corwin, sharing a class together did not make us friends. I'm here to make sure the Princess stays alive long enough for me to return her. That is, assuming you don't get me killed first."

Corwin had never wanted to shout at someone more in his entire life.

"I just think you need to try and see things from another—"

The rest of his words were drowned out by a piercing howl.

What was that?

The howl was loud and wild, very much unlike any sound he'd ever heard come from a human.

He turned his head to get a look at whatever had made the noise, and immediately wished he was still unconscious.

Chapter Twenty-Six — Nightwolf

"Nightwolves are Plyyston's pets: ancient demons of darkness that cannot be tamed. If you see one, you won't likely see anything else."

—PAULINE POURLAND, A.P. 440
<u>A GLIMPSE OF THE SHADOW: THE TRUE STORY OF PAULINE POURLAND</u>

Lurking behind a boulder, a ferocious beast bared its long white fangs.

The beast was large and thick of body, with black, coarse hair that stood on end as if to accent its already obvious state of aggression. The only colour to it was in its eyes, which shone like molten balls of flame. In any other moment they might have been considered beautiful—full of intensity and fire—but right now they were locked directly on Corwin.

"Don't. Move," Sparrow said as she slowly reached for her crossbow, which lay half-buried in the dirt.

A Nightwolf! A real, living Nightwolf!

But he didn't have time to marvel; the Nightwolf licked its lips.

It seemed like all hope was lost, and Corwin braced himself for the inevitable, when suddenly he felt a blast of wind shoot past his ear as Sparrow shot a crossbow bolt straight into shoulder of the Nightwolf.

It let out a roar and spun in a circle as it attempted to bite off the bolt.

"Take my dagger!" Sparrow tossed the blade to Corwin and

struggled to load another bolt into the crossbow.

Corwin didn't have time to hesitate. As soon as he grabbed the dagger, the Nightwolf lunged at him.

In one swift motion, Corwin thrust the dagger upward and stabbed the beast in his chest. At the same time, Sparrow fired a second bolt into its neck.

The now-wounded Nightwolf yelped in pain, stumbled back, and retreated into the valley.

"Nice job!" Corwin exclaimed.

"Not so fast," Sparrow loaded the crossbow again. "We aren't done yet."

Three more Nightwolves had crawled up from the valley and were howling together nearby, creating a most unsettling harmony.

Three more?

Corwin gripped the dagger tightly in his hand, but knew there was no way they could defeat three alone.

But then, just as it seemed they were about to pounce, Akoro jumped down from wherever he was on the cliff and slammed his body directly into one of them. The Nightwolf was crushed under his weight and slid lifeless into the valley.

Akoro tumbled briefly himself, but quickly caught his footing and faced the other two.

In one swift motion, he drew his greatsword, leapt forward, and cleaved off the head of the second Nightwolf.

Incredible.

The headless beast collapsed in the dirt.

But the third had time to think and before Akoro could lift his greatsword again, it leapt through the air and knocked him and his sword to the ground.

Akoro landed flat on his back, and in an instant, the Nightwolf was on his chest, snapping hungrily at his neck. Yet somehow, Akoro managed to catch its mouth with both his hands and, with one great pull, broke its jaw.

"Yes!" Corwin cheered as a mix of disgust and relief flooded through him. That was, until another, much louder howl pierced the sky.

A new Nightwolf, about twice the size of the others, approached.

An Alpha. Corwin cringed.

Sparrow shot a crossbow bolt straight into the back of the Alpha, but it failed to pierce its skin and deflected to the side.

It didn't even flinch! Does it have stone skin?

"Corwin! Do something!" Tray'o shouted as he tried to slide down to them.

But Corwin could not move; he was paralysed with fear.

Move! Help Akoro! He wanted desperately to do something, but what? The Alpha appeared to be impervious to crossbow bolts—how much better would his tiny dagger fare?

The Nightwolf Alpha paced around Akoro, who stood with his sword drawn and ready.

"Go ahead. See what happens, monster!"

The Alpha let out another blood-curdling howl.

And just like that, a fresh pack of three more Nightwolves crawled out, seemingly from nowhere, and surrounded them on all sides.

This can't be happening.

Just when Corwin thought all hope was lost, Skyblind dropped down at his side.

The exiled Prince faced the Nightwolves, slammed his foot down, and shouted at the top of his lungs.

"Nightwolves! To me!" As the words left his mouth, the beasts immediately turned their heads and froze in place.

Skyblind fearlessly approached the Alpha and shouted unintelligible words in its face. The words were not English, but sounded instead like some ancient language.

Or chanting? A a magic spell? Corwin was confused, but whatever Skyblind was saying seemed to be working.

The Alpha cowered and bowed its head.

"Leave here, and do not return!" Skyblind commanded.

The beast growled, let out one final howl, then turned and ran away at full speed with the other Nightwolves following close behind.

When they all had vanished into the valley, Skyblind dropped to the ground and buried his head in his hands, mumbling more foreign words.

This man wields magic with his tongue. Corwin was amazed.

Akoro brushed himself off and wiped blood from his hands before turning to Skyblind. "Whatever you did … Thank you."

"Thank God, not me. I did nothing but access the authority He has given man. By His mercy, the Nightwolves fled," Skyblind said.

Corwin felt as though he was on the verge of throwing up when he surveyed the dead Nightwolves scattered at his feet.

Akoro had fought skillfully, but in the end, it was Skyblind who really won the battle.

We were seconds from death, and he stopped them with words. Maybe there is some truth to his invisible god after all?

Something in his gut warned him that there were probably much greater dangers waiting for them in the Ancient City, and that they were likely going to need the Exile and his invisible god.

"Are you okay to walk?" Corwin stood and offered a hand to help Sparrow to her feet.

"Better than ever," she grunted as she brushed his hand aside. Although she was able to stand on her own, she looked to be in a great deal of pain, and guarded her left side. "Next time we come across a fight, try not to freeze up."

"Hey!" Tray'o called as he and Salana slid down the remainder of the trail and landed next to them. "Did you see that? That was crazy!"

Corwin wasn't sure how she did it, but whenever Tray'o was around, Sparrow's face took on a look of incredulity.

"We saw," she said.

"Is everyone all right?" Salana surveyed the group.

"I am fine. But Sparrow has hurt her arm," Akoro observed.

"What?" Sparrow took a step back. "No, I'm fine."

Akoro slung his greatsword over his shoulder and made his

way over to her. “I will fix it. Stand still.”

“No!” Sparrow shouted. “I don’t need your help.”

This made Tray’o laugh. “What’s wrong? Afraid of looking weak?” he teased.

Sparrow bared her teeth at him, but reluctantly stopped moving. “What are you going to do, then, knight?”

Akoro reached out and touched her shoulder. As soon as his fingers made contact, she flinched and let out a small yelp of pain.

“Hmm. It is not in place. It needs to be reset. This will hurt.” He grabbed her wrist and looked her straight in the eye. “Ready?”

Sparrow ground her teeth together, but did not break eye contact. “Fine. Do it.”

Without hesitation, Akoro lifted her arm up and pulled.

The next sounds Corwin heard were that of bone cracking, then a sickly pop as her shoulder was brought back into place, and her pained scream echoing across the valley.

Chapter Twenty-Seven — Children in the Shadow

"If it hurts to leave, it probably means you mattered."

—ROBYN LANG, A.P. 501

THE HISTORY OF EVERYTHING AND EVERYONE

Of all the things Tray'o had expected to see upon entering the Ancient City, a playground full of children was not one of them.

"They're what?"

"Humans," Skyblind explained. "No different than you nor I."

Tray'o could hardly believe it, but the evidence was right in front of his face.

They'd scarcely been in the ruins of the City for more than a minute before they saw the first child run by. Now they stood in front of a fenced off park where about one hundred children laughed, played, and ran around while an elderly woman supervised.

There could be other explanations, he tried to reason. *Maybe they were stolen and are being raised here to be trained as Dark Ones or something?* But that didn't make sense either. The kids were too happy to be anywhere but where they belonged.

"Whose are they?" Salana asked as she wrapped her fingers around the iron bars of the fence and peered inside.

"They are children; they belong to their parents. But right now, they are in school."

School? Locura children attend school? After what had happened at the Krydor Markets, Tray'o resented the idea that Locura could be anything but monsters.

"Impossible," Akoro boomed.

Sparrow laughed and tapped her crossbow. "We could always test the theory. Let's grab the old one and see if it bleeds red!"

She sure bounced back after that arm thing, Tray'o thought. *Probably trying to look tough again.*

Skyblind scowled at the suggestion. "I've told you this before. Locura—both the name and the disease—were created by the Elders as a way to create fear and expand their control. As you will see, these people are entirely peaceful."

As much as Tray'o hated to admit it, Skyblind seemed to be telling the truth.

The ruins of the Ancient City were cold, dark, and menacing, due largely to the old buildings that towered over them like moss-covered, sleeping giants and blocked out most of the sun's light. The streets were broken and in disarray, and everything about this place felt filthy and forgotten.

And yet, there they were—swarms of laughing, happy children.

It could be a trick. Tray'o wasn't ready to let down his guard just yet.

It was shortly after Skyblind started speaking that one of the children noticed him, waved hello, and ran over to the elderly woman. When she finally spotted the group, she raised her hands to her face in surprise.

"Ellian?" she called after taking a minute to compose herself.

Skyblind waved to her and moved toward a nearby gate the led into the park. "Wait for me," he told the group. "I'll only be a minute."

"Try to hurry," Salana insisted. It seemed the presence of the children did nothing to calm her suspicions, and she kept looking over her shoulder as if expecting some surprise attack.

Better to be safe, especially in a place like this.

Once through the gate, Skyblind was immediately surrounded by some of the children, who laughed and pulled at his robe and beard. He smiled lovingly and said something to a few of them before coming face-to-face with the elderly woman. Without saying a word, he wrapped his arms around her and they embraced. Tray'o wasn't sure, but it looked like she was crying.

"Do you buy it?" Sparrow asked as she twirled a dagger in her hand.

"No," Salana frowned. "And yet … children."

"That does not prove anything," Akoro stated. "The Locura could still be monsters."

"Could they?" Salana asked as she turned her back to the park and leaned against the bars. "Children fear monsters. These ones are too happy to be in any danger."

Tray'o watched as Skyblind conversed with the elderly woman, but he couldn't hear any of their conversation.

She's upset, though. Tray'o knew that much from the expression on her face and the way she kept shifting her weight back and forth.

"Something's wrong." Sparrow observed it too. "We should get out of here while we still can."

Salana shook her head. "Not yet."

Skyblind said a few more words to the woman, then turned away from her and moved quickly through the park.

"We have to hurry," he announced, stepping through the gate and shutting it behind him. "They've just come through here."

"Did she say if she saw Taylee?" Tray'o asked.

"Yes, Taylee and and several others. It is as I suspected, he's dropped the name 'Lunechair' and is once again going by 'Logan Rome', his true name." Skyblind no longer seemed as peaceful or calm as he had been when he first entered the ruins. "That means he's no longer hiding who he is. Follow me, we don't have much time!"

"Time for what?" Sparrow asked. But she was not given an answer; Skyblind was already jogging away, farther into the ruins of the city.

"Come on, and stay alert. We may still be in danger," Salana warned.

Hang on, Taylee. We're coming!

The whole group chased after Skyblind as he led them down a series of narrow streets. For the most part, the city felt entirely abandoned, but as they moved through it, Tray'o gradually became aware of the presence of others. He couldn't get a good look at them, but saw that many were dressed in dirty, ill-fitting clothes and appeared more like the poor of the Outskirts than Locura monsters. They mostly kept to the shadows, and seemed to be more afraid than Tray'o would have expected, but there was no doubt that they were humans.

Maybe they're Dark Ones, and the real Locura are kept chained up somewhere else. But if that were true, then these Dark Ones looked significantly different than the ones he saw burn Krydor.

"Where are we going?" Akoro demanded.

"I don't have time to explain. We must *hurry* if we are to beat him to the bridge!" Skyblind called back.

Suddenly, from somewhere deep within the city, the voices of many men and women chanting rang out, and for a split-second, Tray'o could swear he heard Taylee's voice lost among them.

"Taylee!" Tray'o shouted her name at the top of his lungs.

"Quiet!" Sparrow scolded. "You'll expose us all!"

He knew she was right, but any reproach from her irritated Tray'o.

"That's ironic coming from the girl who screamed so loudly she nearly caused another landslide," Tray'o retorted.

"Shut up, both of you!" Salana ordered before Sparrow could say anything else.

They picked up their pace, but the path was treacherous. In order to keep moving forward, they had to leap over holes in the road, dodge massive clumps of debris, and cut through overgrown weeds.

As they followed Skyblind, the chanting grew louder and

louder, until all at once it came to a sudden and unexpected end. After that, all signs of life vanished, and once again the city felt utterly abandoned.

"Up there!" Skyblind shouted as they approached the ruins of a large, white marble building. Several hundred stairs led up to the building, and after a quick check to make sure no Locura were waiting in ambush, they climbed them as fast as possible.

At the top of the stairs was a single, dark opening right between two white pillars; it reminded Tray'o of a temple, and he wondered if this was where the inhabitants of the Ancient City worshipped Plyyston.

Or whatever god Skyblind claims they serve.

"In there?" Corwin asked.

"Yes. Hurry!" Skyblind rushed past the pillars and straight into the darkness of the building.

Akoro stopped at the doorway. "Are we sure about this? It could be a trap."

Salana pulled out her dagger and stepped past him. "We've come too far to turn back now."

Tray'o agreed, and, with the thought of rescuing Taylee firmly planted in his mind, he followed the others into the darkness, albeit a little more cautiously.

It was pitch black inside. The only light came streaming from behind them, illuminating another set of stairs that descended deeper down into the inky black depths of the building.

"Down here!" Skyblind called from the base of the stairwell.

"I can't see anything." Tray'o mumbled grumpily. He may as well have been blind.

"It's not so bad …" Corwin led the way down by running his hand along the smooth, cold wall.

The group struggled down the steps and through the darkness until they reached level ground.

Now what?

"Over here!" Corwin called from somewhere in the darkness.

In the distance, Tray'o could see a dim glimmer of light

shining from around what must have been a corner.

Tray'o reached out his arms and found a wall, which he followed all the way to the end of a hallway.

When he reached the end and turned the corner, he nearly lost his breath.

It's incredible. Tray'o was overcome with awe. In front of them, illuminating the darkness, a golden door glowed.

The light coming from the door was bright, shiny, and shimmering, almost as if it were a door made of living fire. It didn't matter that it was dark here; the light reflected off the walls of the corridor and cast speckled shadows across everything it touched.

"How pretty," Sparrow quipped dryly. Her injury had done nothing to improve her uniquely sunny disposition.

"What now?" Corwin asked as they approached Skyblind, who was kneeling at the base of the door.

"We … are too late," he moaned.

Too late? Are you kidding me?

"What does that mean?" Tray'o pointed. "The door is right here!"

"We can open it, can't we?" Corwin asked.

"No. Not without the key. They've already passed through." Skyblind's voice was thick with grief.

"How do you know?" Tray'o looked around. "They might still be coming. Maybe we beat them here? Someone watch the stairs!"

"No. They're gone."

No. That's not possible.

Although it was a door, it may as well have been a wall, for there was no handle, hinge, or any visible way to open it.

"I will break it down." Akoro made a fist and pounded against the door with all his might. Each hit against the door created a sort of hollow, thudding sound, but no matter how hard he tried it would not budge.

"What a colossal waste of time," Sparrow said. "At least we can go back now."

Everyone was silent, and, except for Akoro's repeated striking, there was no sound at all.

I can't believe this. All this way for nothing?

Tray'o put a hand on Skyblind's shoulder and shook him. "Hey! Do that thing you did with the Nightwolves. Tell your god to open it for us. If he's so powerful, he could do that, right?"

"He does not work that way," Skyblind stated. Then, lowering his head, he mumbled some inaudible words under his breath.

Some god he is, if he can't even open a little door.

Tray'o grunted in annoyance and turned to Corwin. "What do we do now?"

Corwin's eyes were glued to the door. "I feel like I've seen this before …" he mumbled absently.

Sparrow laughed. "Sure, Corwin. Probably while training as a Dark One spy, right?"

Corwin ignored her and took a step closer to the door. "In a dream …" He reached out his hand and ran his fingers up and around the frame, down the intricate patterns woven into the metal, and across the glowing door itself, until something in the corner caught his eye.

"There," he said, moving toward the right side of the door.

Hidden in the shadows was the faintly painted outline of a red hand.

"Look at that!" Tray'o exclaimed. How had he missed it before?

Skyblind lifted his head. "It is nothing. An imprint of the hand of the man who made the door."

Corwin stared at it intently, then, after a pause, lifted his own hand up to his face. He opened and closed it, then carefully stretched it out and placed it over top of the image.

A loud and sudden chirp rang through the room, and the painted hand lit up and changed to a bright green colour.

"Ouch!" Corwin quickly jerked his hand away; the tips of his four fingers had been pricked and a small amount of blood beaded out.

Tray'o stared in shock as the door suddenly creaked, and,

quite unexpectedly, split in half down the middle. It spread open and then completely disappeared into the frame of the wall on both sides, leaving an open passageway that bathed them all with an ethereal white light from within.

No way.

Tray'o shielded his eyes to block out the light.

"What just happened?" Sparrow gawked.

"I was wrong ..." Skyblind stood and took Corwin's hand in his own. "The Nightwolf was not the key."

"What do you mean?" Salana asked.

Skyblind stared at Corwin with a look of both shock and awe. "It was you; all this time, it was you."

Chapter Twenty-Eight — The Room Beyond the Door

"If doors were built to keep people out, what do we build to let them in?"

—HECTOR THE HOLY, A.P. 730
A TOME OF TRUTH

As soon as the whole group passed through the open passageway, the door reappeared and slid shut, sealing them inside the blindingly bright white room.

Guess there's no going back. Corwin swallowed the lump that was growing in his throat.

The luminous white light was so blinding in contrast to the inky darkness from where they had come that he was forced to squint. But gradually the temporary blindness faded and he was able to open his eyes wider and look around.

They were standing at the end of a long, empty hallway that was illuminated by no visible light source; Corwin suspected that some type of ancient sorcery was at play, and so he shivered despite the humid warmth he felt in the hallway.

Why did the door respond to me? He wanted to ask Skyblind what his words meant, but something about this place felt so secret—almost sacred—that for the moment saying anything at all seemed somehow irreverent.

Sparrow, however, did not share that same sentiment. "How did the door open for Corwin?"

Skyblind lifted a finger to his mouth and let out a soft "*shhh*" to warn that they should remain quiet as he started to sneak down the hallway.

He's right. Master Lunechair – I mean, Logan – might still be here.

Once Corwin was adequately adjusted to the change in light and temperature, he carefully followed Skyblind.

They snuck down the hall as quietly as possible until at last it led them into a much larger room.

It's empty, Corwin realised with a mix of disappointment and relief.

Scattered across the room were several white tables, each one holding an identical black box. The boxes looked solid and seemed to be made of some metallic substance, but other than that, Corwin could not identify what they were or what purpose they may have once served. A thick layer of dust blanketed each one.

The room was square and fairly large—about twice the size of one of his classrooms in Lightspire—and was connected to two hallways, the one they came through and a second one on the opposite side that led somewhere else.

That must lead to the bridge Skyblind mentioned, Corwin assumed.

Various shelves adorned three of the walls in the room, some filled with books, others with potions, and some with unfamiliar objects and relics. The only wall that didn't have a shelf was completely covered with papers, drawings, and markings consisting of different renderings of what looked to be the same spherical object.

"That's a lot of drawings of a circle," Tray'o frowned.

"It's not a circle," Skyblind spoke quietly. "It's a depiction of the Orb of Power."

Salana pulled one the papers off the wall and held it up to get a better look while Akoro searched the immediate area as if he were expecting an ambush.

"I've never heard of this. Is it a relic?"

"More than a relic—it is a source of power so great that it

alone will grant Logan Rome complete and utter rule of all Anaciencia."

"Huh," Tray'o scratched his head. "That's a pretty powerful circle."

Aside from their group, the room appeared empty, and there was really no indication that anyone had been here at all in the last several years.

"You think Logan has it? This Orb thing?" Salana asked as she placed the paper back on the board.

"I'm afraid that he does."

Sparrow scoffed as she dragged her finger across the thick layer of dust that covered one of the black boxes.

"How can you even know if they got in? Just because Corwin could open the door doesn't mean Taylee could."

"She could," Skyblind affirmed. "They share the same blood."

For some reason, this made Akoro laugh.

"What does blood matter in opening doors?"

Before anyone could respond, a friendly yet unfamiliar voice answered the question. "Oh! It matters more than anything."

Corwin looked up and saw a teenaged boy about the same age as him standing at the entrance to the second hallway.

Before Corwin could even blink, Sparrow was already at the other end of the room and had aimed her crossbow straight at the stranger's head.

"Don't move."

"Whoa! Wait!" His eyes grew wide. "I'm not your enemy. My name is Marlo. I came back to grab my bag when I heard some noises and—" Marlo cut himself off when he noticed Skyblind. "Skyblind? Is that really you? This is incredible! You have no idea how hard I've been praying that God would bring you back to us!"

Skyblind smiled. "It is good to see you again."

They're friends ...?

Although this was reason enough to cause Corwin to trust him, Sparrow kept her weapon aimed at Marlo.

"How do you two know each other?" Salana asked as she took

a step toward him.

"Everyone knows Skyblind!" Marlo beamed. "He's the rightful King of Anaciencia!"

This caused Salana to raise an eyebrow and glance at Skyblind. "Is he now?"

Skyblind shook his head. "Don't worry, Salana. It is their wish that I return to rule, not mine," he assured her.

"Nice wish." Sparrow did not sound convinced. "Too bad he won't live long enough to see it fail."

For a second, Corwin thought Sparrow might actually shoot the boy. But before she could do anything foolish, Skyblind stepped in front of Marlo and stared her straight in the eye.

"Put down your weapon. I tell you the truth, this boy is no danger to us."

She laughed. "Yeah, right. He's a Dark One."

"There's that word again." Marlo scratched his head. "Whatever it is, I'm pretty sure I'm not one."

"You aren't," Skyblind affirmed. "There are no Dark Ones or Locura."

"So you say." Sparrow wasn't budging.

Although the boy seemed as friendly as anyone Corwin had ever met before, Sparrow's eyes were untrusting and cold as stone.

Tray'o let out an annoyed grunt and abruptly pushed past Skyblind to get closer to Marlo. "You. Have you seen a new girl around here? Close to my age?"

"A new girl …?" Marlo scratched his head. "Do you mean Taylee?"

Tray'o clenched his fists. "Where is she?!"

"Oh, uh, she's with Logan right now. They're talking to a ghost."

That was all the confirmation Tray'o needed; the next thing Corwin knew, his friend was running out of the room and down the hallway.

Talking to the ghost? While the words were strange, Corwin felt some measure of comfort knowing that his sister was alive and near.

"Wait! Tray'o!" Salana called, but he wouldn't slow down. "Arg! Grab the Dark One!" she ordered Akoro as she ran after Tray'o.

The knight reached over and snatched Marlo by the scruff of the neck.

"Ow! Hey, I'm on your side!"

Akoro, like the obedient man he was, did not waste time arguing, and forcefully took Marlo down the hall as they all moved forward in pursuit of Tray'o and Salana.

"I'm beginning to feel like coming with you all was a big mistake," Sparrow grumbled under her breath as they moved through the long white hallway.

"Hey, how did you guys get in here, anyway?" Marlo glanced over his shoulder at Corwin. "Are you her brother?"

Hmm. So she told him about me.

"I am," Corwin admitted reluctantly.

Marlo smiled the same way a child might when meeting royalty for the first time.

Corwin wanted to believe that this boy was truly harmless—like Skyblind insisted—and was even starting to think that things might actually turn out all right. But then, all of a sudden, he heard the one sound he hated most in the entire world: his sister's ear-piercing scream.

Chapter Twenty-Nine — Logan Rome

"Wise words do not necessarily equate with wisdom; even a fool can have followers."

—THOM PENTITON, A.P. 321
LESSONS OF THE LIGHT

"At long last!" exclaimed Logan Rome, the man Taylee formerly knew as Master Lunechair. Although physically he looked no different, his recent name and behaviour change caused her to feel as though she were staring at a stranger.

How much do I really know about this man? Was everything he ever told me a lie?

"Hmm. Interesting," Roy mused as she and Marlo followed them into the room, along with four other Locura soldiers.

Or Dark Ones, or whatever they thought they were. Even though Marlo, Roy, and the others seemed human enough, Taylee still wasn't sure what to think of them.

They were now entering the second room since passing through the magic door, and although it was identical to the first, this one contained something very different.

Directly in the centre, surrounded by more black boxes, was a glowing ball of fire elevated on a pedestal. It floated freely about two inches in the air, burned the colour of molten gold, and seemed to be almost alive itself. Judging by the look in Logan's eye, this was certainly the thing he'd brought them here to find.

But, strangely, it was surrounded by some sort of bluish sphere of rippling, glass-like, magical energy, and Taylee wasn't sure they'd be able to even reach past it.

"Behold! The Orb of Power." Logan took a confident step toward it as the group murmured amongst themselves.

"So cool!" Marlo grinned with boyish wonder.

"What's that blue stuff?" Roy asked cautiously.

"It looks to be a form of raw Essence. Probably used for the purpose of containment," Logan suggested as he stood a few inches away. "It's nothing to be afraid of; it seems to exist to keep the Orb safe until it's claimed by its rightful owner."

Although he sounded confident, Taylee couldn't shake the feeling that they were making a big mistake.

I wish Corwin were here. She squinted her eyes fearfully as Logan reached his hand toward the blue substance.

But right before he touched the surface, a bright spark shot out from his fingers, and all the light in the room instantly blinked out.

I knew it! She raised her hands to defend herself from whatever might strike in the darkness that now settled over the room.

The only remaining light came from the pulsating glow of the Orb as it shone through the blue sphere of Essence.

At first, it seemed as if all that had happened was that the lights had gone out. But then, almost as if materialising out of the blue substance itself, a glowing blue man emerged.

A ghost?! Taylee's heart leapt into her throat. Until this moment, she'd never really believed ghosts were real.

"How did you get in here?" The ghost-man demanded over the fearful cries of the Locura. His voice was cold and angry, and Taylee wanted nothing more than to run and hide, but all of a sudden, his eyes fell upon her and his whole demeanour changed. "Oh … it cannot be …"

Taylee took a step backward and looked to Logan for help, but he appeared almost as shocked as she was, and could say nothing more than, "Interesting."

"Who are you?" Taylee asked, though as she asked the question, she felt strangely certain she already knew the answer; the ghost-man was the very image of Corwin, though much older and with sadder eyes.

This is the ghost of my father …?

It was the only thing that made sense. The ghost-man would not stop staring at her.

But how? Why? She'd concluded that her mother wasn't a Dark One, but her father's presence here, in this place, brought everything into question again.

Maybe my mother received the necklace from him …?

The ghost-man wordlessly glided toward her and reached out his ethereal hand.

Taylee instinctively leaned away, but he was faster than she expected. She shut her eyes in fear just as he made contact, but felt nothing at all; his hand passed effortlessly and painlessly through her face.

Taylee waited a few seconds before nervously opening one eye.

The ghost—as if suddenly aware of his ghostly qualities—was sobbing on his knees.

"I'm sorry … I'm so sorry …"

Taylee opened both eyes and watched him for a minute, then took a tentative step toward Logan, who had since moved away from the Orb and was poking around with one of the black boxes.

"He's … my father … isn't he?" Taylee asked.

"The ghost of, yes," Logan grumbled, examining the box as if searching for something specific.

Taylee could hardly breathe.

Her whole life she'd wondered about her parents and dreamed of all the things she would ask them if she could. Now, with her father's ghost weeping at her feet, she had no idea what to say.

He looks so sad and defeated.

"Please, don't cry." Taylee tried to sound comforting, but she had no idea how to console a dead man she couldn't even touch.

He looked up at her with ghostly tears in his eyes.

"Forgive me … please, forgive me … you were all I ever

wanted …"

Taylee tensed up. "What do you need forgiveness for?"

He did not answer, and lowered his head to cry some more.

He's destroyed by guilt, Taylee observed. *But over what?*

"What's wrong with him?" Roy asked with a look of disgust.

"He's just the pathetic ghost of an old fool who failed to keep up his end of a bargain," Logan replied unsympathetically.

"No!" The ghost spun to face Logan. "You took her. Everything that happened is because you forced his hand!"

Logan didn't try to hide his contemptuous laughter. "You know exactly why I did what I did. And don't pretend I didn't follow through; the girl before you is proof enough."

The ghost of Taylee's father rose a few inches off the ground and his voice dropped an octave as he said, "You think you've won, but you haven't. I am here, but *he* is far from dead. In the end, you will see who the real fool was. His revenge will be complete when you are left with nothing."

Logan, clearly frustrated and unable to find what he was looking for, cursed and slapped the side of one of black boxes. But as soon as he did, the ghost of her father flickered. It was faint, but Logan noticed it, and a cruel smiled crossed his face.

"Time to move on, ghost. You are no longer needed here."

Before Taylee realised what was happening, Logan picked up the box and carelessly tossed it at the ghost.

"NO!" She screamed as she helplessly watched her father try to catch it.

But he was unable to do anything. The box passed through his hands and shattered into a hundred pieces on the ground.

It all happened so fast.

One minute her father was standing in front of her, begging for forgiveness, and the next, he and the blue Essence surrounding the Orb flashed out of existence, leaving nothing more than a dim mist in the air.

She was stunned.

Gone. Completely and utterly gone.

"What did you do?" she cried as the unnatural white light once again filled the room.

"Do not be upset, dear one. I merely helped your father's ghost ascend to his reward. His grief is over now."

"You killed him!"

"You cannot kill a ghost," Roy mumbled as she kicked the debris from the broken box away from her feet.

My father's spirit was captured within that box. Good or evil, he didn't deserve to be snuffed out like that without a chance to at least explain himself!

Logan took a step forward and tried to put a comforting hand on her shoulder, but Taylee slapped it away. "Don't ever touch me again."

Logan chuckled and turned away from her.

"We're wasting time," Roy reminded him in her irritatingly bland tone.

"Quite right. I've waited for this moment long enough." Logan grinned as he strode over to the now-exposed, pulsating fireball.

As he reached out toward the Orb, Taylee quietly prayed that it would burn his hands. But, much to her dismay, he grabbed it and pulled it painlessly off the pedestal.

Perhaps that Orb contains some evil power that corrupted my father. Maybe that's happening to Logan too? It was the only thing that made sense; the man she knew was a teacher, not a killer, unless she had truly been deceived all this time.

Logan couldn't keep his eyes off the Orb as he cradled it in his arms like one might hold a small baby.

"Taylee, the door, please."

She narrowed her eyes and crossed her arms defiantly. *If he thinks I'm going to help him again, he really is crazy!*

Logan didn't need to ask again.

Roy, along with another Locura, swooped over and took hold of Taylee under her armpits.

"Hey!" she screamed at the top of her lungs as she struggled to get free. "Let me go!"

Unfortunately, Roy was stronger than she looked, and two of the Locura soldiers effortlessly moved her over to the only door in the room.

Taylee tried to make a fist, but they easily pulled her fingers apart and pressed them painfully against the same red symbol of a hand that she was forced to touch earlier.

"HELP!" She shrieked as once again the shock of a thousand tiny needles pricked her skin.

As with the first door, this one reacted to her touch and the light immediately turned green. A second later, the door in front of them slid apart and revealed yet another hallway.

How many of these doors am I going to have to open?! Taylee thought as they shoved her through the doorway.

"Come now, Taylee. You don't need to fight us." Logan followed them into the hall. "Now that I have the Orb, everything will be better. If you'll only trust me, you'll see that I have so much good in store for you."

I'll never trust you again. She wanted to say it out loud, but the pain from the door mixed with the shock of finally discovering her father only to watch him be taken from her caused her vocal cords to constrict in her throat. It took every ounce of strength in her body to keep from crying, but she was determined not to show any weakness in front of Logan.

He and the others started to forcefully move her down the hall, when all of a sudden, Roy stopped dead in her tracks. "Where's Marlo?"

Taylee glanced around the hallway. In all the commotion, she'd somehow forgotten about him.

"Maybe my father's ghost scared him away," she mumbled under her breath. Although she liked Marlo more than any of them, he was still a Dark One, and one less was a good thing.

Logan shrugged. "He couldn't have gone far."

"Wait for me," Roy ordered as she stepped back into the pedestal room. "I won't be long."

Where would he have gone, though? Taylee wondered dimly.

She didn't have much time to consider it, for almost as soon as Roy re-entered, she heard a friendly voice shouting her name. "Taylee? Taylee!"

Her mouth dropped open as Tray'o Sak'ton slid carelessly into the room, followed immediately by Princess Salana, a knight holding Marlo by the collar of his shirt, some girl she didn't know, and Skyblind. She was filled with relief and excitement at seeing them, but it wasn't until she caught sight of her brother that she truly felt joy.

"Cor!" Taylee tried to break free, but the two Locura held her tightly.

Taylee was furious. All that stood between her and all of her friends gathering at the other end of the room was Roy and a handful of Locura.

"Release my brother," Roy warned Akoro as she unsheathed her dagger.

"Return Taylee and you can have him back," Akoro answered in a voice as cold as stone.

Although the tension was high, Logan did not seem to care, and he broke out into gregarious laughter as he stood right in the doorway. "How unexpected. Everyone is together again! Wonderful to see you, Corwin. And Princess Salana—what a surprise. You're a bit out of place here."

Corwin clenched his fists. "What did you do to my sister?"

"Me? Nothing," Logan cooed innocently. "She came with of her own free will and led me at last to the marvellous Orb. It's really quite something, wouldn't you say?" he asked as he held the ball of fire up high for everyone to see.

A threat. Will he try to kill them too?

"Don't you dare hurt them!" Taylee warned.

Logan glanced at her and smirked in a most demeaning way. "Oh to be young and experience the extreme emotions of youth again, right, Skyblind? I must say, you surprised me more than anyone, showing up the way you did back in the Outskirts."

For some reason, Skyblind's presence agitated the Locura, and she felt their grip on her weaken ever so slightly.

"What is *he* doing here?" one asked nervously.

"Who cares," another answered. "He had his chance to lead us."

Skyblind took a step forward, but stopped when Roy pointed her dagger at him. "Brothers, sisters, please hear me. This is not the way!"

Brothers and sisters? What's he mean by that?

Roy laughed. "We tried your way, but peace led us nowhere. Now is the time for war."

"You cannot truly think Logan and his Orb are the answer. He is an Elder himself!"

"Former Elder," Roy reminded him. "And he has proven beneficial to our people. Now, release my brother."

Although Marlo was technically a captive of one of the largest men in all Anaciencia, he seemed quite relaxed. "Don't worry about me, Roy. I'm fine. They're pretty nice."

Taylee wasn't sure if he was just blindly optimistic, or brain-damaged.

A bit of both, maybe.

"All right, I'm kind of done with talking." The girl Taylee did not know raised a crossbow and aimed it straight at Roy.

"I quite agree, though I would put down that weapon if I were you, unless you're anxious to see what my new toy can do." Logan waved the Orb back and forth.

The girl held her position, but, after sharing a look with Princess Salana, reluctantly lowered the crossbow.

"Smart girl." Logan turned his back. "Roy, look away."

Roy turned her face, and, before Taylee realised what was happening, he rolled one of his exploding silver stones into the room.

"Wait!" Taylee exclaimed—but it was too late. The stone erupted in a fury of blinding white light that knocked her friends to the floor.

Taylee stumbled, but the Locura held her tight.

Because she was staring right at it when it went off, she could see nothing but white, and the loud ringing in her ears deafened all her senses.

It took a good minute, but her hearing eventually came back. When it did, she realised that the Locura were rapidly carrying her down the hall while Roy and Logan engaged in some kind of argument.

"… a plan, don't you? We aren't going to leave my brother trapped in there!" Roy exclaimed.

"They will not be trapped for long. If they got in, they can get out," Logan reminded her.

How could they get out? Unless … Of course! The door must act like the Nightwolf necklace. If I can open these doors, so can Corwin. Taylee realised with a new measure of hope.

"So they'll follow us, and then what?" Roy asked.

"It won't matter. Nothing they can do can stop us, not as long as I control the Orb," Logan announced.

Taylee blinked and blinked, and, as her vision slowly started to return, she realised exactly what she needed to do.

Chapter Thirty — The Bridge

"Despite what many affirm, a man is only a man when he is able to channel his anger, rather than having it channel him."

—ELDER RHAMSEY, A.P. 230
<u>THE NINE SINS OF NIGHT</u>

In the same manner as the others, the third door split in half and vanished inside the wall. But instead of another hallway, Corwin now looked inside a completely black room.

"Now what?" Tray'o asked as they all looked down into what seemed to be an empty room with a bottomless pit.

It must be an illusion. Corwin reached a foot out in the darkness, hoping it might strike some hidden, invisible floor. But much to his dismay, he could feel nothing but air.

"So much for a bridge …" Sparrow frowned.

Where could they have gone? Corwin couldn't believe it. *There was only one hallway and it led straight to this door. They couldn't have gone anywhere else.*

"Wait. Up there!" Marlo pointed up.

Corwin raised his eyes and watched in shock as a bright, rectangular white platform descended from above and hovered directly in front of the open door.

The platform was long and wide, and appeared to be somehow suspended firmly over the black abyss. It was completely smooth, an inch thick, and likely able to fit between ten to twelve people, provided they were all standing and didn't require a lot of space.

"A rectangular block?" Sparrow did not sound impressed.

Skyblind leaned forward, stroked his beard and said, "This must be it."

Princess Salana arched an eyebrow. "You think this is the Bridge?"

"In a sense, yes. You saw how it descended. It seems the Bridge is more like a tunnel through the water, and this block is the thing that will carry us to the Island," Skyblind suggested.

Sparrow scoffed. "How do you know it's not some trap and if we step on it we'll fall to our death?"

"I can't," Skyblind admitted. "But Logan's group had to go somewhere."

Only one way to know for sure. Corwin swallowed. "Talking about it won't help us know."

Although the idea of falling to his death was terrifying, he hesitated for only a moment before cautiously stepping one foot onto it.

"Careful!" Salana warned.

It was unsettling, but, as he leaned his weight forward, it felt as solid as any regular floor. And so, once convinced of its stability, Corwin carefully stepped onto the platform completely.

The rectancular platform did not shift even an inch.

"It seems safe to me," he said after a brief pause.

"Good. Move over." Tray'o pushed past the others to climb on as well, followed almost immediately by Skyblind.

Akoro, still holding Marlo by the shirt, turned to Princess Salana and frowned. "I do not trust this platform."

"I don't either," Princess Salana admitted as she boldly stepped on. "But we don't have much choice."

Akoro grunted his disapproval, and then, without any warning, shoved Marlo onto it and reluctantly joined them.

"You coming?" Corwin asked when he realised Sparrow still stood in the doorway.

"Yeah, yeah," she mumbled as she took a nervous step forward.

Although Corwin found it hard to believe she was afraid of anything, it was becoming apparent that Sparrow hated heights.

As soon as she left the safety of the hall, and everyone was firmly planted on the platform, the door slid shut, and they were once again surrounded by darkness. The only light now came from the eerie glow of the white platform.

"So now what?" The fear was thick in Sparrow's voice.

Thankfully, they did not have to wait long to find out, for almost as soon as the door was shut, Corwin could hear a low rumble as the platform started to tremble ever so slightly.

At first it sounded like a heavy gear was stuck and slowly grinding up against metal. The sound grew louder and more strained, until, all at once, the platform shot forward.

Corwin didn't have a chance to take a breath as he and everyone else were forced down to their knees to keep from losing their balance.

Although they were surrounded by darkness, and there was no wind or way to know whether they were actually moving or not, Corwin could feel their speed increasing by the twisting in his gut.

"Do not fear!" Skyblind called out. "God will not abandon us now!"

Oh, to have your faith. Corwin ground his teeth together as he waited for the horrible sensation in his stomach to stop.

CLICK.

A sharp sound rang out.

"Did you hear that?" Tray'o asked.

CLICK.

It rang out again.

Corwin looked around but couldn't see anything.

CLICK.

At first it happened every two seconds, but Corwin realised it was gradually increasing in intervals, until the clicks were less than a second apart each.

CLICK.

CLICK.

CLICK.

It's related to our speed, he realised. *How much faster are we going to go?*

Soon, Corwin became aware of a small blue dot off in the distance.

At first it was nothing but a speck, but as the clicking increased in frequency, so did the distant speck in size. Right when the clicks became so rapid that they were nearly indistinguishable, the dot grew very large and came rushing straight at them.

CLICK-CLICK-CLICK-CLICK-CLICK-CLICK.

"It's going to hit us!" Sparrow screamed as she ducked her head.

Whatever the blue light was, Corwin's fear overpowered his curiosity and he firmly shut his eyes.

A powerfully bright light shattered the darkness, and even though his eyes were shut, Corwin could sense the light of the sun.

"It's beautiful …" Salana gasped.

Corwin opened his eyes and all at once felt his heart leap into his throat.

Where once there was nothing but inky blackness, the white platform they stood on was now surrounded by the most beautiful and vibrant blue of the ocean, which was seemingly held back by an invisible, magical force.

Fish, and all sorts of other colourful underwater creatures, swam past as they stood isolated on the white platform. Here, with the aid of the light, Corwin saw that the platform did in fact ride along some sort of rail, on a track which rested a few feet above the sea floor.

Skyblind was right.

Corwin gasped as he reached out his hand to touch the water that rushed past his head, only to feel the cold, solid resistance of a wall instead.

"This is incredible," he whispered in awe.

Marlo, who was now free and standing next to Corwin, grinned and nodded his agreement.

The clicking, Corwin now realised, was the sound of the platform crossing rapidly over the track, and he let out a quiet sigh of relief knowing that they did not seem to be in danger after all.

They watched with anticipation as their platform glided along the track, past all sorts of underwater life, and toward a distant, mud-coloured shape which Corwin could only assume was the Island.

For a moment he forgot his anger, and the Locura stealing Taylee, and his uncle's illness, and allowed himself to be lost in the beauty of his surroundings.

Unfortunately, it didn't last long.

"Over there!" Tray'o exclaimed as he pointed to another white platform, much farther ahead of them, and riding on the same track.

"Good, they haven't gotten far," Princess Salana affirmed as they caught sight of Logan's flaming Orb. "We should be able to catch up to them on the Island."

"And then what?" Tray'o asked. "He's an Elder—he'll know the Island better than any of us. Plus, now he has that weapon."

Princess Salana shook her head. "It doesn't matter. The Island belongs to Syyris. We will warn him and he will stop them."

I hope she's right.

Glancing around the platform, he could tell by the way everyone looked that they were as apprehensive as he was about the invisible wall that was holding back the crushing torrents of water; everyone but Skyblind, who sat with his back confidently pressed against the invisible rear wall of the platform.

Does this man have no fear at all?

"I'm sorry, Princess Salana. But Syyris cannot save you," Skyblind said.

"Not that again," Tray'o moaned.

"It's true, though," Marlo said. "Syyris is just an idol."

"Uh-huh," Sparrow smirked. "And I suppose Plyyston is not?"

Marlo shrugged. “Nah, he’s an idol too, but I don’t think anyone worships him.”

That seemed to take Sparrow by surprise.

“Is he not the god of Night?” Akoro boomed. “The god of your people?”

“My people? No way. And you’re the ones who created the whole ‘god of Day’ versus ‘god of Night’ thing. Our God is Lord over both seasons, not just one or the other. You’ve told them this before, haven’t you, Skyblind?”

All eyes turned to the Exile, whose face displayed the emotions of someone completely at peace with the world.

“Tray’o Sak’ton,” Skyblind said after a short pause, “you asked me before how I can believe in a God I have not seen.”

Tray’o hesitated. “Uh … yeah.”

“This is another example of what I meant,” Skyblind closed his eyes. “I believe not because of sight, but because I’ve felt His presence. Look at this wall. You cannot see it, but it’s clearly here, holding back the water.”

Tray’o sighed. “Okay … so what?”

“Experience is a great indicator of the validity of a belief. For example, right now, experience tells you that there is a wall holding the water back. In the same way, experience tells me that all the mysterious beauty of the world could not possibly be random and has to have had a Creator.”

“Sure, but wait,” Corwin said. “How can you be sure that Syyris isn’t that creator?”

“Because Syyris is subject to creation in a way that a Creator could never be.”

“Oh really?” Tray’o leaned to one side. “He’s not subject to gravity. He can fly!”

“Yes, he can. Give me a pair of wings, and I too could fly,” Skyblind replied. “The ability to fly does not make a god any more than the ability to walk makes a man.”

“Okay, so what’s your point?” Princess Salana asked.

“My point is that Syyris, while clearly having some power, is not all-powerful. Even in your scriptures you can read that his power diminishes at Night." His words seemed to take on new weight, especially since Darkfall was on the rise. "If you truly wish to find help, then you must turn your eyes to the True God, the God of both Day and Night."

No one said anything for at least a minute, until Tray'o broke the silence. "That doesn't make any sense," he muttered as he got up to watch the other platform again.

Corwin, for reasons he could not explain, could not take his eyes away from Skyblind; something about the sincerity with which he spoke lent an air of authority to his words. But no matter how much he wanted to believe the man, Syyris was proven, and this new god was just a myth.

"So anyway, the thing about our God is—" Marlo started to share, when all of a sudden, Tray'o hissed at him to be quiet.

"Look! Something's happening!" he exclaimed.

"What is it?" Corwin asked as he stood and walked to the front of the platform.

"It's Taylee," Princess Salana stated. "She's attacking Logan."

Good girl. Corwin thought proudly as he saw the distant figure of his sister leap onto the back of Logan.

But his pride suddenly turned to horror as Logan fell forward and the other platform abruptly exploded into a bright ball of light.

"NO!" Tray'o screamed as they all shielded their eyes from the blast.

She must have knocked loose a Flash!

"The Bridge! It's broken!" Akoro shouted at the top of his lungs as Corwin lowered his hands from his face.

The other platform was now sinking toward the bottom of the ocean, and the track they were on was now missing a fairly substantial section.

"What happened?" Tray'o shouted.

"Grab hold of something!" Princess Salana shouted as she frantically looked around the platform.

Sparrow spun around; her face was as white as the platform.

"There has to be a way to stop this thing, right?!"

The look of calm on Skyblind's face had now faded and was replaced with one of uncertainty.

"If there is … I don't know it."

That's it. We're going to crash.

"What do we do?" Tray'o asked.

Akoro dropped flat on his stomach. "Brace yourselves!" he exclaimed as the platform struck the end of the track and derailed.

Corwin was instantly knocked off his feet and slammed straight into the invisible wall—which he now realised was simply made of some strong glass—as their platform fell from off the track and hit the bottom of the ocean.

Everything was a blur as the walls cracked from the sudden strain, and, without warning, shattered under the mounting pressure of the water. Glass and water rushed at them, and Corwin was immediately knocked unconscious by the overwhelming force.

PART III

Chapter Thirty-One — Wrecked

"I love my wings!" cried the fly,
caught inside the web.
"You love them more than life itself?
If so, prepare to die."

<u>BLEU'S FABLES AND FOLKLORE: THE SPIDER AND THE FLY</u>

"… don't let him …" a familiar voice called from the darkness.

"… down carefully!"

"… is Logan?!"

"Stay back!" a fourth voice screamed.

Or was it the first voice? Tray'o couldn't be sure.

Wave upon wave crashed up and under his armpits, lapping against his body and causing his already soaked shirt and pants to cling to his skin. The sound was so methodical and soothing that Tray'o would have gladly lost himself in it if not for the persistent voices tugging at his ears.

Go away. Let me float in peace, Tray'o groaned in his mind. He wanted to stay asleep, but his consciousness was stirring.

"… think the others would wait?"

"… was not the way …"

"… choice did we have?"

Painfully, Tray'o forced his heavy eyelids open.

He was on his back, staring up at a spinning, dark orange sky. In front of him was the sun, which hung dangerously low on the horizon of the sea.

I wish it were rising.

Though he was soaking wet, and could feel himself surrounded by water, Tray'o realised that he wasn't floating at sea but instead lying on the edge of what must have been a beach.

With great effort, he dug his hands into the squishy, wet sand, and attempted to sit up.

The act of movement—though minimal—caused some sort of a painful reaction in his chest, and Tray'o immediately rolled over and heaved up water violently.

Once he had emptied his gut and collapsed onto his back again, he closed his eyes and desperately tried to make the sky stop spinning.

"He's awake!" Taylee's voice called from somewhere far off.

Taylee?

"Don't try to move. You've taken in a lot of water," her voice rang out.

Hearing it again—so kind and gentle—caused Tray'o to smile, and he opened his eyes to see her kneeling over him.

Her hair was wet and tangled, and reflected the glorious red-orange light of the sun; water beaded down her face and caused her skin to glisten bronze, which had the amazing side effect of accenting the brown in her eyes. Tray'o wished he could capture her in this moment and make it last forever.

"You're beautiful," he whispered absent-mindedly.

The sound of Corwin's laughter broke the silence as Taylee gawked wordlessly at him.

"And he's back." His best friend knelt down and said, "You had us worried, Tray. We thought we lost you."

"Really, Cor," Tray'o croaked. His voice was hoarse and cracked inside his throat. "You should know it's not that easy to kill the son of a Lord."

Taylee pursed her lips together. "I'm glad you're okay."

Tray'o smiled at her and, even though the act of moving caused him to feel dizzy again, he reached up and gave her a hug. "You caused quite a mess with that bridge."

What he meant as a joke came out more accusatory than he intended—due largely to the way his sore throat affected the tone of his voice—and Taylee immediately pulled out of his embrace.

"What? Would you have rather I just stood there? He was going to use that Orb thing to kill all of you!"

"I'm teasing," Tray'o insisted. "You did well. I'm proud of you."

The tension went out of Taylee's shoulders. "Oh. Well … thanks."

Tray'o pushed himself up on his elbows and looked around.

Absorbing the crashing waves of the sea was an endless beach of sand softer than anything he could have ever imagined. Behind him rested a rugged, brown mountain, and a thick, bright, vibrant jungle. The landscape here was so very unlike anything he'd ever experienced that it could mean only one thing: they were now on the Island.

As for the rest of their group, Tray'o noticed Princess Salana, Akoro, and Skyblind were standing in a semi-circle, engaged in a heated discussion with Marlo and two strangers whom he vaguely remembered seeing in the hall with Taylee when they first started their pursuit.

Dark Ones, he concluded warily. *The girl was named Roy, I think.*

"Is Logan …?"

"Gone," Corwin answered as if reading his mind. "With three of the Dark Ones. He didn't even try to save anyone but himself."

"That's not surprising …"

Taylee lowered her eyes. "Skyblind, Marlo, Princess Salana, the knight—and that girl you were with—they all helped drag us to shore … we would have died otherwise."

"The knight's name is Akoro, and the girl is Sparrow. They've become kind of friends; we're lucky to have them with us," Tray'o hesitated. "Hey, where is Sparrow? I don't see her anywhere."

"No one's sure what happened to her. We think she went after Logan."

That wouldn't make sense. Tray'o frowned. *She wouldn't leave*

Salana and Skyblind.

"Huh." Tray'o coughed again. It still felt as though his lungs were full of water.

"Can you stand? We have some decisions to make," Corwin asked as he rose to his feet and extended a hand to Tray'o.

"I'll have to sooner or later." He took Corwin's hand and hoisted himself up.

His balance was still off, but he was able to stay on his feet thanks to the help of Corwin and Taylee, who each slipped under one of his arms and walked him over to the others.

They approached Skyblind in the middle of a passionate plea, "… believe me when I say that God would not have us do this!" he exclaimed. "If Logan uses the Orb to kill the Elders, our people will be surely be destroyed in the process."

"How can you know that?" the younger Dark One demanded.

"Because I heard the voice of God myself; we are not to commit murder!"

"You heard him in a dream," the female Dark One named Roy scoffed.

"Yeah," the other one added. "If that was God, how do we know you didn't misunderstand Him?"

"I did not misunderstand," Skyblind was adamant. "We are called to love our enemies, not kill them."

At this, Marlo scrunched up his face. "But the Elders are evil, you know that better than anyone. God would want them to be killed, right?"

Skyblind vehemently shook his head. "No. All human life is sacred."

Marlo frowned again, but said no more.

"Listen," Roy stepped forward. "From the first time we heard about it, the plan was to get the Orb and use it to end the Elder Order. Logan managed to do that before you could, so we went with him. I think you're jealous of that fact."

"It is not for jealousy that I am upset." Skyblind was exasperated. "The plan was never to use the Orb to murder, but to free and enlighten the Kingdom. If Logan claimed to share our ideals, then he is a liar, and our people will pay the price for falling prey to his deception."

"How so?" Roy asked.

"Think about it! If the Orb is as powerful as Logan claims, than what need does he have of our people?"

The Dark Ones had no answer, so Skyblind continued, "I believe Logan is planning to frame us for the murder of the Elders. Using the lie that our people are Locura monsters, he will use the Orb to enslave the Kingdom in ways far worse than they ever could with Syyris."

"That won't happen. Without the Elders or Syyris to stop us, we can finally go to Lightspire and show the Kingdom who we really are," Roy insisted.

"Logan is an Elder still!" Skyblind's eyes grew wide. "He believes in their cause. If he kills the others, it will be because they tried to stop him. But that doesn't mean he won't reinstate some new Elders of his own choosing and continue the process of deception and rule. Only, he'll have the much more dangerous tool—the Orb. Hear me, we cannot let this happen!"

"Are you sure? I mean, do you really believe he'll just continue the Order?" Marlo asked with a look of horror.

"With all my heart, I know he will," Skyblind affirmed.

Silence hung in the air, accented only by the sound of the waves crashing against the shore.

Tray'o still felt a great deal of hatred toward these Dark Ones—even though Skyblind insisted they were innocent of burning the Outskirts—and he could not understand why the Exile would waste time arguing with them, especially after they had captured Taylee.

"Look," Salana interjected. "None of this matters if we go and speak with Syyris. Point me to the Temple, and I will make things right."

"I have told you many times …"

"Yeah, I know, I know. Syyris is just an idol," Salana said. "If that's true, allow me to see for myself."

"Salana, please. We need to be united now more than ever."

"I appreciate all your help in getting us here, Ellian, and I believe you mean well, but I do not share the relationship you have with these Dark Ones." Salana tensed her jaw. "If you intend to continue on with them, then I'm afraid this is the end of our journey together."

Skyblind looked from her to Corwin. "Listen to me! If we don't stop Logan and get that Orb, many people will die! Syyris has no power and cannot save us."

"He can," Tray'o cleared his throat. "I saw Syyris with my own eyes back in the Palace garden. He's real, and he has power." He could hardly believe his words; this was the first time in his life he'd ever said anything like it in regards to Syyris.

Skyblind looked as though he wanted to protest when Roy interrupted him. "Just let them go. They've made up their minds. Why should we care if they want to bow at the feet of a relic? If you're right about Logan, then we don't have time to waste."

Skyblind was visibly torn, but, after letting the weight of those words sink in, he reluctantly pointed toward the mountain. "Walk inland. You shouldn't have to go far before finding a trail that will lead to his temple at the base of the mountain." His voice was thick with sorrow.

He really doesn't want us to go.

"Great, thank you," Salana turned to her allies. "Are you coming with me?"

"I don't think …" Taylee started to say before being interrupted by Corwin.

"Yes," her brother affirmed loudly.

Taylee dropped open her mouth in protest and looked to Tray'o for support. But, as much as he hated to disagree with Taylee, he happened to think Salana was right.

Our best bet is to seek out Syyris. He's the only one who has any real power.

"We've come with you this far. May as well keep going."

"Good," Salana bowed her head respectfully toward Skyblind. "Thank you for your help in bringing us here. I truly hope you are able to catch Logan, but no matter what happens, I promise I will ensure he pays for his crimes."

Skyblind stroked his beard. "When you see Syyris as he truly is, remember my words. There is only One worthy to be worshipped, and He cannot be controlled by man."

And just like that, Skyblind and the other Locura separated from them and started walking down the beach, continuing their heated debate.

Good riddance. Tray'o was beyond tired of all Skyblind's preaching.

"Wait, I don't understand!" Taylee exclaimed as she gave Corwin an irritated shove. "What are we doing? We should help Skyblind chase after Logan!"

"He doesn't matter," Corwin said.

"He does! You don't understand ..." Her eyes filled up with tears. "He killed our father."

Corwin's mouth dropped open. "What?"

"Well, not exactly." She hesitated. "Back in that room. Our father appeared as a ghost and talked with me. He and Logan clearly knew each other and had some history. Before I could find out too much, Logan did something and killed his ghost. He said he was helping him 'move on,' but he didn't fool me."

Tray'o clenched his fists. *Logan will pay for that.*

"What did ... what did he look like?" Corwin asked.

"Like you," Taylee said sadly.

Corwin took a minute to let her words sink in.

"I'm sorry you had to see that, Taylee. But, if that was really a ghost, then he died a long time ago. Uncle Jael is the only father I've ever known, and we still have a chance to save him."

"What do you mean?" Taylee asked as Corwin looked at her with intensity in his eyes.

"You still have our mother's necklace, right?"

"What?" His question clearly took her by surprise. "Of course I do."

“Good. We’ll need it.”

Taylee scrunched up her face. “To do what?”

Corwin smiled at her and, for the first time in a long time, actually looked happy. “After we tell Syyris about Logan’s crimes, we’re going to burn that necklace on the altar and finally save Uncle Jael from his sickness.”

Chapter Thirty-Two — Syyris Sagrado

"Only when you stand to lose what you hold dear are you truly able to discern what is worth the risk, and when to fold and walk away. Unless it involves a woman. Then throw my book out the window. There's no amount of words that'll help you then."

—AALARDIN NEY'RK, A.P. 412
A TRADEMASTER'S GUIDE TO GOODS, GODS, AND GIRLS

Up until now, Taylee didn't realise it was even possible for her uncle to be fully healed. The thought was exhilarating, and even though part of her really wanted to go with Skyblind to pursue Logan, she believed in her heart that going to see Syyris was the right decision after all.

It makes the most sense. Only god could make everything right again.

But as relieving as it was to think that her uncle could be well again, it was also incredibly discouraging to hear that his illness had been caused by the Nightwolf necklace after all.

She had suspected that the relic was the culprit from the moment she'd seen Uncle Jael dying on the floor of Logan's tent, but in the events that followed, she'd allowed her guilt to fade into the background.

Things were different now, though. Now Taylee was the closest to Syyris that she'd ever been, and she felt the weight of it all.

I wonder if Uncle Jael will ever forgive me? Normally, that would never be a question; Uncle Jael always forgave her. But this time was different. This time, her actions had almost killed him.

I wish we'd never met Logan, Taylee thought grimly as she pushed some jungle shrubbery aside. *He's the one who had the relic in the first place.* The origin of the necklace was something he never did explain to her, but evil was clearly involved. *Logan knew much more about the origins of my family than he let on while pretending to be Lunechair. I can't believe I didn't see it sooner.*

As much as she wanted Skyblind to catch and kill Logan for what he did to her father's ghost, part of her still wanted answers from him.

But deep down, she knew it was better to go to Syyris with her questions.

If there's anyone I know for certain that is good, it's Syyris. He won't deceive us. Once we destroy the relic, I know he will explain everything.

Feeling somewhat renewed by the hope of seeing their god face-to-face, Taylee pushed on with a new sense of purpose.

The jungle was a vibrant, green, overgrown mess of thick vines, trees, and bush, and was filled with beautiful, glowing orange and yellow flowers. Everything seemed brighter here, though she suspected the colours might be enhanced by the dull red glare of the sun that burned through the leaves of the trees and warmed her back.

"What are you planning to say to him?" Taylee asked as she caught up to Salana in the lead.

"To Syyris? I don't know yet … I suppose I'll tell him about Logan and the Orb first. That's the immediate threat. But what I need is answers about my father and what the Elders did to him," Salana said.

Taylee furrowed her brow. "What do you mean? What happened to your father?"

Salana stared off into the distance and continued to press through the jungle. "He was killed by Lord Daraak on order from the Elders, if Ellian is to be believed."

The news took Taylee by surprise. *That must have happened after I left.*

"I … I had no idea. I'm so sorry …"

"It is fine." Salana's eyes filled with a deadly intensity. "Or rather, it will be."

Taylee chewed her lower lip. *If the king is dead, that means Salana isn't just a princess anymore.* The realisation made her nervous, and she no longer felt she had anything worthy to contribute to the conversation.

And so the two women walked quietly together in the lead, pushing vines and bush out of the way, until they came across a trail made of tiny stone pebbles. The stones were dirty and pressed down deep into the mossy ground, and Taylee judged that many people had walked this trail before.

She liked that they were no longer slowed by the bush and vines, but wondered if following a path likely used by others was the smartest plan for trying to sneak through the jungle unobserved.

The thought didn't seem to occur to Salana, though, and she did not slow as she stepped onto the path and moved with determination up the gradually sloping hill that led to the mountain.

Skyblind told us to follow it, so it must be okay, Taylee thought reluctantly as she and the others followed Salana up the hill.

As they walked with more space and ease, Tray'o, clearly feeling more like himself, made his way to the front of the group and was soon walking beside Taylee.

"Hey there." He tried to sound casual, but there was a strange uneasiness in his voice.

"Hi, Tray." Although Taylee was happy to see him again, she really wasn't in a talkative mood.

"How're you doing?"

"I'm all right." She sighed. "You?"

"Feeling better." Tray'o brushed his hands through some leaves as they walked. "So … hard to believe we're on the 'sacred, holy Island,' isn't it?"

"Yeah, sure is," she replied. *What does he want?*

"So you're doing well, though? Logan didn't hurt you at all?"

"No, I'm fine. He just confused me a little."

And then vanquished my father's ghost. She wanted to scream it out loud.

"Good. I'm glad … It's really nice to be with you again." Tray'o moved slightly closer to her.

Taylee acted as though she didn't notice and continued to follow Salana up the path. "Uh-huh."

He pursued her for several minutes, speaking vaguely about their childhood, life growing up together, and his appreciation for her friendship. It was all stuff she'd heard him say before, but it was starting to make her feel uncomfortable.

He still likes me. She'd always known it, but up until now he'd never been so obvious about it. *Maybe it was the thought of losing me? Or because he almost died? I hope it's not because he's not going to be a lord anymore …*

Even though she'd always been resistant to the idea of a relationship with him, she'd occasionally found herself wondering what life would be like married to the heir of a castle. But she'd never let those thoughts go anywhere. They'd been friends most of their lives, but he felt more like a brother to her than anything else.

Is that so wrong? she wondered idly.

Soon, everything Tray'o was saying ran together in her mind and turned into rambling as he kept stumbling over his words. After a while, Taylee started to lose focus, which had the unfortunate side effect of causing her to be completely taken by surprise when Tray'o abruptly took her hand and clasped it with his own.

His advance allowed her only a second to let out quiet gasp before she pulled her hand away.

Did anyone see that? she wondered, but embarrassment kept her from looking back to see.

"What are you doing?"

"Oh, I just thought …"

No. Never, Taylee felt immediately. *But I can't just blurt that out, can I?*

She wanted to tell him exactly how she felt, but knew it would crush him.

"Tray ..." Taylee started, but as soon as she saw the look in his eyes, she averted hers.

She couldn't seem to find the words, but her apprehension must have been enough; Tray'o took a step back.

"It's fine. I understand," he said casually, almost as if he didn't care.

They walked the next minute in an awkward silence—which Taylee blamed on Tray'o—until all of a sudden, Salana lifted up her hand and indicated to them all to stop.

She crouched low in some of the tall grass on the side of the trail.

Taylee and the others copied her actions and tried to listen for a sound—all but Tray'o, who was lost in his thoughts and didn't seem to notice.

"Hey, what're you—" Tray'o started to say, but was silenced by Akoro's giant hand, which wrapped easily around his mouth as he pulled him off the trail.

At first, there was nothing but the sound of everyone breathing. But, very soon, a low humming was heard.

It was distant and deep, and unlike any sound Taylee was familiar with.

The sound stopped.

Then started up again.

Then stopped.

"What is it?" she whispered to Salana, who shook her head.

"It's coming from the other side of this hill. If I can get to the top, I should be able to look down and see. Wait here," Salana instructed as she started to carefully crawl through the grass.

Corwin didn't wait, but followed right behind her.

Taylee, not wanting to let her brother outshine her, followed behind him, knowing that if she went, Tray'o would also come.

To her surprise, he did not follow.

"I said stay back!" Salana hissed over her shoulder.

"I want to see," Corwin said.

"Me too," Taylee agreed.

Salana growled, but didn't try to stop them. "Just stay low."

The three climbed the last bit of the path and before long were standing at the top of the hill.

The path widened out here, and the trees opened up to reveal a very large clearing at the base of the mountain. In the centre of the clearing was a long, wide, white structure that resembled a barn. It had a triangular roof, with a massive opening in the front where a wall should have been. Bright light was shining from inside and had to be where the low hum originated.

Just like Skyblind said.

"The Temple of the Holy Flame," Salana whispered.

I wonder if Syyris is in there? Taylee squinted her eyes and tried to see what was inside the building. But from that far away, she couldn't see anything more than the bright light coming from within.

"What are we waiting for?" Taylee asked as she started to stand, but just then, a harsh gust of wind blasted her back.

Taylee hit the ground hard and scrambled to hide with Salana and Corwin in the tall grass surrounding them. But even the tall blades of grass bent to the force of the wind.

No, this isn't wind. It's Syyris!

Without warning, trumpet, or fanfare, their god descended from the sky directly above them. His ensuing roar was so powerful that it caused her to cry out in pain and cover her ears with both hands, but no matter what she did, she couldn't block out the noise.

"It's too loud!" Taylee shouted at the top of her lungs, but even the sound of her voice was swallowed up by the deafening, holy roar.

Taylee forced open her eyes, which she didn't remember closing, and looked up to see Syyris, shining silver and green, complete with his translucent black halo. She watched in awe as he hovered directly overtop of them and glided effortlessly toward the temple.

The size of the Temple of the Holy Flame took on new significance for her as Syyris now appeared to be quite small while landing in front of its opening.

Why does the door need to be so big just for him? Taylee hoped that the thought wasn't blasphemous.

As soon as Syyris had landed, the painful roar started to die down as what had appeared before to be a translucent halo became solid, forming into four black swirling wings which gradually slowed to a stop.

Those are wings, not a halo! Taylee couldn't believe it. *Is that how he flies?*

"Do you think he saw us?"

Salana shook her head, but did not take her eyes away from their god.

I shouldn't have stood. She cursed her curiosity and hoped that he would understand.

Without a word, Salana jumped to her feet and ran at full speed toward the temple.

Taylee stood and was about to chase after her when Corwin grabbed her arm.

"Wait! We don't know what he will do and I won't put you in danger," Corwin insisted as he tried to hold her back.

"What do you mean? Let me go!"

"No. Give me the necklace and I'll appeal for Uncle Jael."

"What? No. Corwin, I have to do this!" She struggled to get free.

"I activated the Nightwolf necklace," Corwin insisted. "Uncle Jael got sick because of what *I* did. This is my responsibility."

As she looked into her brother's eyes, she felt as though time suddenly stood still; guilt washed over her, and as much as she wanted to let Corwin go and take all the blame, she knew she had to confess.

"It wasn't you," she said in a near whisper.

"What?" Corwin's grip on her lessened. "What are you talking about?"

Here we go ...

"Back at home. It was me. I opened the present while you and

Uncle Jael were with the sheep. I was the first to activate it, not you," she admitted.

"I don't understand …"

"I didn't want to get in trouble with Uncle, so I rewrapped it and allowed you to pull it out of the box, knowing it would light up and you'd immediately want to confess. I thought you could take the blame and I could get some answers."

Corwin was visibly stunned as the realisation of her deception washed over him.

"All this time … you let me feel the weight of causing Uncle Jael's sickness, when you were the one who first activated the relic?"

"I didn't know he would get sick." She looked away. "I just thought Uncle Jael would scold me for taking the box but punish you for using the relic. And anyway, I would have told you sooner, but we got separated, and …"

Corwin released his grip. Taylee had never seen her brother so hurt.

I can't look at him.

"I'm sorry," she apologized, and, without another word, turned to chase after Salana.

Blood pumped loudly in her ears as Taylee came closer and closer to their mysterious god. As she ran, she questioned why she had chosen now to confess. She could have stayed quiet and let Corwin tell Syyris. Up until arriving here, she hadn't really seen a problem with letting him think it was his fault.

But Syyris would know, and so would I.

Maybe honesty was what was needed to allow their uncle to be healed? Taylee wasn't sure of anything, but, like Salana, she believed that Syyris was a god of justice. Ultimately, she believed, as long as they brought him the relic, he wouldn't allow their uncle to suffer for her actions.

The guilt she didn't realise she'd been suppressing continued to plague her mind, only causing her to run harder, and she soon caught up to Salana.

Corwin had always been fast, though, and as they approached

the temple, he caught up and was running beside her.

"Taylee!" He panted her name. There was anger in his eyes, but also something she couldn't quite identify.

"I said I was sorry," Taylee answered as they slowed a few feet from where Syyris had landed.

"Listen!" His voice was stern. "We both activated that relic, it doesn't matter who did it first. You're my sister. We're in this together."

He doesn't hate me. She didn't know why it was such a surprise; Corwin was always a loving and forgiving person. But, even still, hearing him say that they were going to figure things out together caused a lot of the guilt she now felt to fade away. *I don't deserve such a good brother.*

"Thanks." Taylee smiled gratefully at him and then, together, they turned to face their god.

Salana was a few feet ahead of them and was boldly approaching Syyris. Although he must have spotted them when he flew overhead, his back was to them all.

His wings were still rotating slightly, with a *thwump, thwump, thwump*, but his terrible roar had finished, and the only sound he made was a soft, high-pitched hum.

"Syyris Sagrado, god of my fathers! Forgive this intrusion! We have traveled a long way to speak with you! I promise you, we are honourable and come here with humble hearts!" Salana said with her hands raised in the air.

Syyris was unmoving, and so Salana carefully made her way around him to look in his face.

Why is he so still? Does he not see us? Or care?

"My Queen! Be careful!" Akoro hollered as he and Tray'o came running from the path quite a distance away.

"My name is Salana E'monton. I am the Daughter of Temchar, the former King of Anaciencia. I know we have broken your law by coming here, but we come with a warning of great danger."

Taylee watched in awe.

He seems so mild up close.

And then Syyris shouted.

Chapter Thirty-Three — The God with Too Many Faces

"Those who love darkness have much to hide, but Syyris is a god of Light; he has nothing to hide."

—ELDER JERAMEE, A.P. 6
HISTORICAL LAWS OF THE FIRST ELDER ORDER

Corwin covered his ears as a high-pitched scream burst out from Syyris; hot air and wind blasted over all of them, causing both him and Taylee to stumble back a few feet. But Salana stood much closer than they did, and when Syyris screamed, she was knocked to the ground.

No!

"Wait!"

Corwin lunged forward and, without thinking, stepped in between Syyris and Salana. "Mercy! Please!"

If he didn't want to listen to Salana, what chance have I got? the voice of logic shouted at him, but it was too late to turn back. Here, in this moment, Corwin was standing at the feet of his god.

Hear me, please. Have mercy on us! he prayed in his mind.

Corwin wasn't really sure what was going to happen next, and in the silence that followed, he half-expected Syyris to obliterate him on the spot.

But Syyris didn't do anything; he just stared with his giant, bulging black eye—unmoving and unspeaking—until, all at once, something in his face shifted.

It was subtle, barely noticeable, like a twitch or a hiccup. But then, right before their eyes, everything changed.

Corwin watched in horror as the entire face of Syyris—eye included—split open from the bottom and lifted up.

It was so startling and confusing that Corwin lost all ability to move or speak; the very face of their god came apart and opened to reveal his sparkling insides.

What's happening?

Corwin couldn't believe what he was seeing as an armoured man climbed out from what appeared to be the very brain of Syyris.

He was the same size as a regular man, but his face was masked by a helmet with slick black tubes that jutted out of it and connected to various points on his shiny, armoured chest.

He almost looks like a Locura.

The man pivoted and leaned against the body of Syyris.

"Who are you?" His voice, while violent and deep, came out muffled and cold, almost like someone speaking with their hands over their mouth.

Salana stood and tilted her head. "Are you … Syyris?"

The man—if he was a man—laughed in a condescending way before stepping forward and reaching for something at his side. The object was solid black, with a square-shaped handle perfectly fitted for him and a long, rounded piece that pointed a few inches past the end of his hand.

Some sort of relic? None of this made any sense. *Why would a man who was inside of Syyris need a relic?*

Corwin wasn't sure if he was more curious or afraid, but before he could decide, or see the function of the relic, Akoro ran up to the man and tackled him to the ground.

The black object went flying from his hand and slid several feet away.

"Akoro! Stop!" Salana shouted.

Akoro, upon hearing her command, released his hold and climbed off the man, who now lay motionless on the ground. "Apologies. I thought he meant to do you harm."

"He may have …" Corwin admitted. *What happened to Syyris?*

"Did you see it?" Taylee asked Akoro. "The face of Syyris opened and this man stepped out. Do you think … Could this be the true form of Syyris?"

Salana pursed her lips together and cautiously approached the motionless, armoured man. Corwin suspected he'd been knocked unconscious by Akoro in the fall.

Could it actually be possible? Is Syyris a human?

"This isn't right …" Tray'o said quietly as he walked up and past the shell of what they believed to be the body of Syyris and straight through the massive temple door.

As much as Corwin wanted there to be a simple explanation for this, everything felt wrong, and his stomach twisted into painful knots as he struggled to comprehend what had just happened.

The sacred sky-beast was completely still; his face was still split open and his wings were unmoving. He no longer seemed so glorious.

Or threatening.

"I don't understand." Salana crossed her arms in frustration.

No one answered her, as they all looked helplessly from the armoured man to the sky-beast.

"Uh, guys? You need to see this," Tray'o called from within the temple.

The group turned their attention toward him and, rather reluctantly, left Syyris.

"I don't believe it," Salana gasped. They stepped through the doorway and under the beam of massive, Essence-powered torches that were affixed to the ceiling.

Impossible.

There were no interior walls or rooms inside the massive Temple of the Holy Flame; it was simply one giant room, filled from end to end with what looked like copies of Syyris Sagrado, carefully lined up row upon row. Some were green while others were black, and a few were covered by tarps. But they all had the same solid black eye, the same shape, and the same razor-sharp wings—

though many were cracked, covered in mud or dust, and even seemed to be missing parts.

"Syyris Sagrado is one ..." Corwin repeated the words of the holy prayer.

"Clearly that writer never visited this temple," Tray'o said.

Taylee gasped at the sight of them and instinctively dropped to her knees. "A chamber of gods?"

"More like a chamber of ghosts." Corwin approached one and very carefully extended his hand. As he expected, there was no reaction when he pressed his fingers against its side and felt the cold, steel skin of what was supposed to be a living, breathing god.

Cold, hard, and lifeless.

"What are they?"

"Relics." Salana was visibly stunned. "There's no other explanation ... Ellian was right."

The shock of seeing all these versions of what they had once believed to be one god was more that Corwin could bear.

How could I have been so foolish? Corwin sat down right in the middle of the temple and put his head between his knees to try and keep himself under control. *Logan told me Syyris could save Uncle Jael. Logan—the man has lied to us since we were kids! How could I have believed him? He knew about this—as a former Elder, he must have! And he used our desire to help get him here.*

"This doesn't make any sense." Tray'o moved from one Syyris to another. "I saw him fly. I saw his power for myself!"

"We all did," Salana said, "a few minutes ago."

A flying relic—that's all he is.

As much as he didn't want to admit it, the evidence was right in front of him.

Uncle Jael will never be well again.

The weight of this revelation was too much, and Corwin was flooded with a sense of overwhelming hopelessness.

"No," Tray'o snapped. "Before. I saw him before, in the garden. He was real."

Salana pursed her lips together. "Apparently not."

Tray'o said nothing in response.

What is there to say? All our lives we've worshipped a lie.

"So … what? Is this supposed to mean there is no god …?" Taylee sounded as confused as Corwin felt.

"It appears we have been deceived," Akoro replied stiffly after another long and painful silence.

The Essence-powered lights buzzed in reply, and although they made the temple quite warm, Corwin's body felt chilled and numb.

"So what about this then?" Taylee pulled out the Nightwolf necklace. "If there's no Syyris, then there's no Plyyston either, right? So how did this relic make Uncle Jael sick?"

Corwin could hardly keep his hands from shaking. His throat constricted, and he struggled to say anything at all.

"I don't think it ever did." He tried to swallow but couldn't. "Whatever happened … Logan did it."

He knew it in his gut.

The words seemed to hit Taylee hard, and she clenched the necklace tightly. Then, she let out an angry scream as she spun around and threw the necklace as hard as she could at the first Syyris.

Corwin watched the necklace soar through the air and then break apart against the side of the thing they had once worshipped; it fell to the floor in pieces.

It was all so strange. Both Syyris and the necklace had seemed to have so much power over his life just moments ago. Now they were only empty, meaningless objects, sitting abandoned in a room.

That was when he glanced toward the entrance and noticed the armoured man was no longer lying on the floor.

"That man is gone!" Akoro exclaimed as he also realised it.

"Does it matter?" Corwin mumbled.

The man was probably just another puppet who could make a relic turn on. The difference was that he at least knew what he was.

"He could warn the Elders that we are here." Akoro turned to Salana. "My Queen, you are not safe."

Salana stared blankly at Akoro, then let out a strange and unexpected laugh that echoed all across the temple and caused the hairs on Corwin's arm to stand on end.

"Syyris is a lie, Akoro," she said after her laughter ended and she caught her breath. "None of us will ever be safe again."

Her words should have scared him, but in that moment, Corwin couldn't feel anything at all.

Everything is meaningless, he realised dimly. *No creator, no god to rule, no law or justice or good or evil. Nothing but magic and games played by those who want to control others.*

"Salana, listen to me." Akoro grabbed her by the shoulders and held her tight. "We have come too far to give up now. You are a queen, and the Kingdom needs you."

"He's right," Taylee agreed. "We can probably still catch up to Skyblind. Maybe we can help him."

"Help him do what?" Salana's voice was distant. "Stop Logan? Are we so sure that him using the Orb is a bad thing?"

Taylee gawked at her. "What are you saying …? Logan lied to us!"

"So did the Elders. But it seems to me that they are the bigger evil here. If Logan's Orb takes them out, then this might be the exact thing Anaciencia needs."

"A strong queen is what the Kingdom needs," Akoro insisted. "You can still be that, even without Syyris. The people will rally to you once you tell them about this."

"The way they rallied around Prince Ellian when he told them his revelations?"

"He was a child then, thought to be mad with the Locura curse. But you are loved by the people."

"For now. People turn with unpopular thoughts. And telling them they've worshipped a relic will be very unpopular."

As much as they all knew it was true, the words were still painful to hear.

"So you would hand your father's kingdom over to the Elders—and the Kaag'ari!—without a fight?" Akoro exclaimed.

Salana averted her eyes.

"If the Elders are powerful enough to control relics of this size and magnitude, I'm not sure we could ever hope to win in a fight against them."

"True, indeed!" a familiar voice sang.

They'd all been so distracted by their recent discovery in the temple that no one had noticed as the entrance became surrounded by Kaag'ari knights.

Him again. Great. Corwin frowned as he caught sight of Lord Daraak. He wore the same green plated armour and looked as goofy as ever, though the bounce to his hair seemed somewhat more restrained, and on his right hand he wore a single silver gauntlet, which shimmered in the glow of the lights above.

And, there was something else that was different. Corwin noticed right away that Lord Daraak was wearing some sort of black chain necklace that wrapped around his neck and split into two points that connected straight to his ears. In fact, all the soldiers were wearing one. They were the strangest looking necklaces he'd ever seen, but there was no time to contemplate their purpose, because as soon as Lord Daraak entered the temple, he was followed immediately by an old friend.

"Sparrow?" Tray'o took a step toward her, but stopped when the knights raised their weapons.

"It's nothing personal." Sparrow's voice was sad. "We had a deal, remember?"

She led them to us. All for a title and a prime spot among the Elites, Corwin realised, though after what they'd just witnessed, her betrayal barely seemed to matter.

"Don't be angry with the girl," the voice of Lord Daraak sang with an irritating lilt. "She only did what was best for the Kingdom in leading me to my bride. I've been searching everywhere for you, sweet one, though I never expected to find you here." He grinned at Salana.

Although he knew Lord Daraak would never have Salana's heart, Corwin felt a pang of jealousy at the sight of him.

“The Elders brought you here?” Salana didn’t even try to mask her incredulous tone.

“Of course! Just one of the many privileges of obedience. A trait I look forward to teaching you,” Lord Daraak cooed as he reached out his hand to stroke her face.

Salana swatted his hand away and spat in his direction. “Unless you’re looking to lose a hand, I’d suggest keeping your distance.”

Her aggressive response caused Lord Daraak to giggle melodically. “How can a woman as beautiful as you be so graceless? Submit to me, my love, and perhaps the Elders will forgive your rebellious behaviours.”

Akoro let a deep growl bubble in his throat. “The throne will never pass to a Kaag’ari.”

Lord Daraak threw his head back and let out the loudest and most guttural laugh Corwin had ever heard. “Do you honestly think she has a choice in the matter?” He turned his attention back to Salana. “But I must say, I am grateful you ran off when you did. After your little stunt with freeing Skyblind, Elder Kaine felt it was time to reward my service with some proper education and enlightenment. You see, he is tired of having an ignorant king like your father. I’m afraid that the reign of the E’monton clan is at an end.” Lord Daraak boldly grabbed her by the arm.

Without warning, Akoro lunged forward and violently slammed his fist into the Lord Daraak’s jaw, knocking loose a handful of bloody teeth.

After that, everything was a blur as the knights rushed on them and forcibly shoved them to the ground.

Corwin tried to resist at first, but his efforts only merited a hard kick to the stomach.

“Akoro, stop!” Salana ordered her faithful knight, who was in the process of being restrained by five men. “It’s over.”

“No!” He struggled to shake the men off his back, but there were too many, and before long, they had him down on his knees at the feet of Lord Daraak.

"Such loyalty should be rewarded. Perhaps there will be a place for you in my kingdom yet. But, until then ..." Lord Daraak raised his gauntleted fist and slapped Akoro across the face. All the strength flooded out of him, and Akoro dropped unconscious.

"Take him to the holding cells. Bring the others with me," Lord Daraak ordered his men. It was a struggle, but the knights that brought Akoro down picked him up and started to carry his body out of the temple.

"Wait! You promised you wouldn't hurt them," Sparrow said as one of the knights forced Corwin and the others to their feet and marched them out.

"As long as they obey they will not be harmed by me. As for the Elders, who can say what they might do?" Lord Daraak's grin looked all the more mischievous with a few missing teeth.

It's unlikely they're going to have mercy on us. Maybe Salana is right. Logan might actually be our only hope now.

But after what Logan did to Uncle Jael, the thought of his help was of little comfort.

Is good only an illusion as well? Is our world full of nothing but evil men fighting for control?

Corwin had never felt so depressed in his life, which made it easy for Lord Daraak and his soldiers to march him and the others back to the trail and down the hill with little resistance. It seemed everyone was in a discouraged state since discovering that Syyris was just a relic.

In fact, it made Corwin suspicious that Lord Daraak wasn't as happy with the revelation about Syyris as he claimed to be, and observed that the man moved differently than he had before. He didn't stroll or glide, but held his body in a more rigid way and took short, deliberate steps. It may just have been the terrain, the crack to his jaw, or the regal feeling of the idea that he would soon be a king. But, whatever the reason, he did not quite seem like himself.

Sparrow also seemed different, and kept her eyes locked straight ahead. He tried to get her attention at one point, but she refused to look back.

She must feel guilty for betraying us, Corwin thought, but it was little consolation. Up until now, he'd considered her a sort of friend.

They walked back down the hill and through the jungle for about half an hour without speaking a word until they came to a fork in the path. The knights who carried Akoro turned down the left side, while Lord Daraak and the remaining knights marched Corwin and his friends down the right.

Sparrow, who hadn't said a word since the Temple of the Holy Flame, turned down to the left to follow after Akoro, but looked over her shoulder briefly and made eye contact with Corwin.

She's trying to tell me something, Corwin realised as he looked into her wide eyes. *But what?*

Whatever message she was trying to convey, Corwin could not understand it, and she looked away and spoke to Lord Daraak. "I'm going to go with them in case he wakes up and tries to make trouble."

"Fine," Lord Daraak sounded disinterested. "Once he is secure, come find me and we'll speak about your reward."

Sparrow bowed her head and disappeared down the trail.

Maybe she means to help us after all?

"Where are they taking him?" Salana demanded.

"Don't be concerned. I would never destroy such a valuable asset, even one who dares strike the future king …" Lord Daraak said.

Salana sneered, but kept the comments she was clearly thinking to herself.

They followed the path for several more minutes before at last coming to the end.

Stepping out of the jungle, they stood at the base of what could only be the Academy. It was a tall building, about 60 feet high, completely square, and made of black, windowless steel. Compared to all the grandeur of Lightspire—or even Pinehouse Castle—Corwin was surprised by how plain and unadorned this building was.

It looks like a giant box.

"This is the Academy?" Tray'o arched an eyebrow.

"Behold, the glorious gem of the Earth." Lord Daraak sounded genuinely impressed. "Before we enter, you need to see with treated eyes. You're now going to put on—arg!" Before he could finish his sentence, he and the rest of his knights dropped to their knees and covered their ears with their hands.

"What's happening?" Taylee asked as their captors fell and writhed on the ground in agony.

"It must be Logan …" Salana suddenly sounded hopeful. "Come on!" She exclaimed as she darted around the Academy.

Corwin and the others eagerly left the Kaag'ari knights and followed Salana around the building. But once they got to the other side, they realised that there was no door or any visible opening there either, so they ran around to the back of the building.

Still, no door.

"Now what?" Taylee asked as they circled all the way around the Academy and could still find no way inside.

Corwin felt a pang of fear when he realised that Lord Daraak and his men were missing.

They must have woken up. They'll be searching for us. We have to hide!

"This must be some sort of trick. There has to be a way in," Salana started to say, when all of a sudden, she let out a yelp of pain and dropped to the ground, followed immediately by Tray'o.

Corwin spun around and saw Lord Daraak standing behind them.

He was surprised to see that he and the knights were holding the same black objects that the armoured man had when he exited the body of Syyris. It looked like some type of Essence-powered crossbow, but before Corwin could do anything to defend himself, one of the soldiers shot him with his.

The bolt struck him in the chest, and Corwin immediately fell to the ground as the pain of hot fire surged through his entire body and completely paralysed his arms and legs. He began to thrash about violently.

"Wait! Listen to me, you hav—" Before Taylee could finish, she too was shot and knocked to the ground.

Chapter Thirty-Four — The Song of Ancients

"Deception: A sin, indeed, but sometimes a necessary one."

—ELDER RHAMSEY, A.P. 230
THE NINE SINS OF NIGHT

"I'm getting really tired of being knocked unconscious," Tray'o grunted as he forced his eyes open.

Much to his surprise, he was lying in the middle of a beautiful, grassy field. It was soft, lush, and a near-blinding vibrant green. Clusters of massive trees erupted with puffy, pink blossoms to his left and were scattered across the many rolling hills in the distance, while tall, dark, snow-tipped mountains lay to his right. But even though it was beautiful here, there was something about the sky that looked strange. It seemed to be somewhat distorted, and took on a faded, bluish-purple hue. The strangest thing of all though, was how the typically low-hanging, red-orange sun now shone golden and hung directly overhead.

The sun doesn't ever get that high.

"Isn't it incredible?" the tender voice of Taylee asked.

Tray'o rolled over and realised for the first time since waking that he wasn't alone. Taylee lay next to him, and his heart pounded faster in his chest at the sight of her.

Keep yourself until control, he scolded himself as he recalled the awkwardness of her rejection.

"Something's not right." The voice of Corwin boomed out from a slight distance away.

Tray'o turned his gaze from the only girl he'd ever loved and noticed Corwin striding toward them. His rugged features were strangely accented by the luminous golden sun, and even though his best friend was walking over with a frown, Tray'o felt completely calm.

"What do you mean?" As Tray'o spoke, he discovered that even the sound of his voice was altered; it seemed to be being absorbed into the air.

"We're trapped in this field by some sort of invisible wall," Corwin explained. "I tried walking toward those trees but no matter what I do I keep hitting something. It's surrounding us on all sides. We're trapped here."

I could think of worse places to be trapped, Tray'o thought with an unavoidable smirk as he redirected his gaze back at Taylee. He was entranced by the way her soft, brown hair was blowing gently in the breeze.

"I can't remember anything after we were attacked," she said as she nervously bit her lower lip.

Attacked? Tray'o vaguely remembered trying to get inside the Academy, and then some excruciating pain. But it was too beautiful here to think about anything negative, and so he shut his eyes and allowed the sweeping, sweet fragrance of the distant trees to fill his lungs.

In and out.

In and out.

Each breath, though long and heavy, felt as refreshing to his spirit as the very presence of Taylee by his side.

The three remained together in the field for an unknown amount of time, trapped within the confines of their invisible cage. Corwin was the only one who could not seem to relax though, and continued to pace around and try and find some way out.

Tray'o cared very little about some solid, invisible wall, and chose instead to rest in this paradise. But no matter how hard he tried to enjoy his surroundings, he couldn't keep negative thoughts from creeping in.

She doesn't love you, a voice in his head reminded him.

Tray'o rolled over and tried to shut it out, but the weight of those words hung heavy on his heart.

"Do you think this place is fake?" Taylee asked. "Like Syyris?"

"I don't know, and I don't care," Tray'o admitted as he sat up. "All that matters is that we're all together."

"I guess," Taylee sighed. "Ever since we found out about Syyris, everything just feels so … wrong. You know?"

"I know," Tray'o agreed, but not because of Syyris.

The moment he tried to take her hand, he felt like he'd lost a part of his soul.

She will never love you, the voice said again.

It pained him to think that he would never be able to share his world with her, not fully anyway. But this had always been the case. Even at Pinehouse, Taylee only took a passing interest in his life. Whatever she wanted, it didn't seem to be something that Tray'o could give her.

But is that true? Could that ever change? The thought was maddening, and even though he knew he shouldn't ask, he couldn't resist.

"Taylee, about what happened earlier …" he started to say, but then let his voice trail off when he saw the sadness in her eyes.

She's looking at me like I'm a wounded bird. He hated that.

"I don't want to make things awkward, Tray. I mean … we're friends."

Although Corwin was technically within earshot, he was thankfully too focused on finding a way past the invisible walls to pay attention to their conversation. Even still, Tray'o chose to keep his voice quiet as they talked.

"Right, I know that. I'm just wondering … do you think we could ever be more than that?"

Taylee averted her eyes. "I don't know. I just … I want to be friends."

"Right. Me too," he lied. "But, I mean, maybe in the future …"

"You're a good man, Tray," she replied, her tone gentle, but cautious. "I really appreciate you, but … I just don't think I can give you what you want."

Her words made absolutely no sense.

"Sorry, but I have to disagree," he smirked. "You're everything I've ever wanted in a wife, and much, much more."

Taylee sighed and looked off toward the distant mountains. "But Tray'o, that's not the way I feel about you. Please don't be hurt."

Of course I'm hurt. What kind of statement is that? he thought, but said, "I get it. I just want you to be happy."

"Thanks." Taylee picked at a blade of grass. "Staying my friend makes me happy."

Friend.

How could such a good word cut so deeply?

Friend is not lover.

It was hard to hear, and all the walls he'd built around the idea of marrying Taylee came crashing down all around him.

No problem, he reasoned. *She'll change her mind once things calm down a bit and we get back to normal.*

But as much as he wanted to believe it was true, he knew deep inside she was never going to change her mind.

"Yeah, that's fine." He struggled to sound casual. "I just thought it was important for you to know where I was at."

Taylee smiled weakly. "Well, I mean, I've always kind of known …"

Tray'o tried to swallow the lump that was forming in his throat. "You have?"

"Yeah."

"Great."

"It's not a big deal," Taylee shrugged.

Maybe not to you.

For years, he could think of nothing other than making Taylee his wife. She was the most important person in the world to him, and he'd do anything for her.

Just stay positive. Girls hate it when a guy sulks.

"Well anyway, if you ever change your mind, just know I'll be around!" he said with a wink.

Taylee forced a smile.

"Thanks, but ... I don't want to give you any false hope. I don't think I'll ever change my mind."

The conversation died after that, and was replaced with an uncomfortable air of awkwardness that lasted far longer than Tray'o had anticipated.

You should never have brought it up. He cursed his desire to know her thoughts.

Just as Tray'o decided to lie back down and try to relax, a blinding white light flashed across the sky and broke silence.

Completely startled, Tray'o sat up and saw Salana standing in the field.

Her hair glowed both black and blonde once again and shimmered in the bright, golden sun. She was dressed in an intricate royal blue dress trimmed with white pearl and cut in such a way as to accent a stunning necklace, a twisted, shiny black chain connected to a small white box that dangled gently across her chest. It took Tray'o a second to realise that the chain wound all the way up her neck and ended in two points lodged firmly in her ears.

Lord Daraak and his soldiers wore this too, he vaguely remembered.

"Are you finding the setting to your liking?" she asked in a voice as cool as the breeze.

Corwin, who seemed the most startled by her abrupt appearance, regarded her cautiously. "What is that chain?"

Salana smiled gently and glided over to him. While her face looked the same, Tray'o couldn't shake the feeling that something more than just the chain and her regal clothing were different.

It's her eyes, he soon concluded. They were glossy, placid, and lifeless.

"Do not fear. You are safe. Are you pleased with your surroundings?" she asked again. This time her voice took on a strange, melodic tone and rang through the air.

"It's very lovely here," Taylee admitted.

"Good. The Elder King thought you would like it." Salana giggled.

Have I ever heard her giggle before?

"The who? I thought all the Elders were equal," Corwin asked and took a step back.

Salana grinned.

"Do not worry about that now. There will be time for questions later. Please, follow me. Oh, and do not be afraid when this world fades." She turned her back to them and glided toward the spot where Corwin had marked the invisible wall.

"There's a wall—" Tray'o started to say, when all at once the vibrant colours of the field drained into the earth. Before he had a chance to blink, the invisible walls became visible, solid stone, and the beautiful world was gone. They were now standing on hard stone in the centre of a black and grey room.

"What happened?" Taylee gasped.

Where the beautiful sky had been, now hung spinning blades in black iron cages.

"I said do not fear. I simply removed the illusion. Take these," Salana stated flatly as she handed each of them a twisted black chain that was identical to the one she wore.

Sensing their confusion, Salana gave them a reassuring smile. "These will help you to be at peace. Place the ends in your ears now. Trust me, no harm will come to you when you wear these."

Tray'o watched skeptically as Taylee examined the bulbous ends and then lifted them up to her ears.

"What? It's Salana. We can trust her," Taylee stated as she slipped them into her ears. Almost as soon as she did, she let out a sudden gasp, and her mouth dropped half-open in awe. "It's … incredible! Do you hear that?"

"They can't hear it until they wear the chain. Please, go on." Salana waited patiently.

Corwin and Tray'o exchanged nervous glances before wrapping their black chains around their necks and placing the ends in their ears.

Much to his surprise, Tray'o found that the ends fit quite comfortably. He didn't hear anything unusual at first, but gradually, he became aware of a sweet humming.

The sound warbled as it rang lightly in his ears, washing over his body and to the inner parts of his consciousness. Rising and falling, a gentle and peaceful flute played melodically as a deep, repetitive drumming vibrated through his whole body. Tray'o could feel his heart beat through his fingertips, and his eyelids felt unusually heavy.

"I feel … safe," Tray'o whispered as the sweet, euphoric humming evolved to include sweeping horns and gently-plucked stringed instruments. It was a form of music so strange and foreign that Tray'o wondered how it was possible he could have lived his whole life and never heard anything like this. It was calming, and caused him to feel as though his whole body were weightless, floating aimlessly down a river of light and beauty where all his previous feelings of disappointment and frustration were washed away.

"Benaural, the Song of Ancients," Salana said. "But we must go. You are expected, and we cannot keep the Elder King waiting," she explained, walking over to a door that seemed to dissolve as she approached it.

The sight would probably have startled Tray'o before, but with the continuous and relaxing music flowing through his ears, nothing seemed unusual anymore. He and his two friends followed Salana obediently down a long, wide hallway.

As they walked, Tray'o noticed some people pass them in the hall. They all wore the same black chains around their necks, and because of it, he felt a certain unspoken kinship with them as they drifted by.

They walked and walked for quite some time before finally arriving at a large, bronze door. Standing in front of it were two of Daraak's green knights.

“Queen Salana. The Elder King awaits,” one of the knights said as they stepped aside.

“Thank you,” she said as she waited for the large door to vanish.

Or did it just slide into the wall? It happened so fast Tray’o couldn’t quite tell. But it didn’t matter. Salana seemed to know what was happening, and she hadn’t led them wrong before, so he shrugged aside any hesitation and obediently followed her through the doorway and into an enormous, sparkling chamber.

As Tray’o looked up, he realised that the sparkling was due to a high, vaulted ceiling that was formed entirely of bright white dots, twinkling down from above.

Those are stars … but how can it be Night already?!

The walls themselves seemed to be made of smooth, solid, black rock, while the seven white marble pillars that filled the room appeared more decorative than functional, as they did not reach all the way to the ceiling.

In the centre of the room—elevated on a crystal pedestal at least ten feet tall—stood a vaguely familiar, middle-aged man. His eyes were golden and his hair was like fire, and he wore flowing, black robes that draped over the ends of the pedestal.

The man glanced down at them with a smile as the pedestal slowly sank into the ground, making him level with the group on the floor.

“I’m glad to see you are now all connected by the chains. Do you enjoy Benaural? How does it feel to hear the Song of Ancients?” The man gingerly strolled toward Taylee, his eyes alive and inviting.

She lowered her head submissively and looked down at her toes. “It feels wonderful, Elder King,” she answered timidly.

The man was silent for a second before breaking out in a heartfelt laugh. With one hand, he reached out to touch Taylee gently on the chin and direct her gaze to his eyes.

“No need for formalities here. That was *their* game. We are all family now. You may call me by my true name,” he said to all of them.

Tray'o thought he should feel jealousy or something by the way that this man touched Taylee, but for some reason he couldn't feel anything but calm.

"Forgive me. But I don't know your name."

The man laughed. "I am Logan Rome, formerly the Elder of Knowledge. But now, I am the Elder King."

Logan. Tray'o tried to recall where he had heard that name before. It was somewhere in the desert, with his friends. But the faces were blurry and unfamiliar, and the song in his ears washed the memory away.

"I know you …" Corwin said at length.

"Yes, you do. In the old world, I was known to you as Master Lunechair." Logan grinned.

"But … you looked …"

"Older? Yes, well, that was a necessary deception to keep my identity secret. If the Elders had found me, our salvation would never have come," Logan spoke lightly.

Salvation? Tray'o thought, but said, "Did my father know who you were?"

"Of course he did," Logan grinned. "Rai'o helped protect me while I searched for a way to rescue the Orb. Little did I know that Corwin and Taylee were the answer to my problem all along."

"What does this have to do with them?" Tray'o asked abruptly.

Logan is dangerous, his inner voice reminded him.

But as soon as he thought it, the music in his head swelled, and Tray'o was hit by a wave of euphoric pleasure that replaced all former doubt.

"A valid question, my young friend. You see, Corwin and Taylee are the children of an old friend of mine, Rowyn Batale'ord."

At the mention of their father, Taylee tensed up. "But … you killed him."

Logan touched his hand to his chest and appeared genuinely offended by her accusation.

"I did no such thing!"

"Yes, you did," her voice was strained, but her eyes were

intense. "You killed his ghost!"

"That was not your father's ghost." Logan's smile was inviting and gentle. "It was a pre-recorded projection that he must have left to scare people away if they ever tried to steal the Orb. I know it's hard to understand, but that was not your father."

"So … if that wasn't his ghost then … is he still alive?" Taylee asked.

"I'm afraid I don't know the answer to that question. All this time, I'd assumed he was dead. But seeing as the lab was empty and he'd left a projection, it's quite possible that he is still alive, somewhere."

Still alive? It was a crazy thought. *I wonder if he would like me more than Jael does?* Tray'o wondered.

"You were friends?" Corwin asked after a brief pause.

"Yes, indeed, we were. Your father was a great man." Logan said. "Rowyn was the one who managed to restore some of the most intricate relics in this marvellous Academy. One could even say that it was he who found the solution to the greatest problem the Kingdom of Anaciencia has ever known."

Taylee's eyes grew wide with wonder. "What problem is that?"

She was captivated. They all were.

This man has our answers.

He is better than Syyris.

He is real.

Chapter Thirty-Five — The Problem with Scarcity

"Gambling is the worst possible way to earn Essence—unless you cheat."

—AALARDIN NEY'RK, A.P. 412
A TRADEMASTER'S GUIDE TO GOODS, GODS, AND GIRLS

Corwin didn't notice it right away, but sometime after they entered the room, the stars above their heads started to swirl. By the time he realised what was happening, they were all spinning together at such a rapid rate that he was immediately disoriented and had to grab one of the pillars to reduce his dizziness.

Then, all at once, the stars collided and exploded into a bright flash of blinding white light. The next thing he knew, the pillar had vanished, and they were back standing in the same grassy field where they first woke, with the only difference being that Logan was with them.

"What is this place?" Tray'o asked with a look of confusion on his face.

And how did we get here? Corwin was completely disoriented and spun around to try and gather his senses.

"Life was significantly different for our ancestors," Logan explained as he paced back and forth across the field. "A thousand years ago, when things were whole, this is how the world looked."

That makes sense. Corwin glanced up at the sun's high position in the sky. *This is before the sun was wounded.*

"Imagine living in this world, where green trees grew in abundance, creatures of various sizes covered the land, and there were more people than stars." As Logan spoke, the very ground they stood on shifted. Suddenly, they were no longer in a field, but standing in the heart of what looked like the Ancient City before it was destroyed. The towering buildings were no longer covered in vines or overgrowth, but were clean, bright, and reflected the sun's light, while scores of people walked freely all around them on the streets. At first, Corwin tried to get out of their way, but to his great surprise, the people walked right through them as if they weren't even there.

We're the ghosts here.

"There were powerful kingdoms, and kings in control of massive islands, religions, magic. Comfort was the cry of the people, and many fought and died to bring it about." Logan spread his arms out and breathed it all in as he spoke.

"Oh, the power these people wielded. True magic, unlike anything in our wildest imagination. They could create life—and take it—all in a matter of seconds. Hot or cold were environmental choices, and they even found ways to travel through space! Weapons were created that could wipe the planet clean of life eight times over. Some of the greatest minds walked the land, and endless knowledge was at the tips of their fingers."

Suddenly, the thriving city faded from view and was replaced with a dim, red glow.

Fire, Corwin realised.

"But they grew greedy, and as time passed they began to drain the Earth of all its resources." As Logan spoke, the fire leapt up and consumed a forest right before their eyes.

It's not real, Corwin reassured himself as he watched the fire spread.

"Once one resource ran out, they'd find a way to use another, until that one would run dry too. So much was taken, stripped, and robbed from the land that it started to fight back with natural disasters unlike anything we'd ever known."

As if to illustrate his point, the smoke from the fire suddenly swirled together and formed a frightening funnel that reached from sky to ground. As the funnel formed, several others appeared behind it, ripping trees from the soil as they raced across the horizon. Just when Corwin thought it couldn't get any worse, several cracks appeared and spread out across the surface of the sky, bringing with them bright flashes, loud rumblings, and chunks of flaming rock that came crashing to the Earth.

"Spinning torrents of rock and fire fell from the sky, while the very core of the Earth erupted, opening its mighty jaws and swallowing whole cities and civilisations. Yet still our ancestors continued to find ways to fuel their lusts."

Corwin watched helplessly as the largest rock he'd ever seen came hurdling straight at them. Taylee let out a yelp of fear as all of them—except for Logan and Salana—covered their faces in vain defence.

But as soon as the rock hit the ground, everything vanished again, and they were back in the Ancient City, only now it was black and burnt while dead bodies littered the streets.

"As the resources of the land became more and more limited, wars became frequent, and bigger and more destructive weapons were created. Economies crashed, and whole cities fell into anarchy. The land was in chaos, and a line was drawn between the three remaining kingdoms. Sides were taken, and the biggest war this planet had ever seen broke out. Hundreds of lives were lost every second, and no one seemed any closer to victory. The scarcity was too great, and mankind was virtually destroyed because of it."

Corwin knelt down and stared at the face of one of the dead bodies.

It's not real, he reminded himself, but still he couldn't keep from feeling sad at the sight of it all.

"How did humanity survive?" Taylee asked timidly.

Logan seemed to like the question, and he dramatically waved his hand in the air. The destroyed city faded away and was replaced with a beautiful, peaceful landscape once again, within which a group of men and women were in the process of building something. Corwin noticed right away that the sun hung low here, not high like in the other visions.

This is after the Purge.

"The survivors—not more than one hundred men and women—gathered together on the mainland of what we now know as Anaciencia. It was the only place left on the planet that was protected from the destruction, due to a magical, domed shield that encompasses the land. The survivors formed the Code of Anaciencia, by which they swore to give up their magic forever and live off what was left of the land as simply as possible. And their plan worked, for a time …"

Logan stopped moving and grinned in a most unusual way, but it didn't matter. Corwin was enraptured by the man and his tale of their history, even though some instinctual doubt produced sharp pains in his gut. A significant part of him was concerned and wanted to run away from Logan, but there was also something in the back of his mind that kept assuring him that Logan was in fact good and that there was nothing to fear.

"There is nothing to fear," Corwin found himself whispering softly.

"What happened next?" Taylee asked, her eyes wide with wonder.

Logan, who was visibly enjoying the telling of this story, twirled around and looked out at the land.

"A small group of former wizards decided that it would be foolish to eliminate the use of that great magic. Instead, they believed they could control it. So they moved across the waters and came to the Island. Here, the First Elder Order was formed."

The world around them shifted once again.

They now stood on the water itself, directly across from the Island. From where he stood, Corwin could see the Syyris' temple and the Academy, as well as a dock, which jutted out from the Island a few feet into the ocean.

"As time went on, they realised that as long as magic was used wisely, under the careful control of one group with a common vision, the ancient power wasn't dangerous at all, but rather, a valuable gift. As time passed, the Elder Order used some of the more powerful relics to invent the idea of Syyris, a mighty sky god."

Corwin and his friends watched in awe as Syyris Sagrado launched himself from the Island and soared high into the sky. Even though he knew Syyris was not a real god, he couldn't shake the wonder and awe he felt as he watched the mysterious relic fly.

"The people on the mainland had long since forgotten the old power, and when they saw the relic and what it could do, they fell into immediate submission. They have been under Elder protection and control ever since." Logan ended his speech as the image of Syyris hovered directly over his head.

"But you lied. That's … evil." The words sounded strained as they came out of Taylee's mouth, almost as though she had to struggle to say them.

"Evil? No, not at all." Logan's posture was open, but his tone was somewhat stern. "Is it evil for a father to impose rules on his child? Or, Corwin, is it wrong for a shepherd to keep his sheep inside a fence to protect them from danger?"

"No. It's not wrong."

"There, so you understand."

"So… " Taylee hesitated. "So, there really is no god then …?"

Logan laughed, and as he did, the image of Syyris and the rest of the world faded from existence. They were once again standing in the black room with the white pillars and the stars shining down on them.

"What is a god? One who provides protection, creates life, has control, and is all powerful? By those definitions, I am more a god to you than Syyris ever was." Logan stopped speaking for a minute to let that sink in. "Syyris was an image—a tool—used to keep our people safe. There is nothing to fear—this is how things have worked for hundreds of years."

Somehow, it all made sense.

"You mentioned a problem," Tray'o reminded him.

"Yes … well, my predecessors did a fine job of restoring the shape of the world. With control of the magic relics, the resources of this land began to replenish themselves naturally. But the sun was not as easy to control." Logan sighed.

The stars started to swirl above them once again, and Corwin noticed dark shadows of men and women lurking all around them.

"Darkfall has plagued us for centuries. As you know, it's a time when evil chooses to manifest itself. Since we gain our magic Essence from the sun, Night is hard on us all. With no sun, we have no power to fight."

Corwin felt a chill run down his spine, and he realised for the first time that he was grateful for the relaxing music.

I wish I'd had this chain my entire life, he thought wistfully.

"As the Elder of Knowledge, I did my best to protect our people using what little Essence we could store. But every six months, when the darkness falls, the Locura continue grow stronger while we grow weaker. This is our great problem." As the words left his mouth, the room became strangely quiet, except for the steady rhythm of the music racing through their ears.

A memory of the playground full of children briefly flashed before Corwin's eyes, but was quickly replaced with the very unnerving sight of the dark shadows looming all around them.

"Is that why Rowyn—I mean, my father—created the Orb?" Corwin asked as skeptically as he could manage. He wanted so badly to hate this man, but in his heart he felt nothing but respect.

"Rowyn, a most brilliant man, spent his entire life working on a solution, until at last, he found it. He came up with the idea to harvest a rare mineral on the mainland and use it to create an Orb of endless light, one that would be able to harness the power of the sun. This great power would eliminate our need for Essence, he explained, and would be enough to keep us warm and powered during Darkfall. He promised that for the first time since the Purge, we would have unlimited magical energy."

"But the Elders stopped you," Tray'o stated.

Logan wrinkled his nose. "Yes. They didn't see the scarcity of

Essence and sunlight as a problem. They liked using its lack to form the economy, create power struggles, and ultimately rule over our people. But I knew the truth. In my studies, I discovered that scarcity is what caused the Purge in the first place. Scarcity is what caused our ancestors to drain the planet of life; abundance is the only solution.

"In an attempt to keep up the illusion of unity, I voted against the project with the other Elders, but secretly funded Rowyn in his hidden lab in the Ancient City, where many of the necessary materials were in abundance. Things were going well, until the Locura caught wind of it. Before I knew what was happening, they put aside their masks and madness to make an alliance with the other Elders to stop Rowyn."

Corwin still found it so strange to hear his father named and spoken about as if he were anything but a shepherd. Up until now, when he thought of his father, he pictured a man similar to Uncle Jael.

I never expected he was someone who worked on the Island.

"Your father went missing, and I was to be executed for my part in funding the project. But I managed to escape—thanks to the help of Lord Rai'o—and remained hidden in Pinehouse Castle for years."

Condemned for trying to save the world. It didn't make sense. *How could the other Elders be so selfish?*

"Tell them the rest," Salana insisted. It was the first time she'd spoken since entering the room, and Corwin had almost forgotten she was even with them.

Almost.

"Without your father, I thought my dream of unlimited, free magic was lost forever." Logan cleared his throat, almost as if the very thought was causing him to get emotional. "The Orb was sealed away in his lab by some spell that only allowed him access. Why he chose to flee in the first place confused me for years. It wasn't until recently that it all started to make sense."

Logan stepped toward Taylee and then turned her head slightly to the left. Materialising out of thin air was a woman with similar hair and features to his sister. She wore a beautiful white gown, and looked at them with tenderness in her eyes.

Mother? Corwin was stunned; this was the last thing he was expecting to see.

"As a part of the initiation to the Academy, men and women were required to drink a potion that eliminated their ability to reproduce. This was done because the other Elders believed that having children would cause distraction from work. I never suspected that Rowyn could have found a way around this with his lab partner."

Taylee reached out her hand to try and touch the woman, but her fingers passed right through the image. "Our mother?"

A smile spread across Logan's face. "Indeed. The two of them fled the lab, but what happened after that is a mystery. Whatever he did, it was all for the purpose of allowing his pregnant love to escape."

Corwin could not take his eyes off her. Until this moment, he didn't think he would ever know anything about his mother and what she looked like.

"How did she get to Pinehouse?" Taylee asked.

"After I escaped from the Elders, I found her wandering the Borderlands. Together, we went to Rai'o for help. She died shortly after giving birth to you at Pinehouse. Sadly, she never told me what happened to Rowyn, and so we placed you under the care of her brother, Jael."

Corwin tensed at the mention of Uncle Jael. *How did I not think of him sooner?!*

"How do we heal him?" he demanded. "You said the necklace needed to be destroyed by Syyris, but Syyris is not real."

Logan sucked in air with his mouth and slowly let it slip out his nostrils as he formulated his next words. "I'm sorry, Corwin, but I needed you to believe there was hope in order for you to come with me. I never intended to deceive you for so long, but you must understand that for years I wrongly believed that there was no way to rescue the Orb. I'd never considered that it was possible for someone of Rowyn's lineage to gain access. When you two activated the necklace relic, I realised for the first time that you could likely open the door, and so I lied to you for the greater good of the Kingdom."

Corwin wanted to be angry, but for some reason it was impossible. As Logan spoke, all he felt was compassion and understanding.

It must have been so hard for him to not tell us the whole story.

"It must have been so hard for you not to tell us the whole story," Corwin echoed the voice in his head.

"Very," Logan agreed.

It made sense to Corwin, but for some reason Taylee was still resisting. "But, why lie? You could have told us the truth."

"It was too much for you at the time," Logan insisted. "You would have thought me insane if I'd told you Syyris was not real back then. I needed you to have hope and trust me if we were going to rescue the Orb. But now we have it, and if you are able to help me activate it, I strongly believe we can use the power within to find a cure for your uncle."

A cure. So there still is a way to save him.

Corwin looked away from Logan and focused on the image of his mother as it flickered under the light of the stars. She was beautiful, but in a different way than Salana. Her face was gentle, and she seemed like a happy person, but there was deep sorrow trapped behind her eyes.

I wonder if she would be proud of who we've become.

"Do you understand what I'm saying?" Logan stepped in front of the image of their mother, which had the unfortunate side effect of causing her to fade from existence. "Finding a cure for your uncle is just the beginning. As children of Rowyn, you can do so much more than just open doors and turn on a necklace; you may not see it yet, but you are Anaciencia's last hope for survival."

Chapter Thirty-Six — The Chains That Bind

"There can never be true peace in the world so long as greed exists."

—HECTOR THE HOLY, A.P. 730
<u>A TOME OF TRUTH</u>

You are Anaciencia's last hope for survival.

The words of Logan Rome echoed in her head as Taylee drifted down another winding corridor with Tray'o and one of the Academy guards. The guard had been ordered to escort them to their rooms, but—even though he was tall with bright blue hair and striking gold eyes—Taylee found him uninteresting and they did not speak to one another, which was probably for the best because after everything she'd learned from Logan, she couldn't seem to keep her thoughts focused.

Syyris Sagrado was a lie.

Uncle Jael may yet be healed.

The Elders are a group of evil men keeping us in poverty by restricting magic, but my father was not evil; he created a source of unlimited energy to save the world, and only we can activate it.

It was a lot to comprehend, yet Taylee felt completely at peace.

"Do you think Corwin will be okay?" she asked as they turned down another hall and continued to follow the guard.

"I guess so … I don't really know what to think," Tray'o admitted with a blank expression.

After Logan had explained to them the secret history of Anaciencia, Corwin volunteered to go with him to something called the Reaktor Room and, once there, to help figure out how to activate the Orb.

But before they left, Logan had insisted that Taylee and Tray'o remain together and in safety in case there were any problems when the Orb was activated. So they were now being escorted somewhere else.

What happened next took both Tray'o and Taylee by surprise.

Like a flash of lightning, Skyblind and Akoro burst through a side door and rushed the guard.

The guard barely had time to pull two short, curved swords from the sheaths on his back before the exiled prophet swung a long, thin staff at his head.

Crack!

Wood splintered in every direction as the guard crashed into a far wall.

He lay there stunned as his lip split open and the side of his blue hair started to turn red with blood.

Without any hesitation, Akoro reached out with his massive hands, grasped the guard by his shoulders, and repeatedly slammed his head against the wall.

Taylee was stunned by the brutality of it all, and stared wide-eyed at her friends.

Friends? No. These men are dangerous.

"What are you doing?" Tray'o demanded.

They are working against Logan!

The music pumped vigorously through her ears and Taylee felt a sudden spike of anger in her gut.

"We are here to help," Akoro stated gruffly.

"Help? We are not in trouble." Taylee felt the words fall dully off her tongue.

"I'm afraid that you are in more trouble than you're able to realise." Although Skyblind sounded sad, he looked furious.

I thought he was a good man?

That's when she noticed that the two men were not wearing the chain.

That explains it! They can't hear the music!

"Get back!" Tray'o shouted as he stepped between Taylee and Akoro. "Stay away from us. Help! Guards!"

Tray'o shouted at the top of his lungs until Akoro abruptly punched him in the gut. Her friend keeled over into a heap on the floor and gasped in an attempt to catch his breath.

"Stop!" Taylee had never felt so much fear. *I trusted you!*

"You have been tricked," Akoro firmly gripped her shoulder. "You must remove the chain from your ears."

"No!" Taylee pulled away from him. "I like the music."

"The music produced by the chain is crafted from a dark magic that is falsely colouring your view of things. Please, the longer you keep it in, the more it will consume your mind. You must remove it now!" Skyblind implored her.

He wouldn't hurt me. He couldn't. Taylee reminded herself of all the kind things Skyblind had done for her, and wondered if perhaps he was telling the truth.

No! He's lying. The chain is good!

"You're lying," Taylee repeated automatically. "The chain is good."

"Do you think so? Touch your ears and tell me if it still *feels* good."

Don't listen to him! her inner voice protested, but something about the passion in his voice caused her to doubt.

Maybe it wouldn't hurt to try? She cautiously raised her hands to her ears. But as soon as she touched the chain, hot pain seared through her fingers and she recoiled in shock.

"It hurts!"

"Yes. But to be free it must be removed," Akoro boomed.

Fear overtook her as a chorus of flutes and trumpets swelled all around her.

Taylee hid her face.

"No. Maybe later."

"There is no later." Skyblind's voice was strained. "You must remove it. Time is running short. Trust me, I have never deceived you before."

He's right. He hasn't ever deceived me, Taylee reminded herself despite the overwhelming ringing in her ears. She chewed her lower lip, reached up toward the chain, then immediately drew back her hand.

"I can't. It hurts too much. If it's so evil then take it out for me, please!"

"I wish I could. But since you're the one who put it in, only you can remove it. Hurry, before we attract more attention," Skyblind warned.

Taylee hesitantly touched her hands to her ears again, but as soon as she did, the stabbing pain returned. "I can't!"

"You must!" Skyblind's voice echoed through the halls, making Taylee feel small and insignificant.

He's trying to shame you. Don't let him!

Tray'o had finally caught his breath and bared his teeth in anger.

"Don't trust them," he sneered.

Taylee gave him a sideways glance and looked back at Skyblind as her eyes filled with tears. *If you take it out, you will die!* the voice hissed inside her head.

"How can I be sure that taking this out won't kill me?" Taylee asked.

"How can you be sure that if you leave it in it won't kill you? You felt the heat when you touched it, and you know it has the power to harm. Please, remove it now so we can save your brother!" Skyblind urged.

That caught her attention. "Corwin? Why? What's wrong with Corwin?"

"Stop stalling," Akoro boomed. "Take it out, and we will explain."

Taylee looked back and forth between the two men before taking a deep breath. The closer her hands got to her ears, the more inner pressure she felt building inside her head and the louder the music throbbed in response.

Taylee gasped. *How long have I not been breathing?* she thought as she filled her lungs with air. *This is a mistake!*

"Tray'o," Taylee squealed his name. "I can't do this without you."

Tray'o met her eye. "They're trying to kill us! Don't you see?"

Skyblind kept his gaze fixed on her as he spoke. "I promise, I will let no harm come to you. You must have faith." Something about the way he looked at her—with such love and urgency in his eyes—compelled Taylee to action.

"If it's a trick, and we die, at least we die together," she squeaked, her voice feeling foreign and unsteady.

Tray'o shook his head. "I won't let you die." He stood, but before he could do anything, he was grabbed from behind by Akoro and held tightly.

Tray'o fought and struggled to get free but Akoro was much bigger and kept a firm hold.

"Please, Taylee. Believe," Skyblind begged.

Believe. The word echoed in her mind amidst other cries of *Liar,* and *He wants to kill you!*

Grinding her teeth together, Taylee used every ounce of her will to stretch her fingers out as far as they could go and touch the ends of the chain. Extreme pain pulsed through her, and the inner pressure caused her ears to ache as though they were about to explode.

"You can do it, Taylee Medisto. You are strong. I believe in you," Skyblind reassured her.

That was all it took.

In one swift, determined motion, Taylee snatched the chain and ripped it out of her ears.

Blinding white light flashed behind her eyes.

Taylee fell.

The next thing she knew, she was on her knees, panting.

Her whole body felt cold and drained.

Tray'o was screaming.

He sounds … different.

Although she could hardly see through the tears that blurred her vision, she felt in her soul that everything was better.

"It's gone …" she whispered, hearing for the first time in hours complete and utter silence.

There was no music: no throbbing, pumping melody which seemed to drive her every thought. Now, there was only silence—and a dull longing in her heart to be connected to the song once again.

And, now that her mind was clear, she started to realise that things weren't as they had originally seemed. Where at first these halls seemed beautiful and bathed with glorious light, they now appeared dark, dreary, and void of life.

The thing that disturbed her the most, however, was how the blue-haired guard whom Akoro had seemingly beaten to death was actually unharmed and lying unconscious against the wall.

What other lies has this magic made me see?

Taylee threw the chain as far away from her as possible.

"Oh Tray! We've been deceived. We've been horribly deceived!" She buried her face into her hands and wailed.

Logan is a liar and a deceiver. How could I have been tricked by him again?

Skyblind kneeled next to her and placed a comforting hand on her back while Akoro spun Tray'o around.

"Your turn!"

Chapter Thirty-Seven — The Problem with Abundance

"The more you think you need, the less you'll be satisfied; anyone who tells you otherwise is a liar or a salesman— which is why the best salesmen are liars."

—LADY LYNDA Q'BEE, A.P. 646
<u>A WAVE OF WONDER</u>

I preferred the music, Tray'o thought glumly.

It had taken several minutes for Tray'o to calm down enough to remove the chain himself, and when he finally did, he collapsed in a heap next to Taylee.

"I feel awful," Tray'o murmured.

Akoro gripped his shoulders and pulled him back up to his feet. "You'll live."

Despite his best efforts, Tray'o could not seem to steady his legs. He felt as wobbly as if he'd been drinking for hours.

"Taylee, Tray'o, are you well enough to walk?" Skyblind asked compassionately as Taylee too struggled to regain her balance.

"I think so," she said.

"Good. We have much to do and very little time," he stated as he beckoned them to follow him down the dimly lit halls.

Tray'o couldn't believe how differently everything appeared now that he was free of the chain. Whatever magic was in that music, it had somehow kept him oblivious to the darkness of the halls and the foul stench that saturated the air.

How could we have been so deceived? Tray'o thought of Logan and his flashy smile.

"I'm glad you got free," Taylee said to Akoro. "I wasn't sure what was going to happen when those knights took you away."

Akoro kept his eyes locked straight ahead. "I did not free myself."

"What? You didn't?" Taylee inquired. "How did you get away?"

Akoro grunted, but gave no reply.

Maybe Skyblind saved him and he doesn't want to admit it? Tray'o mused.

After walking for several minutes down various corridors and hallways, they arrived at last at a black door covered with a series of numbers and an unreadable inscription.

"What's behind this door?" Taylee sounded apprehensive.

I guess that makes sense. We've been opening a lot of doors lately …

"Much has changed," Skyblind said as he knocked three times on the door. "Do not be afraid of what you're about to see."

After a brief moment, the door slipped into the wall and revealed Sparrow on the other side.

"About time!" she snapped

Tray'o narrowed his eyes when he saw her. "Wait, what is she doing here?"

"Relax, Pinehouse. I'm not going to bite you."

"She's safe. She freed me from the knights," Akoro admitted reluctantly. "Come, we don't have time to waste."

Safe, eh? We'll see about that. Tray'o couldn't help but feel skeptical. After what they'd been through with Logan and the chains, he resolved to never be deceived by anyone again.

The others moved past him and into the room without hesitation.

"Coming?" Sparrow asked impatiently.

If you betray us again, you're done, he tried to say by making his face as menacing as possible. It didn't seem to have any effect, though, because she just rolled her eyes and left him standing alone in the doorway.

As Tray'o stepped into the room, he was surprised to find it was filled with many of the same black boxes that were in the secret lab where Logan found the Orb. The only difference was that these ones were all stacked on top of one other against one wall. Each box contained a glowing, whitish-blue square in the centre with many red and green dots blinking to some unknown pattern along the frame.

More ancient relics, I guess.

But he didn't take time to examine the boxes too closely, because facing them were the two Dark Ones, Marlo and Roy, and a vaguely familiar old man in a robe beside whom Sparrow took her place.

The light from the boxes faintly illuminated the old man's weary face and outlined every wrinkle and scar. His hair was grey, his eyes dull, and his mouth curled upward in what could only be described as a cruel smile. But the most alarming part about him was the cut of his robe.

He's an Elder.

Somehow, Taylee recognized him right away, and she recoiled in alarm.

"That's Elder Kaine!"

The man glanced over his shoulder at her and grimaced.

He's wounded, Tray'o realised.

The Elder's shirt was stained red with blood and he was leaning on Sparrow for support.

"Don't worry. He's harmless," Marlo assured them with a grin.

Tray'o scratched the back of his head. *I thought the Elders were the bad guys.*

As he stepped deeper into the room, he realised that the glowing squares inside the black boxes were not just bright colours but actually various illuminated images.

There must be a hundred of these, he thought in awe as walked over and scanned the various pictures in the boxes. *There must be a picture of everything in the entire Kingdom here!*

In one he recognized the ruins of Krydor, and in another the courtyard of Pinehouse Castle. There were more images than locations he knew, and each box contained something different. It wasn't until he saw one showing Corwin and Salana walking through a corridor that he realised these were not actually still pictures, but rather pictures in motion.

"What are these? Magic portals?" Tray'o asked in awe as he reached out to touch one. As he did, his fingers came in contact with what felt like glass.

A hoarse laugh intermingled with coughs from the Elder was his reply.

"I don't understand," Taylee crossed her arms. "What's he doing here?"

"When we were separated, I led my group into the Academy and tried to warn the Elders about Logan and his Orb," Skyblind said, his voice thick with grief. "But they would not believe me, and called for the guards. By that point, Logan must have already hijacked the chain and used it for mind control, because the guards turned on the Elders and slaughtered them all. We tried to help, but we were unprepared. Elder Kaine was the only one we could save, and he brought us here to hide."

All the Elders—except for Kaine—are dead? It was hard to believe. Up until recently, he'd always kind of believed the Elders were powerful sorcerers practically immune to illness or death. But now they seemed like nothing more than weak old men who hid behind powerful relics.

I guess that's why they hated my father for having so many.

"But why save him?" Taylee asked. "I mean … he's the one who tried to kill you." She said the last bit under her breath.

"If I let everyone who ever opposed me die, there would not be many left for my God to save," Skyblind stated somberly.

This made the Elder scoff. "This is a waste of time. You need to go."

Akoro nodded in agreement and turned to Marlo. "Are the doors open?"

"This system is a lot more complicated than what I'm used to back home, but thanks to Kaine, we've managed to open a path," Marlo stated without looking up from whatever he was doing to the boxes. "I still can't seem to shut down the music remotely, though. I'll need more time."

"Just do your best, Marlo," Skyblind affirmed. "Roy, we could use some help. Are you with me?"

Roy shrugged and stepped away from the boxes. "Better than standing around here watching Marlo try to be a hero."

"Wait! Where are you going?" Taylee rushed over to them.

"If Corwin activates that Orb, we need to be ready," Skyblind answered as he opened the door. "Stay here and work with Kaine. He will explain everything."

"I don't understand ..." She looked at Tray'o, but he couldn't think of anything to say.

Skyblind lovingly placed a hand on Taylee's shoulder and stared deeply into her eyes. "Have faith, Taylee. God has not forgotten us."

And with that, the three of them slipped out of the room.

Who would have ever thought I'd be hanging out in a room with a Dark One, a dying Elder, and a back-stabbing Elite with delusions of grandeur. Tray'o frowned. *Oh well. At least Taylee's here.*

"You should go with them," Kaine said to Sparrow.

"No!" Her reaction was immediate. "I won't leave you."

"It doesn't matter." He coughed. "I'll be dead soon anyway."

"Don't say that. You'll be fine." Sparrow was clearly in denial; the man was turning whiter every minute.

What's the deal there, anyway? They know each other?

"Are you still hoping to get in his good books?" Tray'o couldn't help but mock her attempts to console the man. "There doesn't really seem to be anyone left in the Elder Order to reward all your 'hard work.'"

Sparrow shot him an angry look. "Shut your mouth, Pinehouse."

Ha! That struck a nerve.

"What's wrong? Afraid the final Elder will find out that you don't care about anything beyond building your reputation?"

Sparrow looked like she was ready to attack him when Kaine put his arm out to stop her.

"Do you have a problem, son of Rai'o?" Kaine glared at Tray'o.

Tray'o shrugged again. "Not with you."

For some reason, this made Kaine smirk. "Sparrow is my daughter, so if you have a problem with her, then you have one with me."

That was unexpected.

"What? Seriously?" Tray'o and Taylee exchanged a look.

Sparrow didn't say anything, but by the way she stiffened, Tray'o knew it must be true.

"I thought people on the Island couldn't have children?"

"You've thought a lot of wrong things," Sparrow stated plainly.

"People on the Island are not *supposed* to have children," Kaine agreed. "But we Elders make the rules, and we can also break them."

Tray'o leaned against the wall. *I guess it makes sense. All this time, she wasn't trying to please the Elders, she was trying to please her father.*

"Well," he said after a brief pause, "happy reunion then."

"Enough of this!" The stress in Taylee's voice was obvious. "Can someone please tell me what we're doing here?"

"We're trying to stop Corwin from activating the Orb for Logan," Marlo replied as he pushed some buttons on one of the black boxes. "But we need your help. Stand over by the map, please." He directed her attention to a white wall.

"Uh, what map?" Tray'o asked just before the wall transformed into a brightly-coloured map filled with many green and blue shapes framed by glowing white lights.

As Tray'o and Taylee approached the wall, he realised that there were names written on the green shapes, and thin black lines dividing each one. The largest and most prominent names were The Republic of Meric, United Camerida, Euroica, and Caspia. The names meant nothing to him, and none really stood out, until all at once he noticed a large green mass at the very bottom with the word 'Anaciencia' scrawled across it.

"What is this?" Tray'o gawked.

"A map," Marlo stated plainly.

"Obviously. But a map of what? This thing is huge!" Tray'o exclaimed. "What are all these other shapes and names supposed to be?"

"Green. For land," Taylee said as she traced her fingers along the word 'Anaciencia.'

"The shapes are land masses belonging to the other kingdoms of the Earth," the Elder confirmed.

"Other kingdoms?" Taylee looked as confused as he felt.

Marlo nodded. "This planet is much bigger than we'd ever thought! There's lots beyond the border of the sea."

How can that be possible?

"There were once many other kingdoms, but they were all eradicated by the abundance of energy produced by the Orb," the Elder hissed through his teeth. "Your father, Taylee, was not the first to create that power. But I'm sure Logan didn't tell you that in his little history lesson, did he?"

"Not exactly," Taylee squeaked.

Lies and more lies. When will it end? For the first time, Tray'o was actually starting to miss his ignorant life at Pinehouse.

"Logan told us the world was destroyed because of scarcity in the land," Tray'o explained, "but that now that we have the Orb, there will be no war or suffering."

"There will always be *suffering*." The Elder's voice was thick with disdain. "But Logan is blinded by lust. He knows as well as I do that the only thing abundance creates is parasites."

That doesn't sound good. Tray'o tilted his head and said, "Parasites?"

"Unlimited, free Essence—or public access to 'magic,' as you know it—makes you people lazy. Rai'o was a good example of what happens when a common person gorges on such power." Kaine looked at Tray'o with disgust in his eyes. "If Corwin activates the

Orb, no one will need to work. Yes, there are those here in the Academy who could have used this abundance wisely, but a vast majority would abuse it, as history proves. The Ancient Kingdoms crumbled as common men indulged themselves to death." Kaine had to stop speaking to cough. Though his voice was unwavering, his body appeared to be getting weaker.

He doesn't have much longer.

"The problem isn't with abundance," Marlo remarked. "It's when people worship abundance instead of worshipping God."

"Not you too," Sparrow groaned.

"This is why the Elder Order swore to limit the usage of 'magic' by making Essence into currency," Kaine continued without responding to Marlo. "This is also why we did everything in our power to stop Rowyn from recreating that blasted Orb in the first place."

Taylee lowered her eyes and said quietly, "So that's why my father's ghost was begging for forgiveness."

"Hang on," Tray'o held up his hand. "You can't blame him if it was Logan's idea. Her father was probably deceived like we were."

"He was not deceived," Kaine insisted.

Taylee chewed her lower lip, then took an apprehensive step toward Kaine. "So … if Logan was evil, does that mean my father was too?"

"I wouldn't exactly call him evil. Rowyn broke many vows, beginning when he fell in love with Kyla. They resented our rules and desired to have a child. Logan promised to allow it if Rowyn would build him the Orb."

That's not what Logan told us. Tray'o was about to mention it, but then realised that at this point it seemed very unlikely that anything that came from Logan's mouth was truth.

"Once Kyla became pregnant," Kaine continued, "Logan locked her away and used that as motivation to force Rowyn to complete the Orb. So you see, if he had not desired children, we would not be in danger now."

"Seems like he wasn't the only one who desired children,"

Tray'o said under his breath. If Kaine heard him, he gave no indication.

"So my father was *forced* to build the Orb." This seemed to bring Taylee a measure of relief.

"Even so, he recreated the very thing that destroyed the Ancient World, and if we don't stop Corwin, then our kingdom will suffer the same fate as the others."

Taylee took a deep breath. "How can we help?"

Kaine motioned to Marlo, who had stepped away from the boxes and was now in the process of building a 4-foot, three-legged tower with a rectangular object on top that he pointed directly at Taylee.

"Tell Corwin the truth." Although Sparrow spoke with authority, her voice quivered with doubt. "And hope he can still hear you."

Not much chance of that if he's got that music in his ears.

"What's that?" Tray'o asked as Marlo pressed down on the rectangular relic and a little red light started to blink.

"It's your magic portal," he replied with a grin.

Chapter Thirty-Eight — Slayer of Darkness

"The man who fears failure is the one who worships victory; such a man does not act in the interest of god, no matter how moral he may appear."

—THOM PENTITON, A.P. 321
LESSONS OF THE LIGHT

There was little doubt in Corwin's mind that the words of Elder King Logan Rome were anything but the absolute truth, and he now felt quite convinced that— even though Logan was only a man—he was the closest thing to a true god that Anaciencia would ever know.

Being in the presence of such a man was intoxicating. Despite the fact that his age was impossible to determine, Logan had accomplished more in his lifetime than Corwin could ever dream. He felt unworthy to be in his presence, but followed obediently as Logan led him and Salana through the intricately lit and adorned halls of the great Academy.

In his right hand, Corwin held the fiery Orb of Power. It was surprisingly cool to the touch and weighed barely anything at all. When he stared down into the golden ball, he was filled with a most unusual sense of awe and dread.

In my hands is a source of unlimited power crafted by my very own father. It was hard to wrap his mind around the reality of it all.

"I'm proud of you, Corwin," Salana leaned over and whispered as they climbed up a set of winding stairs. Her lips brushed his ear, and the warmth of her breath sent a shiver down his spine.

She had stayed close beside him ever since they'd separated from Taylee and Tray'o, and together they'd been following Logan to what he called the Reaktor Room. Once there, Corwin was supposed to place the Orb on a pedestal and usher Anaciencia into a golden age of light and prosperity.

And in this age, Uncle Jael will surely be healed and whole.

"Thank you. Actually, it's really incredible." Corwin could hardly take his eyes away from the fiery sphere in his hands. "At first, I was so disappointed when I learned Syyris was false. But now I see how small and useless he really was. This Orb will do so much more for us than Syyris ever could." He couldn't understand it, but his words felt strange and foreign as he spoke, almost as if they weren't really his own.

"Yes. You will activate the Orb and finish your father's work, eliminating poverty, illness, and war from the Kingdom," Salana stated. Whatever he was detecting in his own voice was amplified when Salana spoke. Beyond that, she was acting even more kindly and gently than ever before.

It's nothing. She's just beginning to see you as more than a poor shepherd, a voice in his head insisted.

The thought caused his heart to beat faster.

"We are almost there." Logan's voice echoed down the staircase. "Steady yourself, Corwin. They will write songs about this moment: Corwin Medisto, Slayer of Darkness, Bringer of Light."

Corwin wanted to be excited, but for some reason he couldn't seem to shake the sickening tension that was growing in the pit of his stomach.

Since when do you care for fame? a distant voice inside him whispered.

When they finally reached the top of the staircase, Corwin found himself standing in a massive chamber, where dozens of golden pillars reached so high in the air that he couldn't even see the ceiling (and trying only made him feel dizzy).

At the other end of the chamber, Lord Daraak and a few of his knights were waiting next to a black door with the now-familiar, red image of a hand in a box on its side.

Salana tensed at the sight of the Kaag'ari men. "What are they doing here?"

"Have no fear," Logan reassured her. "Although they were once pawns of the Elders, they are now under my control."

I hope so. Corwin couldn't help but feel a twinge of jealousy whenever he saw Lord Daraak.

"Is he still going to try to marry Salana?" Corwin asked.

For some reason, the question made Logan laugh. "Of course not. Now that I am the Elder King, she is free to marry whomever she chooses."

Salana bowed her head gratefully. "Thank you."

Ha! Corwin couldn't help but feel smug. *I hope he heard that.*

"Now," Logan placed a hand on Corwin's back and started to guide him toward the door. "Let us go and fulfill your destiny."

"I'm ready," he affirmed, then added, "What happens on the order side of the door?"

"We will walk across the platform, place the Orb on a pedestal, and you will touch another hand marker. The Orb will then power an ancient machine that will fuel Anaciencia with enough energy, power, and light to allow us to thrive for generations to come!" Logan declared.

Corwin, now excited beyond belief, eagerly walked toward the door. *Not too quickly,* he reminded himself. *You don't want to look like a little child.*

But with each step he took, the louder and more triumphant the music in his head became. It swelled around him and urged him onward with such a zeal and energy that he could hardly contain himself.

You and Taylee may have caused Uncle Jael's illness by activating the necklace, but you'll make it all right again with this Orb.

Corwin was just starting to think that things couldn't get any better, when all of a sudden, a loud shout rang out and caused him to stop a few feet away from the door.

"Wait!" His sister's voice echoed through the chamber. "Don't open the door!"

Taylee?

Corwin searched with his eyes but couldn't seem to see her anywhere.

Am I imagining it?

Just then, a rectangle of light materialized above the door, revealing a picture of Taylee and Tray'o standing in front of what appeared to be some sort of map.

It's magic! he realised. *How did you two get in there?* Corwin tried to ask, but the words caught in his throat. Something in his gut still felt wrong, but his brain was screaming at him to keep walking toward the door.

"There's been a breach in the security room!" Lord Daraak shouted to a few of his knights, who wasted no time scrambling toward the staircase.

"Corwin, Logan is lying to you!" Taylee appealed to him. Her voice, normally so compelling, now had little effect.

"Ignore them," Logan pointed up at the projected image of Taylee and Tray'o. "They are not wearing their chains."

Of course. That explains why she looks so upset.

"You took off your chains?"

"That music is dangerous and confusing you. Both you and Salana! Take them off, please!" his sister insisted.

"They're trying to steal this from you," Logan waved dismissively at the image on the wall. "Taylee wants to be the one to activate the Orb, not you. You know how your sister is. She wants the attention for herself."

Corwin's mouth dropped open.

How dare she be so selfish!

"I can't believe you!" He scowled at the image of his sister. "It doesn't matter which of us activates the Orb. You should just be happy that Uncle Jael will be healed.

"No! Logan's lying to you!" Tray'o shouted. "Look behind us. See this map? This is what the world looked like before. All of this was wiped out when the Ancients used the Orb's power. It's dangerous!"

"Your father built the Orb, not the Ancients," Logan shook his head. "Open the door and let us finish what he started."

Corwin, who was now feeling very confused, nodded apprehensively and resumed his approach.

"He's trying to confuse you! Our father wouldn't want this!" Taylee pleaded.

Logan knows best, a voice echoed in his mind.

"Logan knows best," Corwin repeated.

The next thing he knew, he was standing at the door with his hand hovering over the red symbol.

"No!" Taylee whined.

"That music is still confusing him!" a distant voice that sounded like Sparrow snapped. "Can't you stop it?"

"I'm working on it!" an unfamiliar voice replied. "I need a few more minutes!"

"We don't have a few minutes!" she shouted again.

What's going on? He wanted to know where those voices were coming from, but at the same time, he knew he shouldn't let himself be distracted.

Open the door, Corwin.

"Open the door, Corwin," Salana echoed the voice in his head.

As much as he wanted to obey, something still didn't feel right.

"I understand Taylee is jealous, but what about Tray'o? He has no reason to resist this," Corwin asked Logan. The symbol pulled at him, and it took everything he had to keep from touching it.

"He'll say whatever it takes to make Taylee happy," Logan growled. "This is why we Elders forbid romantic relationships. I'm afraid that by removing themselves from the music of Benaural, they have put their own selfish desires over the greater good."

He's right. They've always been selfish.

Salana gently placed her hand on his shoulder.

"You deserve better than them."

I deserve better than them, the voice in his head repeated.

"No! Corwin, please!" Taylee pleaded.

"Once you activate the Orb, you and I can restore life to Anaciencia." Salana's words were honey, and they dripped with the sweetness of truth.

In that moment, Corwin realised that he wanted nothing more than to please his Princess.

No. My Queen.

Without another thought, Corwin turned and placed his hand on the symbol.

A sharp pain shot through his fingers, and a loud chiming rang through the chamber. The red light flashed a bright green, and the heavy, iron door slid open.

Corwin could hear the distant murmuring of Taylee's voice calling out to him, but whatever words she now spoke were completely drowned out by the music that was triumphantly ringing in his ears.

I am Corwin Medisto, Slayer of Darkness, Bringer of Light.

Chapter Thirty-Nine — The Weight of Worship

***"If you want to rid yourself of disappointment,
love no person or thing or place;
this world cannot compare with what the next will bring."***

—LADY SILVER E'MONTON, A.P. 705
A WORLD WITHOUT WOMEN

The door slid shut behind him, and all light vanished; there was nothing but the pulsating glow of the fiery Orb to light his path. But he wasn't afraid.

"What now?" Corwin asked as he turned to look at Logan.

"I'm not sure," the older man admitted. "I've never been here before."

They did not have to wait long to find out. As if in response to his question, two yellow lights opposite one another turned on right in front of them. As they did, another pair appeared, and another, and another, until a trail of golden lights shot out into the centre of the room and illuminated a metallic walkway.

The glowing lights that now illuminated the path were at the base of a waist-high railing made of thick metal beams that had likely been constructed to keep people from falling off the walkway.

"That's a long way down," Salana observed as she leaned over the edge of the railing and stared into the dark abyss below.

There's nothing to fear; the Orb will protect us, Corwin asserted as he confidently stepped between the glowing yellow lights and toward the centre of the room. With each step, a lively, musical echo rang through the chamber and seemed to mix perfectly with the music flowing in his ears.

This place is incredible!

Every step past one set of glowing lights seemed to trigger another piece of the music, and he found himself overjoyed at the thought of his movements playing a part in the Song of Ancients.

Taylee and Tray'o don't know what they're missing. But they'll understand once they see how this Orb will save Uncle Jael and all of Anaciencia.

The musical tones increased in pitch, the drums boomed, and the strings swelled louder and more triumphantly as he took one final step and came at last to the end of the walkway.

Directly in front of him stood a bright white pedestal made of some shiny, unknown metal.

"This is what you were born for," Logan whispered in his ear. "Now do it for your father. And more importantly, do it for Uncle Jael."

Without hesitation, Corwin lifted the flaming Orb high above his head and placed it firmly on the pedestal.

It clicked in place and started to rotate ever so slightly.

"Ready?" Corwin asked as he stared down at the red hand symbol which glowed near the bottom of the pedestal.

Salana gripped his shoulder and gave it a reassuring squeeze. "Ready."

Corwin grinned back at her and then reached for the symbol.

In the same fashion as the others, he placed his hand flat against it and felt the now-familiar sting.

All at once, the red symbol turned from red to green.

Then …

… nothing.

Other than the colour, there did not seem to be any immediate change.

Shouldn't the Orb do something? Corwin wondered.

It didn't burn brighter or spin faster, or grow in size.

The Orb didn't do anything at all; it simply glowed as it had before.

"Is it done?" Salana asked with a look of confusion.

"I … don't know." Corwin leaned forward to try and get a better look.

As soon as he got closer, he noticed that it was, in fact, starting to glow brighter.

That's better, he thought to himself with a feeling of relief.

The music also was increasing in volume and tempo as it built toward a triumphant conclusion, and Corwin allowed himself to be swept up in the euphoria of knowing that he was about to be the cause of the restoration of the world.

And then the fiery light inside the Orb fizzled out.

Wait, what?

"What happened?" Salana echoed the confusion he now felt.

"Stay back!" Logan pushed Corwin out of the way and placed his hands on the Orb. Now that it had ceased to produce light, it appeared to be nothing more than a hollow ball of dull, dirty crystal.

"What did you do?!" Logan snapped.

"I—uh …" Corwin stammered. "Nothing!"

Seeing the Orb so lifeless and empty shocked and horrified Corwin, but the music insisted on remaining upbeat and pleasant.

"Maybe that was supposed to happen," Salana suggested. "Maybe the energy flowed into the pedestal."

Good thinking. That must be it.

Logan thought about that for a second, then shoved the lifeless Orb into Corwin's hands. "Hold this," he grumbled as he crouched down next to the pedestal and tried to see if there were any switches or levers to pull. But, much to their dismay, the pedestal was solid and smooth, and aside from the hand icon, there was no way to interact with it.

None of this makes any sense. Why is the Orb dark?

For the first time in hours, Corwin felt anger rise up in his chest, which had the unfortunate effect of causing the music to swell louder and more triumphantly than before, almost as if it were trying to calm him or keep him at peace. But Corwin was too frustrated for that to work, and he found the music annoying and distracting.

"What are you doing?" Salana asked as Corwin put the Orb down at his feet.

"I can't think with all this noise," he said as he placed his hands on his ears. But as soon as he did, a stabbing pain tore through his head.

"Ow!" he exclaimed as everything in his body cried out for him to stop.

Fool! Leave it alone! the voice in his mind rang out.

Part of him wondered if he should obey, but when he looked down at the shell of the Orb and heard the peaceful, calming music in his head, he was filled with so much frustration that he aggressively yanked the chain out of his ears.

White light shot in front of his eyes as Corwin let out a startled gasp and dropped to his knees. All at once, the music ceased to play and there was nothing but silence for the first time in hours.

"I feel … different." His voice sounded hoarse, almost like he was waking up from a deep sleep.

Lighter, maybe?

"How dare you …" Logan spun around and stared at Corwin. "You think to trick me!?"

The self-titled Elder King looked more the way he had when he had gone by the name Lunechair, except that his face was more sunken and pale, his eyes were hollow points, and his formerly inviting grin was now a disdainful scowl.

In that moment, Corwin realised that it was they who had been tricked.

"Salana, Logan lied to us! You have to take out your—" Corwin tried to warn her, but before he could finish, Logan picked up the Orb in his hand and, in one swift motion, cracked it hard across Corwin's jaw.

Pain shot through him and blurred his vision as Corwin tumbled back across the platform and away from the pedestal.

"Hey!" Salana's voice rang out, followed by a loud cracking sound and a cry of pain.

Corwin struggled to focus his eyes and see what had happened, but his vision was blurred and splotchy. From what he could tell by the way Salana was leaning against the railing, it seemed as though Logan had hit her as well.

He'll regret that.

"What did you do to my Orb?!" Logan growled as stormed over to Corwin.

"Nothing ..." Corwin grasped at the railing and tried to pull himself back to his feet, but Logan was too fast. He picked up Corwin by his collar and shoved him back even farther down the walkway.

"You did something," Logan snarled. "Reactivate the Orb!"

"I don't know what happened!" Corwin exclaimed as he tried to crawl away, but Logan was relentless and was soon towering over him once again.

"Liar! You're just like your father." Logan grabbed Corwin and punched him in the face.

Corwin staggered backward a few more feet, tripped, and fell hard on his back.

You have to do something. His mind raced. *Logan is going to kill you!*

Then, all at once, Corwin caught sight of the green handprint next to the door behind him.

Without a second thought, he crawled across the platform as quickly as he could and stretched out his arm toward the hand symbol on the door. It was higher than he was able to reach, and so he had to pull himself up by the railing to try again.

This time, his hand made contact, and the door slid open.

He expected to see Lord Daraak and his guards on the other side. What he didn't expect was that they would be standing and talking with Skyblind, Akoro, and the Dark One named Roy.

"My Queen!" Akoro's voice boomed when they all realised the door had opened.

"I'm okay" Salana replied weakly. She sounded as disoriented as he felt.

She took her chain out, Corwin realised as he looked back and saw her holding it tightly in her right hand.

"Stay back!" Logan hissed as he stopped his assault and retreated back on the walkway toward the pedestal. "This is my Orb and you will not have it!"

Skyblind ignored the directive and dropped to his knees in order to help Corwin stand.

"You took the chain out," he smiled. "Good work."

Although the words were encouraging, very little of the last few hours felt like good work to Corwin.

"It's too late," he groaned. "I … activated the Orb …"

"Really?" Roy mused as she laid eyes on it. "Looks kind of dead to me."

The dull, grey ball that once held so much promise looked like nothing more than a trinket now in Logan's hand, and yet he clutched it tightly to his chest.

"Guards! Defend your king!" Logan shouted into his wrist. But Lord Daraak and the others just stared blankly at him.

"You cannot control them anymore. Marlo just turned off your song," Akoro said as he stepped past Corwin and moved across the platform.

"That music was controlling us?" Salana sounded disgusted as she closed her fingers around the chain.

"Yes, my Queen," Akoro said.

Without a second of hesitation, Salana threw the chain on the floor and crushed it under her foot.

"Never again," she hissed at Logan, who was now standing between her and Akoro.

Logan scowled at them and repositioned himself in a defensive stance, grasping the Orb like it was a weapon.

"Stay back. It's dark now, but it still contains great power!" he sneered.

"No." Skyblind's voice was distant and sad. "I don't think it does."

What happened to the Orb? Why would my father make something that did nothing?

As Corwin tried to sort through his thoughts, Lord Daraak and some of his guards took a few steps toward the doorway.

"I wouldn't come any closer if I were you," Roy warned as she held up two thin swords in their direction. Corwin expected them to put up a fight, but, oddly enough, the Kaag'ari knights listened.

They look as confused as I feel.

It appeared as though the knights had somehow been cut off from the music.

"It's over, Logan. Time to face reality," Skyblind called. "It seems that the Orb was just another useless idol."

"You are the one who worships useless idols, Exile!" Logan seethed. "Yours is a god of shadows! But I hold the key to illumination."

Salana stared at the hollow Orb and shook her head. "Ellian's right. It's powerless."

Corwin's heart raced in his chest. "Are you saying this is the same as Syyris?"

"No. Worse." Salana's nostrils flared. "At least Syyris could fly. All this Orb did was look powerful."

"How dare you …!" Logan screamed as he rushed to Salana and struck her in the face with the back of his hand. She was not expecting the blow, and stumbled back and against the railing.

"That was a mistake." Akoro cracked his knuckles and moved faster across the walkway. But his approach stopped when Logan pulled a knife out of his boot, grabbed Salana by the hair, and held the weapon to her throat.

"Come any closer and I will end your little princess," Logan warned as he dug the tip of the blade into her neck. A small trickle of blood oozed out from where he pierced her skin.

He's going to kill her, Corwin realised in horror.

Akoro clenched his fists together.

"If you think to harm her …"

"You will what?" Logan laughed maniacally. "I'm the Elder King. All power and authority still belong to me. Daraak, seize these men, and whatever you want will be yours!"

But the knights did not move.

"What have you done to us ...?" Lord Daraak pressed a finger to his forehead.

Without the music to control us, he has nothing. Corwin looked over his shoulder at the green knights. It seemed that in their confusion, not a single one of them was willing to risk fighting Roy.

"Release me," Salana said through gritted teeth. "I may yet show you mercy."

Logan scoffed. "You foolish girl. Don't you get it? There is no monarchy. Your family name means nothing unless I say it does!"

Salana flinched ever so slightly, but managed to remain calm and controlled.

He may not have the music or the Orb, but he still has his pride. It dawned on Corwin that this might be the only way to save Salana.

Steadying his legs, Corwin took a few steps away from the door.

"Stay back!" Logan warned. "I will kill her."

"I don't think you will." Corwin tried to sound confident. "You need her alive. Without your relics to control us, this threat is all you have. You are weak."

Logan flared his nostrils. "What did you just say to me?"

That struck a nerve.

"You're a liar and a thief," Corwin continued. "I'm glad the Orb failed so we can all see how pathetic you really are. No wonder the Elders got rid of you."

Logan's grip on Salana's hair loosened.

It's working.

"It was you." The man locked his angry eyes on Corwin and his face burned red. "You did something to ruin my Orb."

Good, let go of Salana so Akoro can take you out.

"Of course I did," Corwin lied. "You don't deserve that kind of power."

Logan ground his teeth together, and for the first time, Corwin felt a twinge of fear; he'd never seen so much hatred before.

"You're a useless coward, just like your father," Logan seethed. "I may not have been able to kill him, but I can certainly—"

But before Logan could finish his threat, Salana took advantage of his distracted state and slammed her left elbow into his gut.

Logan gasped for air and doubled over in pain just as Salana punched him straight in the face, knocking him flat on his back.

"I'm not some princess needing to be rescued," Salana declared as she stood over him. "I'm Queen Salana. Elder or not, you will bow your knees to me."

Corwin was stunned; he had not expected that to happen.

The Elders were fools to think she was incapable of ruling on her own.

Logan writhed on the floor, holding his very likely broken nose with his hand in an attempt to stop the steady stream of blood that poured down his chin. It was the most undignified Corwin had ever seen him.

"Did he hurt you, my Queen?" Akoro asked with deep concern in his voice as he rushed over to her.

"I'm fine," she insisted as she wiped the blood from the small cut on her throat. Once Akoro verified that she was unharmed, he turned his attention back to Logan, who was struggling to get back to his feet. But before he could stand, Akoro placed his foot on the old man's chest and held him firmly in place.

"Not so fast." Akoro's snarl practically split his face in two.

Corwin, still feeling somewhat disoriented by his separation from the music, couldn't help but stare at the Orb, which Logan still clutched in one hand. Without the glowing light, it looked so insignificant.

How could we all be so tricked into thinking it had so much power? The more he tried to think, the more his head hurt.

Skyblind placed a reassuring hand on his shoulder as if to say he understood.

"Hey," Roy called with cool indifference as she turned away from the door. "Those green knights ran away."

Salana glanced at her and let out a quiet sigh. "I'll deal with them later. Daraak has nowhere to go."

"Great." Roy pointed one of her swords at Logan, who was still pinned under Akoro's foot. "So what's the plan for him?"

As much as Roy made him uncomfortable, Corwin was happy she asked the question; he'd been wondering that very same thing.

"My Queen," Akoro spoke up. "Allow me to honour you and remove him from this world."

"A tempting thought." Salana paused to think on his words before turning her attention to Skyblind. "What would you suggest?"

Skyblind had remained strangely silent the last few minutes, and now that he had been addressed, he looked at her with compassion in his eyes. "You are the rightful queen; the decision is yours. But may I suggest that—even though he has done us a great evil—he be brought back to the mainland?"

Salana pursed her lips together. "For what purpose?"

"As a wise young woman once said on my behalf, every man is entitled to a fair trial."

For some reason, this made Salana smile. "Lift him up," she ordered Akoro. "He will stand before the Court, where all will see him for what he truly is."

Akoro's grin faded away and disappointment washed over him, but he bowed his head and did as she commanded. "Yes, my Queen."

With little resistance, Akoro hoisted Logan up and back to a standing position.

"Foolizh girhl! Releaze me!" He gurgled through his bloody nose in a way that made his demands seem comical.

It's hard to believe that only a few minutes ago, he was the most powerful man in the Kingdom.

"Let's go," Salana ordered, ignoring Logan's pleas as she pried the Orb out of his hands. "There is nothing here for us anymore.

"What about the Orb?" Corwin asked as Akoro started to escort Logan away.

"It was all an illusion," Skyblind stated. "There is no power in it. Never was."

"Lhiar!" Logan sputtered and tried to get free, but Akoro's grip was too tight, and he easily shoved Logan through the doorway.

Salana stood next to Corwin and handed him the Orb. "This belonged to your father. Do you want to keep it?"

Corwin took it from her hands and held it tightly. It felt like nothing more than a trinket now. Whatever connection this thing had to his father, Corwin couldn't sense it.

"No, I don't," he answered as he lifted it over the railing.

He hesitated for a minute and allowed himself to feel the weight of all that had just happened.

All this time, I thought it was the answer to our problems. And what good did it bring? I nearly died for this thing …

A few moments ago, he had believed this thing was going to change the world. But it turned out to be just another deception, and he was done with being deceived.

He let go of the Orb.

They all watched as it tumbled down into the abyss below and fell for a good ten seconds before the sound of a distant clang was heard.

Corwin raised his eyes from the deep pit and met Salana's gaze. She regarded him silently before giving an ever so slight nod of approval.

"So what now?" Roy asked through a big yawn.

"Now?" Salana folded her hands in front of her face and pondered her next words. "I guess we go home."

Chapter Forty — The Return

"Oh my heart is but a magnet of curiosity
Yet it lingers ever closer to some poor atrocity.
Creation longs for healing, and chaos for His stillness.
But everything is longing for a cure for all its illness."

—The Sanctification Song
Author unknown

"For a building titled 'The Temple of the Holy Flame,' it's surprisingly easy to burn," Tray'o whispered to Taylee with a look of amusement.

"Shhh …" Taylee brushed him aside.

Now's not the time for jokes, Taylee thought.

Taylee had thought it a bit strange, but Sparrow had insisted that the body of her now-deceased father, Kaine, the Elder of Justice, be burned along with the relics they once knew as Syyris.

"In many ways, he was the real Syyris," Sparrow said to the group as they watched the flames engulf the building. "It only makes sense that they go together."

Taylee wasn't really sure how she felt about Salana's decision to burn the former relics, but she knew better than to argue with her. And, even though she'd been devout in her lifelong worship of the sky god, she found it pretty easy to say goodbye.

And Kaine was kind of a jerk, so I won't miss him either.

There was only one thing about the non-existence of Syyris that still bothered her.

"If he was just an idol," Taylee leaned over to Corwin, "do you think there's even an afterlife?"

"Don't be stupid," Roy grunted her annoyance before Corwin could respond. "Just because one god was proven false doesn't mean there isn't a real one."

No one asked you. Taylee bit her tongue to keep from speaking. Even though Roy had helped them out in the end, the two still didn't really get along.

"You're still defending the idea of a god?" Tray'o scoffed.

"Why not?" Marlo chimed in with his opinion. "Counterfeits can't exist without a source for them to copy, right?"

The look on his face told Taylee that he clearly disagreed, but before Tray'o could make some wisecrack about the futility of religion or belief, Sparrow glared at him.

"May I honour my father in peace without the sound of your voices chattering in my ear?"

Tray'o closed his mouth and quietly swallowed any sarcastic comments he may have been forming.

Too bad that didn't work more often.

Taylee turned her eyes to Skyblind, who stood silently next to Salana. Although he was healthy and appeared unharmed, something about the look in his eye told her that he was sad.

"Is Skyblind okay?" Taylee whispered to Corwin.

Her brother exhaled deeply. "I don't know. He was tricked into thinking the Orb had power, just like the rest of us. It's a pretty weird feeling to know you were so wrong."

True. Taylee still struggled to believe that the Orb had done nothing once it was activated. *I wish I could have seen it for myself.*

The fire lasted for quite a while, and it wasn't until after it had died down that Salana asked Akoro to go inside and break off one of the more recognizable pieces of Syyris and bring it out to her.

"What's that for?" Taylee asked as Akoro slung the piece over his shoulder.

"Proof," Salana stated plainly. "My people will struggle to understand Syyris was a relic. This will make it much easier."

That makes sense. Taylee had seen with her own eyes that

Syyris wasn't a god, and yet it still felt strange. *It's going to take the Kingdom a long time to adjust to this.*

After the funeral was over, Salana led the others to the docks, where scores of former residents of the Academy were all filing onto the E'monton ship *Deliverance*. Taylee was surprised at how little resistance there was from them when it came to leaving the Island, but, as Skyblind pointed out to her some time later, all of these people had been living in slavery to the musical chain for most of their lives and believed that they would never see their homes or loved ones again. When the music ended, and Salana liberated them from the Elder rule, the choice to leave was easy.

It wasn't until just before they were about to leave the Island that Lord Daraak and his knights chose to come running out of the forest.

"Wait! Please, forgive our actions," Lord Daraak shouted. "We were manipulated, just like you. We would never truly try to bring you harm."

Salana said nothing in response and just stood there, watching them in icy silence.

Taylee suspected she was debating whether or not to leave them behind, and part of her hoped she would. But, at the last possible minute, Salana lowered the walkway.

"Your wisdom and mercy will be sung about for ages, Salana." Lord Daraak caught himself when he saw the look of rage in Akoro's eyes. "Er—I mean—my *Queen*." He bowed his head.

"No weapons," she stated before allowing them to step onto the ship.

"Oh. But … surely you can't be serious?" Lord Daraak whined, but Salana and Akoro were unwavering.

And so, one by one, the green knights tossed their weapons onto the beach.

"Happy?" he asked with a slight snarl to his voice.

"Delighted," Salana replied as she turned away from them. "Ellian, can you join me for a minute?" she asked Skyblind.

"Of course." He nodded solemnly, and the two of them descended into the lower cabin of the ship.

Deliverance was a big ship, and even with all the residents of the Island onboard, Taylee found that there was plenty of room to move around and avoid Lord Daraak and his slimy smile.

Thankfully, she thought to herself as she found Corwin and Tray'o, who were leaning against the railing on the top deck to watch as the ship pulled away from the Island.

"So that Orb really did nothing?" Tray'o asked Corwin.

"Nothing at all."

Taylee didn't think it could be possible, but Corwin had never looked more sombre in his entire life.

"Do you think your father knew?" Tray'o asked. "Or did he also believe it had power?"

"He must have known," Corwin answered. "He made it."

"He knew," Taylee affirmed.

"Well, why go to all the trouble of creating something that doesn't even do anything? And then locking it in a secret room?"

"Who knows?" Corwin leaned his elbows on the railing. "Maybe he needed it as a distraction to get away ..."

"I guess ... But then why would he leave your pregnant mother behind?"

"I don't know, Tray," Corwin hung his head. "I wish I did but ... I just don't know."

Tray'o scoffed. "And all this time I thought my father was messed up."

There's more to the story. There has to be.

"I don't think he left her behind," Taylee answered abruptly. "I bet he thought she was dead."

"What do you mean by that?"

"The ghost of our father was so surprised when he saw me, he couldn't have known that we lived," Taylee explained as she recalled the conversation they had in the room where she and Logan found the Orb. "Later, Kaine told me that Logan locked our mother up and kept her hidden away to force our father to finish the Orb ... so he must have believed she was dead. Otherwise he would never have left it locked up like that." Taylee chewed on her lower lip as she processed her thoughts.

"That still doesn't explain why he made an Orb that did nothing," Tray'o said.

"When the ghost of my father saw Logan," Taylee continued, "he said, 'His revenge will be complete when you are left with nothing.' I didn't understand it at the time, but I think our father sealed the Orb away to drive Logan mad with desire. And then when Logan finally got it and found it did nothing, it completed his revenge."

"That's a pretty elaborate plan," Tray'o said. "I would have just made it blow up in his face."

Taylee looked at him and shook her head in disgust. "Then I'm really glad *you* didn't build the Orb, or Corwin and Salana would be dead right now."

For some reason, that made Tray'o laugh.

Taylee broke eye contact with him and watched the white-tipped waves as they crashed against the side of the ship. This was the first time she'd ever been on a boat before, but after traveling through a tunnel under the sea, sailing wasn't nearly as exciting.

"Do you think he's alive still? Our real father?" Corwin asked after a minute.

"I don't know. I hope so." Taylee leaned against the railing and let the wind blow her hair. "After seeing his ghost, I would really like to meet him for real."

"Me too," Corwin echoed her sentiment.

"At this point, I just want to get out of these clothes and take a good bath!" Tray'o interjected with a wink.

Taylee knew he was trying just to take some of the edge off the serious conversation, but his casual attitude in light of everything they'd just experienced was really starting to bother her, and she couldn't help but question his sanity.

"Everyone, can I have your attention please?" Salana announced as she and Skyblind returned from the lower cabin and stood at the front of the ship.

It took a few minutes, but eventually, Akoro was able to get everyone assembled on the main deck to hear what Salana had to say.

"You all know who I am, and know that since my father was king and is now dead, that I should be named Queen of Anaciencia. But, I have come to learn a hard truth on this journey—I am not the rightful heir to the throne."

The crowd murmured their confusion, and she had to speak louder to be heard. "My father had a brother, Ellian E'monton, the man you see before you now. He was exiled and branded a criminal because he discovered what we all know now to be true—that Syyris was nothing more than a relic and a tool used to enslave our people for generations."

The crowd responded well to this and many nodded or shouted their agreement.

What's going on? Taylee exchanged a confused look with her brother.

"Therefore, I have decided that when we return to the mainland, I will be giving full rule back to my uncle until the time comes for me to rightfully take the throne. I am requesting your full support for my decision in order to more effectively transition into this new age for our great kingdom."

The reactions on the ship turned negative, and many of the people murmured their confusion as they tried to understand what this would mean.

"A branded man, our king?" she heard someone say.

"Has she lost her mind?"

"He's a savage!"

Taylee felt her heart beat faster.

Salana turned to Skyblind and motioned for him to speak. He cleared he throat and took a minute to gather his thoughts.

"It was never my desire to lead. Though I may technically be the next in line, I was raised in the wilderness, with the people you know as Locura. My home is not in a palace." He gave a heavy sigh. "But since Salana is so insistent that this is the right and just thing, I find I have no choice but to accept her decision, with one condition: Salana must keep her title as Queen, and she will rule with me as an equal, to aid me in the things that I do not know and to help me restore peace to Anaciencia and among our people."

The crowd continued to murmur, and Taylee suddenly felt afraid that there might be a riot onboard the ship.

The last time Skyblind tried speaking to a crowd like this, they tried to beat him to death.

But then, the abrupt sound of a single person clapping broke out from beside her, and a smile spread across her face.

Corwin had taken a step forward and was clapping his approval.

Taylee wasted no time in joining him.

Many faces of the crowd stared at them like they were crazy, and Taylee felt afraid they might still be in danger. But then, Sparrow stepped out and joined in the clapping, followed by Akoro.

"Couldn't be worse than anyone else we've had, right?" Tray'o mused as he stood beside Taylee and joined them.

Shortly after that, others started to clap as well, and before long, the entire ship was clapping and cheering their approval.

Corwin leaned over to speak to her. "It's hard to believe."

"What is?" Taylee asked over the roar of the crowd.

"Not that long ago, we were a divided land, with a false god, corrupt Elders, and a fat, useless king. Now, for the first time in Anaciencia's history, power is in the right hands."

Epilogue — The Final Exile

As soon as *Deliverance* arrived back at the Lightspire docks, the Kingdom of Anaciencia was changed forever.

From the moment they stepped off the boat and onto the mainland, Queen Salana was bombarded with questions and accusations. For the first time in their history, the Kingdom was without any god or Elder rule, and this panicked the citizens of Anaciencia beyond belief.

But, as was to be expected, Queen Salana handled herself quite well, and soon the truth of the Elder deception was common knowledge. As a result of her calming presence and strong leadership, there were no outbreaks or riots when she announced to the world that Ellian was the rightful heir to the throne and that they would be ruling Anaciencia together, though the final say and authority would be his.

Things in the Kingdom had never seemed better. The only real trouble came when King Ellian invited the individuals formerly known as Locura to rejoin the kingdom and be made full citizens. Marlo and Roy helped a lot when it came to showing the citizens of Lightspire that the Locura were not actually monsters, but it wasn't until several of the Kaag'ari knights came forward and confessed that Lord Daraak had paid them to dress up as monsters in the Krydor attack that people were really able to accept the outsiders.

"You mean, all this time, Lord Daraak was the one who burned Krydor?" Tray'o took the news hard when Queen Salana announced it to the Court.

"I'm afraid so."

All the lords and ladies broke out into mass hysteria, and it took a full ten minutes before they could calm down enough to allow King Ellian to pass judgement. But, when Akoro sent some knights to bring Lord Daraak to stand trial, he was nowhere to be found.

It seemed that when the Kaag'ari clan members learned about Lord Daraak's involvement with the Elders and how he and his men were the ones who had orchestrated the attack on Krydor Markets, they took him away and he was never seen or heard from again. When Queen Salana demanded proper justice, they promised her that Daraak already received adequate punishment for damaging the family name, and that she would never need to worry about him again. Though it did not satisfy her desire, there was little she could do; the Kaag'ari were still a powerful clan, and they insisted on dealing with their own.

Without Daraak or his knights to patrol the Palace, Akoro was promoted to Chief Guard and Warden of the Anaciencia army—though now that everyone realised there was no true Locura threat, the army served very little purpose.

But, traditions must be upheld! Tray'o mused whenever he'd see them training.

As for Syyris, the Kingdom survived surprisingly well without him. No one missed living in terror of the great sky-beast, but that was not the end of religion. A large majority still chose to worship Syyris and insisted that he could still exist even though he was formerly represented by a relic. Several smaller sects broke out in the days that followed, all with varying beliefs on his true nature.

The formerly-named Locura did their best to spread King

Ellian's beliefs throughout the Kingdom. Some did turn and accept it, but it was definitely a minority religion, even though the King himself practised it.

Tray'o still couldn't wrap his mind around the idea of worshipping another god—especially one who was invisible. As far as he was concerned, he'd had quite enough of worship for one lifetime.

As Night progressed, things between him and Taylee became even more awkward, mainly because the reality of Taylee's disinterest in him had finally clicked, and also because she started dating Marlo midway through Darkfall. Tray'o was incredibly jealous at first, but, upon seeing how happy Marlo made Taylee, the decline of their relationship was somewhat easier to bear.

But, of all the things that changed since returning from the Island, it was Sparrow that surprised Tray'o the most. She never finished her studies, or became great like she so desperately wanted. It didn't make any sense to him, but, as she explained to him some time later, the only reason she'd ever wanted to be the best was to make her father proud.

"That's a lot of pressure. Kaine didn't seem like a man who was easily pleased," Tray'o observed.

"No, *Lord* Pinehouse, which was all the more reason to try," she said with a wry smile.

"Ugh." Tray'o grimaced. "Don't call me that."

"Why not? It's true, now."

Despite his many protests, Queen Salana had restored the title of Lord to Tray'o, and Pinehouse Castle was once again returned to his lordship.

But, he found there was very little about the place that pleased him anymore. The halls were empty reminders of a life he never truly appreciated and a father he never really loved. On top of that, he sensed echoes of Taylee everywhere.

"I never asked for this," Tray'o said.

"Of course not, but you were born to it," Sparrow reminded him. "I don't understand why you hate it so much."

Tray'o struggled to find words which would accurately describe how he felt. "Being a Lord always meant … a restricted life."

"You mean, a life without Taylee."

Her words hit him hard. "Yeah, I guess."

Sparrow scowled and turned her eyes away. "You're unbelievable."

"What?"

All at once, her mood completely changed. "After everything that's happened, you're still brooding over that girl. It's time to grow up. We're all sick of that story."

As much as he hated to admit it, he knew she was right; just like Pinehouse, Taylee was part of the past, and that was where they both belonged. So, shortly after that conversation with Sparrow, Tray'o established Roy as guardian over Pinehouse Castle and decided to make Lightspire his permanent home.

Although Roy was now accepted as a full citizen of Anaciencia, she still preferred to keep herself distant from people, and so she happily took up residence in the Outskirts.

She's tough and moody—a great fit for Pinehouse. My father would have liked her.

It worked out better this way; Tray'o much preferred the city. "It's like one big, Krydor Market," he often said.

Plus, living in Lightspire kept him closer to his friends.

Unfortunately, Corwin had become so distant that it was hard to even consider him a friend anymore.

It seemed Corwin never got over the guilt he felt over Jael's illness, and so he stayed by his side constantly. Tray'o suspected his friend was turning toward King Ellian's God as a way to cope, as evidenced by the way that he was constantly reading the little red book that the King also carried around wherever he went. But whenever Tray'o attempted to ask about it, Corwin got irritated.

"You'd just mock it," Corwin said.

"I won't. I'm just curious about what's so great about that book—you can't stop reading it!"

"King Ellian believes this contains the words of God," Corwin finally said. "If there's any truth here, then it's my responsibility to search it out."

Tray'o eventually had to stop asking about it, because Corwin was right. The temptation to mock it was too strong. Because of this, the two gradually drifted apart.

Since their return, Corwin and Jael remained with Holland and his family. Holland's son—formerly known as "the Last Holland" and now called "the Returned Holland"—was one of the people rescued from the Island, and so the Holland family was happily together again and told Corwin that he and his uncle were welcome to stay with them as long as they wanted.

The Holland family took extra good care of Uncle Jael, but in all the time that he spent at their home, he never once woke. There were no improvements through the entire season of Night, and just before the sun started to rise on a new Day, he passed into death.

Queen Salana insisted that his funeral be held in the Palace garden, and everyone gathered together to remember and honour his life. It was the first time they'd all been together in one place since Salana was pronounced Queen.

"The death of Jael marks the end of the era of our fathers," she informed the crowd at the end of the ceremony. "It is now up to us to rule and care for this land."

Although Corwin came to the funeral, he stood in the back and, as soon as it was over, he shared a few quick words with Queen Salana, hugged her, and slipped away.

"I'm worried about your brother," Tray'o said to Taylee after seeing Corwin abruptly leave.

"I know. I worry about him all the time."

"What do you think he'll do now?" Tray'o wondered out loud.

"Who knows," Marlo answered as he stepped over and put an arm around Taylee. "I'm sure the queen will find something meaningful for him to do."

Nobody asked you.

"He still blames himself for everything that happened." Taylee frowned.

"It's not his fault," Sparrow reminded them. "Logan deceived everyone."

"It doesn't matter," Taylee said. "He always takes things too seriously."

Marlo shrugged his shoulders. "He'll have to get over it sooner or later. He just needs time."

"Which is exactly why I granted his request," Queen Salana stated as she and Akoro joined them.

As soon as they approached, everyone dropped to one knee and bowed. Queen Salana regarded them with a quiet smile and gestured for them to stand. "My friends, no formalities, please. I am still Salana."

Taylee nodded and did as she was bid. "Of course."

"What do you mean? What request did you grant?" Tray'o asked.

Akoro looked confused. "Did Corwin not tell you?"

"Tell us what?"

"I assumed you knew." Queen Salana hesitated. "Shortly after Jael died, Corwin asked us if he could take *Deliverance*."

"What? Why would he want the ship?" Tray'o asked, but before an answer could be given, Taylee spun on her heels and took off running in the direction Corwin went.

Tray'o shot a confused glance at Marlo before both boys and Sparrow chased after her.

They ran with Taylee all the way to the docks and arrived just in time to see Corwin walking up the plank of the ship, *Deliverance*.

"Wait! Corwin!" she shouted.

"Taylee …?"

Tray'o hated the way Corwin said her name when he was depressed.

"What are you trying to do?" Tray'o called.

"Please, go back to the city." Corwin waved them away. "I'm fine."

Taylee rushed up the plank to his side and, quite unexpectedly, slapped his face. It was then that Tray'o understood. "You're leaving?"

Corwin rubbed his cheek. "Yeah."

"But … why?"

Corwin didn't say anything at first, but looked out at the sea. After a long intake of breath, he opened his mouth to speak. "Marlo told me that my father spent some time in the Ancient City after he locked up the Orb. He requested a boat, which they provided, and he sailed off to the old lands marked on that map you found."

"He thought he'd lost everything," Marlo said. "Logan made him think you two died when your mother did … But if he knew his children lived, there's no way he would have left."

"Which is why I have to go now," Corwin stated. "Our father might still be alive out there, somewhere."

Taylee scowled. "You're going to try to find him?"

"Yes. And maybe while I'm searching I'll learn the truth behind King Ellian's god. His book speaks of far-off lands where this god walked with his people. Perhaps he's out there."

"Come on," Tray'o groaned. "You can't seriously want to go search after *another* god?"

"Why not? Someone made this world. If it wasn't Syyris, then who?"

"Why does it matter?" Tray'o shook his head. "Just come back and let's talk about this."

"No. My decision was made when Uncle Jael died."

It's useless. He's too stubborn.

"Thanks for telling me." Taylee looked genuinely hurt.

Corwin stared at his sister with deep love in his eyes. "I couldn't say anything to you because I knew you were the only one who could stop me."

Taylee crossed her arms. "Who said anything about stopping you?" She pushed past him and boarded the ship.

Corwin scratched the back of his head. "You mean …?"

"Of course, you idiot!" she snapped. "Marlo, let's go!"

Marlo didn't hesitate to run up the plank and join her on the ship.

You've got to be kidding me. Just like that?

"If you think we're all going to support you on your little god quest …"

Corwin forced a smile, but the sadness in his eyes was overpowering. "I don't expect you to understand, Tray'o. But please, respect my choice. This is something I need to do."

Before Tray'o could say anything further, Sparrow punched him in the shoulder and said, "Don't be stupid, stupid."

"Ow!" He grumbled as he rubbed his arm. "What's that supposed to mean?"

"You know. Let her go. It's over." Sparrow's eyes practically drilled a hole through his head.

She knows I want to go with Taylee.

Tray'o quickly looked away from Sparrow and addressed Corwin again. "What about Salana? I thought you two were finally starting to hit it off?"

"We're just friends, Tray." Corwin sighed. "And anyway, she doesn't need me. She's got Akoro and King Ellian and a whole kingdom to rule."

More than anything, Tray'o wanted to tell Corwin that he wanted to go with him. Seeking out new lands and forging his own destiny was beyond appealing. *And it's not like Taylee's married. Her thing with Marlo is bound to end when she realises how boring he is.*

But despite all the arguments in his mind, he knew Sparrow was right; he had to let them go.

"Take care of yourself." Tray'o was looking at Corwin, but meant it for Taylee.

"Thanks." Corwin nodded, then added a quick, "Don't worry. We'll be back."

But from the look in Corwin's eyes, Tray'o wasn't so sure his friend was prepared to ever return. *Maybe it's for the best Taylee is going. I don't think Corwin could survive this trip on his own.*

Tray'o and Sparrow watched in silence as Corwin, Taylee, and Marlo waved goodbye from the balcony of the ship and the captain finished his final checks. Then, without any fanfare, the heavy ship pulled away from the dock and slowly moved away from the mainland.

"You made the right choice." Sparrow affirmed.

Tray'o flashed a grin, but inside, his heart was breaking.

Whether this was a foolish quest, or the beginning of something more significant than he could yet understand, Tray'o couldn't help but look on with sorrow as his closest friends separated from the Kingdom and became the first-ever self-proclaimed exiles from Anaciencia.

If there is a True God, I hope he's out there. Otherwise, they're in for a really boring trip.

THE END

Acknowledgements:

First off, I must give thanks to my Lord and Saviour Jesus Christ for all that He has done for me. You are the One True God, and none but You can withstand the weight of worship.

To my parents, I thank you for your continued support. You taught me to love story from a young age, and if it wasn't for you, I wouldn't be where I am today. Mom, thank you for encouraging my creativity and always believing in me. Dad, thank you for reading the very first draft of this novel and for your endless support during the revisions.

Chris Hansen. Words cannot express how deeply grateful I am for your incredible mentorship and faithful friendship over the years. You cared for me in one the hardest seasons of my life and demonstrated the unconditional love of Christ in a way I had not experienced before. I can say with absolute certainty that this book would be nothing more than an abandoned file on my computer if it wasn't for you. Thank you, thank you, a thousand times thank you.

And to everyone else who read early drafts of this novel or sacrificed time to help make this project a reality, I thank you from the depths of my heart. Friends like you are precious, and I'm so glad to have had so many people join me on this journey. I'd name you all, but I'm afraid I might forget someone, and that just wouldn't do!

56446870R10221

Made in the USA
Charleston, SC
23 May 2016